The Red Hat Club
Rides Again

ALSO BY HAYWOOD SMITH

The Red Hat Club
Queen Bee of Mimosa Branch

The Red Hat Club
Rides Again

HAYWOOD SMITH

St. Martin's Press 🐾 New York

The characters and events in this novel are purely fictional. Any resemblance to actual persons or events is coincidental. Though this novel is about a group of women in a Red Hat Club, there is no affiliation or endorsement by the Red Hat Society.

www.stmartins.com

Library of Congress Cataloging-in-Publication Data

Smith, Haywood, 1949–
    The red hat club rides again / Haywood Smith.—1st ed.
      p. cm.
    ISBN 0-312-31691-7
    EAN 978-0-312-31691-4

    1. Female friendship—Fiction. 2. Recovering alcoholics—Fiction. 3. Middle aged women—Fiction. 4. Women alcoholics—Fiction. 5. Women—Georgia—Fiction. 6. Surgery, Plastic—Fiction. 7. Online dating—Fiction. 8. Atlanta (Ga.)—Fiction. 9. Psychological fiction. I. Title.

PS3569.M53728R45 2005
813'.54—dc22

                                                                            2004051440

First Edition: March 2005

10 9 8 7 6 5 4 3 2 1

This book is dedicated to God's most precious creations: grandchildren—born and yet to be. I'm told the world goes golden the first time a grandmother touches those tiny toes. I can't wait!

Acknowledgments

First and foremost, a huge "thank you" to all my readers who purchased *The Red Hat Club* in the first few weeks, putting me onto the print *New York Times* Best Seller List! God bless you, every one. I wrote this book with you in mind, and I did my best to make it funny and heartwarming.

So many of you wrote and e-mailed kind words about my books. I can't tell you how much it means to me. If you wrote and didn't receive a reply, I apologize. Now that I'm moved into my new Back Bay home, I'm better organized.

To Betty Cothran, my faithful critique partner, I couldn't have done this without your wonderful insights and sharp pencil. You are the best.

To Patti Callahan Henry, a name to be noted in the world of fiction: Thanks for letting me be one of the midwives at the birth of a superstar.

To Mary Trautman, thanks for your friendship, your enthusiasm, and for picking up the tab. And to wonderful Julie Brogdon, my precious friend and favorite sculptress in the whole, wide world, thanks for introducing us.

As always, thanks go to my editor and associate publisher at St. Martin's Press, Jennifer Enderlin. And to Sally and Matthew and Kim and John, and all the rest of the wonderful team I work with.

Once again, I can't begin to express my gratitude for the expertise and generosity of Glen Havens, Maryland, and the staff at the Ark in Roswell, Georgia, for making sure I don't lose my laughter, no matter what.

My appreciation also goes to the reference staff at Emory law library for digging up the law school calendars I needed. And to Ginger at the Swan Coach House for helping me set the particulars straight about that wonderful institution.

Special thank-yous go to Robin and Travis and Pat and Kristin and Ennio and Helder and Tom and Chris, and all the other wonderful people who take such good care of me in my new Boston home. I love it here.

And thanks to my son and daughter-in-law for, God willing, making me a grandmother in May of this year.

My gratitude to Georgia and Jim for helping me pack up the last of my belongings for the drive to Boston. I wish you all good things together. And to Betty and Joe Mitchell for putting me up in Richmond on the way.

When it comes to business, people are usually quick to complain when things go wrong, but not to compliment when things go right. So I'd like to extend special thanks to the staff of Maaco in Lawrenceville, Georgia, for restoring my wonderful old Queenie car back to her former glory after I knocked out her front teeth and put a big dent in her fanny in separate SUV encounters only weeks apart (the perils of driving a regular car these days). Queenie never looked better.

Before I close, I can't resist one complaint: Raspberries to the state of New Jersey for having the most misleading road signage ever, which got me lost at least five times (hauling a trailer) when all I wanted to do was stay on dad-gummed I-95. Clearly, the New Jersey Department of Transportation is riddled with passive-aggressives. Just had to get that off my chest.

The Red Hat Club
Rides Again

Here We Go Again

O NE OF THE NICE THINGS ABOUT BEING A GOODY TWO-SHOES
Buckhead housewife is that nobody would ever guess I'd com-
mit a crime, much less kidnap anybody. I have the ultimate
mommy face and "comfy" physique. All four of my best friends and I
look like the respectable, middle-class, middle-aged women we are.

Okay, with the exception of SuSu till this year, but even she has
gone respectable lately.

I still can scarcely believe we pulled it off—a real Keystone Cops
kidnapping, complete with security guards chasing me and a desperate getaway. The law and conscience aside, my mother—a true lady—
brought me up better than that.

But as SuSu always used to say (before she became a law student
last fall), "Rules are made to be broken," and boy, did we ever break
them. We're talking high crimes and misdemeanors. Not that we were
strangers to the occasional well-intentioned misdemeanor, especially
when it involved helping out one of our own.

But I'm getting ahead of myself.

First, let me put this all in proper context.

If there's to be any hope for higher civilization, some things in this
life have to be held sacred, and for me and my four best friends (Teeny,
SuSu, Linda, and Diane) it's our second-Tuesday, monthly Red Hat
luncheons at the Swan Coach House tearoom in Buckhead. The only
acceptable excuses for absence are death, incarceration, or nonelective
hospitalization.

Through all the triumphs and tragedies of more than three decades—including Junior League, potty training, wayward husbands, wayward children, menopause, aging parents, and the frightful resurrection of seventies clothing—our commitment to meeting monthly, for ourselves and one another, has kept us close. That, and the Twelve Sacred Traditions we've evolved since we were fellow Mademoiselle pledges from Northside, Westminster, Lovett, and Dykes high schools back in the sixties.

But the most amazing thing about our monthly luncheons is, no matter how well we know one another, there's no telling what surprises are going to crop up over the Coach House's white tablecloths and fresh centerpieces.

Take last April. . . .

Swan Coach House tearoom, Atlanta. April 8, 2003. 10:55 A.M.
As always, I got to the Swan Coach House Restaurant before the valet parking, so I saved myself a tip and pulled into a slot under a canopy of blooming dogwoods and towering, newly tasseled oaks across from the main entrance. Spring—a precious, unpredictable event in Atlanta—had come early this year, confusing the plants into a glorious, out-of-synch display that sent the pollen count soaring along with the spirits of the populace.

As I crossed to enter, I savored the warm air perfumed by narcissus and hyacinths. The clouds of oak and yellow pine pollen would come later, driving everyone inside and providing a bounty for car washes and sellers of antihistamines, but for now, the day was perfect.

Once inside the gift shop, I made my usual cursory circuit to see what was new since last month in the tempting array of gorgeous things. Fortunately for my budget, nothing sang to me, so I proceeded down the short flight of stairs to the restaurant foyer.

Funny, how you fall into ruts without ever realizing it till they're interrupted. I've always liked to get to our Red Hat luncheons first, before the tables fill and the floral padded walls rumble with a polite roar of female chatter and chairs scraping on the dark wood floors. Our regular waitress, Maria, always seats me at our usual banquette in the back corner and brings me fresh, no-cal hot lemonade right away, which I load with Sweet'N Low and sip slowly, taking advantage of the waiting quiet to shake off the mundane concerns of my life and focus on friendship.

But that morning when I entered the dining room from the bright yellow foyer, I saw that SuSu had already beaten me there for the third time in as many months—a total turnaround from her pathological lateness of the past two decades. I shook off a tiny stab of disappointment that I wouldn't have my settling-in time.

She waved, looking like a just-ripe Lauren Bacall in a red cashmere beret and bulky black turtleneck sweater over slim black slacks. She'd finally gotten with the program about wearing a red hat a year ago, but the purple clothing thing was still a no-go.

Talk about a makeover. Gone were the brassy red hair and too-young clothes from SuSu's bitter, wayward years following her divorce. With the help of Teeny's generosity, she'd aced her LSAT, gotten into Emory Law School, and adopted a whole new, professional look. Classic to the core in her smooth, shining, dark-honey, chin-length hair and elegant wardrobe (most of which came from Teeny's *Perfect* line of real-woman clothes) SuSu already looked like the domestic relations lawyer she would be when she graduated in another two years. Every time I saw her this way, it made my heart swell with pride for her.

As always, an aura of smoke-tainted perfume surrounded her. She'd reformed, but not completely.

"How's school?" I asked.

We'd been busy praying all year for good grades, though SuSu had always been brilliantly book smart. It was just men she didn't have a lick of sense about.

"Brutal," she grumped. "And, Georgia, you'll never guess what my study group did to me."

I knew it was major; she rarely called me by name.

After all our years as friends, I fell instantly into the tried-and-true rhythm of our conversations. "No. What did your study group do to you?"

"They invited in a new guy without even asking me, then stuck me with him as a study partner for tort review," she fumed. "Probably stuck me with him because he's even older than I am. I guess the legal eaglets think it's pretty funny, but I sure don't."

The old SuSu would have cussed a blue streak next, but the new SuSu bottled that all up and minced out a tame, "I am *so* annoyed."

Maria arrived with warm mini muffins and took advantage of the break in conversation to ask me, "Excuse me, but would madam like the usual, or perhaps some fresh-brewed coffee this morning?"

Mmmmm. Coffee sounded good for a change. Iced tea season was still a few weeks away. "Coffee, please."

I returned to our conversation, surprised that SuSu would mind studying with a man "full-growed." Last fall she'd solemnly sworn off stud puppies, a resolution she'd already broken several times, but Tradition Eight (No beating ourselves up—or each other—when we blow it) had kept us from mentioning her "slips."

"Is he a problem?" I asked her.

"I'll say." SuSu adjusted her beret with her perfect American manicure. Gone were the red talons of the past. "He's the stupid, embarrassing Mattress Man!"

I tucked my chin. "The guy on those cable ads?" The one who stood there dressed in a blue baby bonnet and matching footed pajamas, singing mangled lullabies with his ukulele to promote his chain of mattress stores?

"Yes," SuSu bit out. "And he's as big an idiot as he looks."

Having been the gullible brunt of many a prank over the years, I eyed her with suspicion. Last time I looked, they didn't let idiots into Emory Law School. "You're kidding. This is some April Fools' joke, isn't it?"

SuSu glowered. "Do I look like I'm kidding?"

Mouth pursed, I shook my head.

"The joke's on me, kiddo, and the only April Fool is him. The guy's totally annoying. Always joking around when we should be studying." Her nostrils flared. "Not everybody has a photographic memory like he does."

I injected logic, futile though it was. "Ah. A photographic memory. Maybe that's why your study partners thought he could benefit the group."

SuSu would not be appeased. "Maybe so, but they at least should have asked me first."

I had to bite my lips to keep from laughing at the idea of SuSu, trapped, studying with a man who was famous for wearing a blue baby bonnet and footed pajamas on late-night TV ads. "I always thought he was kind of cute, in an older sort of way. Nice dimples."

"Well, he's bald as a mango under that baby bonnet," she grumbled.

"How can he go to law school and run those stores?" I wondered aloud.

"He doesn't. He sold them."

"But I just saw him on a new ad a few days ago."

Her mouth flattened. "That was part of the deal. They paid him a fortune to keep making the ads. At his age, you'd think he'd be embarrassed."

This, from the woman who'd come back from the bathroom at a charity fund-raiser at the Piedmont Driving Club dragging a toilet-paper comet, with her dress caught up in her sheer pantyhose, exposing half her fanny to high society. But SuSu's memory worked in adverse proportion to her alcohol consumption, so she probably didn't even remember it.

I looked up to see Linda stomping toward us, her usually sunny round face grim as thunder and her broad-brimmed red hat askew on her soft gray curls.

SuSu abandoned the subject of the Mattress Man. "Whoo," she murmured as Linda approached. "Looks like she's got a bee up her butt."

Very out of character for our level-headed Linda.

Linda dropped her open-topped Kate Spade bag by her chair as she plunked down into her regular seat beside me, then started fanning herself vigorously with her napkin, her plump neck red and mottled.

SuSu and I exchanged knowing looks, recognizing the symptoms immediately.

"At last," I crowed. "She's having a hot flash. Coming to join the rest of us on the shady side of the hill."

Linda glared at me like a bull eyeing a toreador. "It is *not* a hot flash," she snapped out. "And just because y'all have all gone through the change before me doesn't mean I have to."

"Oooooh," SuSu gloated. "Moody, moody, moody. Been there, done that. It's the hormones talking, baby. Estrogen in the major minuses." She patted Linda's arm. "Time to crank up the old HRT, and you'll be right as rain."

Linda recoiled from her touch, irate. "Contrary to your personal experience, SuSu," she snapped, "some people don't try to solve everything with a pill. Or a drink."

Whoa! Serious personal foul! We never discussed SuSu's drinking. Granted, it had grown progressively worse since her second husband had left her in the lurch, but SuSu was still fully functional. We accepted the drinking as her problem, and hers alone, to deal with. "Fixing" each other (unless it was a life-or-death situation) was strictly taboo.

Why Linda had said that was beyond me. I doubted even menopause would have sent her for the jugular that way. There had to be something else.

A look of deep concern overrode whatever offense SuSu might have felt. She leaned closer. "Linda, honey, what's the matter?"

Linda looked like she was about to burst into tears.

Please God, not Brooks. It couldn't be. They had the perfect marriage. Linda's plump little urologist husband adored her. (Maybe because she still got up cheerfully at five every workday of the world to make him a hot breakfast before his hospital rounds.) If he'd gotten tangled up with some chickie-boom, I'd kill him with my bare hands.

Linda seemed to be searching for something to say, then blurted out, "It's Osama Damned Boyfriend," her nickname for her daughter Abby's live-in boyfriend of eight years. "Who else?"

Abby, six months before graduation at the top of her class at Agnes Scott, had abdicated her role as Jewish princess and dropped out to become a hairdresser, moving to Virginia Highlands with Osama (his real name), a first-generation Iranian-American, Rastafarian tattoo artist ten years her senior. (A very confused, but laid-back young man.)

At least he didn't eat pork or drink. They had that in common.

But he was still a Jewish mother's nightmare. Brooks and Linda had kept open the lines of communication (and, against my advice, their pocketbook). Now, eight years later, the unlikely young couple seemed genuinely happy, in an underachieving, counterculture sort of way. Still, he'd always been Osama Damned Boyfriend to Linda. "Abby is wasting herself on that pot-smoking loafer."

SuSu eyed her with lawyerly shrewdness. "I don't think that's really it. Abby's been doing fine. Has something new happened?"

Linda scowled and went pale.

I offered her the basket of tiny muffins. "Take one," I mothered. "You look like your blood sugar just tanked."

She went green around the gills and shook her head. "Back off, Georgia."

Only something really serious could make a polecat out of our placid Linda. Something big was bothering her. My overactive imagination projected the worst. "Ohmygosh. Is Abby pregnant?"

Linda all but took my head off. "No! She is not pregnant! That would be good news. At least I'd have a grandchild." She fanned herself harder. "Tradition Five, y'all. Leave me alone. Quit ganging up on me when I'm feeling unsteady."

She said the last so loud that several heads turned at nearby tables. SuSu's expression clouded.

Afraid she'd make things worse by trying to pin Linda down, I called a Do Over. "Tradition One, then." I motioned for Maria. "Linda, do you think a cup of tea might make you feel better?"

The minute I said it, I realized how condescending it sounded, but Linda was through attacking. She just looked miserable and nodded.

"The usual," I told Maria. "And a couple of extra napkins, please." The way Linda looked, I might have to put a cold compress on the back of her neck.

If this was the start of menopause, she was in for a lulu.

Teeny provided a welcome distraction when she glided in wearing a lightweight, red faux-suede skirt with a matching jacket over a cutwork purple shell (size 3), topped by a gaucho-inspired flat-brimmed red straw hat that made the most of her blond coloring. I recognized the design as one Diane had done for the petite division of *Perfect*.

When our pal Diane had ended up a displaced housewife, Teeny (the mogul of our group, who had parlayed her nest egg into twenty million during the market's zenith) had taken advantage of Diane's bone-deep Southern class and penchant for organization by hiring Diane to supervise and design *Perfect*, a line of elegant, comfortable, easy-care clothing for real-women's bodies. The concept had hit pay dirt with America's baby boomers who longed for the return of clothes that made you say, "What a gorgeous outfit! It makes you look so *slim*!" Not that Teeny needed to look any slimmer than she was.

But watching her approach us, I wasn't focused on her outfit. I was focused on the uncharacteristic frown that drew her precise blond brows together.

Even when she'd been stuck married to philandering Reid, Teeny had presented a genteel mask of pleasantness in public. What was up with her?

Maybe the cosmic nasties were just in the air.

All three of us watched her take her place. "I haven't seen you frown that way since the divorce, Teens," Linda ventured, her genuine concern tempered, no doubt, by the chance to shift our attention away from herself. "What's up?"

"I really couldn't say," Teeny murmured, tacitly evoking Tradition Five. (Mind your own business.)

I really couldn't say had been our socially acceptable alternative to "don't ask," since we'd had it drilled into our heads as Mademoiselle pledges back in high school. It warded off unwanted questions and avoided hurting feelings when somebody asked a question best left unanswered, like, "What do you think of my tattoo?"

Oooooh. My mind took a left back to the previous subject. Maybe Linda was upset because Abby had gotten a tattoo.

Nah. Whatever it was, it was something worse than a mere tattoo.

Teeny looked down at the table. "Right now, it's confidential. But y'all will be the first I call on if anything develops."

Again, I projected the worst. "You haven't lost all your money, have you?" Could a person lose twenty million all at once? Probably not. Still . . . " 'Cause if you did, you can move in with us."

Not that she'd want to stay in our humble little Collier Hills ranch after life in her gorgeous double condo on Peachtree, high above Buckhead.

Careful not to skew my red fedora with her wide-brimmed gaucho hat, Teeny gave me a sideways hug, her face aglow with affection. "Bless your heart. No, honey. I'm set for life, no matter what happens to the economy." She drew back. "Someone I care about is in trouble, that's all. I want to help, but sometimes helping is hurting, if you're rescuing them from the consequences of their actions."

I wondered about her two hard-drinking, high-living sons. They adored their mama, but were following in their wayward father's footsteps.

Maria emerged through the swinging doors beyond our table, with a tray bearing fresh muffins, Linda's tea, and Teeny's orange juice. Maria knew all our individual preferences, as well as the predictable patterns of our luncheons.

As patrons began to filter into the dining room, Teeny and I started chuffing muffins and butter. I'd been on Atkins for six months and dropped twenty pounds, then switched to South Beach, but when the Red Hats got together once a month, I ate whatever the heck I wanted.

Linda took only tiny sips of her tea.

"So," I said to Teeny from behind my napkin before my mouth was decently empty. "How are those precious grandbabies?" Grandbabies were always a safe topic. Teeny had two granddaughters, honeymoon babies both, born ten and twelve months after her sons married gorgeous, high-powered businesswomen in a double ceremony. "How old are they now?"

"Caroline is three months, Catherine is five. And they're both adorable. Caroline's so interested in everything, but she'll happily entertain herself with a toy. The only time she cries is when she's wet or hungry. Catherine, though, that's a different story. She's a wiggle worm, already reaching for things. Busy, busy, busy. Her mama's going to need that nanny I gave them."

"I'm green with jealousy about those grandbabies," I confessed. The way my son and daughter were dragging their feet, I'd be on Social Security before I got a grandbaby of my own.

At thirty, my son, Jack, showed no signs of settling down now that he'd completed his MBA at State and gone to work for Home Depot Corporate. And at twenty-five, my daughter, Callie, was in the throes of getting her doctorate in English at Georgia, which seemed to leave no time for serious relationships, much less marriage and kids. (Marriage, then kids, was the preferred order in my conservative Christian household, thank you very much.) "Can I borrow yours sometime?"

"Sure." Teeny patted my arm in sympathy. "Want one, or both?" She was serious, even though I really hadn't been. Her heart was as big as her fortune.

I shifted the topic slightly. "How did your DILs"—daughters-in-law—"react to the nannies you gave them?" I would've leapt for joy at such a gift, but the boys' wives were both real estate attorneys, used to running things themselves.

"They were delighted," Teeny said. "The DILs are real career women. Couldn't wait to get back to work. And I think it helped that the nannies are both in their fifties and so wonderful."

Teeny's sons had said she was crazy to fork out an annual salary of seventy-five thousand for each of the nannies, but there was method in her madness. No daycare for her precious grandbabies. Teeny's grand-daughters—and their brothers and sisters to come—were going to learn solid values, good manners, and personal responsibility at home, whether their parents were willing to take the time to teach them or not.

I slathered plain butter on a mini muffin and popped it into my mouth, then chased it with a robust slug of coffee. "Mmmmm."

The room was beginning to get crowded, and I looked up to see Diane breeze in past a large group, flushed and smiling in an elegant dark purple, washable mock-linen tunic over matching drawstring pants (another of her designs). Topping it off was her divorce hat, a red-sequined ball cap that declared FREE AT LAST in zircons above an appliqué of a white dove in flight, a sure sign she was full of herself and raring to go.

Thank goodness. Somebody in a *good* mood.

"Hey, y'all. What're we talking about here?" Diane asked briskly as she took her seat.

"The DILs like the nannies," I informed her.

Teeny cocked her head at Diane. "You're awfully sparkly for this time of day, even for you. What's up?"

Diane blushed to the faint white roots of her brown hair. "I'm happy, that's all. It's spring. Everything's gorgeous. I love my job. Isn't it okay for a girl to be happy?"

Girl? We exchanged sidelong glances. "Sure," I said. "Long as you tell us what's put that cake-eatin' grin on your face."

She flushed even deeper. "Not yet. I mean, really, there's not really anything to tell," she dithered. "Yet."

SuSu reared back. "Oh, honey, I know that look. Diane's got a guy." Big news, since decent, unattached men—who weren't looking for twenty-somethings—were scarcer than unbleached teeth in Buckhead. "Tell. Tell."

Clearly busted, Diane invoked, "Tradition Five." (Mind your own business.)

"Tradition Six," I countered. (Girls first. No man shall come between us.)

"Tradition Seven," SuSu couped. (No secret affairs.)

"Oh, for goodness' sake," Diane flustered out. "Who said anything about an affair? It was only a phone call. Not even a date."

At the mention of the word *affair*, heads turned at nearby tables, and Diane shrank, flaming. "So a guy called me," she whispered tightly. "Now you've probably jinxed the whole thing by making me talk about it."

Linda did a dry ceremonial spit to ward off the jinx. "Tui, tui, tui."

Brims converging, we closed into a tight huddle over the tiny vase of alstralemeria at the center of the table.

"Get real," SuSu said, clearly enjoying the opportunity to put Diane on the hot seat. "Talking about men doesn't make a bit of difference, and you know it. They do what they want, regardless."

"So," I prodded, "who is he?"

"Where'd you meet him?" Linda asked atop my question.

Good thing Diane had low blood pressure, or I might have been afraid she would stroke out, red as she was. She got all prissy. "On the Internet, if you must know."

I straightened, aghast. "Don't tell me you've been going to *chat rooms*." The virtual equivalent of bar-crawling! And it was common knowledge that chat-room people lied their heads off. Heck, you couldn't even be sure the guy you were talking to was really a guy! Not that I knew from personal experience, mind you. I was *very* happily married since recently falling in love with my long-suffering husband. More about that in a minute.

Diane shook her head in vehement denial, but all the subtle signs told me she had, in fact, been chatting. "Nothing like that." She crossed her legs. "I was just noodling around on the Web and found this site where you could register to contact old classmates, so I registered my class at Westminster. And lo and behold, this guy I knew in grammar school e-mailed me."

"And?" Teeny's brows rose in anticipation.

Diane's blush shifted to a glow. "And so, we've e-mailed for a while."

"What's a while?" SuSu cross-examined.

Diane buttered a roll with inordinate concentration. "A few months."

"A few months?" SuSu blustered. "And this is the first we're hearing about it?"

"Oh, back off," I chided. "Tradition Eight." (No beating ourselves or each other up over anything.) "Can't you see, she's happy?"

At least she had been, till we'd started grilling her.

Maria arrived with menus (as if we needed them) and refills. After making sure we all had what we needed, she discreetly vanished.

By now, the level of chatter in the dining room was so high, we no longer had to worry about being overheard.

"So," I coaxed Diane with a sly grin, "who is he?"

Diane went coy as a teenager, quite a contrast to her usual no-nonsense self. "Clay Williams. My sixth-grade boyfriend. I wore his ID bracelet the whole school year. Then his father got transferred to Cleveland."

"Ooooo. An old flame." I lifted my coffee in a toast. "I smell a real love story brewing here."

Diane deflected the embarrassing attention by shifting to me. "Speaking of love stories, how high have you gotten those hearth fires burning lately?"

Now it was my turn to color up. SuSu wasn't the only one who'd turned over a new leaf at midlife. Thanks to Teeny's intervention the year before, I'd fallen head over heels in love with my husband for the first time, after thirty years of taking his quiet devotion for granted. I never told him that I hadn't loved him as I should have before then; I just did my best to show him how I loved him now, body and soul.

John had been shocked, but delighted by my newfound ardor, and we'd both been having fun spicing things up. "Well, I'm considering a really sexy little Easter Bunny outfit," I confessed.

"That ought to put John in a hoppin' good mood," Teeny said.

"If that doesn't, nothing will." SuSu waggled her eyebrows, her voice low. "I hope it's a crotchless number with ears and a fluffy tail. The old Easter egg hunt will take on a whole new meaning."

"SuSu!" Blood flooded my face in embarrassment. "There is no need to get crass."

She may have adopted a professional persona, but my childhood friend still had a ribald streak. That's why I'd asked her to come with me to the adult toy store the next time I went to pick out an outfit. But I knew better than to get all huffy. This bunch would never leave you alone if you got all huffy. "I think we can come up with a few exciting rites of spring," I said.

Loosening up at last, Linda rolled her eyes at me. "If I showed up in that sexy little getup, Brooks would laugh his head off. Or have me committed."

"As well he should," SuSu said. "You're Jewish, for cryin' out loud, even if you do have a nonpracticing Iranian Rastafarian common-law son-in-law. You can't be the Easter Bunny." She narrowed her eyes at Linda in appraisal. "But maybe something in a silver lamé menorah . . ."

The thought of plump Linda in nothing but a few strips of lamé was daunting enough for Teeny to revert to Diane's Internet guy. "So, this childhood sweetheart." Teeny leaned forward, her blue eyes dancing with speculation. "Does he still live in Cleveland?"

"Actually, no." Diane finally decided to be forthcoming, in typically brisk, organized form. "Graduated from Yale, then did his doctorate in history at Duke, where he married and had two daughters. Taught there till his wife got cancer six years ago, and he retired to take care of her. Lost her three years ago." Her eyes went soft with sympathy. "She sounds like a wonderful woman. Poor guy took it really hard."

The rest of us exchanged pregnant glances.

Oblivious, she went on. "He's been doing research and spending a lot of time with his two granddaughters, but I think he's awfully lonely."

"Bull's-eye with the boyfriend," Teeny exhorted.

"Ohmygod." SuSu spread her demure American manicure for emphasis. "One mouse click, and Shy Di comes up with the Holy Grail of men: a devoted, literate widower at the perfect stage for a fresh start—who had a crush on her once. I hear wedding bells."

"SuSu." Diane bristled. "Back off, and I mean it. He called me. One phone call. Granted, it was a nice one." Her posture mellowed. "A great one, as a matter of fact. But now you have to go all overboard and spoil it." She opened her menu and scowled at the selections we all knew by heart.

Chastened, Teeny and I followed suit.

SuSu at least had the decency to apologize. "Sorry, honey. I didn't mean to push. Can I call a Do Over?" (Tradition One.)

The question was rhetorical. Any of us could call a Do Over at any time and get a fresh start. It was the first and best of our Twelve Sacred Traditions, since forgiveness is the primary requirement for lasting friendship. More about those later.

Diane's face cleared. "Sure." Even if she should decide after all these years to hold a grudge, she wouldn't have a place to put it, bless her heart.

Linda, pinked up but still a bit pale, smoothed the napkin in her lap. "Who's got the joke? Let's hear it. I could use a laugh."

In all the years we'd been lunching together (long before we were Red Hats), we'd taken turns bringing a joke to our monthly get-togethers. Teeny was terrible at it, Diane and I were fair with occasional inspirations, SuSu tended toward the crass, and Linda was hit-or-miss. But it gave us something to laugh at, one way or the other.

We all looked around at each other, shrugging. When nobody came forth, we went for our pocket calendars and came up with a universal "You," pointing at Linda.

"Damn," she grumped. "I completely forgot." Her neck mottled.

"Okay," I deflected. "Who's got a pinch-hitter joke?"

This had happened before, and we usually got a good laugh out of trying to come up with something. But with Teeny distracted and Linda all grumpy and SuSu ticked off at her study group, the odds weren't good.

"Okay," I volunteered. "Here goes: What did the skeleton say to the bartender?"

SuSu offered an anemic "What?"

"Bring me a beer. And a mop." I grinned, nodding.

Moans all around.

"Okay," I defended. "Joke's done."

SuSu leaned past Linda for an exaggerated "Ha, ha, ha."

Linda reared away from her with a fresh frown. "Phew. M.O."—makeover. Tradition Five. "You smell like an ashtray."

Without invitation or warning, SuSu delved into Linda's open purse. "Got any gum?"

Linda responded with a look of panic and a vehement "No!" that clearly had nothing to do with the gum, but she was too late.

SuSu had already come up with an unopened early pregnancy test in her hand. "Ohmygod!" Her gaze snapped to Linda's. "This is for Abby, isn't it?"

Our precious goddaughter, pregnant out of wedlock! By a Rastafarian Muslim tattoo artist!

Flushed to a shade just shy of her purple jumper, Linda snatched the narrow box and jammed it back into her bag. "No. This is not for Abby." A dozen emotions warred in her usually placid face. Then two fat tears rolled down her cheeks as she forced out a thick, wavering whisper. "It's for me."

2

The Twelve Sacred Traditions

BEFORE WE GO ANY FURTHER, I THINK IT'S BEST FOR ME TO EXPLAIN the Twelve Sacred Traditions.

My mama always said that if you can count your close friends on three fingers, you're luckier than most people in this world. Our little Red Hat group fills a whole hand, and we know how blessed we are. But we didn't stay friends by accident. It took work to survive the usual arguments, blabbed secrets, hurt feelings, conflicts about our kids, marital disasters, denials, and peccadilloes of the past thirty-plus years. It took our Twelve Sacred Traditions.

Some of them (the first six) go all the way back to high school, when we were fellow Mademoiselle pledges. The rest have evolved over the seasons of our lives.

As with everything, there are the exceptions that prove the rule, as noted. Only three involve penalties, and of those, only Tradition Four results in banishment. Breaking Nine or Eleven means free lunches or movies for the rest of us, so we pounce on those infractions with glee, and there's no right of appeal.

So here are our Twelve Sacred Traditions. As the saying goes, "They work, if you work 'em."

TRADITION 1: DO OVER

Any one of us, at any time, can ask for a fresh start and get it: change of subject, change of attitude—no matter how bad we might have screwed things up (in which case, immediate apologies are in order). No grudges allowed.

We stole this concept from the boys on the playground, who duked it out, then ended up buddies once the fight was over. Unlike we girls, who cherished our grudges along with the silver charm bracelets in our jewelry boxes. So we took a leaf out of the boys' book—substituting a verbal element for the fistfights and contact sports. A simple "D.O." or "Do Over" is all it takes to make us retract our claws, whether we like it or not.

This works amazingly well, by the way.

TRADITION 2: MAKEOVER

Anybody can call a makeover (M.O.), provided there's a consensus and immediate improvement can ensue. This excludes weight, physical deficiencies, and cosmetic surgery. Clothes, jewelry, makeup, accessories, hair color (especially hair color), nails, and hairstyles are fair game.

Not that it's easy to be the object of an M.O., but if you can't trust your friends to tell you your new outfit is too tight, or that new lipstick makes you look ten years older and runs into the teeny wrinkles around your lips, who can you trust?

Personal grooming is one case where truth must always take precedence over illusion. The number one offender these days, demanding instant attention, is low-carb-induced Death Breath. It has edged out wearing Capri pants (on anybody over 100 pounds) as the biggest insult to polite sensibilities.

Our red hats are the only exception to this rule of good taste—for Linda and me, at least. When it comes to our *chapeaux rouges*, anything goes, even sequins before lunch. But Linda and I usually reserve our ostrich feathers, beads, bangles, boas, fake leopard fur trim, and rhinestones for special occasions like birthdays or the arrival of grandchildren.

TRADITION 3: NO LIES

We must be able to trust each other for the truth.

But that does *not* mean we have to tell everything we know, especially if it would spill the beans or hurt somebody's feelings unnecessarily. In those cases, we're morally obligated *not* to give an honest answer. The only proper response is, "I'm sorry. I really couldn't say," a phrase that was drilled into us as Mademoiselle pledges back in high school. Even after all these years, though, those words are never my first inclination.

So if one of us (can we say SuSu?) buys an overpriced, small house near Brookhaven and doesn't ask our opinions until after the fact, she will surely hear a subdued chorus of "I really couldn't say."

TRADITION 4: NO TELLING

Never, ever, ever will we rat out one of the group, even anonymously to the IRS when there's a huge contingency fink-fee involved. Our shared secrets are to be kept secret. We do not pass them on—even to blood sisters, therapists, priests, ministers, rabbis, the police, the FBI, grand juries, congressional committees, lawyers, husbands, or mothers. *Especially* not lawyers, husbands, or mothers!

The penalties for breaking this tradition are immediate banishment from the group and eternal damnation featuring perpetual upper-lip electrolysis, freezing feet, and ill-fitting underwire bras.

TRADITION 5: MYOB (MIND YOUR OWN BUSINESS)

If a Red Hat doesn't want to talk about something, she doesn't have to, and that's that. (Well, it's supposed to be, anyway.)

Further, a Red Hat has a perfect right to be wrong without being judged or bullied.

This tradition is the hardest one to keep, since we care so much, and all of us but Teeny are "fixers" at heart. Mainly, this tradition binds us in a solemn covenant *not* to try to fix each other. (Another guy thing we have borrowed.) Impossible for many women, but it's the ideal we strive for.

As you shall see, we sometimes blow this rule to smithereens. But always with the best of intentions. Like last year, when Teeny found my long-lost first love and gave me the chance to see my old flame and finally realize that I really loved my husband. And the time Diane seriously considered taking out a contract on her crooked, faithless ex-husband. We'd convinced her to go for a safer, more elegant revenge. And most recently, when Linda decided to report Osama Damned Boyfriend to the IRS (based on nothing) in an effort to get him out of her daughter's life. Fortunately, we'd convinced her it would only make him a martyr.

TRADITION 6: GF (GIRLS FIRST)

No male, including husbands, lovers, sons, fathers, brothers, bosses, or pals, shall come between us. Conversely, we know better than to bash errant husbands or boyfriends—no matter how much they might deserve it—since reconciliations often occur, and then there you are, left standing with all your insults hanging out.

TRADITION 7: NO SECRET AFFAIRS

Despite the fact that it seems to contradict Tradition Five, this tradition is the exception that proves the rule. Affairs are far too dangerous to be waged without backup and advice, especially these days. (You never know where his thing has *been*.) So if one of us is contemplating a fling, she doesn't have to tell everybody in the group, but she *must* tell at least *one* of us so the voice of reason and responsibility will be represented.

The only one of us who broke this tradition was quiet, devout Teeny, though to this day, she swears she never did (on mere technicalities). Based on her "rogues' gallery" of separate vacation photos showing cute, obviously adoring men, I sometimes wonder. But aside from that, only SuSu kept this particular tradition's motor hot. Until she turned over her new leaf as a law student last fall and swore off casual sex. (With spotty success, but it's the thought that counts.) The rest of us were either too happily married (Linda), too traditional (me), or too content alone (Diane) to even look at another man.

TRADITION 8: NO BEATING OURSELVES OR EACH OTHER UP WHEN WE BLOW IT

Pretty self-explanatory. The second part is fairly easy. The first is hard, hard, hard, since it seems to be our curse to feel personally responsible for everything that happens within a mile. (Except SuSu, who does better than any of us at "live and let live," maybe because she rebelled against her strict upbringing when she was widowed with two toddlers.)

TRADITION 9: NO GENERAL DISCUSSIONS ABOUT RELIGION, ABORTION, OR POLITICS

When it comes to religion, our little group ranges from shake-your-fist-at-God, ex-Presbyterian atheist (SuSu) to guilt-driven Catholic (Teeny) to nonpracticing Jew (Linda) to born-again Protestants (Diane and me). Our differences never mattered much until ten years ago, when Teeny and I, along with 600 other Buckhead matrons, got involved in this great interdenominational Bible study and started having sidebar discussions about the Scriptures at Red Hat luncheons. Diane ignored us, but Jewish Linda and atheist SuSu took umbrage, so we agreed to cool it, content to leave the dispensation of each other's souls to the Lord God Almighty, where it belongs. Brief mention of church activities is allowed for planning purposes only.

As for abortion (RU-whatever included), we cover the board on that topic, too, but our convictions have always been too deeply held and polarizing to make discussion anything but anguish for us all. So we agreed to disagree and let it lie. At least, until Linda turned up possibly pregnant, as you shall see.

Usually, Teeny and I just keep her devout Catholic and my fundamental pro-life sentiments to ourselves and pray for the others behind their backs. So there.

Regarding politics, we span the spectrum from right-wing reactionary (SuSu) to active Republican (Diane) to middle-of-the-road apolitical (me and Teeny) to yellow-dog Democrat, bleeding-heart tree hugger (Linda). When the Clinton administration put an end to our ability to have polite, objective political discussions, we decided, in the interest of harmony and mutual respect, to add a political ban to the religious and abortion restrictions. The only exception regards local elections and referenda, provided comments are based on recorded fact or issues, not editorials or image.

Anybody who breaks this tradition by bringing up politics, abortion, or religion—even in a subtle, indirect way—is promptly and glee-fully declared out of order, then forced to pay the bill for the whole table.

TRADITION 10: WITH THE EXCEPTION OF ALCOHOLIC
BEVERAGES, ALL CALORIES SHALL BE IN CHEWABLE FORM

This tradition is not observed by Teeny, who would probably shrivel up and blow away without the sugar in her sweet tea, and Linda, who is fluffy but doesn't care, but the rest of us who constantly fight the Battle of the Bulge outnumbered them and voted it in on principle anyway. Our artificial sweetener rule restricts real sugar to foods we can actually chew. Hence the diet sodas with our ice cream sundaes, artificially sweetened iced tea with our chocolate éclairs from Henri's Bakery, or coffee with Sweet'N Low to wash down the huge, decadent apple pancakes at The Original Pancake House. (Yum. I *dream* of those éclairs and apple pancakes.)

TRADITION 11: NO "I TOLD YOU SO'S"

Simple to say, but maybe our biggest challenge to obey. This extends beyond words to gestures and facial expressions. (SuSu swears it will take plastic surgery to keep me from rolling my eyes whenever she mentions having casual sex—a far less frequent occurrence than it used to be before she went to law school—but the verdict's still out on how long she'll be able to keep up her new conservative trend.)

Infractions are punishable by having to pick up the tab for the en-tire table or taking everybody to whatever movie the victim wants to see, at the victim's choice.

TRADITION 12: THE SUBJECT OF WEIGHT WILL NEVER BE
MENTIONED OR EVEN IMPLIED

In our group, "my body, my choice" means no pointed looks when fried foods, junk foods, heavy sauces, second desserts, or alcoholic beverages are consumed or abstained from in our presence. We are not responsible for what any of the others chooses to put into her body—

our obligation extends only to taking the car keys if it's drugs or alcohol. But as an extension of that individual responsibility, those of us who've let ourselves go are banned from whining about tight clothes and resulting health problems, or obsessing about diets. Bor-*ring!* If and when one of us does decide to lose weight, she must let the results alone speak for themselves.

Conversely, our well-meaning slender sisters are prohibited from offering us helpful hints or harboring secret feelings of superiority. Nor shall the fluffy resent the svelte for their self-discipline and/or enviable genes.

CODICIL: EXERCISE AND WORKOUT FADS MAY ONLY BE MENTIONED ONCE

Once is informational. Any more is duress. And boring, boring, boring. (This restriction does not extend, though, to details about hunky instructors or good gossip gleaned in a health and fitness setting.)

*I*n summation, these Red Hat Twelve Sacred Traditions are the bones of our lifelong friendships, resilient enough to survive an occasional break and heal, yet strong enough to weather our own frailties—not to mention enduring the greatest peril to friendship of all: change.

And honey, if I can keep them, anybody can!

3

Whoa, Baby!

Swan Coach House. April 8, 2003. 11:20 A.M.

SUDDENLY OBLIVIOUS TO THE CROWDED, FLOWER-FILLED TEAROOM around us, the four of us sat, stunned, our eyes fixed on Linda as she shoved the pregnancy test deeper into her purse.

SuSu exploded first. "What do you mean, it's for you? How? *Why?*"

Diane glared at her. "You, of all people, know how." The catty reference to SuSu's numerous relationships was totally out of character, an indication of how shocked we all were.

From Linda's dire expression, it was easy to see this was the menopausal woman's nightmare, unplanned and unwelcome.

My own heart was pinging like a Ford Pinto running on bad gas. Linda couldn't be pregnant. Brooks was only six months away from retirement. He'd been planning for years to take Linda around the world. A baby would ruin everything.

Noting our expressions, the women nearby instantly zeroed in on what was going on at our table.

We all leaned into a protective huddle over the bud vase of fresh flowers.

Linda, pregnant? Please, no. For so many reasons.

"We do not need to panic," Diane whispered. She peered earnestly at Linda's grim expression. "This kind of thing happens all the time, and it turns out to be menopause."

"Oh, hell, Diane," SuSu argued, incapable of whispering discreetly.

"She ought to know the difference." Then she turned on Linda with, "How could you let this happen? Brooks is a *doctor*, for God's sake. What about birth control?"

Linda went scarlet. "It was only one time, and we were at . . . well, we didn't have anything with us."

Away from home? Linda hadn't been out of town for months. "What do you mean, you didn't have anything with you?" I heard myself ask. "Where *were* you?"

Linda cocked a fierce look at me and bit out through pursed lips. "At the Fox frickin' Theater, if you must know."

Brooks had been on the board there for years. My perverse mind wondered if he'd been "on the boards" there with Linda.

Plump Brooks and Linda, stealing a risky quickie *at the Fox Theater?* "You are lyin'," I challenged, knowing she wasn't. Not about a thing like that.

Diane chortled. "A grown human being can barely fit into those dinky little seats, much less—"

"Where were y'all?" Teeny asked in amazement, her bright blue gaze sparkling with curiosity. "In the balcony?"

Flat-mouthed, Linda took refuge in, "I really couldn't say."

The rest of us promptly threw Tradition Five (Mind your own business) out the window. "Oh, don't give me that," I scolded. "This is *us*. Spill it."

Seeing our eager expressions, Linda let out an exasperated sigh, then whispered tightly, "In the orchestra pit, if you must know. After a wrap party for the opera."

All three of us recoiled almost imperceptibly in shock. *Not* an image of shy, anything-not-to-be-noticed Brooks I would ever have imagined!

Linda defended, "We'd both had too much to drink, and we slipped back into the theater to watch the sky effects. One thing led to another, and . . ."

The thought of Brooks getting silly and enticing Linda into the orchestra pit was so funny I would have laughed, had the possible consequences not been so dire.

"It doesn't matter where it happened. The only thing that matters is if it took or not." SuSu brushed off the sidetrack with a wave of her hand. "And if it did, what you're going to do about it." She peered into Linda's face. "You don't have to have it, you know."

Since SuSu's effort at a whisper was louder than my regular speaking voice, Linda and Diane glanced around to see if anyone had overheard, but there was no indication anyone had. The women at the next table seemed engrossed in their own conversations, and the elegant little old lady who lunched every day, almost always alone in her St. John suits at the same little double nearby, was safely out of earshot, staring politely into the middle distance as she always did.

"SuSu!" I hissed, my pro-life convictions sorely tested. I remembered the days before she was widowed, when we'd marched side by side against Roe v. Wade.

Teeny bristled up to the full extent of her tiny, devoutly Catholic self.

"Well," SuSu justified, "she doesn't have to go through with this."

Teeny flicked a vicious swat with her rolled napkin at SuSu's arm, eliciting a muffled yelp. "Bite your tongue for saying such a thing!"

She turned to Linda. "God's timing may not be our own, sweetie, but this could be a great blessing to you and Brooks. Think of Abraham and Sarah."

Linda's brows shot up. "Yeah, well, Sarah laughed when she found out. You won't catch me doing that."

Teeny leaned even closer. "But—"

"Teeny!" Diane clamped her hand across Teeny's mouth. "You're as bad as SuSu. Leave Linda alone. She's an intelligent woman. She knows what her options are."

I knew I should keep my mouth shut, but that's never been my strong suit. "You don't have to do anything drastic," I murmured close to the gray hair curling softly over Linda's ear beneath the turned-up brim of her red hat. "Plenty of childless couples would die for a baby from wonderful parents like you and Brooks."

"Georgia!" Diane turned on me. "Please. Leave the poor woman alone."

"Y'all . . ." Miserable, Linda raised her palms in a staying gesture. "Stop fighting. I feel bad enough as it is."

"How many times have you missed?" came out of my mouth, completely on its own.

"Three." Since menopause was a major topic of conversation at these get-togethers, we all knew she was the last one of us still having periods.

"Maybe Diane's right," I comforted. "Maybe it's just menopause."

Linda shook her head in denial. "Not unless that comes with morning sickness."

"Oh gosh, Linda." Teeny's eyes went huge. "Remember how sick you got on rice pudding when you were carrying Abby?"

Eeeyew.

Linda turned green at the gills. "Thanks so much for reminding me of that."

Abashed, Teeny patted her arm. "Oh, honey. I'm so sorry. I wasn't even thinking."

A long-suppressed memory surfaced from my own pregnancy. I'd gotten so sick from the dressing and spices in a loaded foot-long sub that, to this day, I can't bear the smell of a sandwich shop.

But pregnancy might not be the worst of Linda's worries, my internal Chicken Little ranted. Nausea and missed periods could signal some truly sinister possibilities at our age.

"We may be getting all het up for nothing." As usual, it was Diane who injected some rationality into the situation. She pointed to Linda's Kate Spade purse holding the pregnancy test. "Let's take that instant thingie downstairs to the bathroom and find out where we stand."

Never mind that Linda might prefer to take the test in the privacy of her own home, alone. "Do it here?" Linda whispered. "Are you nuts?"

But this was one cat that couldn't be put back in the bag. She'd kept mum for at least two months. If she didn't want us butting in, I reasoned, she wouldn't have said the pregnancy test was for her.

And I was just as eager to find out immediately as the others.

"If we do this here, it'll be all over town by suppertime."

"No, it won't." Taking Linda's arm and urging her up, Diane rose, a tight smile on her face for the benefit of all the surreptitious glances that turned our way. "Georgia will stand guard."

I stood and murmured through my own determinedly cheerful expression. "Speak for yourself. I want to be there."

Linda pulled free of Diane's solicitous grasp. "I can still walk by myself, thank you."

In all our years of lunching at the Coach House, we'd never gotten up en masse before, and the regulars noticed. Big time. Conversations all around us lulled with curiosity.

"Do you think we should all go at once?" Teeny questioned in a whisper. "People are starin'."

SuSu rose. "Oh, for cryin' out loud, Teeny. Let's just go."

The two of them followed as we headed for the stairs. We made such a spectacle wending through the tables in our red hats and purple outfits, that before long, everybody in the place was watching.

Maria came out of the kitchen and frowned in confusion. I detoured close to her and whispered, "Don't worry. Everything's under control. We'll be right back to order in a few minutes." I made a mental note to add an extra five to the fifty we always gave her to make up for monopolizing her table all day.

She nodded, but her expression remained confused.

Fortunately, there was no private party going on downstairs in the ground-level dining room, so we snagged a chair to block the door and headed into the elegant bathroom.

While I positioned myself to block anybody who might try to come in, SuSu took Linda's shoulders and steered her into the stall.

"Take your time," SuSu instructed her, "but when you finish, bring the thingie out here. We're all with you, sweetie." She gave Linda a hug, then closed the stall door and waited outside.

"Oh, y'all," Linda groaned out. "What if it's positive? I am way too old for this nonsense."

"Everything's gonna be fine, sweetie, no matter what," I told her through the stall door. It had taken me twenty years to train my husband to say that whenever I thought the world was falling apart, but even as I said it to Linda, I wondered how anything could ever be okay if the test was positive.

"Diapers. No sleep. Spit-up," she whined.

SuSu chimed in with a brisk, "You've got plenty of money to hire help. You could just kiss its little head every night at cocktail time, then send it back to the nursery. It'll adore you."

SuSu had been getting witchier and witchier as law school had progressed, a phase we'd all endured with the confidence that she'd eventually come back around, but this was beyond ignoring.

"Linda could no more ignore her own child," I scolded, "than you could have."

SuSu sniffed. "Well, she might not even have to." She leaned toward the door to the stall. "Hurry up and get this thing done."

Teeny lifted a finger in inspiration. "Maybe Abby and Osama Damned Boyfriend could raise it." Now, *there* was an ironic twist. Let the grown child raise the unplanned sibling, instead of the grandparents getting stuck with the unplanned grandbaby.

"Oh, Gawd!" echoed from the stall. "Just when I thought this couldn't get worse."

Diane rolled her eyes. "Can we please give the woman some peace?"

Teeny's sharp little features condensed in regret. "I was only tryin' to help."

Taut silence filled the room.

After a brief rustle of fabric, we heard Linda open the box. Then nothing. And more nothing. And more nothing.

"Y'all," Linda's plaint echoed from the stalls. "I can't do anything with you hovering out there listening. You've got to go outside. I promise, I'll come get you as soon as I'm done."

"Okay." Diane herded us toward the door. Outside, we congregated in an anxious huddle at the bottom of the stairs.

"I am serious, y'all," Diane told us in her teacher-at-the-parent-conference voice. "No matter what happens in there, don't push her. Just let her know we love her and we'll be there for her."

"Ohmygod," SuSu murmured, "the *orchestra pit*?"

A chortle escaped me and Teeny.

"A baby, at our age?" Diane mused aloud, but not loud enough to carry up the stairwell. "I'd have to jump off a bridge, that's all there is to it."

"But why would it be so much worse than a grandchild?" I argued. "Y'all can't seem to get enough of your grandkids." And I was so jealous.

"The P words, honey," SuSu said. "Pregnancy: we didn't have to carry them or deliver them. And they're not permanent; we can send them home with their mommies when we get tired. After a day with Peyton—"

The conversation came to an abrupt halt when a hapless thirty-something wearing Ann Taylor arrived on the landing above us. She halted. "Oh. Is there a line?"

I offered a sympathetic grimace. "Sorry. Are you urgent?"

She shook her head, no.

"Oh, good, cause the bathroom's temporarily out of order," I lied smooth as eye cream, "but they're fixing it. Should be done in twenty minutes."

Surely it wouldn't take longer than that for the test to give us the verdict. I had no idea. The last time any of us had been pregnant, you had to go to the doctor and kill a rabbit to find out.

The woman nodded, just registering our red hats. "Are y'all some kind of club?"

The four of us turned to her with a clearly dismissive "yes."

"Ah." She literally backed up. "Well, I'll try again later." She headed upstairs.

The bathroom door opened. "Okay." Linda was holding the plastic stick.

We all rushed inside and barricaded the door.

Diane peered at the little opening in the stick. "How long does it take?"

Linda frowned. "The box said three minutes. If the line shows up on the square, it's negative"—which, rumor had it, wasn't necessarily conclusive—"but if it turns up on the circle, it's positive." Now, *that* would be conclusive.

She checked her watch. "It's been two minutes."

"Hope it took more than two minutes to get this way," SuSu blurted out in a tactless attempt to lighten things up.

We all glared at her, then crowded around Linda for a better look at the dreaded section of the plastic wand.

Linda's mouth trembled. "Oh, y'all, I can't stand this. Here." She handed me the wand. "Just tell me what it says. No comments. Just tell me, positive or negative. That's it."

We nodded as she paced away from us, her arms crossed over her ample chest and her hands gripping her rounded biceps.

I stared at the indicators. Nothing yet.

SuSu shot a wide-eyed "better her than us" look my way. At least Brooks was devoted to Linda. There was no question that he'd support her no matter what.

Linda paced, her eyes averted.

Nothing yet. I pointed to the pregnancy test. "Maybe it's defective."

"Oh, Lord," Linda moaned out. "Please don't make me have to get another one and do it again. I drove all the way out to Decatur so I wouldn't run into anybody I knew."

I'd have gone to Macon.

Then, slowly, a line started to form on the wand. Across the circle.

We exchanged looks of dread, then turned our eyes to Linda.

Shades of *It's Never Too Late*, one of my favorite movies about a middle-aged pregnancy, starring Paul Ford and Maureen O'Sullivan came to mind. But this wasn't Hollywood.

Sensing our attention, Linda pivoted. One look at us was all it took. "Oh, no." The words seemed to catch in her throat, cutting off all her air. She went so pale, Diane and SuSu leapt forward to catch her if she fainted.

"Quick, the chair!" Diane ordered.

I managed to get it under Linda just as she sank down heavily. Pale as a paper towel, she focused her frustration in the safest place. "Damn, y'all. You act like I'm gonna faint. I never fainted in my life. Jewish women only faint if their children marry out of the faith." Her haggard appearance said otherwise. "What is, is," she declared as much to herself as to us. "This is not a tragedy. I can deal with this. It's not like something happened to Brooks or Abby." She dry-spit three times at the mere mention of such a thing.

"Never mind that I'll be sixty when she goes to kindergarten," she went on, a note of surreal giddiness creeping into her voice, "and seventy-three when college comes around." Her eyes widened. "Oh, Lord. What if it's a boy? I don't know anything about boys. What if he wants to do sports? The only sport Brooks cares about is golf. You can't play golf with a two-year-old."

SuSu laid a consoling hand on her shoulder. "Aren't you gonna cry?" she prodded. "Or wring your hands and curse fate? It's okay. We'll understand."

SuSu had a point. Linda was being entirely too calm.

"At least cuss!" she went on. "If you don't do something, this'll eat you alive."

Linda slumped. "I'm too damned tired to act up. And what good would it do, anyway? None."

We presented quite a bizarre picture, huddled around her in our red hats and purple, contemplating what life would be like for Linda with a fresh crop of stretch marks, baby fat, morning sickness, and high-risk complications. Not to mention breast-versus-bottle, midnight feedings, colic, dirty diapers, and finding a decent nanny.

"If it's a girl, don't name her Georgia," I chimed in, compelled to personalize this child-to-be—if in fact there was one. "She'll hate it."

"Or Tina," Teeny added. "I never liked my name."

Linda shook her head, half-dazed. "We're Jewish. We only name our children for dead people."

I'd forgotten. "Oh, yeah."

"Well, maybe Linda's not going to be naming anybody anything," SuSu declared.

"SuSu!" Diane warned. "Tradition Nine!"

"Nine, schmine," SuSu shot back without rancor. "We've all shot the traditions to smithereens already."

"Oh, settle down," I told her, still not able to accept the fact that this might really be happening.

When we'd all had our babies, our friendships had helped us through. But now, and only one of us facing motherhood? "Linda shouldn't do anything till she's been to a gynecologist and made sure of exactly what's going on," I said. "I still think this could be a hormonal hiccup."

Linda looked to me with doubt and gratitude. "Georgia's right." My favorite thing to be. "The only trouble is, my OB/GYN died of an aneurism two weeks ago. Had some poor woman in the stirrups and fell face-first right into her unmentionables. How awful is *that*?"

I guffawed, eliciting looks of reproach from the others. "Oh, lighten up, y'all. At least Linda still has her sense of humor."

Teeny patted Linda's arm, going misty. "The best times in my life were pregnancy and having little ones," she said with nostalgia.

"Yeah," SuSu countered, "but you were in your twenties. Linda's only ten years away from Medicare."

All of us, including Linda, glared at SuSu for yet again bludgeoning us with the obvious.

"This is not a catastrophe," Diane said, logical to the last. "We're with you all the way. Brooks can find you a wonderful OB/GYN to check things out, somebody discreet."

Linda's brave façade began to crumble. "I'm not sure I want to tell Brooks. Not until I know exactly what I'm up against. And what I want to do about it."

That caught us up short. Brooks and Linda were practically joined at the hip. I couldn't conceive of her keeping something this important from him, even for a little while.

We all thought it, but Diane was the one who blew Tradition Five yet again with, "But you have to tell him. He's the father. You can't not tell Brooks." She paused, a wicked gleam in her eye. "He *is* the father, isn't he?"

"Oh, for God's sakes," Linda blustered, trying not to smile at the preposterous question. "Of course, he's the father!"

"Of course, he is," Teeny appeased.

The tension broken, Linda blinked in that deadpan way of hers. "Any of y'all know a good obstetrician who specializes in geriatrics?"

Teeny raised a finger. "No, but I sure like mine. She's so nice, and only fifty-eight, so she won't stroke out on you. And she knows from experience that a hot flash is a hot flash, not a power surge."

"Let me get something to write with." Linda rummaged up a pen and little notepad from her purse. "What's her name?"

"Sandra Castellano. She's in with four other women at Piedmont. I like them all."

"You should try my doctor," SuSu offered. "He's single, gorgeous. Has the greatest dimples, and he flirts with all his patients. Makes me feel like a queen."

Leave it to SuSu to turn a pelvic exam into a recreational experience. Can we say "Wrong!" Frankly, the *last* place I want to be flirted with is when I'm trussed up in the stirrups.

"Only you," Linda retorted. Then she turned her attention back to Teeny. "Do you know Dr. Castellano's number?"

"Sure." Teeny rattled it off by heart. "And she gives you her home phone number, too, when you become her patient."

"Sounds too good to be true." Linda stuck the pen and tablet back into her purse.

"Here." I wrapped the pregnancy test in a paper towel and handed it back to Linda. "Wouldn't do to leave this lying around where somebody could find it. The gossips would have us all preggers."

SuSu sniffed at me in a most superior manner. "Do you honestly think anybody would root around in the trash for something like that?"

"Yes," Linda and Diane and I said in unison, eliciting the first genuine laugh since Linda had dropped her bombshell.

"I can see it now." Diane crooked her pinkie and peered down into the trashcan. "Lucretia Hottentot, special operative from ALTA"—that's the Atlanta Lawn Tennis Association, for all you nonnatives—"breaks out her rubber gloves and Purel, and dumpster dives for the scoop of the century." She mimed a banner headline, dead serious. "Respected Buckhead urosurgeon and Fox Theater board member impregnates wife in the orchestra pit after a rousing performance of *Aida*."

Linda grinned, the life returning to her eyes.

"This momentous conception," Diane went on, "was accomplished without the benefit of Viagra."

Linda covered her face, embarrassed, even as she nodded in confirmation.

Diane's tone dropped to FM levels. "Breaking with Jewish tradition, the child will be named for an inanimate object, not a dead person. If a boy, Bassoon. If a girl, Timpani and Glockenspiel are front-runners."

I flashed on the dead gynecologist with his face in his patient's privates, and let out a peal of semihysterical laughter.

"Easy, girl." Diane motioned us toward the door. "Come on. This calls for white wine." She pointed to Linda. "For everybody but you."

Linda bristled. "I drank a glass of wine with supper the whole time I was carrying Abby, and it didn't hurt a thing. So count me in."

We'd all indulged (in moderation) during our pregnancies, but at least we'd had the good sense to stop smoking.

"Well," Diane capitulated. "Maybe just one glass. Just this once."

As we started up the stairs, we met the woman from the landing, who greeted us with a cheery. "Oh, good. Everything back in order?"

"Honey," Linda said, "everything's about as out of order as it can get, but the toilets work just fine." With that, her tickle box tumped over.

Her giggles were contagious. We all dissolved as the confused woman edged by at a safe distance.

"Come on," I told the others, wiping happy-sad tears of release from my cheeks. "Double frozen fruit salads are on me." After all, Linda was eating for two.

Maybe.

4

Autumn

Our first monthly luncheon. Swan Coach House. Tuesday, October 8, 1973. 10:50 A.M.

*H*AVING LUNCH AT THE SWAN COACH HOUSE WAS A BRILLIANT idea, even if I do say so myself. One of my better inspirations, prompted by SuSu's coming home to show off her pregnant self. We'd even talked Diane into taking time off from teaching to come down from Chattanooga, where they'd been for the past two years since Harold had graduated from law school.

Not that Teeny and Pru and Linda and I didn't see each other often. We talked almost daily on the phone and got together, one on one, in a piecemeal fashion. But with motherhood looming for all of us but Linda and Diane, I'd felt a need to stake out some group time that would be sacred just for us. SuSu's visit had provided the perfect excuse.

And the Coach House was the perfect spot. Since the Forward Arts Foundation had converted the old Swan House garage into a tearoom and gift shop back in '65, the restaurant had instantly become *the* place to lunch for Old Atlanta, a welcome alternative for the gently impoverished (like our little group) who didn't belong to the Standard Club or Brookhaven or Cherokee. Staffed by a diverse mixture of socialite volunteers and down-to-earth professionals, the service was uneven. But the food was good, thanks to the feisty cook (Cookie, of course) who thought my mama hung the moon for giving Cookie's cousin a job in an era when nobody else would hire a young black woman pregnant out of wedlock.

I arrived early to make sure we got a good table, but the volunteer hostess would have none of it.

She straightened to the full extent of her book-on-the-head posture and condescended, "I'm so sorry, but your full party must be here in order to be seated. Policy, you know."

Give some people a little power . . .

"Is Cookie here?" I asked sweetly. Nobody, I mean nobody, dared to cross Cookie.

The hostess faltered. "Of course. She's in the kitchen, as always."

No doubt cracking the whip over the volunteers.

"Could you please ask her to come out for just a second? Tell her it's Georgia Peyton Baker." I batted my eyelashes. "Or, I'd be happy to go for her myself, if you'll just show me where—"

"Oh, no," the volunteer hostess hastened. "I'll go ask her. But I doubt she'll come. This is the busiest time for her."

The hostess disappeared into the kitchen. She'd scarcely gotten inside before she came back out with Cookie right behind her, perfuming the air with an offering of her heavenly little cinnamon rolls.

"Lord have mercy." Cookie spread her arms to embrace me. "Would you look at you, child! Gonna be a mama."

At only five months, my stomach muscles had already cried uncle, putting me into Empire maternity dresses, but the most alarming development was that my butt was spreading to gargantuan proportions. Nobody had warned me about that butt business. Mine had been too wide *before* I got pregnant.

Suddenly feeling self-conscious and anything but beautiful, I placed my hands over my spreading middle. "Yep. I'm gonna be a mama."

Cookie drew me into a giant hug that smelled of Clorox and cinnamon, then thrust me to arm's length. "I bet your mama can hardly wait."

I grinned. "She's pretty excited."

"When's it due?"

"Not till February."

She eyed me in surprise. "Woo-eee. Must be a boy, then, big as you are. You want Cookie to see what it is?"

Mama swore up and down that Cookie's method of telling whether a baby would be a boy or a girl was foolproof, but it was hardly appropriate for the Coach House. I chuckled. "Cookie, darlin', I don't think the good ladies of Buckhead are ready to walk in and find me lyin' on a table while you dangle a pencil by a needle and thread over my pregnant self to see if it circles or goes side-to-side."

The image appealed to me in a perverse way, but that was back when I still cared what people thought of me. "Thanks anyway, though. But it's a great idea. Maybe we'll go back to my house after lunch and do it on all four of us."

"All four of you?"

"Yep. Pru Bonner and Teeny Grantham and SuSu McIntyre. We're all expecting." Out of habit, I used their maiden names; that was how Cookie knew them, anyway, from our bridal showers here. But with babies in the works, the time had come to "remember their mizzes" as Cookie would have put it. I needed to start referring to us by our married names. "SuSu's home from Beaufort for a visit, so the whole bunch of us from high school are getting together for lunch."

"Well," Cookie declared. "Idn't that just fine?" She pointed to my tummy. "I don't need no pencil to tell that's a boy, though. I discerns it."

Cookie was famous for "discerning" things, a talent she attributed to the Holy Spirit.

"Dr. Velkoff thinks it might be twins, but it's too early to know." I grinned and patted my belly. "I hope it is. I've always wanted two kids." (Never have more children than you have hands.) "It would be great to get it all over with at once." So far, my pregnancy had been no picnic, so it wasn't an experience I looked forward to repeating.

Unlike Teeny, whose first pregnancy and delivery had been a piece of cake. She'd glowed like a field of sunlit daffodils all the way through, the shadow of secret sadness erased from her shy smile for the first time since I'd known her. Now, she said, she wanted ten little stairsteps.

Her and Reid's families had been delirious with joy over the first grandson of the Witherspoon developer dynasty. They were almost as thrilled when she got pregnant less than a year later, interpreting it as yet another evidence of divine *benedictus*.

Oy. I just didn't get it. Can we say, "Recovery time?"

Cookie cocked her hairnetted head at me. "Ain't no twins in there, I'm tellin' ya." She handed me the basket of cinnamon rolls. "Here. Feed that boy some of Cookie's good rolls. Give him sweets, so he'll be sweet."

Sounded like a great concept to me. "Thanks." I leaned close and whispered conspiratorially, "Cookie, I need a favor. I'd really like to get a table right away, but this woman here says it's not 'policy.'"

Cookie turned on the hapless hostess. "What you mean, keepin' this precious child out here when she needs to be sittin' at a table with some tea so she can eat Cookie's nice, hot rolls?" She turned back to me. "How many of y'all is there gonna be, honey?"

I counted off on my fingers, "Me, Teeny, Linda, Diane, SuSu, and Pru. Six."

She placed her fists on her hips. "Mmmm-mmmm! Let's get y'all a table close to the kitchen so's I can keep an eye on you."

Ignoring the hostess's look of disapproval, Cookie ushered me toward a sixer in the back corner by the window. "You just sit yourself down, and I'll send one of those little dilly-tunts out with some nice Constant Comment tea to settle your stomach."

I sat, trying not to gloat at the frustrated hostess. She'd get over it. Soon the lobby would be filled with women she could keep from seating till their parties were complete.

Cookie headed back toward the kitchen. "And some iced water. Babies bring up the heat in a woman, that's for sure."

"Thanks so much. And thanks again for the rolls." She always remembered just what I liked.

I watched her return to "her" kitchen.

My tea and iced water were out in no time, delivered by a curious volunteer server who clearly wasn't impressed by my connections in low places. I was glad when she left me in peace.

Sitting there with only the clash of pans and Cookie's muffled orders to break the pleasant silence of that sunny spring morning, I had no idea that thirty years later, all but one of us would still gather monthly in that same, exact spot for the sacred ritual of friendship that started that day.

I just sipped my tea and wolfed down those delicious little cinnamon rolls before the others got there and I'd be forced to share.

Truth be told, I've always been greedy about my food. I confess it. Maybe because there had always been just enough, never extra, at my house growing up. But I savored each and every crumb of those warm little rolls.

I'd just finished the last one when Teeny waddled into the foyer from outside wearing a maternity dress with a floral Banlon, long-sleeved top, a yellow sash tied in a bow at the Empire waist, and a ballooning navy blue skirt big enough to slipcover a VW bug. On her tiny legs, poor Teeny looked "big as a tick," as my country grandpa used to put it.

I waved my napkin, forgetting protocol, and called, "Woo-hoo! Over here!" (I'm the only one in my family who didn't get the discreet sensibilities gene, a fact that has prompted much eye-rolling long-suffering in my genteel mother.) Unable to resist annoying the hostess, I raised my voice again. "I pulled strings and got us a table early."

I didn't worry about embarrassing Teeny. She was unflappable, and way too pregnant to care about anything but her approaching due date in two weeks.

She waddled over and pulled out a chair. "Whew. I sure am glad you went ahead and got us a place to sit down for good. I do not want to have to get up any more than absolutely necessary."

She said it with a smile, though. Even now, when there was more baby than Teeny, she radiated excitement. It was contagious. Fatherhood had mellowed Reid. He'd even cut back on his drinking and started coming home more.

She collapsed into the chair with a plunk. "Whuff. I think I'm about ready to put this baby *down*," she said without a shred of complaint.

Frankly, gravity being what it is, I'd have bet my house she'd never make it to her due date, especially since this was her second. And especially since she'd had to have a C-section with Christian, which had come as no surprise to anybody, since Christian weighed almost eight pounds. This time around, she was stuck having another C-section, but she'd opted not to schedule it ahead of time, saying God, not some doctor, would be the one to decide her baby's birthday.

So I'd put $5 on the week-early slot of our Baby Pool. (We hadn't told Teeny about the pool, just to make sure nature took its course. She might have held out for full term, just to prove she could.)

She sniffed. "Mmmmm. I smell cinnamon rolls."

Busted. A hot tide of embarrassment rushed to my face—a common occurrence since I'd entered my second trimester. "Sorry. I scarfed them all."

Teeny smiled her sweet little smile, a devilish glint in those big, innocent baby blues of hers. "How'd you manage to get 'em? I'm starved."

"Cookie. That's how I got the table, too."

Teeny grinned. "Good old Cookie." She craned toward the kitchen doors. "Do you think she'll—?"

As if by telepathy, two volunteer waitresses merged with butter, five waters, a fresh basket full of hot cinnamon rolls, and another hot tea.

Teeny brightened. "Oooo, goodie." She plucked a tiny cinnamon roll and popped it into her mouth. Her eyes closed in pleasure. "Yum."

I took another look at all that baby in her lap. "How there's room in your stomach for one atom of food is a mystery to me."

"Me, too." She put four sugars into her teacup, then poured and stirred. "But just these past few days, I'm ravenous."

There was no justice. The woman had had not one iota of morning sickness, fatigue, or heartburn, while I'd had enough for both of us, and I was only halfway.

"Eat up, then." It occurred to me that Teeny's sudden appetite might be significant, so I made a note to ask Cookie if sudden appetite augured anything in her pregnancy lore.

Changing my slot on the baby pool would cost me another $5, but that would bring the pot up to $80, enough to buy four decent maternity dresses or 320 gallons of gas, all of which had top priority at our house while John was finishing his doctorate at Tech.

After a trickle of customers came in, SuSu and Linda arrived together. We'd all offered to have SuSu stay with us while she was in town, but Linda had won out since she had the most room. (Thanks to her and Brooks's parents, who'd donated the down payment on a nice house—one *they'd* picked out—when Brooks had started his surgical residency at Emory.)

Watching the girls come in, I scarcely saw Linda—trim as ever in a blue Chanel suit—for the sight of our no-longer-lanky SuSu, clearly showing at six and a half months despite her roomy beige chemise. We hadn't laid eyes on SuSu in the three years since her adorable husband had taken her away from us by buying a vet practice in Beaufort, SC, where SuSu was now making money hand over fist as an Avon lady.

Teeny and I waved, then motioned them over.

"Look at you," I exclaimed at the softened lines of her face, her thickened upper arms, and her newly prominent behind. "You're almost fluffy."

She giggled and gave me a hug. "Ditto. You're bigger than I am, and five weeks behind me."

While the three of us fell into a baby fest, an unusually subdued Linda slipped quietly into the chair beyond SuSu.

"So," Teeny said, bright with curiosity despite the fact that we'd all talked to SuSu at least once a week since she'd left. "What's it like as the premier makeup lady and wife of a beloved Low Country, small animal vet?"

Grinning, SuSu wrinkled her nose. "Colorful. And smelly." Her eyes went distant with adoration. "But wonderful. Perfect."

Linda dry-spit three times to keep from tempting fate with such bold talk, but if ever two people were made for each other, they were Tom Harris and SuSu. His love had helped heal the pain of SuSu's past hurts, and for that, she worshipped the man. So did I (in a strictly platonic way, of course).

Teeny waggled her naturally blond eyebrows at SuSu. "Things that good, eh?"

SuSu's expression glowed with pride. "Amazing. I love my life, making a home with Tom right next door at the clinic and meeting all the local women at makeover parties. It's just like the Donna Reed Show." She seemed almost shy, but so, so happy. "And best of all, we've found a really wonderful little community church nearby."

This, she hadn't told us, but SuSu had always played it close to the vest about religion.

"What denomination?" Diane asked.

"None, which I like." SuSu radiated peace and hope. "Plain faith, without a lot of rules. It's almost like going back in time there," she told us. "Things are simple and good. The pastor's truly humble and so encouraging."

I never would have guessed that SuSu, of all people, would find comfort in any church, but she clearly had. "SuSu, I'm so glad," I told her, despite a skeptical nag of concern. I was still searching for my own answers in that department, but the calm assurance on her face made me wonder if I might not need to give the organized religion another look.

"The church is the center of everyone's social, as well as spiritual, life," she went on. "We love it. Just love it. And Tom's been nominated as an elder." She grinned. "Can you see me as an elder's wife?"

Teeny squeezed SuSu's hand. "Absolutely."

A small commotion at the entry to the dining room drew our eyes to Pru—our own version of Cher with long, wildly curly dark hair—who on this particular fall day had on wide-striped hip-hugger bell-bottoms, platform shoes, a "Mama Cass" floppy hat, a macramé vest, and a clearly braless peasant shirt. She'd just spilled the contents of her macramé shoulder tote at the feet of half a dozen waiting customers, who sidestepped the scattered belongings.

I watched her snatch up a plastic bag of what looked like herbs, while several nearby patrons did proper Geisha stoops to help corral a giant bottle of Tums, a snarl of love beads, a pipe—a *pipe?*—a pack of Newports, an Afro pick, a can of Aqua Net, and three half-eaten tubes of fruit Lifesavers, among other things.

Oblivious to the stares prompted by her counterculture couture, Pru bent down—her striped ass high, exposing six inches of "bad skin" above her hip-huggers—but her efforts hindered more than helped. Things kept falling back out.

"Oh, Lord," Linda muttered with uncharacteristic disdain when she saw the pipe.

"What?" I glanced from Pru to Linda and back again. "She's always been a klutz. That never embarrassed you before." Teeny's and SuSu's expressions echoed my confusion.

Linda shook her head at us, then heaved a sardonic sigh. "Oh, never mind. Maybe ignorance *is* bliss." My, but she was grumpy.

Ever-demure Diane entered the foyer just in time to see Pru's striped butt pointed skyward in her direction. Smooth as a figure skater, she promptly made a U-turn back out into the parking lot to avoid being part of the spectacle.

I started to get up and go help, but SuSu motioned me back into my chair. "She's okay."

Her floppy hat askew, Pru had finally started toward us, the knotted fringe on her shoulder bag lashing diners along the way.

Pru had the biggest heart of us all, so we—like everyone who loved her—easily forgave her lack of social graces. Only those who didn't know the woman underneath assumed she was merely a hippie and an airhead—which she was, but there was more to her than that. True, she'd been behind the door when the book smarts had been handed out, but she was the kindest person I'd ever known, even with those who didn't deserve it—most notably, her lazy, controlling husband, Tyson.

When she reached the table and looked up, she zeroed in on Teeny and hooted, "Oh . . . my . . . God! Quick, boil some water! This woman is surely gonna pop, on the spot."

When everybody in the room turned to see for themselves, Teeny colored up, but her laughter held no reproach for Pru. "Not according to my OB." Teeny smoothed her hands across the expanse of navy blue fabric. "He swears I'll go another two weeks."

Pru and I exchanged brief, guilty Baby Pool glances, then stifled laughter, but Linda merely put on a pained smile.

Meanwhile back in the foyer, Diane held open the door for an older lady, discreetly checking to make sure the coast was clear, then headed over. She made it to the table in plenty of time to get in on the hugs and exclamations.

"Sorry I'm late, y'all," Diane said as she air-kissed me. "Mama's so glad to have me home, she all but handcuffed me to the sofa to keep me from leavin'."

"Glad you got away." I hugged her extra hard. "Can you believe we're all here? Is this too great, or what?"

As the official keeper of ties and maker of traditions for our group, I reveled in having my best friends together after three years. Even Pru's little mishap hadn't put a dent in my high spirits. I could scarcely believe the six of us had finally managed it. Or that four of us were expecting at the same time, excluding Linda—for whom a pregnancy now would be a disaster, since Brooks was only midway through his surgical residency—and Diane.

We hadn't planned to reproduce *en masse*; it just happened. SuSu swore it was divine providence. My mama said it must be something in the water. (Periodically while we were growing up, everybody on College Circle would just turn up pregnant. Of course, that was before the pill.) Diane had teased us that babies were contagious. She claimed that Pru and I and SuSu had seen how happy Teeny was with her first pregnancy and perfect-baby Christian—What other kind of baby would our angelic Teeny have?—and gotten the bug ourselves.

I couldn't answer for the others, but to be honest, I'd gotten pregnant because it was what came next. Tired of working at menial jobs, I'd opted to do what my mama had done before me: raise my family. I mean, heck, I'd put John through graduate school, and his dissertation was finally submitted. We could manage fine on a Tech professor's salary. I clipped coupons, did my own decorating, and sewed.

Unusually flushed, Diane took the seat next to Linda and gulped her iced water. Then she grinned at us so hard she showed her molars.

Teeny cocked her head, eyes narrowing. "And what's put that thorn-eatin' grin on your face, young lady?"

With that, the rest of us hushed right up and turned to hear the answer.

Diane inhaled, scanning us one by one with bright expectation, heightening the suspense. "Well, I did it," she blurted out at last. "Y'all aren't the only ones expecting. I'm pregnant."

We all exploded. Except Linda, who looked miserable. But the rest of us were too caught up with Diane's announcement to deal with it.

"Aaagggh!" Teeny waved her napkin rather than get up, but the rest of us surrounded Diane with hugs.

"When?" SuSu demanded.

As usual, I stuck my foot in my mouth. "I thought Harold didn't want any?"

Diane laughed. "He doesn't, but I said it was my way or the high-way."

Pru punched a fist skyward. "Right on, sister."

So much for romantic illusions about marriage. (Not that I had any of those, myself.) But Diane had always said she married Harold be-cause she wanted to. With no other suitors, she'd been grateful for what she had and said yes.

She took a delicate sip of tea. "I did sweeten the deal, though. Of-fered him all the blow jobs he wants."

"Bwah-ha-ha." Pru spit tea halfway across the table in delight.

Hearing that crass proposition come out of Diane's prim little mouth shocked the rest of us as much as it must have shocked Harold. I all but broke up laughing.

"What did he say?" SuSu asked, aghast.

"What *could* he say?" Diane answered. "I told him I would be in charge of the child, anyway. Harold never lifts a finger at home, as it is. All he's responsible for is the money." She bit into a cinnamon roll. "Mmm. These are yummy."

A totally crass rejoinder connecting the comment to her "deal sweetener" with Harold came to mind, but I actually thought better of blurting it out. "Obviously," I said instead, "he decided to go along."

Diane nodded. "I think the blow jobs were the deciding factor."

This time, I did laugh, along with the others, even gloomy Linda.

Diane's mouth flattened. "He countered with some stipulations: he refuses to change any diapers or get up in the night or put it to bed or feed it or babysit it alone."

Pru sat erect in outrage. "The man's a male chauvinist pig."

This whole no-bra feminist thing was the latest nonsense Pru had picked up from Tyson's hippie friends, but we didn't hold her respon-sible. She always had been gullible.

"Pooh," Teeny deflected. "Reid doesn't do any of that stuff either. I don't care. The baby's worth it."

Diane nodded. "I'm sure Harold expected me to argue with him about all that, but I didn't. I just said, 'Fine.'" A smug smile eased her expression. "My mother will be delighted to come help out as long as I'll let her, but I saw no need to mention that to him."

A delicious irony, since there was no love lost between Harold and

Mrs. Culpepper. Midnight feedings and poopy diapers might not look quite so bad if it meant getting rid of his mother-in-law.

"It took a few days for him to decide," she explained, calm as you please. "Mostly to make sure I was serious about leaving him if he didn't go along."

Divorce was a no-no in the corporate world. Not to mention the fact that Harold had political aspirations. So Diane had brought a really big stick to the negotiations. "But then he agreed," she concluded. "That was in May, and boy, did it happen fast. I'm almost four months." She giggled. "Lord, it was hard to keep this a secret till I got here. I was dyin' to tell y'all, but I wanted to wait and surprise you."

"What's Harold's attitude like now?" Teeny asked her.

"Fine. I make sure it doesn't interfere with his routine. We still go sailing and entertain a lot." She wrinkled her nose. Boy, was she in for some jealousy when Harold went from being the center of her attention to being a daddy. But if anybody could manage him, it was Diane. "I knew Harold was spoiled when I married him, but we have a lot of fun together. It's a very nice life."

Not unlike John and me. After my high school sweetheart had disappeared, breaking my heart, I'd dutifully gone to college, where I'd met and married my husband because he adored me and he was safe—gentle, industrious, steady, and dependable. It hadn't mattered to him that I didn't return his depth of feeling. We, too, had "a nice life."

Carrying our child, I prayed I would feel the fierce devotion for my baby that I could not give its father.

"Wow. How brave of you to confront your husband like that." SuSu's fingertips went to her lip. "But what if he doesn't come around? What if he hates having a child?" Unthinkable, but Harold was awfully spoiled. Susu's green eyes went wide. "What if he leaves you?"

In that day and age, the most horrible of fates.

"Then I'll have my child and plenty of alimony," Diane said with impressive conviction. She always had been the most flat-footed of all of us. "There's no doubt in my mind that Harold will make plenty of money in the banking business."

Diane straightened. "I don't want to talk about Harold, anyway. Let's talk babies."

"Has anybody decided what kind of delivery they want?" I asked.

"Besides Teeny, of course." Pru raised her hand just like she used to in school. "I'm going natural all the way, at home with a midwife," she announced.

I'd thought midwives went out with the turn of the century.

"You are kiddin' me," Linda challenged with more than a little edge to her voice, which was understandable, as the wife of a doctor. "What if something goes wrong?"

"Millions and millions of women all over the world have babies without hospitals." Never comfortable with confrontation, Pru toyed with the deep ruffle that fell from her elbow. "The midwife can always call in help if she sees signs of trouble." She finally looked us in the eye, sweet as ever. "I went to see this fortuneteller in a spiritualist commune near Suches, and she said I'd have three girls without a hitch, and we'd move to Montana and make a fortune."

She smiled with perfect assurance. "So I'm going with natural breathing and Zen for pain control. And then I'm gonna breast-feed. No synthetic chemicals for this baby."

"Speak for yourself." I spread my napkin across what was left of my lap. "I want an easy delivery: knock me out with the first contraction and don't wake me up until it's time to go to the hairdresser." I wasn't kidding.

Diane took a sip of her water. "Not me. We're making the drive up to Vandy. They've got that new epidural method. Much easier on the baby than a general, but hardly any pain. That's what I'm going for."

"Pooh," I disclaimed. "Northside has that, too, but when they told me they were the first hospital in Atlanta *insured* to do that procedure, and I could go back to my room *when I could move my legs*, I wanted no part of it. Plus, you have to dilate to five before they'll even give it to you. My big sister was plenty miserable before she got that far with her delivery, I can tell you."

Diane sniffed. "Oh, pipe down, George. They wouldn't do the thing if it wasn't safe."

I waggled a cinnamon roll in her direction. "That's what they said about laser circumcisions, and a bunch of poor little boys got their thingies fried off before the doctors went back to the old way."

The others winced. As usual, I'd gone too far and said too much.

Our mothers would have died if they'd known we were discussing such unladylike matters in a public place, much less the Coach House. But it was the seventies, after all. Let it all hang out.

Well, most of it. We *were* Southern girls, so we still had rules, not the least of which were the five sacred traditions we'd developed since we were pledges in Mademoiselle.

In an effort to shift to a more acceptable topic, I went from the frying pan to the fire. "How's your morning sickness, Pru. Any better?"

"Awful. Death on wheels. But I finally got it under control." She glanced from left to right at the tables filling with women in their best lady-lunch Puccis and Howard Wolfs, then leaned in close to confide. "I was afraid to take prescriptions for it. I mean, can we say, 'thalidomide?' Then I found something that works. All natural." Another glance from side to side, then she pulled out the little bag of "herbs" for a peek. "Acapulco Gold, honey. No more morning sickness."

Acapulco Gold?

This was Atlanta, mind you, not San Francisco, so I had no idea what Pru was talking about. Marijuana and cocaine were just finding their way to the golden ghettoes of Buckhead, thanks to transplants like Tyson.

"Oh, good grief," Linda scolded in a tight whisper. "Get rid of that. Are you trying to get us arrested?"

"Pot, is that pot?" SuSu's features congealed in righteous indignation. "Are you nuts?" I was sure Pru hadn't come up with this on her own. "I knew Tyson Fouché was nothing but trouble," SuSu fumed, pointing an exact replica of our mothers' Finger of Judgment at Pru. "That's *illegal*," she whispered tightly. "You can go to jail just for having that stuff in your purse."

Pru dismissed our objections with the same carefree spirit that she'd used when dismissing our concerns about marrying Tyson. "It's strictly medicinal. And anyway, look around. Do you see one cop?"

I couldn't believe she was being so cavalier about getting caught with illegal drugs, or so cynical. "Never mind about that." Feeling very self-righteous (having given up my precious menthols for my unborn child's benefit), I felt compelled to scold, "Have you even considered what that stuff might do to your baby?"

"Oh, this is not nearly as damaging as tobacco," she rattled off.

"And it's a lot safer than those prescription drugs. Purely organic." She leaned in to whisper, "I grow it myself, just to be safe." She smiled. "Tyson knows loads of people back in L.A. who used it for morning sickness. They all had perfectly healthy babies."

Lord, help us. Typical Tyson malarkey.

We'd known he smoked dope occasionally in high school and college, which some people (not us) thought was cool as grits. But Pru never even drank. It hadn't occurred to us that Tyson might turn her on to marijuana.

An awkward lull settled over us. I mean, what in the good, green earth do you say to somebody who's smoking marijuana for morning sickness?

The waitress arrived, providing a welcome distraction. "May I bring you ladies something to drink?" she asked, meaning soft drinks.

It was 1973, and you had to go to a private club to get wine or Bloody Marys with a meal before happy hour in Buckhead. Not that any of us would consider drinking in the middle of the day. We'd outgrown that with spring break and fraternity weekends.

We all ordered sweet tea; then Diane directed the conversation to safer ground. "What did I miss before I came in?"

I gave SuSu an affectionate nudge. "SuSu here has been telling us how much she loves her little church in Beaufort. And her husband, who has been nominated as an elder."

"And our dogs," SuSu added. "We have a great golden retriever and two Irish setters. Tom has them so well trained, they're a joy to be around." Her mother had never let her have any pets. "And Tom's beside himself about the baby. Says he'll be happy with anything. Long as it's human."

"Oh, SuSu," Pru beamed for her. "I'm so glad. Nobody deserves more happiness than you do."

Except maybe Pru. A few years as married women had given us new perspectives on the "anything goes" atmosphere at Pru's house, where we'd all flocked in our teens. And on Mr. Bonner's drinking, attributed to his stint in a German POW camp during The Big One.

"What about you, Diane?" I asked. "What's the latest scoop from Chattanooga, besides the baby?"

She shrugged. "I miss Nashville, but Harold says we'll be able to transfer back in a few years. I'm still teaching kindergarten, for as long as they'll let me." Visibly pregnant teachers were still a no-no in a lot of places. "But we can manage just fine on Harold's salary. He's doing really well at the bank, probably because they love the same shades of gray."

It was the first time she'd ever acknowledged his penchant for shaving corners. Personally, I'd always thought Harold was way too slick, but Diane had steadfastly accepted him as he was. Until this baby business.

"What about you, SuSu?" Diane asked her. "Any ideas about what kind of delivery you want?"

SuSu's green eyes sparked with mischief. "Tom says we can save tons if he does the delivery in his surgery. He'll just knock me out, then when it's all over, send me home with a cardboard funnel around my neck."

After a heartbeat of silence, we all got the unexpected joke and laughed, but Linda's was forced.

As conversations broke out around us, I leaned over to Linda and whispered into the side of her brown bouffant. "Are you okay? I know you must feel a little left out, but your time will come." I pulled away to let her see my concern.

Oh-oh. Shouldn't have said anything.

Big tears spilled over onto her cheeks and her face contorted so badly that she hid behind her napkin.

Linda never cried.

Instant guilt made me kick myself for asking, as if it was all about me. "Oh, honey, I'm so sorry. I shouldn't have pushed."

The others instantly zeroed in on us.

Linda wasn't supposed to cry. Linda never cried.

She inhaled deeply, struggling to regain her composure, and wiped the napkin briskly under her Leslie Gore–eyelinered eyes. "No. No. 'S okay." Another deep breath. "I'm fine. Just give me a minute." But her mouth didn't cooperate, flivering like a worm on a hot sidewalk. She waggled her napkin at us. "Talk. Just talk. Please." The last was a plea, but the one time women can't make small talk is when someone they love is in trouble.

"Honey, what is it?" Pru coaxed. "Brooks hasn't gone and done anything stupid, has he?"

Brooks? Fooling around? More likely the pope than Brooks!

Linda's pitiful expression went rock-solid. "Of course Brooks hasn't done anything stupid. Don't be ridiculous." She faltered again. "It was me who did something stupid."

That made us all sit up and take notice. Linda, fooling around?

Nah!

Her eyes welled huge again, her mouth taut. "I took the bleemin' pills. Never missed a one. Just like always. Ninety-nine-percent effective. That's cold comfort when you're in the one percent."

Pru frowned in confusion, but I knew exactly what Linda was talking about.

"Agh," I gasped. "The pill." Oh, good glory! Were we *all* pregnant, every last one of us?

Linda's case of the pitifuls gave way to tight anger. "Yes. It didn't work. I'm officially pregnant, dammit."

No guessing how she felt about it, no siree. Brooks still had three more years of surgical residency, then years of building his practice.

"How does Brooks feel about it?" SuSu asked.

"Oh, he's delirious with joy. Says it'll be fine," Linda railed. "The man's a genius at medicine, but an idiot when it comes to money. He has no idea how much it takes to keep that house up and pay the bills, as it is. And there's no way the store will let me stay on after I start showing." She worked for an exclusive bridal shop and loved her job.

But there was no question that Linda would have her baby, regardless. We were respectable married women. Respectable married women in our world had their babies and brought them up, loved them, no matter what. We were the Boomers, privileged beyond any generation before us, well-educated and well-indoctrinated in our roles.

But at that moment, none of us knew what to say.

Not that it was the end of the world, but I thought better of reminding her that God's timing is always better than our own. Judging from her threatening expression, she'd probably attack me bodily across the table, which would give the Ladies Who Lunch something to chat about, yes siree.

Teeny—her instincts impeccable, as usual—got up and lumbered over to hug Linda. "Oh sweetie. It'll be okay," she crooned. "It really, really will be okay. You'll manage, and we'll all help you."

The perfect response to any crisis.

Now it was Linda's turn to argue that it *wouldn't* be okay (a necessary part of the process) and she obliged. "No, it won't. I'll be all by myself with a little baby to take care of. I'll be up to my neck in diaper service and formula and sterilizers, and too tired to do anything but lie there if Brooks should actually make it home, and God be praised, want to do something besides sleep." She gathered steam. "Poor kid probably won't even know he has a father."

She spread her stubby little hands. "I can see it now, at the bar mitzvah: 'Mom, who's that guy next to Gramma? See? That one there. Gramma's picking lint off his suit with one hand and force-feeding him cake with the other.'"

Suddenly, for the first time in her life, Linda sounded like one of the comediennes on the comedy album, *You Don't Have to Be Jewish,* as if conception had sucked the Southern right out of her and replaced it with New York. The effect was mesmerizing. And highly disconcerting.

"Oh, don't worry, dahling," Linda went on to her imaginary son. "That's just your fahtha. You remember him. He's the guy with the stethoscope who came to Passover three years ago."

At least she was cracking wise.

"Oy." She threw up her hands just exactly as her mother always had, with the same inflection and expression. "Oy, oy, oy."

"That does it." I motioned across the table. "You have officially turned into Miriam Bondurant."

Linda let out an exaggerated moan, but the tension was broken. "And I thought things couldn't get any worse."

"So," Pru asked. "What're you gonna do about it?"

Linda looked at her, blank, lapsing back into her Southern self. "What do you mean, do about it?" She frowned. "Last time I looked, being pregnant meant I'm gonna have me a baby. Works that way for everybody."

"Not everybody," Pru said, as innocently as if she were announcing the weather was nice. "I've been reading Gloria Steinem, and she says our bodies are our own, and we don't have to have children unless we're ready for them, and there's no shame in it. We've just been brainwashed by a repressive, male-dominated society. Particularly religion. Religion has been an instrument of feminine oppression since its inception."

Oppression? Inception? These words were actually coming out of Pru's mouth?

Pru, reading anything she didn't have to, much less a godless radical like Gloria Steinem?

I was so shocked, I didn't even consider the heresy she was parroting smack in the middle of this enclave of traditional Southern womanhood.

For the second time that day, she'd rendered the rest of us speechless.

So we did what all good Southern girls do when somebody lays a big, fat egg. We politely changed the subject.

And after lunch, we all went over to Linda's, where we threaded a needle, stuck it into the eraser of a pencil, and dangled it over our babies, one by one.

Mine had a little trouble making up its mind, but eventually settled into a strong crosswise pendulum. Sure enough, I had Jack. When I carried Callie six years later, it circled.

Teeny's swung strong and true, straight across. Reid was a lot of things, but he did make sons, and another son Teeny did have. Right smack dab on her due date, winning the Baby Pool, which she'd known about all along, herself.

With Linda, the pencil circled slightly, then went still. A week later, she lost the baby. Brooks was home and said it was for the best, since she'd been taking the pill for the whole first month she'd been pregnant and not known about it. Three years later, the pencil circled strong for daughter Abby, the light of their life.

Diane's showed a boy, and a mighty smart one he turned out to be. And believe it or not, his daddy turned out to be a half-decent father. Only half-decent, mind you, but you've got to consider what you're working with there.

SuSu's circled hard from the get-go. Girl. Her daughter was born four months later, as lively a child as her mother had been timid. SuSu's star athlete and scholar of a son came later, his gender accurately predicted by the pencil.

Pru's pencil swung sideways. She scoffed, arguing that the psychic had never been wrong (more malarkey). But apparently, smoking marijuana for morning sickness didn't nullify the predictive effect of the dangling pencil, and sure enough, she had a boy. But the pot might have had something to do with the fact that little Bubba turned out to be a rovin', tokin' career Deadhead. Either that, or Pru and Tyson's getting busted on the six o'clock news for wholesaling cocaine.

5

I Always Wanted
to Be a Princess

The Playpen adult novelty superstore, Piedmont Road. Thursday, April 10, 2003. 11:00 A.M.

TURNED OFF PIEDMONT, IGNORING THE EMPTY PARKING SPACES BY the front door, and took the narrow side drive to the cramped rear lot.

A word to the wise: If you ever find yourself going to an adult toy store, park in the back, especially if you have a license plate everybody knows. Even in a big city, you never know who'll come driving by.

My first time (this was only my second) I'd made the mistake of pulling in right up by the front door, and one of my church circle members spotted my prestige license tag. At our next meeting, she waited until we were all seated with our coffee and I was drinking mine to lean over and whisper—in front of everybody—that she'd spotted my "Mooma" prestige tag outside the "porn store," and felt it her duty to warn me that John had borrowed my car for illicit purposes.

I managed to keep from spraying the room with coffee, but the mouthful swallowed like a concrete block. It took all my self-control to smile benignly, then whisper back that I appreciated her concern, but there must have been some kind of mistake.

Lord knows who else she'd told. Frankly, I was more than happy to let John take the fall. But I was so embarrassed, I had the mother of all hot flashes—in spite of my hormone replacement therapy—and was stuck there, acting as if nothing was wrong, for another hour. (No way was I turning tail and ceding the room to that gossip in sheep's clothing, even if I spontaneously combusted.)

So definitely park in the back. And go early, during the week, as soon as they open (ordinarily, 10:00 A.M.). Aside from a lone—usually sleepy—salesperson and a few die-hard porn fans who can't wait to swap out their videos, you'll have the place to yourself.

Forget going at lunch. They're slammed with workers (many of them professional types who look like they should know better) swapping out *their* porn flicks.

And speaking of porn flicks, for the record, I've never even considered renting, much less buying, any. I get embarrassed enough at R-rated movies. As far as I'm concerned, sex is not a spectator sport. Plus, the few stag movies I saw in college were sad and sleazy, so contributing my money to the porn industry always seemed like shopping in pawn shops—taking advantage of somebody else's misery. Not to mention perpetuating some seriously destructive concepts about women.

For that matter, I'd never even considered going into a sex shop until some woman I met at a sustainer luncheon a few months ago invited me to an adult toy party she was hostessing, à la Tupperware or Mary Kay. Mind you, I don't even talk to my best friends about stuff like that, and here this woman was, a virtual stranger in $5,000 worth of designer clothes, asking me to help her make her dildo quotient so she could qualify for a deep discount with the supplier. Oy.

I did what I always do when someone completely blindsides me: I stared at her in absolute astonishment, speechless.

She just laughed and blew me off with, "Don't get your knickers in a knot, sweetie. I can see it wouldn't be your cup of tea, anyway." She said it with such *Sex in the City* condescension that I got really mad. I mean, how in blue blazes was she supposed to know what was my cup of tea and what wasn't, just because I reacted with surprise at being invited to a sex toy party by someone I barely knew?

So I decided then and there to go, all by myself, to the biggest adult toy store in town, to see if anything inside *was* my cup of tea.

And maybe to find a little something to ring John's chimes, in a conventional sort of way. (Wouldn't want to give the boy a heart attack.

Not now that I had finally fallen head over heels for his sweet, steady self.)

I didn't even tell a single Red Hat I was going. It took me a few weeks to work up the nerve to go, but I did it, on a cold, rainy morning. (The perfect excuse to wear a scarf and raincoat.)

As for what I discovered there, I have to confess I found a lot of it fascinating. Not the porn videos, of course. Those looked perverse and appalling. But the costume section—several of those were a hoot. As were quite a few of the "toys."

I had no idea what some stuff was for. And some things, I simply found degrading and wondered why anybody would want to use them.

But I did pick up a hilarious little French maid getup and a few other silly things, and tried them out that night with John.

My, oh, my, did they go over well. Far from being appalled or amused, John reverted to his twenties, and a good time was had by all.

So here I was again, after a decent (or would that be *indecent?*) interval. Mind you, I didn't want props to become a substitute for good old-fashioned creative lovemaking—but on special occasions, or maybe an occasional holiday . . . That's why I was back. Easter was upon us, and I thought John might need a little cheering up, since for the first time ever, both our kids would be away with friends for the holiday. So I'd asked SuSu to meet me.

I'd broken down and enlisted her help, partly as an excuse to see her, but mainly because I needed an objective eye. I wanted to look sexy, not hilarious or ridiculous. She might have decided to straighten up lately, but her colorful past gave her a perspective on such matters that I lacked, and I knew I could trust SuSu to tell me the truth and not to tease me about trying to spice up my love life.

I was browsing the Easter section (the Easter section of the adult toy store? Oy.) when she came up behind me and hollered, "Yoo-hoo! Georgia?" so loud everybody in the store turned to watch her walk over. "Oh, there you are! In the Easter Section."

I flash-flamed, mortified, and turned around to get a shock that made me forget my embarrassment. "Ohmygod!"—usually *her* line— "You cut your hair!"

She ran her long fingers through the shining, tousled, dark-blond layers. "Like it?"

Frankly, it didn't do a thing for her, but since it was done, I broke Tradition Three (No lies.) without a qualm. "It looks adorable!"

She hadn't had short hair since we were kids. Not that it didn't look nice. It was fashionably layered and attractive, and went with the rest of her serious student persona.

Elegantly casual in slim camel pants and a rich brown cotton turtleneck, she nailed me with a wry smile. "Liar. I did it for convenience, but it may not suit me."

Not wanting to betray how wholeheartedly I agreed, I changed the subject back to the way she'd ambushed me and attracted curious gazes from everybody in the store. "Why did you holler at me that way? You did that on purpose, didn't you? Just to embarrass me."

"Oh, honey," she said with a mixture of affection and gentle chastisement. "You have *so* got to get over yourself. What do you think they're gonna do, grab their cell phones and call the media?" She raised her voice again. "Alert AP and UPI! Upstanding conservative and *Bible study* attendee *Georgia Peyton Baker* spotted in adult toy store." She scanned my outfit. "Dressed in the ever-popular Whitney-Houston-skulks-about-Atlanta-incognito style."

Did I mention I'm really working on lightening up? After all, anybody who saw me in there was there themselves. So I couldn't help laughing and grabbed SuSu's arm, raising my voice to the same crowd-control level as hers. "Well, if it isn't Emory law student SuSu Virginia McIntyre Harris Cates! What brings you in today, SuSu? A little something to relieve the tension of tort review?"

A flash of approval brightened her answering grin. "There you go. A-plus for that one."

It sure was good to see a glimpse of her old hell-for-leather self. Granted, her wild days had gotten out of control, prompting her to reassess and go to law school, but we all loved her free spirit—and envied her the open anger that had prompted her to thumb her nose at the very Southern proprieties that still affected the rest of us.

"Okay," she said in normal tones. "So what are we looking for?" She glanced at her watch. "I wish I could give you more time, but I have a class in an hour, so let's hop to it."

I still couldn't get used to her newfound punctuality. Or maybe, if the truth be told, I secretly resented the fact that law school, not consideration for us, had brought about the change. How petty was *that* on my part?

I held up a frisky little bunny costume that was barely more than a mesh of strategically placed furry white ribbons, bows, and a puffy tail. "What do you think?"

She shook her head.

I was counting on her honesty. In my middle-aged condition, less was definitely not more. "You're right. Too skimpy." I poked through the other Easter selections. "All of these are."

SuSu shrugged. "It doesn't *have* to be Easter, does it?"

"It probably shouldn't," I said, my conscience pricked.

"So, what do you have in mind?" She did her eyebrows like Groucho Marx. "Something sexy, I presume?"

"Exactly." At least we were on the same page. "Preferably opaque, with sleeves."

She frowned in consternation. "Oxymoron, kid." Then she brightened. "Unless you think John might go for the whole leather thing. I dated this jockey one time, hung like a racehorse, and you wouldn't believe what a leather body stocking and that crop—"

"Whoa." I stopped her before it got too deep. "We're just talking costumes here. And John. I do not want to scare the man, just spice things up."

"Sexy, opaque, with sleeves." She glanced at her watch. "In thirty minutes or less." I got her legal-eagle look of concentration. "Let me roam. I'll come up with something." She wagged her tastefully neutral manicure toward the wall of dildos. "Meanwhile, browse over there. Let your imagination go, and see what comes to mind. If something looks fun, get it."

I'd already picked up plenty on my first, solo trip, but didn't feel the need to tell her. Instead, I just cruised the displays for anything new (none that I could tell), then worked my way back over to the costumes just in time to find her at a "Star Warps" (as opposed to *Star Wars*) display.

"Oooo, I like this one." She held up a deep-sleeved white gown of sensuous knit that also included a dark wig with a distinctive roll of hair wound over each ear like a bagel. "The Princess Lay Ya model. Sexy, opaque, with sleeves."

SuSu laughed and raised the "Han So Low" costume that went with it, complete with a black hole where Han could show off his wares to the universe. "Wait'll you see the light saber that goes with this one!"

"Ouch." Still, from a theological standpoint, I supposed outer space theme would be less blasphemous than Easter, even if it was only the pagan Easter Bunny part. Embarrassed despite my resolution not to be, I grabbed the Han So Low getup, including a thirty-inch pink rubber "light saber" that used two D batteries for more than illumination. (Yes, thirty inches. It wouldn't be much of a light saber if it wasn't, but I was sure only the business end was meant to be employed.) "Mission accomplished."

The checkout clerk was alone up at the register, and I had plenty of cash. Maybe if we hurried, I could get out before anybody else came up.

"Wait." SuSu lifted the Princess Lay Ya. "You're not going to try this on?" She frowned, skeptical. "I think you ought to try it on. After all, that's why I'm here, isn't it?"

It was. I shot a wistful glance at the still-deserted register, then turned to scan for the dressing rooms, half expecting to find some inadequate curtain draped across a cheaply paneled cubbyhole where I dared not touch anything.

"They're over there." SuSu pointed to a sign on the wall. "I'll go get the key and meet you there."

I only waited a few seconds before the clerk came and unlocked the one marked WOMEN. I was relieved to find the spacious red Formica cubicle clean and well-lit, with a sturdy bench, a three-way mirror, adequate hooks, and a door that locked, leaving no cracks. I checked the featureless walls and ceiling for signs of a hidden camera lens, but saw nothing suspicious.

It was, though, the first dressing room I'd ever seen with a condom machine. And a box of disposable underwear hanging on the back of the door under a sign that read, PLEASE WEAR PANTIES AT ALL TIMES WHEN TRYING ON. THANK YOU—THE MANAGEMENT AND YOUR FELLOW CUSTOMERS.

Curious, I daintily extracted a pair with two fingertips. "Oh, good grief," I called to SuSu. "They have disposable thongs in here." Paper *thongs*. What in the world good would those teeny things do, I ask you?

"Oh, yeah." She chuckled. "I'd forgotten those."

I dropped the thong into the empty trashcan, then broke out the waterless sanitizer and some tissues to clean a safe zone where I could put my clothes on the bench. Only then did I carefully disrobe. I was buck naked and about to put on the costume when it occurred to me to ask, "SuSu! What if somebody else has tried this on?"

It was a question I'd never thought to ask before in all fifty years of dressing rooms I'd used, with any of the zillion hats and dresses I'd blithely tried on. But circumstances alter cases. This *was* a sex shop, not Marshall's.

After a brief pause, SuSu's voice came over the door. "Good question. It's white. Check it. You'll probably be able to tell."

I checked the cuffs and high neckline. No signs of soil or makeup, but I wasn't convinced. "It looks okay, but I don't know. Maybe I should just try it on at home, where I can wash it first. If it doesn't look good, I can bring it ba—"

"All sales final, sweetie," she informed me. "In a place like this, I'm sure you can understand."

"Oh, Lord, yes." What was I thinking?

I bit the bullet and put the outfit on, noting that all the closures were Velcro. Of course.

It didn't help that I'd worn black granny pants under my usual black-knit Kmart slacks that now lay safely folded with the rest of my clothes in the germ-free zone on the bench. Still, standing in front of those mirrors draped in clingy white nylon with nothing decorating the bodice but my nipples (a few inches lower than I would have liked), I had to admit the cut was flattering, even on my size 12-going-on-14 self. But the sexy effect evaporated when I put on the cheap wig with its ear-buns. My tickle box tumped over for real.

SuSu knocked. "Is that good laughter or bad laughter?"

"Both." The total effect was hilarious—not exactly what I was going for.

She knocked harder. "C'mon. Let's see."

"Okay," I said, wiping tears from my eyes, "but you asked for it." Standing concealed behind the door, I opened it just enough to let her in.

SuSu glanced back to be sure nobody was watching, then slipped inside and relocked the door. Only then did she turn for the full effect. One look at me in that wig, and she dissolved into wordless, pointing hilarity that culminated in a huge inhale of "Ah-ah-ah-ah!"

She's the only person I've ever met who can laugh on the inhale.

When she could manage it, "M.O., M.O., M.O.!" (Sacred Tradition Two: Makeover.)

"This *is* the M.O." I struck a lurid pose that kept her going and set me off again, too.

It had been too long since I'd laughed so full and free, especially at myself.

We were on a roll when the male clerk hollered cheerfully over our cackling, "You ladies okay in there?"

We halted abruptly in mid-hoot, wide-eyed, our hands over our mouths.

"Can I bring you anything?" he asked in a pleasantly conversational tone. "Need any sizes swapped out? Maybe some other selections to try? We have a special on red crotchless teddies."

That set us off again, so I could barely manage a distorted, "No, thank you. Please, just leave us."

"Okay. But remember, you try it, you buy it."

"Awp!" I tucked my chin and clammed up and turned to SuSu. "He thinks we're . . ." I couldn't even speak it.

"Who cares what he thinks?" SuSu straightened up, rubbing the muscles of her face, our tickle boxes empty at last. "Oh, man, it feels good to let go and rip like that. I'm so stressed out and brain dead studying for exams, and that idiot Mattress Man distractin' me all the time with his corny, totally unfunny jokes. This was a godsend."

She glanced at her watch, and the old SuSu exited abruptly in favor of the new, responsible one. "The dress looks great, but I'd hold off on the wig till after the fireworks." She gave me a brief hug. "This has been real, but I've gotta run."

"Oh, no, you don't," I countered with a shard of panic. "Don't run out on me, please. Not till you walk me through checkout." I opened the door and motioned her out so I could change. (I haven't gotten naked in front of anybody but John or my doctor in a decade, and that includes sisters and girlfriends, thank you very much.) "I mean it. Please do not leave me."

"Okay. But you've got to learn to check out by yourself sometime," she teased.

"I will." Of course I'd checked out alone that first time, but that time, the clerk hadn't practically accused me of trying out the merchandise on another woman. This time, I needed SuSu for moral support (which until lately, would have been an oxymoron in itself, bless her heart).

I was dressed and out in record time. "Done. Let's blow this joint." I handed SuSu the "light saber." "Here. Would your future lawyership mind carrying this?"

"Not atall." She wielded a convincing lunge and parry.

As we started for the register together, she leaned over to say quietly, "I've got plenty of cash, if you need any." Despite the financial hardships she'd endured after losing everything in a bitter divorce, SuSu was unfailingly generous with the "start over" bankroll Teeny had given her—even for a cause as "bad" as this one.

Touched, I hoped my smile showed how much that meant to me. "I've got plenty. Thanks."

Another helpful hint for all you out there: Always pay cash at an adult anything store, or you'll end up getting an avalanche of heinous "plain brown wrapper" solicitations in the mail, stuff you definitely won't want your grandchildren to get hold of. Or your grown children, for that matter.

"How about I follow you back over to Emory," I suggested to SuSu, "and we have a cup of coffee before your class?"

"Great." We reached checkout, which, I am happy to say, was empty except for us and the multi-pierced, tattooed clerk.

SuSu slapped the "light saber" across the counter with a leer. "Ring 'er up." I could have killed her, but reminded myself to lighten up, so I managed a halfway-convincing smile.

After I paid for everything, the clerk rolled the light saber in brown paper and twisted the ends like a giant doobie, then handed it back to SuSu. "Paper or plastic for the rest?" In one hand, he held up a plain brown grocery sack, in the other, a plastic bag emblazoned in neon colors with a lascivious female grin with a long pink tongue licking the upper lip.

I glared at him. "What do you think?"

He whipped open the paper sack. "I was just messin' with ya." He laid in the costumes. "Just havin' a little fun." He actually had the nerve to wink at me! "That's what we're all about here, fun. Like y'all was havin' back in the dressin' room."

Outraged, I inflated to the full extent of my biddieness. "Listen, you!" Heads turned all over the shop. (Well, *head* turned. There was only one other person there, and he looked pretty seedy, but I was still outraged.) "I'll have you know that nothing, and I mean *nothing* happened in that—"

"Okay." SuSu jerked the bag of merchandise from the counter and thrust it into my hands, turning a blithe face to the clerk. "Why don't you just have a little fun with yourself, sonny boy. You have a nice day, now, hear?"

He frowned, unsure she'd meant what that sounded like.

Trust me, she had, which left me feeling more than a little vindicated.

Urging me toward the back door, SuSu said to me through a forced smile. "Remember our New Year's resolutions? I'm gonna *straighten* up, and you're gonna *lighten* up? I'm doin' my part. Now you do yours." She put on a fake pout. "Of course, if anybody from the *Tattler* gets word of this, you're out of that run for the White House in '08."

She always knew how to get me outside of myself. I tried to act mad, but couldn't. "Oh, Tradition Five," I grumbled. (Mind your own business.)

"Oh yeah?" She smiled. "Well, Tradition Eight right back at ya."

"What do you mean, Tradition Eight?" (No beating ourselves or each other up when we blow it.) "I didn't blow anything. And neither did you."

Her smile deepened. "Precisely. So lighten up." She held open the back door for me.

Just as we stepped outside into the sunlight hazed with pine pollen, my cell phone rang. I groped in my purse to find it, but as usual, I didn't get to it till it stopped ringing.

The screen said, *1 missed call.*

I punched *Options*, and Teeny's home number appeared, replaced by *1 text message.*

I punched the button to retrieve the text message.

Please call Red. Ever the lady, she said *please* even in urgent text messages. Red was our code for the special Red-Hats-only cell phones she'd given us all.

"It's Teeny," I told SuSu. Teeny had called from her penthouse on Peachtree, so I tried that number first. "Something's up." She hadn't used Code Red since Abby—Linda's daughter and our collective goddaughter—had been taken to the hospital last fall with a hot appendix.

Curiosity lit SuSu's expression. "Hope it's not something bad like last time."

I got the "Sorry, I'm on the other line" message, so I speed-dialed the Red Hat number. One ring shy of the "I'm on the other line" message, she answered, somewhat breathless, "Hey. Where are you, and whatcha doin'?"

Goodness. That was out of character. "I'm . . ." I almost told her I was leaving a sex shop, but I caught myself. "I've just finished a little shopping with SuSu. What's up?"

"SuSu? I thought she was studying for exams." There was a disconcerting pause.

"She was, but I needed an opinion, and the store wasn't far from Emory, so she came." I prayed Teeny wouldn't ask what I was buying. I knew it would hurt her feelings to get, "I really couldn't say," in return. "What's up? You sound kind of disconcerted."

Another odd pause. "Actually, I've been packing. Could I please speak to SuSu for a second?"

I shrugged. "Sure." I handed her the phone. "She wants to talk to you first."

SuSu took it, then listened for a while. "Um-hm." Pause. "Oh, sure." Pause. "No, my feelings aren't hurt. And you're right about exams. I couldn't possibly leave now." She smiled. "No, really, it's fine. Y'all have fun." A grin. "Okay. Win some for me. Bye."

She handed me the phone. "Put a quarter in the slots for me." Then she waved her keys at me and headed for her car. "Take pictures, and you can tell me all about it when you get back and exams are over."

"Teens? What's up?" I clicked my car unlocked and slid into the warm interior, activating the wipers to brush away the pollen that had coated the windshield.

"I need y'all to go to Vegas with me for a few days, a week at the outside. Can you do it?"

She'd used the word "need," not "want," and Teeny rarely asked anything of anyone, so I didn't hesitate. "Sure. When?" Only as an afterthought did I grope in my purse for the two-year pocket calendar we all used to keep track of our busy lives.

"This afternoon."

Big gulp. "Whoa."

Nothing major on my calendar for the next week, but to leave *this afternoon?*

Normally, it took me as many days as my trip was long to pare down to three suitcases and pack. "Travel light" was not in my vocabulary.

When pressed for time, I'd been known to dump my entire lingerie drawer into my suitcase. I had to have at least two pairs of granny pants for every day: one pair of black for day wear under my slacks, and another pair of beige for nighttime. (I cannot stand to have on dark underpants with my pastel sleep shirts. It's just *wrong*.)

"I need to be in Vegas tonight," Teeny explained, "and it's important for y'all to be with me. Don't worry about SuSu; she's fine with staying behind. I wouldn't dream of asking her to leave right before exams, anyway. But I sure could use the rest of you."

That was all it took. "I'm in, then, sweetie." My mind splintered into a frantic checklist, at the top of which was calling John and telling him I was leaving for who-knows-how-long.

"Thanks so much," Teeny said. "I knew I could count on you."

"I'm on my way." As I inched my way out of the crowded rear parking lot, I shot a wistful glance to the wrapped light saber and the plain brown sack on the seat beside me. Oh, well. I hadn't planned to use it till Easter, anyway.

"When's the flight? I'll need some time to get packed and run some errands."

"I've chartered a jet out of Peachtree DeKalb. It's ready when we are, but luggage space is limited, so try to keep it so down to a mini-mum. Two bags each, if possible, and that includes the carry-on." Wishful thinking, on her part. I usually required three bags for a long weekend. But for Teeny, I squelched the mini–nervous breakdown that threatened at the mere prospect of such radical condensation. "Two bags it is."

Okay. Only ten pairs of underpants. Five black, five beige. I could start there.

And one pair of shoes per day. I could manage that.

"Great." Teeny sounded quite relieved. "Take whatever time you need, then come on over to my house. Linda's packing now, and Di-ane's leaving the office shortly, under duress." Teeny chuckled. "Our Miss Executive said she couldn't get away from work, but her boss"—Teeny—"told her she had to. It'll do her good to see how well she's trained her people."

I spotted a slot in the traffic and gunned it into the tight lane, elicit-ing a screech of brakes and a hand gesture from the young man who'd been speeding up to the next red light.

"Are you driving?" Teeny asked in concern, all too aware of the many fender benders I'd had while trying to use the phone and navi-gate Atlanta traffic at the same time.

"It's okay. That was the only hard part," I lied so she wouldn't worry. Traffic or no traffic, no way was I hanging up till I'd asked why we were running off to Vegas. "So, what's this all about?"

I turned onto Lindbergh on a yellow arrow.

"Do you mind if I wait till we get to the plane," she asked, apolo-getic, "so I can explain everything to everybody at once? I'm not trying to be mysterious, but I've got a jillion things to nail down, myself. Once we're airborne, I can catch my breath, and we can all relax. Is that okay?"

Like I said, Teeny rarely asks anything of us. "Sure. Anything you want." As usual, I'd been thinking of things only from my perspective.

All I had to do was pack. She had to make sure all her holdings were in good hands.

"I'm on my way," I said, already mentally absent as I ran though my wardrobe. A fashion alarm almost sent me off the road. Clothes! "What's the dress?"

"Nice casual will be fine. People wear everything in the casinos. Bring layers. It's warm in the daytime out there and quite cool at night."

Casinos. I'd never been in a casino in my life, but the idea appealed to me. Along with getting there in a private jet. What an adventure.

I only wished SuSu didn't have to miss it. "SuSu said for me to put a few quarters in the slots for her."

"Do it, then, by golly," Teeny said, distracted. "Now get off the phone. I want you here in one piece."

"Hanging up now," I said, then hit the button.

Oh, Lordy. Two bags!

Never mind the rest of it. Had I really promised to bring only two bags? My *pillows* and *shoes* would take up one of them!

Oy.

Triple oy.

6

The Wind Beneath Our Wings

A T MY AGE AND IN MY CONDITION, GOING OUT OF TOWN RE-
quired a series of brief, but urgent, errands: drugstore, bank,
and cleaners. Navigating the ever-present uptown traffic on
my way to have my prescriptions topped up, I called John to let him
know where I was going.

His cell phone rang. And rang.

He wasn't going to be happy when I told him I was off on a junket,
but it was probably just as well that I couldn't give him advance notice. He always sulked when I left him alone for more than a night—
something that used to irritate me, but now I saw as evidence that he
depended on me and would miss me.

There was a click, and the ringing stopped.

"John?" He'd answered his cell phone, but all I could hear was the
brush of fabric against the microphone and muffled conversation.

I called it "put on shoulder," John's version of putting unwelcome
interruptions on hold. How many times had I seen him answer just to
stop the phone ringing when he was busy, only to wedge the receiver
into the side of his neck while he finished what he was doing, oblivious to the person on the other end?

I hated when he did that to me. I never called him at work unless it
was really important. But, to be fair, he never looked at the caller's
number when he was preoccupied, so I couldn't take it personally.

"John!" I yelled really loud, fully aware that he wouldn't hear, but it was cathartic to vent in the privacy of my car. "John! Answer the damned phone!" I hollered. "Dammit!"

Beside me at the red light, a woman in a Mercedes convertible with the top down heard me even through my closed window and glared over at me.

A jolt of embarrassment distracted me momentarily from my aggravation. I aimed a sheepish "Sorry" in her direction and was glad when the light changed.

"Hello?" John's voice was a mixture of annoyance and concern. "Who is this?"

That's the trouble with those Bigbrain boys: it takes a lot to get their attention, and they don't suffer interruptions well.

A sappy gush of affection replaced my irritation. "It's me. I'm sorry to interrupt you at work—"

"No," he hastened, his voice warming. "Don't apologize. You can call me anytime." What a honey the dear man was. "Is everything okay?"

Ah. Acknowledgment that I never "bothered him with the small stuff," as Steve Martin put it in one of our favorite old-comedy videos.

"I'm fine, honey. But something's come up." No sense beating around the bush. "Teeny needs the Red Hats to go with her to Las Vegas for a few days. A week at the outside. We're flying out as soon as we can all get packed."

I could almost hear the mental gears grinding as that physicist's brain of his shifted, fully and painfully, from academic to mundane. "Today?" Aghast.

The ordinary doesn't come easy to men like John. He'd grown dependent on me to take care of life's mundane details for him. Though he was working on a clean hydrogen energy source, I had to lay out his clothes every night and be sure he put on socks. The same color socks. And the same color shoes.

"Don't worry, honey. I'll fix up all your clothes. And you can eat at the Picadilly. I'll be back before you know it."

Another long pause. "Well, okay, then." Only a little pout in it.

He reverted to the comfort of statistics. "What's the airline and flight number?"

I braced myself for male frustration deflected into protests about safety. "Well, actually, we're flying charter. Teeny has a jet waiting at Peachtree DeKalb."

John surprised me, responding with humorous envy instead. "Dang. When's that woman gonna get remarried so I can pal up with her new husband, and *we* can fly off on a private jet to Vegas?"

My grin was automatic. "I wouldn't hold my breath. You know what Mama always says: 'It takes a helluva man to replace no man at all.'"

It was just banter, but felt like flirting, and a twist of desire sprouted low inside me. I sure would miss the comforting warmth of John's long, lean body against me every night.

"Well, Teeny's a helluva woman, and she deserves a helluva man," he said with conviction.

"Find her one, then."

I could almost hear that "aw, shucks" boyish grin of his. "Don't know any more. You married the last one."

So I had. It had just taken me a quarter of a century to appreciate it.

The plain brown sack beside me reminded me of my Princess Lay Ya costume, and a sharper stab of longing hit me. "Well, when I get back, Mr. Helluva Man, I've got a little Easter surprise for the both of us. And that's all I'm gonna say about that."

He laughed like a twenty-year-old.

Lord, it felt good to hear that. "I'm on my way home to pack, then we're all congregating at Teeny's. I'll call you from the airport as soon as I find out the particulars about the flight and the hotel."

"Great." He did his televangelist imitation, his sole successful effort at humor. "Be careful with that gambling, though. It can steal your soul. Yea-ah. Sin City, that's what Las Vegas is. Guard yourself, young lady. Guard yourself."

"I hate to tell you, but I'm getting two rolls of quarters at the bank, and I plan to spend every one of them on the slots."

"Oh, woe. Down the slippery slope," he said in character, then reverted to himself. "Seriously, try not to lose more than a thousand, okay?"

"John. Don't be ridiculous. Twenty dollars is plenty."

"That's peanuts. Splurge a little. Splurge a *lot*. I mean it." I could tell he did. "You never spend anything on yourself. Kick back and have some fun at the casinos. Doctor's orders." Ph.D.'s, at least.

"Bye. I love you."

"You do, don't you?" he said with the satisfaction of a man who finally knew it was true.

I laughed and hung up, just in time to turn into the drive-up window at the drugstore.

An hour later, I emerged from my tidy little house on Muscogee Drive with only one twenty-nine-inch suitcase and a drag-along. Miracle of miracles! Of course, the drag-along weighed forty pounds (I checked it on the scale), but you can't have everything.

I'd made the ultimate sacrifice by bringing only one of my favorite synthetic down pillows and limiting myself to five pairs of shoes. And five outfits: three with identical slim black-knit slacks and assorted shells, man-shirts, and blazers; one two-piece dress (in case we went to a show); and one flashy dress blazer with velvet jeans and ankle-high Sam & Libby pointy western boots, just for the hell of it.

This may not seem to be a great accomplishment, but trust me, it represented a lifetime breakthrough with my "be prepared" compulsion to bring everything I *might* want with me whenever I leave home. But I had pared my selections down to the almost bare essentials.

All waistbands, of course, were elastic, and all but one pair of shoes were comfortable. I have my priorities.

My only difficulty was getting the drag-along—the equivalent to a sack of concrete—into the backseat by myself. (The trunk was too high.) But I managed without losing my bladder tack. After that, the suitcase was a piece of cake.

A little over two hours after Teeny had called me, I pulled off Peachtree into the Plaza Towers parking area.

Teeny's driver, Kal—a soft-spoken Serbian refugee in his thirties—was waiting outside the south tower. He stepped to my door and opened it. "Good afternoon, Miz Baker." (We'd coached him long and hard to master that "miz.") "Only two bags this time?" he noted with admiration.

Proud of myself, I nodded. "Only two. And I packed in less than an hour, I'll have you know."

He applauded with a courtly little bow. "If you shall be so kind as to leave your keys," he said in barely accented English, "I shall gladly take care of the car and transfer your luggage to the minivan."

Teeny had twenty million dollars, but her favorite vehicle for our outings was her deluxe Town and Country Chrysler minivan. All those years of practicality and frugality had gotten her where she was, and she wasn't about to change horses.

Except when it came to helping people. She was generous beyond all reason in that. Like paying Kal more than enough to support his aged parents, wife, and three kids Teeny had brought to this country.

I got out, leaving the car running. "Great." It was so nice having "people" to take care of things.

Kal bowed again. "Mrs. Witherspoon is expecting you upstairs."

"Thanks."

The security guard held the lobby door for me. "Good afternoon, Miz Baker. Please go right on up."

"Have any of the others arrived?" I asked as I crossed the high, wood-paneled foyer toward the elevators in the back.

He nodded. "Miz Williams and Miz Murray are already there."

I was the cow's tail.

I looked at my watch, wondering if I was subconsciously filling SuSu's place as the late one in our little group now that she'd returned to the compulsive punctuality of her youth.

When the elevator opened on the twentieth floor, I crossed the elegantly appointed hallway to two sleek, white doors devoid of hardware. I placed my palm on a plain, faintly illuminated box on the wall beside them. A bar of blue light scanned my palm print, then the right door began a leisurely outward swing. Teeny's personal assistant, Connie, was waiting just inside. "Please come in, Georgia."

Teeny considered her staff to be team members in her life, not underlings, so we were all on a first-name basis.

I stepped inside the spacious, elegantly neutral apartment accented by superb touches of color in art, fresh flowers, and sculpture. Teeny was on the phone in her study at the far side of the apartment, beyond her all-white fabric-draped bedroom.

When she saw me, she waved, hung up, and hurried over for a

proper society hug. "Hey! I am so proud of you. Kal called up and said you'd only brought two bags. And on such short notice. I am truly humbled."

"Well, you should be. This is a red-letter day in my life," I gloated. "From now on, no more *la voiture*"—our French guide / driver's sarcastic name for my huge hardsider suitcase on our eighteen-day Red Hat sojourn through the south of France. It meant *the automobile*—"I'm gonna learn to travel light, if it kills me."

Teeny cocked a skeptical blond eyebrow. "Light?"

Kal must have told her about the hernia-maker drag-along.

"Well, with fewer bags, anyway. It's a start."

"We were just waiting for you to have some lunch, then head for the plane." Teeny motioned me toward the balcony beyond the dining area's glass wall, where Linda and Diane sat drinking iced tea in the bright sunlight at a glass table. Artistically arranged pots of blooming tulips, daffodils, hyacinths, and azaleas surrounded them.

A loud growl from my stomach reminded me that I hadn't eaten since my three scrambled eggs with cheese at 7:30 A.M. "Great. There wouldn't happen to be any of my brown chicken salad around, would there?" It was one of my favorites, even if I *had* made it up myself—a celestial mixture of minced chicken thighs, minced celery, and toasted pecan bits in equal measure, held together with sugar-free, home-made sweet mayo, spiced with coarse-ground fresh pepper, then tightly rolled in buttercrunch lettuce leaves. Beautifully legal on my low carb diet.

Teeny grinned. "I swear, that Laura's psychic." Laura was Teeny's cook, a culinary force of nature from Cabbagetown. "She started making a batch before we even knew you were coming."

Things always taste so much better when you don't have to fix them yourself, and Laura could duplicate all my favorite recipes to perfection.

"Yum." I salivated like a cat in a caviar factory. "I'll have a double."

Connie noted the request. "Coming up." She held open the frameless glass door for Teeny and me, admitting the faint scent of hyacinths and the sound of traffic from Peachtree below.

"Well, if it isn't herself," Diane said when we stepped beyond the mirrored reflections on the glass. She turned to Linda. "You win. I owe you a dime." Our standard bet.

"How long did you think I'd take?" I asked Diane.

She grinned. "At least three hours. But I'm proud to lose. Good goin', girl."

I looked to Linda, who clearly wasn't at her best. "Are you okay for this?"

She nodded. "Beats sittin' home twiddlin' my thumbs and wondering what y'all are up to. The high-risk OB couldn't see me for two weeks."

"Yeah," I said, "but you do not look well."

"I wouldn't feel any better here than I will with y'all, so could we just drop it, please?" she snapped, still clearly hormonal.

She had a right to be testy. Getting pregnant at fifty-five will do that to you.

Since we were all there I finally broke the news: "Well, I've got a major revelation for y'all. SuSu cut her hair. Seriously short."

They weren't impressed. "Um-hmm." "Yep." "We know."

Crestfallen, I sank to a chair. "And I was the last to find out?" She was supposed to be my best friend!

Obviously, my feelings showed, because Diane patted my arm. "She wanted to see the look on your face when she met you this morning."

I felt myself flush. If she'd told them where, she was dead meat. "Did she mention where we met?"

"Nope," Linda said, guileless. "Just that y'all were going to get together between her classes."

Thank goodness. "Well, it looks pretty sad, but she knows it."

Teeny plopped into the chair beside me, clearly worn out. "Whew. I'm almost afraid to sit down. I was up all night working out a plan, then putting this trip together."

"Speaking of that," Linda asked, "what the heck is all this about?"

Teeny's lopsided little smile looked awfully fragile. "Do you mind if we wait till we get to the plane? I'd really like to eat something in peace, first." Aware of our curiosity, she added, "I promise, all will be revealed. And you'll see why I wanted to wait."

It was a question of trust, and with Teeny—despite the secrets she'd kept from us in the past—there was no question.

"Sure." "Okay." "Fine by me."

My cell phone rang, showing SuSu's cell number on the screen. "It's SuSu," I told the others, then answered. "Hey."

"Hey, SuSu," Teeny and Linda and Diane called out across the table.

She responded with a perfunctory, "Hey, everybody," then addressed me. "Where are you?"

"We just sat down to eat at Teeny's. Where are you?"

"Between classes and study group." I heard her slurp something through a straw. "So what's the scoop?"

Laura and Connie arrived with our plates, but the others remained focused on me.

"There is no scoop. We're going to Vegas." I don't know why it made me so uncomfortable for her to ask me in front of the others, but it did, so I deflected with, "I've brought two whole rolls of quarters to play the slots with. John told me I could spend up to a thousand dollars, but that's absurd. I might go a couple of hundred, though, if it's fun."

"Stay away from the roulette," SuSu advised, experienced in such matters from her "good-girl-gone-bad," post-divorce phase. "And the craps. Don't play craps unless you know what you're doing. And forget poker; your face is an open book. Just stick to the slots at first." Expert advice, from somebody who'd never come back from Vegas with two nickels to show for it. "But don't sit down to one that's just paid off. Watch for one where somebody's been feeding it for a long time without winning, then take their place and stick with it."

That didn't make a lick of sense to me. "You mean, deliberately pick a loser?"

"They all have to pay off within certain time frames. If you get one that's eaten a lot of silver without paying, it's bound to go eventually. The progressive pots are the best. Look for the ones with a lighted sign over a group of them that shows a big jackpot. They pay the most, especially if you're playing three quarters a spin."

"Okay, then. I'll pick a loser with a progressive pot and play three quarters to win." It was Greek to me.

"And if you need to improve your luck, cross your fingers and use the pull handle."

"Oh, please." I believed in divine providence, not luck, and that sounded suspiciously pagan. Of course, what could I expect from an angry atheist like SuSu?

Connie set down a generous arrangement of chicken rolls garnished with ripe mango and strawberries at my place. I nodded my thanks to her and told SuSu, "My chicken salad is here, so I've gotta go. Don't study too hard. I wish you could be with us."

"Me, too." She hung up, never one to suffer long good-byes. Or being left out.

Things never felt quite right without the five of us in full. As I so often did, I consoled myself with food. "Mmmm. The chicken wraps are perfect."

Conversation centered on the safe topic of what we'd all packed and Brooks's and John's reactions (both good). In no time, we cleaned our plates of everything but the parsley and, too full even to resurrect our curiosity about why we were going, headed for the airport.

I've got to tell you, charter is the way to fly. While Kal cleared our bags, we went through security without a wait, then were driven across the apron to a sleek twin-engine jet that was bigger than I'd expected.

A uniformed flight attendant helped us get settled in the comfy buff leather recliner seats, then offered us a selection of first-run in-flight movies. By the time we'd decided on *Sweet Home Alabama* (again), we were taxiing to the runway. I called John and left a message with all the flight particulars and the hotel where we'd be staying: the Parthenon.

That accomplished, I looked to Linda to make sure she was all right, just as the others did the same.

Even that was enough to set her off. "Would y'all please quit starin' at me like I'm gonna throw up or drop dead?" she grouched. "I told you, I'm okay." She poked in the pocket on the side of her seat. "Where are the barf bags on this thing, anyway?"

The flight attendant arrived with two, a little compress of ice chips, some ginger ale on the rocks, and a few captain's crackers. "Try small sips at first," she murmured reassuringly, then melted discreetly back to her little flight attendant's cubby.

Man, it was nice to have "people" who knew what they were doing to do things for you.

Linda accepted the tray without comment, laid the cold compress across the base of her neck, then sipped cautiously on the ginger ale. Her color improved immediately.

Only when I was sure she was settled did I turn to Teeny. "Okay. We're airborne. Could you tell us now what this is all about?"

Teeny nodded, rubbing her tiny, perfectly manicured little hands down her face to conceal a yawn. "Sorry. I've only had a couple of cat naps since I left the Coach House."

That was Tuesday; this was Thursday.

Fatigue bloomed, harsh and aging, in her features. "Everything's just been so crazy, and I dared not explain until we were safely on our way, for fear SuSu would find out. If she did, I know she'd want to come, but that would be disastrous. She can't leave school now. And as a future officer of the court, she shouldn't have anything to do with this. At least the Vegas part."

She was talking. I heard the words, but they weren't really making a lot of sense. "What Vegas part?"

Teeny struggled to collect herself. "It's Pru. She's been doing so well, making such progress, but she didn't want me to tell y'all. Not yet. She was afraid she'd fail again." Empathy softened Teeny's eyes. "She's held down a good job since the Mademoiselle reunion, and done so well working her steps from NA." (Narcotics Anonymous.)

She heaved a long sigh. "But lately, she hit a rough patch, 'Jonesing' they call it, nearly jumping out of her skin, and wouldn't you know? That useless son of hers decided to take off without a word."

Bubba had been dropping off the world periodically since his fourteenth birthday. He always turned up later, without apology or explanation.

"Normally, she takes it with a grain of salt," Teeny explained, "but this time, she went bonkers."

We sat, poised, intent.

"Pru gave her counselor permission to discuss her case with me from the beginning. When this happened, he said she'd been working through some tough emotions about her past, including how Bubba turned out, issues that brought up serious feelings of worthlessness.

And fears of abandonment. So when Bubba disappeared, the voice of her addiction used that as an excuse for her to jump back into the drugs, even though she knows they'll kill her."

"Damn." I thought back to the sweet, trusting girl Pru had been when she married Tyson. "Do y'all remember back when she and Tyson first met, how we all thought it was so fascinating and urbane that he smoked pot?"

Linda nodded. "It was right up there with the fact that he was from L.A. and had actually surfed the beaches of California."

Atlanta was seriously provincial back then. We'd all laughed our way through *Reefer Madness*, but Tyson was the first person we'd ever known who actually smoked grass, and he was too cool for Antarctica.

Teeny sighed. "It seemed harmless at the time."

Pru had been so smitten that Tyson could do no wrong in her eyes. In turn, he—like most pot smokers of that day—was motivated by zeal and paranoia to convert her to his own bad habits.

"I have a confession," I said. "Considering the fact that Pru's daddy was a drunk, I figured pot was safer for her than booze, and told her so."

Diane bristled. "You told her her daddy was a drunk?"

I bristled back. "No. I told her pot was safer than booze, which was even worse."

Diane stood down. "Big Tradition Eight on that one, honey. Quit kickin' yourself. That was over thirty years ago. The statute of limitations ran out a long time ago." She took a sip of iced tea. "None of us knew anything about drugs back then. Heck, the doctors were prescribing addictive levels of sedatives and Dexedrine to most of the housewives in North Atlanta."

The rest of us had stuck to our gin, rum, and bourbon, but we hadn't judged Pru for toking with Tyson and his Land of Zoar pals. After all, it was the tune-in-and-turn-on seventies.

I shivered. "I still can't believe I actually worked in their shop all that time without a clue of what was really going on."

"None of us suspected, and why should we?" Linda said. "Stuff like that never happened in our world."

After Pru and Tyson had married, his wealthy parents had set the newlyweds up in business, never dreaming that the cozy import shop was an almost-perfect cover for Tyson to smuggle in drugs among the enamelware teapots and oriental vases so he could support his own growing heroin and cocaine addictions. As the months had passed, Pru had become more paranoid, jumpy, and withdrawn. When we'd tried to talk to her about it, she just flew off the handle. Before our eyes, she was becoming someone we no longer knew.

"It did seem funny that they weren't more concerned by the lack of customers," I admitted, "but I didn't want to embarrass them by mentioning it." An alarming thought occurred to me. "Ohmygosh! I paid for my first washer and dryer with *drug money*."

Teeny made the sign of the cross. *"Ego te absolvo."*

"Georgia, get off that martyr thing, sweetie," Linda scolded gently. "This is about Pru, not you."

"I'll never forget that night on the news," Teeny said.

Everybody who was anybody watched WSB at six o'clock back then. Except Diane, who was living in Nashville.

I nodded. "Who could forget it? I was setting the table, and John was studying."

"I was cooking supper," Linda said. "Brooks never got home from the hospital before seven."

A pensive silence settled as Teeny, Linda, and I revisited the three minutes that had shattered our safe, cozy view of the world.

"At first, I didn't recognize the house," Teeny said.

"Oh, I did," I said. "I'd gone with Pru when they were looking to buy it. And John and I had had dinner with them just two weeks before the bust." The first live, televised wholesale cocaine bust in Atlanta history, and it was Pru and Tyson.

Linda shook her head. "I didn't know it was them till they showed that policewoman jerk Bubba out of Pru's arms, and I saw Pru's face in the camera lights."

"What a face it was," I remembered. "No remorse. No shame. Just fury." Our girlhood friend was barely recognizable, screaming profanities at the police.

"The way she kicked that cop when he put her in the squad car," Linda said. "She was like a wild animal."

Tyson had gotten ten years. Pru had gotten probation and, after rebuffing our efforts to help, had dropped out of sight to battle her own demons for the next quarter of a century.

That was why we had been so hopeful to see her clean and sober at the Mademoiselle Reunion a year and a half ago, working hard (with Teeny's help) to reclaim her dignity.

And that was why it broke our hearts to hear that she had given in to the demons that would degrade and kill her.

"Y'all, we can't let her go this time. We have to do something," I said, tears welling.

Teeny shook her head. "Pru's choices are still her own. She'd done so well. . . . It's such a shame that Bubba disappeared right when she was so vulnerable."

"Why would he do that to her? Leave that way, without even calling her?" Linda challenged. "Surely he knew—"

Teeny shook her head. "He had no way of knowing how fragile she was." Her face softened with empathy. "They never talked about Pru's problems. Too dangerous. She was so ashamed, so afraid he'd abandon her if he ever knew what she was really going through."

I cut to the chase. "So, what happened then?"

"She came into work Tuesday morning high as a kite," Teeny said, "and quit her job. Then she left her apartment, her furniture—everything she'd worked so hard to attain—and spent all she had on airfare to Vegas because a couple of Bubba's Deadhead cronies thought that was where he'd gone."

"How can we help?" Diane asked. "You said her choices are her own."

"Only up to a point," Teeny said. "The detectives found her in Vegas. She's gotten hooked up with some really bad characters, but I've hired plenty of help to coax her away from them and into a safe place where we can do an intervention."

Diane frowned. "She knows she's an addict. What good would an intervention do?"

"The counselor said it would show her how much we care," Teeny explained. "That she's not alone. She feels so alone."

Teeny's mouth flattened. "Realistically, the odds aren't good, but maybe if she knew we'd be there for her, she might have a chance. If we can talk her into going back into treatment, we can act as her family, help support her."

"Whether she wants us to or not?" Diane asked.

Teeny nodded, her blue eyes wide with the enormity of what we were facing. "Unless she gets away from her suppliers, she'll die, and soon, according to my investigators. The people she's mixed up with are notorious for using addicts till they get too sick, then driving them to a sleazebag motel out of state and overdosing them to avoid problems. We have to get her out of there and into treatment."

We all sat pressed into our seats by the weight of what we were hearing. "Down the rabbit hole with Alice," I said, remembering the words from a seventies song: *Just ask Alice; I think she'll know . . .*

"What about Bubba?" Linda asked. "Wouldn't it help if we could find him?"

Teeny nodded. "I have a dozen excellent investigators hot on his trail. But it isn't easy to track a hitchhiker. They've narrowed it down to the Aspen area, though, and we're pulling out all the stops to find him. I've offered him and anybody who finds him fifty thousand dollars reward for coming in."

I whistled low. "That ought to do it."

"What if you do find him," Linda asked, "but Pru doesn't want to come with us?"

Teeny seemed to catch a second wind, regaining her prim posture. "We kidnap her," she said, calm as you please.

That sat us all up straight. Yes, siree.

As usual, my Chicken Little projected the direst of extremes. "As in federal offense, FBI, *felony* kidnap her?"

"No," Teeny answered. "As in, she'll be dead within the week if we *don't* kidnap her."

"You're serious," Linda said, assessing Teeny's expression. "This is truly a matter of life and death."

"It's the suppliers we're getting her away from, not herself," Teeny clarified. "We can't just let her go, let her die. You haven't known her for the past few months. She'd found herself, reclaimed her dignity, and I know she can do it again."

A reassuring peace transformed her. "I just know that if all of us go to her together and promise to help her, it won't be so easy for her to blow us off. The choice to change is still hers. She'll just be making it in a safer place."

"Count me in," Diane said without reservation. "I don't think I could look myself in the mirror if I let Pru die without trying to save her, even if it means kidnapping her."

"I'm in, too," Linda said. "As for the kidnapping part, I wouldn't worry." She motioned to us all. "I mean, look at these innocuous, mommy faces. Pillars of our community. Charity workers. Not so much as a jaywalking conviction among us. What DA in his right mind would press charges against these faces for trying to save our wayward friend's life?"

My head was still unconvinced, but my heart won out. "Count me in, too." John would never believe this. Assuming I'd ever tell him, which I probably wouldn't—unless we ended up getting arrested by some politically suicidal DA who had an axe to grind with his mommy.

So we were all for one and one for all.

Except for SuSu, who, as a future officer of the court, had been wisely excluded for her own good.

Teeny relaxed in earnest. "I knew I could count on you." She pressed the service button. "This calls for champagne." She glanced at Linda. "For everybody but you, my missy."

Linda sat up abruptly, catching the now-warm compress in her hand. "Make mine a Diet Sprite." She looked more like herself than she had since the meeting. "Ladies, we have a mission, and failure is not an option."

"The Right Stuff," I compulsively identified the quote's origin.

She shook her head, some of her wry humor returning. "Tom Hanks, *Apollo Thirteen.*"

Maybe focusing on Pru was just what Linda needed right now.

The flight attendant arrived with a bottle of cold champagne, three flutes, and a Diet Sprite on the rocks.

Diane lifted her glass in a toast. "Here's to safe travel, a long nap, and success at the end of the line."

We added our glasses. "Hear, hear."

We settled back to watch the movie with our drinks.

Within thirty minutes, we were all sound asleep and stayed that way till we landed, which was good, because Teeny was right. There was no sleeping once we got there . . . and all hell broke loose, thanks to me.

7

A Trip to Ancient Greece, Vegas Style

The Parthenon Casino, Las Vegas, Nevada. 8:00 P.M.

STANDING WITH TEENY THROUGH THE OPEN SUNROOF OF OUR white limo, I took in the gaudy splendor of Electric Avenue on the way to our hotel. The air was cold and dry on my skin, but the show was worth it. I felt like we'd been shrunk to the size of grasshoppers and dropped into the most grandiose, surreal, overdone *Around the World in Eighty Days* goofy golf course imaginable.

"This is the only way to see Vegas," Teeny advised me soberly, as if she'd done this a dozen times instead of just once. But her once was one more than mine. I'd never been to Vegas. Or Atlantic City. Or even to the Harrah's in Cherokee.

I scanned the road ahead. On the left was a roller-coastered replica of Manhattan, including a Statue of Liberty; on the right, a massive Lego-looking rendition of a medieval castle; then pseudo-Roman Caesars Palace, resplendent with columns; then an erupting volcano at the home of Sigfried and Roy; then two ships in a genuine-water harbor where a pirate battle with cannon-fire was going on. Beyond that, Barnum & Bailey on acid. But the sight that dwarfed the others for scale and impact was a towering, floodlit replica of the Parthenon-capped Acropolis, with hundreds of windows in the sheer "cliff" walls. "Oh . . . my . . . gosh." I grabbed Teeny's arm. "Is that where we're staying?"

Teeny had been so worried about Pru, she'd scarcely smiled since we'd started out, but this brought on a grin. "Yep. Newest on the Strip. Isn't it amazing? And awful?"

That pretty much summed it up.

Beyond it lay Paris with its Eiffel Tower, then the Venetian and the towering Stratosphere with its change-your-underwear thrill ride on the top, interspersed with less spectacular holdovers from days gone by, all interspersed with marquees touting Celine Dion, Wayne Newton, and countless headliners. At the far end of the Strip stood a massive curve of turreted plaster with dancing fountains out front. But it was the Parthenon that dominated even its most extreme of its neighbors.

I felt a tug on my black knit slacks.

"Quite hoggin' the sunroof," Diane shouted up, to be heard over the air rushing past us. "Give the rest of us a look."

"Sorry." I surrendered my position, and Teeny followed.

Linda had seen it all at least a dozen times before with Brooks on medical conventions, but Diane insisted she stand up with her. "Come on. The cold air'll feel good."

Still a bit green in the gills from our flight—"crossing the Rockies on a gnat's back," as she'd described it—Linda relented.

Teeny and I were reassured to hear them talking and laughing. Teeny picked up the receiver for the intercom. "Driver, please take us to the end of the strip, then circle back to the Parthenon."

Diane and Linda didn't come inside till we'd made the circuit and neared the Parthenon's colonnade. Breathless, rosy, and renewed, they tumbled into the seats beside us.

"Here we are. Operation Red Hat Rescue commences," Teeny said as we slowed to turn in. "My investigators picked this hotel because it's so new that its security force hasn't been fully staffed, so there's less chance of interference if we hit a snag." She gathered her purse into her lap. "When we check in, please let me do the talking. I've registered as Rose Pendergrass."

"Who's Rose Pendergrass?" Diane asked.

"The twelfth richest woman in America," Teeny said. "I picked her for a cover because we're the same age, and nobody knows what she looks like."

As always, she'd nailed down the details, even on such short notice.

And God was in the details. Little wonder Teeny had succeeded in amassing millions without anybody suspecting—even us.

The limo rolled to a halt beside the tall, palm-framed double doors with MAIN LOBBY carved into the marble above them.

An entourage of tanned, gorgeous bellmen stood waiting in short white polyester doubleknit tunics and sandals sporting leather strips that criss-crossed their tanned, muscular calves.

Pure kitsch.

But the one who helped me out of the limo sure knew how to pour on the charm. "Goodness, what a lovely group of ladies," he said as he drew me to my feet with a strong, warm grip. "Welcome to the Parthenon. If you need anything, anything at all, please ask for Jules."

"Oh, I will."

Word of Rose's coming must have preceded us. We were certainly getting the royal treatment.

Still, I couldn't resist a catty whisper to Linda when she joined me. "This is the tackiest, most vulgar place I have ever seen in my life."

"Tacky, maybe," she whispered back, scoping out a particularly buff bellman whose muscles rippled as he hoisted my suitcase out of the trunk. "But you gotta like the view."

"Amen."

As soon as we were all out, the buff bellmen divvied up our luggage and preceded us while the doorman—doing his best to look dignified in a white polyester toga and wreath of gold plastic olive leaves—welcomed us inside.

The Parthenon Hotel and Casino was even more awful and amazing inside.

Linda and Teeny trailed the parade of bellmen toward the white marble front desk, but Diane and I stopped in our tracks just inside the soaring atrium. Talk about marble and "gold" overkill, with pseudo-ancient-Greek finery that went way beyond wretched excess.

Palm trees, gaudy mosaics, and mirrored walls with scads of columns defined the ground floor, but the center of attention was a two-story marble replica of Diana, complete with golden helmet and spear. Well, near-replica. I was pretty sure the Greek master Phidias had done a much better job with the original.

"Gawd," Diane breathed when she saw Athena. "Phidias must be rollin' in his grave." (We Red Hats know our art history.)

"Amen." Glancing around, my brain drew a comparison with the overblown, overgilded sets of that awful "big-hair" religious channel with that weeping woman in the huge lavender wig. Everything at the hotel and casino seemed geared to impress in a garish way and bolster the blue-collar ego. The place just tried too hard, but I guess that was Vegas.

I couldn't resist a brief detour to tap on one of Athena's massive toes to see if she was really marble.

"Fiberglass," I mouthed to Diane as we caught up with the others behind the parade of tight-assed bellmen.

Tacky though the hotel was, they sure knew how to make a fuss over their guests, though. I felt like an Oriental potentate as we arrived at the front desk to find the fawning general manager waiting, flanked by two regular clerks.

"Good evening," Teeny said politely. "We're booked into the Alexander the Great suite."

"Welcome to the Parthenon, Ms. Pendergrass," the manager effused. "We are honored, indeed, that you chose to break your seclusion with us."

Diane and I looked to each other. Was he onto us?

"Thank you. These are my close personal friends. Please extend the same courtesy to them that you would to me."

He made a brief bow to us. "Ladies. We are at your disposal." Hands clasped like an undertaker, he turned back to Teeny. "I hope madam's charter flight was uneventful."

"How did he know we flew charter?" I whispered into Diane's ear.

"Everybody knows everything in Vegas," she whispered back as if she knew what she was talking about, which she didn't, because she'd never been there, either. "They even have cameras in all the rooms," she told me. "Including the bathrooms."

"They do not!" I said in alarm, loud enough for Linda to hear.

She leaned over. "Yes, they do." She should know. "Now keep it down. You look like a couple of yokels."

Cameras in the bedrooms? And the *bathrooms*? That, I did not like.

Linda saw my expression and smiled, superior. "Just think of your time here as a brief experiment in exhibitionism."

Not!

The clerk handed the manager a stack of gold keycards, which he passed on to Teeny. "These are your premium service access cards, both to your suite and to a fifty-thousand-dollar line of credit. Apiece. No cash or credit cards are necessary within the entire hotel complex. If you desire more, it's yours for the asking."

Did people really spend that much? Two rolls of quarters were more my speed, never mind what John had told me I could spend.

The manager motioned toward an elaborate temple façade in the mirrored wall across the atrium, guarded by a burly security man in white slacks and a bright blue blazer. "Please allow me to personally escort you to your suite. It occupies the entire upper level of our Parthenon penthouse."

Good grief! I dared not think what Teeny was paying for it.

"As you requested," he went on as we started across the lobby, "there are five bedrooms, including the master suite, a fully stocked kitchen with personal chef, and a butler."

Teeny paused. "I thought I made it clear, we require absolute privacy."

She looked like she was about to turn down the butler, so I tugged on her sleeve and whispered, "Oh, please, let's keep the butler. I've never had a butler. We won't say anything in front of him, I promise."

Since she always got a kick out of it when I enjoyed the luxuries she could provide, she hesitated only momentarily before turning back to the manager. "The butler may stay. But I trust he is discreet."

The manager beamed. "Ms. Pendergrass, what happens at the Parthenon *stays* at the Parthenon."

She nodded and resumed our progress. "Several of my personal bodyguards will be joining us in the casino later. Will that pose a problem?"

"Not at all," he hastened to assure her, "as long as they are unarmed and check in with our security when they arrive."

Crossing to the "temple," we saw guests of a dozen nationalities, everything from scruffy twenty-somethings in jeans and halter tops, to mom-and-pop tourists in shorts with Las Vegas T-shirts, to elegant cosmopolitan couples in expensive evening wear, to fat old men with major bimbos clad in outfits more fitting for a show biz revue than a date.

Across the shining marble floors and garish mosaics, we arrived at the deadpan security guard. The manager slipped a gold keycard into an unmarked slot beside the ornately embossed bronze doors, and they slid open with almost-silent precision. "This elevator is security controlled exclusively for our penthouse guests. Your keycards are required to open and activate it. If you are expecting guests, simply call down to the desk and we'll have the security guard send them up."

He motioned us into the mirrored twelve-by-twelve elevator that was anchored at the four corners by elongated versions of the famous portico statues, their breasts clearly outlined (and noticeably larger than the originals') through their carved gowns.

After we stepped onto the elevator's elaborate mosaic of nymphs and satyrs, the manager used his keycard to set us in motion. Surrounded by infinite images of ourselves and the statues, I leaned over and asked Diane, "Is it just me, or have these statues had boob jobs?"

She looked, and folded her lips inward to keep from laughing.

"It's not you," Linda murmured.

I tapped one. More fiberglass.

My mind conjured the image of some snockered high roller going for one last thrill on his way to the penthouse, getting frisky with one of the Greek ladies, and a chuckle escaped me. Worried that the manager would think I was laughing at his hotel (which I was), I sobered and stole a glance at him.

He just smiled politely and nodded. For what Teeny was paying, I guess he didn't care whether I laughed at his hotel or not.

As we ascended at a leisurely pace, I searched for signs of a hidden camera, but couldn't find any. Probably behind a two-way section of the mirrored ceiling, I reasoned.

Unless Linda had been pulling our legs about the surveillance. Having been the gullible brunt of one too many whoppers from my friends, I remained skeptical.

I decided to get the answer from the horse's mouth. "I've been told we're being observed at all times," I said to the manager, eliciting glares from Linda and Diane. "Is this true?"

He didn't flinch. "Our hotel has the finest security to guarantee the safety of our patrons and their winnings," he rattled off, clearly not for the first time or even the fiftieth. "We spare no expense to assure both the privacy and the security of our guests."

I probably would have pressed him, just for the fun of it, but the doors opened, and what was waiting beyond made me forget completely about hidden cameras.

Gleaming white marble covered expansive interior walls and floor, and a private balcony filled the space between the penthouse's glass walls and the Doric columns that marched down all four sides of the penthouse.

The view of Vegas was breathtaking.

Inside the fifty-by-fifty common area, low furniture in white leather surrounded a marble fire pit in the living room, and a long glass dining table was held up by Corinthian capitals and surrounded by white-leather upholstered chairs on casters. Palms and exotic arrangements provided the only color besides a few strategically placed mosaics that defined the various areas of the room.

But the pièce de résistance was the white poker table that sported a micromosaic of *Venus Rising* on its octagonal top.

The butler, a distinguished older man in white tie and tails, appeared from the kitchen carrying four crystal flutes of frosty champagne.

"I don't think we'll be indulging just yet," Teeny said. "I'll have a regular Coke, and please bring some cold Diet Cokes and diet ginger ale for the others."

He smiled and retreated to the kitchen, returning with a bar cart stocked with ice and sodas. He circulated, softly introducing himself as Charles in a cultured British accent and taking our drink orders.

The manager hovered by Teeny. "I trust everything is to madam's satisfaction?"

Teeny looked around, visibly amused by the wretched excess. "It'll do." She graciously shook the manager's outstretched hand. "Please see that you and the staff are adequately compensated. Just add it to my bill. I'll have my assistant review the charges thoroughly when we get back."

Smooth as polished travertine, she'd shifted the chore of tipping to the manager, but put him on notice that the added charges would be scrutinized.

That was our little mogul.

The manager bowed slightly. "Of course."

"Oh, and please make sure our car is kept ready. We may be going back out at any time, on short notice."

He bowed again. "Absolutely, Ms. Pendergrass."

Teeny waited till he left, then turned to us. "So. Here we are." She motioned to the hallway that had to lead to the bedrooms. "Y'all pick out your rooms. I'll take what's left. I've got to make a few calls." She took her cell phone out onto the balcony.

The butler reappeared. "If the ladies will please make their room selections, I shall be happy to unpack and iron their belongings."

Linda and Diane exchanged impressed looks, but I hesitated. No male besides John and my gynecologist had ever laid eyes on my granny pants. And though the five pairs each of black and beige briefs were neatly sealed in zip-close freezer bags (as were the rest of my un-mentionables, a packing tip that appealed to my obsessive-compulsive nature), there was no guarantee the butler might not take them out and discover that the elastic lace was frayed on most of them.

No, I definitely didn't feel comfortable with a complete stranger in white tie and tails—especially a British one—passing judgment on my underwear.

I was a secure, very happily married woman, I reminded myself, and I'd never see this guy again after we left. What did I care what he thought of my underwear? But I did, brainwashed by all those motherly admonitions about ER technicians judging me by the condition of my lingerie.

"I think I'd prefer to unpack myself," I told him, feeling my face flush with unexpected insecurity. "I *would* like my hanging things to have a press, though." No sense passing that up. "Maybe you could do those last."

Charles the butler smiled, devoid of condescension or sarcasm. "Certainly, madam. As you wish." He motioned to the elaborate master bedroom, then the hallway to its left. "Your rooms are ready. If the ladies find anything amiss, please let me know immediately, and it will be rectified. We have a selection of pillows in down, foam, and synthetic down. Simply mark your preferences as to type and number on the card beside the bed, and I shall make certain your tastes are accommodated."

Mercy. I hadn't needed to bring my own, after all. I decided to ask for six synthetic downs.

Since Teeny was paying, none of us even considered taking the master bedroom. And frankly, I wasn't too keen on the idea of a round bed and satin sheets, anyway. It just seemed *wrong*, somehow. Wouldn't things hang off—or slide off—when you slept?

The other three bedrooms were fancy enough, each with a white-draped, columned canopy bed open to the mirrored ceilings, plus semi-artistic murals of ancient Greek vistas on the walls, and its own private marble spa and balcony overlooking the city.

Being the sort of person who likes corner booths at restaurants (nobody can talk about you behind your back) and end-unit condos at the beach (only one common wall), I picked the last room and went inside to stow my stuff before the butler showed up. After all that angst deciding what to bring, unpacking came as a three-minute anticlimax.

Even so, I was the last to join Teeny and the others on the balcony that overlooked Electric Avenue in all its neon splendor. "So. Where do we stand?"

Teeny patted the cushioned chaise beside her. "We have some time to kill." It was only 8:45.

Charles circulated with a selection of hors d'oeuvres that included a pile of midget-sized low-carb chocolate peanut butter cups. "Only two net carbs in three of them," he murmured when he saw me eyeing them.

I helped myself to three of them, with several strawberries to balance the nutritional scale, then sampled a mini-bite proportionate to its size.

"Oh, yum," I rhapsodized. Chocolate is my favorite substitute for drink. The candy almost tasted real. I nibbled away, trying to make them last, but before I knew it, I was on my ninth little peanut butter cup.

Linda looked at me and frowned. "I'd go easy on those. The reason they have so few net carbs is that there's tons and tons of stuff that acts like a laxative in them."

I held my ninth and final peanut butter cup in my fingertips, pinky crooked. "That's okay. An occasional purge never hurt a girl, especially one our age."

"How many of those things have you had?" she challenged.

"Tradition Twelve," I countered. (No discussion of weight or diets.)

Linda, still grumpy and hormonal, arched a gray eyebrow. "This has nothing to do with diets and everything to do with digestion. Don't say I didn't warn you."

"Tradition Eleven," I chided. "That sounds suspiciously close to an 'I told you so' in advance."

"Maybe it is." She tried to be huffy, but wasn't successful. Instead, she simply came across as miserable, which I could hardly blame her for under the circumstances.

Obstetricians hardly let expectant mothers eat or drink much of anything fun these days.

I savored every teensy remaining bite of my synthetic candy, then licked my fingers clean. Meanwhile, Teeny and Diane munched and talked shop about the clothing business to pass the worried, waiting minutes.

"So, what's the exact plan?" Linda asked her at the first lull in conversation.

"Everything's set for midnight or thereabouts down in the casino." Teeny stretched. "We couldn't try to take Pru anywhere near her suppliers. They'd kill her for sure if they thought anybody was sniffing around her. But she'd been gambling on the Strip before, so we're banking on the fact that they won't be suspicious if she goes again. My chief investigator called in two women operatives to pose as users and lure Pru here to the casino. They've promised Pru they'll feed her quarters at the slots till midnight. The moment they cut off her cash and leave her alone, we move in and offer to take her to rehab."

"How do you know Pru will go with them?" I asked.

"They're already on their way," Teeny said. "The decoys are wired so my chief investigator and his men can hear everything."

My Chicken Little poked holes in that scenario right away. "How did they explain staking her to the slots? Wasn't she suspicious?"

Teeny shook her head. "They staged a fake incident where Pru helped them escape with a lot of cash from a make-believe pimp. Then they gave her a methadone pill, just enough to ease her up out of with-drawal, and offered to take her to the casino to thank her, but just until midnight." She sighed. "That's when we move in and offer to take her to that great rehab facility in the Smokies."

"Why do we need to wait?" I asked. "Couldn't we just go down and get her right away?"

Teeny shook her head. "We're giving the methadone time to take hold in her system. You can't reason with an addict who's frantic for a fix. And her counselor said she'd be more receptive to us if she'd worn herself out losing."

"What happens if she wins?" my Chicken Little asked. "I mean, she might. What then? How do we stop her from taking the money and leaving to buy more drugs?"

"Oh, for heaven's sakes," Diane fussed. "How many people really win at those things? I think we're safe, there. She won't win."

Chicken Little is nothing if not persistent. "If nobody won at the slots, nobody would ever play them," I argued, compelled to articulate the what-ifs. "John said they offer the best odds in the casino. And he ought to know."

"John's a physicist, sweetie, not a statistician," Linda put in.

"Children," Teeny scolded benignly. "If Pru wins, we'll punt and come up with something. Those agents with her are really sharp." She lifted her cell phone and started scanning down her recently called numbers. "As a matter of fact, their partners probably have a contin-gency already. I'll check." She pressed the button and waited, then moved away to talk to "her people."

"Pru is *not* gonna win," Diane said with confidence, then popped a ripe strawberry.

Linda didn't look so sure. She lifted her hands and eyes skyward. "Your mouth to God's ear."

"I think you're aimin' that in the wrong direction," I told her. "As my country granny used to say, cards and gamblin' are the devil's do-main."

"Well, poor Pru ought to feel right at home, then." Sadness perme-ated Diane's words.

We were dancing with the demons on this one, for sure. Which re-minded me. . . .

"Since nothing's going down till midnight, I want to give those slots in the casino a try, myself."

"I don't think that's a very good idea," Diane cautioned. "What if Pru spots you? It could ruin everything. Remember, we're supposed to keep a very low profile."

She had a point.

Charles chose just that moment to appear with coffee. "Would the ladies care for some fresh Colombian coffee, decaffeinated or regular? Or perhaps some decaffeinated iced tea? Sweet or unsweet."

Boy, he sure had our Southern number.

"No, thanks," I answered for myself. "But I *would* like a couple of progressive slot machines, please. I don't suppose you could have some brought up?"

He laughed as if I'd just made the drollest little joke. "I'm afraid not. But I know the casino would be delighted to indulge madam."

Rats.

Maybe I could slip in a few quarters while we were staking Pru out. Not just for myself. After all, I had promised SuSu I'd play a roll of quarters for her.

I looked at the clock. Less than two hours, and we'd be back up here, trying to reason with Pru. If only she'd listen. But cocaine was supposed to be the hardest addiction to break.

I sent an arrow prayer heavenward. *Please, Lord, hold her in Your hand and make a way where there is no way.*

Then I settled back to wait for midnight.

8

Plan A

W HAT DO THE TOUGH DO WHEN THE GOING GETS TOUGH? WE Red Hats break out the cell phones (especially if it's toll-free after 9:00 P.M.). As soon as we flopped on the white leather sectionals to wait for further developments with Pru, we all called home to check our messages and touch base with family.

Meanwhile, Charles kept our sodas filled with unobtrusive perfection.

Teeny, of course, had a dozen urgent business calls to answer. Apparently, even if you hire the best people, you still have to keep in touch. But between calls, her cell phone rang.

We all poised.

"Hello?" Intense concentration congealed her expression. "Great. And she doesn't suspect anything?" Relief. "Fabulous. And the guys at the door?" Concern. "I thought we had four?" Skepticism. "Well, if three's it, then I guess that's it." Pause. "Did you have any trouble with casino security?" Nodding. "Good." Pause. "I know. Of course you are, and for that, I am truly grateful. We just have to pull this off without making a scene or tipping her suppliers." Great relief. "Oh, they are? Thank goodness."

A longer pause. "Okay. Let me know if anything comes up." Pause. "Oh, they don't?" Pause. "All right then, call us from outside if you need to. You have my friends' cell numbers, just in case?" Teeny nodded. "Great. And the doctor will be here by then?" Pause. "And he's free for the whole trip." Another nod. "Perfect. Unless I hear different, we'll be down at the elevator waiting for you at midnight. Have Mr. Phillips meet us downstairs at the penthouse elevator." More nodding. "Great. Bye."

"Did you just say Mr. *Phelps*?" Diane teased. "I know you hired the best, but 'Mission Impossible'?" Her attempt at humor was lame, but it broke the tension.

Teeny grinned. "That's Mr. *Phillips*, the chief investigator, and he looks like Barney Fife. But he's ex-FBI, a crack shot, a black belt in several martial arts—as are his female partners keeping an eye on Pru— and he has a master's in criminal justice."

"What doctor?" Linda asked.

"One who specializes in addictions," Teeny said. "I've hired him to supervise Pru's transition to rehab."

"What was that about calling from outside?" I asked.

"Oh," Teeny said, "Mr. Phillips says that regular cell phones don't work in the casino. His decoys are wired with radio transmitters so he can monitor the situation, but he has to go outside to call us on cell."

"The casinos probably do that on purpose," Diane reasoned, "so nothing will distract people from their gambling."

Blocked cell phones. Wired decoys.

I started to feel a tingle of mixed anxiety and excitement as the reality of our situation sank in. We were really, truly about to participate in a plot with black belts and crack shots and people pretending in deadly earnest to be who they weren't, all to help an old friend.

How thrilling was *that* for a middle-class Goody Two-shoes from Buckhead, like me?

I didn't pray for guidance, afraid that the answer might not jive with our plans. Instead, I asked for divine protection, which is very shaky theologically, I can tell you. Still, the good Lord can accomplish His will even through the shortcomings of His children, and our hearts were in the right place.

It had to work out. The pros were on it.

As Linda had said, failure was not an option.

But just to be safe, I went back to my suitcase and put on the auburn China-doll pageboy wig I'd brought along just for fun because its deep bangs and thick sides covered a lot of my face.

When I came back out onto the terrace with it on, the others didn't even tease me about it, a sure sign they were as nervous as I was.

Somber, we all returned to the reassurance of the mundane.

Forgetting the time difference, I called John and woke him from a dead sleep. He wasn't nearly as impressed with my description of Vegas and the hotel as I wanted him to be, but, to be fair, it was pretty late there. Despite his sulking whenever he found out I was going somewhere without him, once I was gone, it was out of sight and out of mind with John (a common Bigbrain trait). One of my nicknames for him was Oblivious George (the opposite of Curious George the monkey). He never required "I'm here safely" check-in calls, assuming that no news was good news.

I wish I could do that, but I think the worry gene is on that extra X chromosome that makes us women.

Linda didn't want to wake Brooks up (he conked at 9:30 during the week), so she called Abby to check on her and Osama Damned Boyfriend, night owls both. Ever helpful, Osama got on the phone and tried to teach her how to play roulette, but after a while she politely thanked him and hung up. "I swear," she grumbled. "I wish that man wasn't so dang nice. If only he didn't smoke pot and have all those tattoos."

She left out the Muslim / Iranian part, which I considered a definite sign of softening.

I hit the speed dial for SuSu. Just before the message would have kicked on, I heard a click and a fumble as she opened her cell phone. "Hey," I said. "Did I wake you up?"

"No," she answered, belied by the fogginess in her voice. A long inhale. "I'm just clobbered from studying."

I heard what sounded like the rustle of sheets in the background, not loud enough to be SuSu, then some heavy steps, then a distant door closing. I winced.

"Oh, gosh. Did I interrupt something?"

"No." Her voice sharpened, doubtless defensive about her already twice-broken chastity resolution. "No. I was just taking a little cat nap. What's up?"

More like a tomcat nap.

SuSu had fallen off the celibacy wagon again. But I said nothing, in observance of Tradition Five (Mind your own business.) and Tradition Eight (No beating each other up when we blow it.). Instead, I thumbnailed a gossipy account of the flight, the city, the gorgeous bellmen, and our amazingly awful hotel, hoping she wouldn't pick up on the fact that I was keeping something from her. I'm such a wretched liar.

Of course, SuSu was keeping something from me—I knew the sounds of postcoital male—so we were even.

She lit a cigarette, then exhaled. "Did you win anything with my quarters?"

Uh-oh. "Actually, we were so tired from the trip and getting settled that we haven't gone to the casino yet."

A distant door opened to the sound of a toilet flushing.

"Ohmygod, I can't believe y'all," she said louder than necessary to cover the noise. "Y'all are actin' like a bunch of little old ladies. Midnight is noon in Vegas. Get up, take a cold shower, and go down there and play my quarters. I have a premonition that something big is gonna happen with y'all out there."

Major uh-oh. She *had* picked up on something.

"Down, girl." I did my best to keep my tone light. "We were just coolin' our jets. We plan to go down at midnight, as a matter of fact."

"That's more like it. I like the midnight thing. Very dramatic."

You don't know the half of it.

I heard the heavy creak of springs, then more rustling sheets, another confirmation that she was not alone in bed.

"Are you there?" she prodded.

"Yes," I hastened. "Yes."

"You're not on that damned laptop, are you?" she scolded. " 'Cause if you are, that is so rude. Callin' me up at this hour, then only givin' me half your brain."

I scalded with guilt from past transgressions, but realized it was better for her to think that than realize why I was distracted. "Sorry. I'm turning it off right this minute."

Seeing my anxious expression, Linda intervened. "Gimme that phone." She grabbed it. "Hey," she said brightly. "Whatcha doin' back there at law school?" Pause. "Studyin', huh?" She smiled. "Well, we're hobblin' around like a three-legged dog out here without you." Pause.

"Good grief. Only eight hours in three days? Girl, you'd better do something for stress relief, then get some sleep and take your vitamins, or you won't be any use to anybody, includin' yourself, by the time those exams roll around."

Sex was definitely a stress release. I wondered who SuSu's latest stress-releaser was. Probably some cute, blindly overhormoned undergrad.

And no, I was not jealous. SuSu's latest escapade merely provoked a fillip of desire attached to the image of John's ecstatic face from our recent adventures in the bedroom.

"Okay." Linda nodded. "I mean it, though: Take care of yourself. Here's Georgia."

I accepted the phone. "Well, I won't keep you. Just wanted to check in and let you know we got here safe."

"Thanks. I was just wonderin' why I hadn't heard from y'all."

Now, there was a whopper. I smiled. "I'll call tomorrow and fill you in on all the details."

"Great." SuSu took a deep drag, then exhaled, followed by a muffled male cough that I knew perfectly well was no accident.

We see you, Tom, my mind quoted from a children's book, *we know you're there.*

SuSu coughed, herself, to cover, but I knew what was what. I think men really like it when someone calls while they're in the throes of whatever. It's like dogs peeing on their territory; the guys subconsciously want the person on the other end to know they're there and what's been going on. It's a pride thing.

"Don't forget to play my quarters," SuSu admonished. "As a matter of fact, play mine first. I'll split anything you win fifty-fifty."

"Okay."

"Swear," she challenged.

I came back with our most sacred vow from childhood. "Double-pinkie-lock, hope to die."

"Okay. 'Bye."

" 'Bye." I hung up, to hear Diane talking to her son in Germany, where it was already morning.

He was such a gorgeous, smart kid that girls had thrown themselves at him since he was a boy. Now that they were women, nothing had changed, so it was little wonder he was so blasé about settling down. But he dearly loved his mama, as Southern boys should, and was unfailingly sweet to Diane.

All of us but Teeny (who was still leaving messages at various offices) eavesdropped while Diane chatted with him about his high-powered business ventures. From Diane's repeated, "Oh, and where did you meet *her*?" he was clearly still in the mega-eligible, rich young bachelor mode, dating everybody and nobody in particular. Even so, he never failed to come home for two weeks at Christmas, showering Diane with expensive gifts and plenty of attention.

But even budding tycoons want an heir, so some girl was bound to land him eventually and give Diane the grandbaby she wanted. We all believed that for her.

By 10:00 P.M. our time, we'd all finished our calls, and Teeny told Charles he could go to bed. Her chief investigator reported back that Pru was zoned out at the slot machine, and everything was going as planned. So we all grabbed satin comforters from our rooms and adjourned to the balcony's chilly desert night to wake ourselves up a bit.

Bundled on the balcony's cushioned chaises, we watched the lights below and tried to dilute the tension with conversation. We were all worried about the dire events that were now in motion.

"So," Teeny asked, her cell phone clutched in her hand just in case something went wrong. "How was SuSu about our going off without her? Really?"

I tucked my feet closer inside my comforter. "I doubt she'd even given us a thought. She was definitely in bed, and definitely not alone."

All ears immediately zeroed in. Linda's jaw dropped. "You didn't say anything to me about that when she hung up."

I shrugged. "I was trying to mind my own business. Tradition Five. Remember?"

"You can tell *us*," Diane said, her feelings obviously dented by my failure to share this latest juicy tidbit.

I refused to fall for it, saying equably, "I just did."

Linda leaned forward. "So?"

"So, that's all I know," I said. "She acted like she was alone, but I heard him get up and go to the bathroom, then get back into the bed."

Okay, so we were talking about SuSu behind her back. We may be Red Hats with Twelve Sacred Traditions, but we *are* still human—and very much women.

Diane arched a critical brow. "So much for good intentions. I thought she was gonna be celibate till she got out of law school so she could focus her time and energies on studying."

I doubted I could pass so much as a driver's test at this stage of my life. It made my head hurt just to think about the academic grind SuSu had taken on. Emory Law was notoriously difficult.

Linda shook her head, flat-mouthed. "All that talk about keeping her life free of distractions so she could make dean's list."

"She has so far," Teeny reminded us, positive as ever. "And she'll do it again. SuSu's brilliant."

Diane shook her head. "Well, I hope she does better with that than she has staying away from men. First, that tall intern last September. And that blond teaching assistant in November."

"Surely you didn't expect her to quit cold turkey," I defended. "It takes time to break old habits." SuSu had been sleeping around since her wretched divorce. "Considering the fact that for the last few years she's gone through men like cheap pantyhose, I think cutting down to two studmuffins in a whole semester is definite progress. And as far as I know, this is her first slip since."

Clearly uncomfortable with the conversation, Teeny changed the subject, concern written on her heart-shaped face. "What do you think she'll do when she finds out the reason why we came? And that I asked y'all to keep it from her?"

I knew the answer to that one without hesitation. "Honey, we all forgave you for a hell-of-a-lot bigger whopper than that." Teeny's secret fortune and separate-vacation "friendships." "SuSu'll forgive you. She'll forgive us all." SuSu's grudges were reserved for God and her sorry-assed ex. "Especially if I win some money for her on the slots. I brought a whole roll of quarters with her name on it, and she made me swear to play hers first."

Teeny frowned. "I'm not sure we'll be able to gamble if everything goes as planned."

Right on cue, her cell phone rang. We all went on alert.

"Hello?" Pause. "Yes, this is Tina Witherspoon." As the caller spoke,

Teeny slumped, eyes closed, which scared me, but her next words eased my concern. "Thanks be to God." She turned to us with weary gratitude. "They found Bubba. He's with my people on the way to the Denver Airport, ready to come to his mother." Back to the caller. "How did he react when you told him?" Nodding. "He does? Oh, that's so wonderful." Pause. "Okay. I'll call as soon as we know for sure where we're going and when." Pause, tiny frown. "And he doesn't mind waiting?" Smile. "Yes, I guess for that kind of money, I wouldn't mind hanging around the airport for a while, either. Well done, Ms. Atkinson. Well done." She hung up. "What a relief."

"No hock, Sherlock," Linda said. "At least now Pru has a compelling reason to get back on track."

"Thank you, Lord and Saint Anthony." Patron saint of lost things— one of Teeny's favorites. Revived, Teeny shivered. "Man, it's getting cold out here. I think we're all waked up enough. Let's go back inside."

"Dibs on the fire pit," I claimed in earnest, a victim of "froze toes" as my daughter Callie used to call them.

It wasn't much of a fire, just some anemic gas logs—which shouldn't have surprised me, considering the hazards of having an open flame in the vicinity of so much polyester upholstery. But it felt good.

After toasting our toes, we freshened up, then scanned through two dozen first-run movies so fast you'd think we were men, trying to decide which one to choose. We ended up watching a little of everything, and a lot of nothing, not unlike Diane's son's dating style. Frankly, the selection in the high-roller suite wasn't geared to a bunch of middle-aged women, anyway. It leaned heavily to the car-chase, T & A, shoot-'em-up genre.

"Mr. Phelps" called in a report that Pru was still rooted to her seat at the slot machine, flanked by the two "user" agents who were feeding her a steady stream of quarters and making sure she knew the gravy train ended at midnight. Pru had won just enough to keep her coming back for more. Everything was going as planned.

When Teeny told us, Diane refrained from saying, "I told you Pru wouldn't win," but we all knew she was thinking it.

At ten till midnight, Teeny marshaled us to the elevator. I stood ready, my purse heavy with the two rolls of quarters that I carried along with all my other earthly belongings, just in case. (Be prepared!)

"Okay." Teeny looked at the diminutive Piaget on her wrist. "Let's synchronize our watches."

Diane readied her Citizen for resetting. "I can't believe somebody really said that."

Deadly earnest now, Teeny didn't respond. "I have exactly eleven fifty-one fifteen."

I adjusted my Timex, while Linda's plump fingertips struggled with her Seiko.

"Crud," Linda muttered. "I have no idea how to adjust seconds. I'm gonna set this thing for eleven fifty-two. Somebody tell me when that comes, so I can push the stem back in."

We stood poised, then said, "Now," in near unison.

"Close enough." Teeny ruled. She took out her keycard. "Everybody make sure you have your keys."

We all held ours up.

"Okay, here's the deal," she went on. "Mr. Phillips will take us to the row of slots just before the one Pru's on. Her back will be to us, so she shouldn't spot us coming. The aisles are crowded, and it's easy to lose somebody, so we'll split up on the row before hers, then approach her in pairs from each end."

No need to assign who went with whom; Teeny and Diane had always been as close as Linda and I were.

"Then," Teeny went on, "after the decoys leave Pru with no money, we move in from either end. I'll talk to her, tell her we've found Bubba. Offer her food, drink, whatever it takes to get her back up here."

Chicken Little wanted to know what happened if Pru refused to come with us, but I managed to sling the feathered freak-out back into her little henhouse of doom and padlock the door.

"Sounds like a plan to me." Diane smoothed her impeccable blazer. "Let's do it."

This was no game; it was a matter of survival for someone I'd once loved very much. Pru and I had grown apart over the years, but that didn't mean I didn't care. The possibility that we might fail set my heart beating hard and heavy with performance anxiety.

Despite a soul-deep conviction that God can and will work His pleasure using the means available, I suffered from the time-honored Southern woman's delusion that He needed me, personally, to help Him.

Talk about hubris, but there you are. It's what kept Southern women from starving or going crazy through the Civil War, the Great Depression, race riots, the death of the textile industry, the emergence of the international New South, and an epidemic of men who go shiftless and wayward at midlife.

So it was with great trepidation that I followed the others into the elevator and rode down to our date with destiny.

Five minutes later, Mr. Phillips (who did, in fact, look like a taller version of Barney Fife in khakis, with an earpiece firmly in place and a microphone dangling into the vee of his golf shirt) led us deep into the darkened world of noise and neon that was the casino. Walking behind Teeny and Diane, we passed row after row of individual slots on the way to the progressive ones near the back. I couldn't help noticing the wide range of people there in every imaginable type of clothing, from fresh-faced twenty-ones to wrung-out oldsters.

"Most of these people sure don't *look* like they're having fun," I confided into Linda's ear over the din. "They look like they're at war with the machines."

Linda's brows lifted as she scanned the rows. "I guess they are. Compulsive gamblers actually believe that what they do or don't do can affect their luck. They're convinced the big payoff is just around the corner if they just handle themselves right." She shook her head with a sad smile. "Their superstitions are endless."

She wasn't kidding. I spotted a sun-seared bear of a man with his cowboy hat turned backward and then a little granny rapping precisely three times on her machine after she won a small payoff. Another woman crossed herself, kissed a rosary, then turned around three times in place, hand to heaven and what I assumed was a prayer on her lips, before she sat down to play.

"I even have a few of my own good-luck rituals," Linda confided.

"What are those?" I asked, wondering where Pru was.

"The main one is to stop playing when I run out of money," Linda answered.

Before I could respond, we almost ran into Teeny and Diane, who had stopped. Wary, "Mr. Phelps" shepherded us into the next row of slots. He spoke into his microphone, then told Linda and me to go to the far end of the aisle and wait for his signal to come around on Pru's row.

I couldn't resist a peek between machines as we got into position, but I didn't recognize any of the women with their backs to us.

Good thing Teeny had offered to do the talking. My throat felt like it had swelled like a toad-frog's. And my heart hammered like the backbeat at a Stones concert.

Please God, let this work. And don't let us get arrested for kidnapping, I added with just as much sincerity.

Linda and I stood poised, our eyes locked to "Mr. Phelps." He pressed his finger over the earpiece and spoke into the microphone, motioning for us to hold. Then two overmade-up, skanky women with wild hairdos and dark roots emerged from Pru's row of slot machines, the plastic containers they carried almost empty of coins.

The make-believe addicts. Had to be.

"Oh, my gosh," Linda said as they spoke briefly to Mr. Phelps. "That one on the right has on the same outfit you just bought at Filene's Basement."

Good grief. She was right. "Perfect. I just spent two hundred dollars, no returns, on designer druggie chic."

The women nodded to "Mr. Phelps" and split up, presumably to act as backups should things go wrong.

Then "Mr. Phelps" signaled us to move in.

Half-wild with anticipation, I looked down the row to Diane, who gave us the thumbs-up.

Linda and I rounded the corner to the next row and started threading our way through the players and observers who clogged the aisle.

Unable to spot Pru, I zeroed in on Teeny for guidance. She stopped beside a hunched figure with dark hair and laid her hand on the woman's shoulder.

I watched Pru's face, already haggard with despair, crumble at the sight of Teeny's sympathetic smile. Pru curled in on herself as if she wished she could implode to nothingness. Linda and I moved in close from our side, but not too close. We didn't want to pen her in.

"It's okay, honey," Teeny said to her without condescension. "You've had a setback. Those happen. But everything's going to be okay, I promise. We've found Bubba, and he's just fine. He wants to see you. To help you get back on track. We all do."

Like a cornered animal, Pru glanced up to see us standing all around her. But her response was anything but grateful. A flash of mortal shame was replaced immediately by anger. She straightened, hands fisted. "Get out. Leave me alone. You're lying about Bubba. He's dead. I know it." She whacked at her chest. "I can feel it. A mother knows when her son is dead. Now go away and leave me alone!"

People looked over from their machines. And I saw a casino security guy go heads-up, scanning for the source of the disturbance.

Teeny firmed, but dropped her voice. "That's just the drugs talking," she said, "lying, like they always do to get you to use. Bubba's fine, and I'll prove it. I'll call him right now so you can talk to him." She opened her cell phone. No service. "Damn. The phones don't work in here. If you'll just come over to the hotel with me, we can call him."

Clearly, Pru was not convinced.

"Pru, we care about you," Diane said. "That's why we came. We want to help you lick this thing."

"You don't have to do it alone," I told her. "We want to be there for you."

Pru's spine stiffened. "Bull shit! Where were y'all after we got busted that time? You disappeared, just like everybody else. Didn't want to dirty your hands with us."

Not true! We'd all offered to help, but she'd turned us away. Yet somehow, I knew it would be futile to argue with her. Blame was part and parcel of the addict's psyche, rewriting past, present, and future.

Pru turned to sneer at us. "Where were you when I was trying to feed my child while his father was in prison?"

That hit a hot button in me, putting me on the defensive. I'd offered to help her with groceries back then, but Pru had wanted only money, so she could keep herself in cigarettes, booze, and drugs. How dare she accuse me of being so unfeeling, when it was she who'd put her addictions above her child's welfare!

My frustration must have showed, because Linda grabbed my forearm and squeezed, hard, to silence me even as she said to Pru in an even tone, "Pru, none of us can change the past, but we're here now. And we want to help."

My intellect told me that Pru was only trying to pick a fight with us so she'd have an excuse to reject our help, but my heart bled from her baseless accusation. At that point, the best I could do was draw back, wounded, and let the others try.

Teeny put her arm around Pru's shoulders. "Please, just come with us upstairs. We've got the whole penthouse to ourselves. There's plenty to eat and drink up there, and we can call Bubba. I swear, Pru, he's okay. Once you talk to him yourself, you'll know it's true."

I saw a blessed shard of hope warring with the determined despair in Pru's eyes, but then her face hardened with bitterness. "Leave me alone." Her voice got louder as she went on. "You think I don't know you'd tell me anything to get me up there, out of sight, so the men in white coats can bundle me up and cart me away?" We were attracting unwelcome attention. "Well, it won't work. I'm sick to death of being your charity project, so scram! And take the Junior League, here, with you! It's too little, too late!"

She reached into her bucket for a quarter and found it empty, then stood to leave.

"Wait. Don't go." I grabbed for a roll of quarters and broke it open over her bucket. "Use these. I know this machine is lucky."

Pru shoved the bucket back toward me. "I don't need your charity. Take your measly quarters and get out."

This time, the security guard zeroed in on us. He motioned for another to move in as he approached. "Is there some sort of problem here, ladies?"

"No," Teeny said. "My friends and I—"

Pru spoke on top of her. "These women are *not* my friends." She jerked back the bucket and sat, feeding them into the machine as she spoke. "They're trying to make me leave, and I'm not finished gambling."

"That's not true," I defended. "I just *gave* her those quarters."

Pru's expression went sly and evil. "That is a lie. I never saw these people before. They're just a bunch of do-gooders who want to stop me gambling."

Linda made an "oh, no," face, and I found out why.

The security man's expression set in concrete. None too gently, he took Teeny's upper arm in one hand and Diane's in the other. "I'm afraid I'll have to ask you ladies to leave the casino. Immediately. This is a legal form of entertainment, and we have a zero-tolerance policy about harassing our customers."

His buddy latched onto Linda and me in like fashion, and they all but lifted us off the ground heading toward the exit.

Oh, Lordy, we were about to be given the bum's rush to the sidewalk!

Where was Charles the butler when you needed him?

Chicken Little went stark, raving berserk inside me.

People stopped and stared, making way.

Three rows down, "Mr. Phelps" moved in to intervene, blocking our progress, but Teeny motioned him to wait. "It's all right, Mr. Phillips." She looked to the security man. "As you know, this is my bodyguard, Mr. Phillips."

"*Your* bodyguard?" The man's grip loosed immediately. Clearly, he wasn't anxious to step on such powerful little toes as Rose Pendergrass's. But our guy held on to Linda and me.

Teeny rubbed her arm. "Thank you." She shot a pregnant glance to "Mr. Phelps" before addressing the guard. "I'm sure we can clear this up without any further disturbance." She looked just put-upon enough to keep him off balance. "Contrary to what the lady in question told you, she is an old friend of ours, down on her luck. When we saw her in the casino, we came over and tried to convince her to have dinner with us in the penthouse. Clearly, she has some serious personal problems, because she misinterpreted our efforts. I'm sure you can understand what an unfortunate misunderstanding this all is."

Man, she was good. And to think, I'd once believed her incapable of the slightest falsehood. But I guess all those years of covering up for a high-profile, abusive, philandering, alcoholic husband had given her plenty of training.

The guard nodded, but still didn't back down.

"Of course," Teeny said, all honey, "I shall be happy to compensate the casino, if necessary, for any unpleasantness we may have inadvertently caused." She extended her gold keycard. "Shall we say, five thousand?"

Mr. Phillips stayed where he was, but relaxed, with a nod of admiration toward Teeny.

The security guy knew which side his bread was buttered on. "Well, I'll speak to the manager. Please wait here. I won't be long." He left us to his stone-faced buddy.

The guard was right; we didn't have to wait long.

The general manager rushed over, oozing apology, trailed by a dark-haired tree trunk of a man in a silk suit and tinted glasses who had to be some muckety-muck from security. The tree trunk nodded to the guy holding me and Linda, and he immediately released us, turning his attention to dispersing the few remaining curious. "Nothing to look at here. Please enjoy the casino."

"Ms. Pendergrass," the manager gushed, his tone and posture for all the world like Fagin's from *Oliver Twist*. "We so regret this little misunderstanding. I trust you and your friends are all right?"

In her best duchess mode, Teeny nodded. "Thank you so much for your concern. We're fine."

"Then of course, we shall be happy to overlook the entire matter."

The tree trunk shot him a warning look.

The manager squirmed, raising one finger. "There is just one little thing." I could tell, he was definitely caught in the middle. "We'll have to respectfully request that you keep your distance from your friend. Otherwise, we'll have to ask *her* to leave. Clearly she's somewhat disturbed, and we really don't want to have another disruption upsetting our guests."

Teeny blanched, but remained serene. "Oh, no, we wouldn't want that. But I don't want to interfere with my friend's entertainment, either." I saw a light go on in her eyes. "As a matter of fact, I'd like to subsidize her play at that particular machine. I would be most grateful if you could inform her that because of her inconvenience, the house is staking her to free play on that machine"—she paused—"in twenty-five-dollar increments." Smart move. Teeny batted her eyelashes. "Under the circumstances, I'm afraid she wouldn't accept anything from me."

"Certainly," the manager said, "we'd be delighted to do as you wish." I'll bet they were; it was more money in their pockets.

Can we say, brilliant? That should keep Pru where she was—for a while, anyway.

Mr. Phillips spoke up. "Was there a limit you were thinking of, Ms. Pendergrass? Monetarily or time-wise?"

Teeny considered, then told the manager, "Let her play till she's five thousand down." That should take quite a while on a slot machine.

Unless she won.

Diane must have read what I was thinking in my face. She edged over. "I'm telling you," she said in a stage whisper, "she's not going to win."

"How very generous and thoughtful of you, Ms. Pendergrass," the manager fawned.

The tree trunk snapped his fingers, and one of the guards took off, presumably to take care of staking Pru.

"Now, if you ladies will excuse me, I must return to the hotel. Please notify me immediately if there is anything further I can do. We want you to think of the Parthenon as your home away from home."

"Thank you ever so much," Teeny dismissed.

Linda and Diane and I waited until he was out of earshot before we mocked his "Home away from home," but Teeny was in no mood for levity.

She corralled us and Mr. Phillips and made for a palm-secluded table by a fountain in the lobby, where we couldn't be overheard as we started brainstorming alternative plans.

Meanwhile, the decoys moved back in to keep Pru company, but she was so hostile, she ran them off, too, and kept feeding the slot machine with the quarters the house had provided.

We brainstormed for what seemed like an hour, but was only fifteen minutes. Under so much pressure, none of us came up with anything brilliant. The one thing we all agreed on, though, was that we couldn't let Pru go back to her suppliers. When they got word of tonight's incident, they'd probably eliminate her on general principle.

This wasn't an adventure anymore. It was so deadly that I didn't even notice I was up five hours past my East Coast bedtime.

Mr. Phillips said there was little choice left but to "gunny sack" Pru, as we called it in the South. His male operatives would drug her, then "help" her to the penthouse. But Teeny raised the valid point that security would be on Pru like white on rice till she left the casino, so that wouldn't work. Not to mention the guard at the private elevator.

He countered that they could try to nab her outside when she left, but security on the Strip was as tight as it was inside the casinos. Anything suspicious drew immediate police attention.

Stymied, Teeny rose. "I can't think here. Come on, girls." We stood. When Mr. Phillips rose with us, she motioned him to stay. "If you'll excuse us for a little while." She turned back to us. "There has to be some way to get Pru to let us help her." She pointed to the casino lounge and said with uncharacteristic assertion, "To the bar. I need some liquid inspiration, and we need a plan B."

9

Sirens

W E HEADED INTO THE LOUNGE TO REGROUP. DIANE AND LINDA were so preoccupied trying to come up with alternatives that they didn't even look up as Teeny led us to a table.

Fortunately, the place was deserted except for a lone thirty-something cowboy in formal wear and a black Stetson at the bar. Something about him drew my attention. As if he sensed my looking at him, he shifted his lanky six-foot-plus frame so I caught the full impact of him.

My breath caught in my throat. Taut as a long-distance runner and tanned to a burnish, he was all-man gorgeous in the Sean Connery, Clark Gable mold. Chicken Little immediately evaporated in favor of Princess Lay Ya. "I wonder if he'd like to play Han So Low?" I mused.

Teeny frowned in confusion. "What?"

Rats! I'd said it aloud. Ears flaming, I shook my head. "Never mind."

Normally, I'm not one to scope out men young enough to be my son—or any men, for that matter (well, those bellmen, but that was really just admiration for what a nice job God had done making them. No, really; it was)—but this guy was drop-dead sexy, and his subdued formal wear fit that lean, muscular body like custom-made.

I looked closer at his boots. (Footwear is a dead giveaway with men.) They were clearly expensive, elegantly tooled black leather in a conservative style.

While Linda and Diane and Teeny powwowed, I sat down at the seat that gave me the best view of the gorgeous cowboy, feeling sexy and mysterious in my auburn wig (which was a good one, by the way, and flattering).

Gorgeous cowboy caught me looking and grinned, spiking dimples deep enough to hide a dime.

Woof! I melted on the spot.

My inner Miss Manners countered with a sneer: *Rude, rude, rude! He has his hat on indoors.*

But those dimples more than made up for that.

The waitress arrived, her erect nipples the only decoration on her gracefully draped white polyester Greek minidress. Without consultation, Teeny ordered for everybody. "A double black Russian for me." She pointed to me and Linda. "Two Diet Cokes for them." A nod to Diane. "And a double frozen margarita, no salt, for her."

Whoa. This was serious. Teeny never acted bossy. That was my job. And Linda's. And, on occasion, Diane's.

Putting the cowboy on the back burner, I fulfilled my Red Hat role as the asker of the obvious. "What do we do about Pru now?"

Teeny put her forehead to the table. "Ask me after I've had that Black Russian."

I sighed. "Man, I wish SuSu was here. She's always great with Plan Bs."

Diane nodded. "Especially if the plan involves attracting a man. Throw in a man, and she makes the Pentagon look slapdash."

At the mention of SuSu's male fixation, Linda's grumpy little frown gave way to a glow of pure inspiration as the spirit of SuSu descended upon her like a tongue of fire. "Of course. That's it. A man."

She zeroed in on the cowboy at the bar, who turned around and tipped his hat in our direction. Teeny and Diane followed her line of vision, and Diane had the same reaction as mine. But Teeny was too worried to react.

"Pru won't come with us," Linda said with the resonant conviction of a prophetess, "but I'll bet she'd come with him."

"Damn," Diane breathed, too smitten with the cowboy to stick with the subject. "Forget Pru. I'd go with him myself, anywhere, anytime."

I'd never seen her react that way. But then, I hadn't reacted that way before, either.

I noted the scattered peanut shells and two empty shot glasses on the bar beside the gorgeous cowboy. "Looks like he's been there awhile."

"What a waste," Diane said. "Why in the world would a man that good-looking be sitting alone?"

Chicken Little provided a possible answer. I dropped my voice to a whisper. "Do you think he might be a gigolo?"

"Who cares? Time's a'wastin'," Linda said. "Let's ask him."

Completely misunderstanding what she meant, I hopped to my feet. "I'll go." Before they could stop me, I was on my way to the bar.

Close up, he was even better, with eyes so blue they didn't look real, and tiny white smile lines radiating from the corners of his eyes. I readjusted my age assessment to early forties, which only made him that much more attractive.

He spoke first. "I was just sittin' here thinkin' you ladies look too purty to be in a place like this all by yourselves."

The accent was cultured Texas.

My ears throbbed. "My friends and I were just wondering something," I blurted out, awkward as a teeny bopper. "You don't have to answer if you don't want to, but—"

"Ask away, little lady." He grinned. Oh, dimples, dimples, dimples. "I'm at your disposal."

Gorgeous and courtly. I could hardly stand it.

I leaned in confidentially. "You're not . . . well, an *escort* or anything, are you?"

He let out a strangled sound and reared back.

Oh no! I'd mortally offended the man. He'd never help us now.

Then the humor returned to those azure eyes. "No, ma'am. I am definitely not an escort." He stuck out his hand. "The name's Cameron Hodges." I shook it, and he held my hand just long enough to make an impression, but not too long.

I wanted to dissolve into a puddle. "Oh, I am *so* sorry. Please forgive me. It's just that you were alone, and so good-looking, and . . ."

His forehead cleared at my inadvertent compliment. "That's okay. I guess I should be flattered." He cocked his head toward the casino. "I had a few days free and decided to test out mah new car and come see what the shoutin's all about up here." Wry smile. "Frankly, I'm not impressed. This place is tacky, even to a Texan, and that's sayin' somethin'."

Those dimples erased my mortification.

"And throwin' away mah hard-earned money is not mah idea of entertainment."

Gorgeous, courtly, and *sensible*. Catch me before I faint.

Spellbound, I shook my head and heard myself say, "You are the most gorgeous man I have ever seen in my life."

Oh, Lord! I'd said it aloud. That did it. I reverted to the awkward, insecure thirteen-year-old I had once been.

He laughed. "Well, you're mighty purty, yourself."

Now he was just patronizing me. Suddenly all too aware of my middle-aged self, I backed away, almost too embarrassed to speak. Tradition Eight completely evaporated from my brain. (No beating ourselves or each other up when we blow it.) I just wanted to go hide. "Thank you so much for being so understanding," I managed to get out. "Again, I apologize. I . . . my friends and I wanted to ask you something else, but I think I'll let them do it. And I swear, it's not insulting." I was rattling on like an idiot.

I could tell my face was flaming when I got back to the table. "Well, he's not a gigolo. I asked him."

Linda shot erect. "You *what?*"

"You told me to ask him, so I did, but I don't think it was a very good idea."

She swatted at my upper arm. "You nudnik. I meant ask him to *help* us, not ask him if he's a male prostitute!" Her voice carried clear across the room.

I set a new world's record for horrified embarrassment. "Oh, shit." I not-so-gently pounded my auburn bangs on the table. "Damn, damn, damn. I am so sorry, y'all."

"Tradition Eight," Linda grumped.

I straightened to find Cameron the Cowboy watching us, obviously amused.

"Oh, sweetie." Teeny patted my back. "It was an honest mistake. We'll all have a good laugh about it one day."

I doubted it. More likely, I'd wake up sweating in the night for years to come, tingling with the echoes of mortified adrenalin that pulsed through me.

"All is not lost," Diane declared. She turned to Teeny. "How much more cash is in that little bag of yours?"

"Enough," Teeny answered. "Why?"

"How much do you think we should offer him?" Diane asked. "It needs to be enough to get him to do it, but not so much that he'll be suspicious."

"Oh, y'all, I don't know about offering him money," I fretted. "Especially after I asked him if he was for hire. I think he'd be really insulted."

"He doesn't look upset to me," Linda observed.

Eyes glued to the cowboy, Diane said a distracted, "We can't just ask him to do it for nothing. Why should he?"

Teeny thought a minute, then counted out ten crisp hundreds. "Here's a thousand. We'll need to feel him out about compensation, but be delicate about it."

"Don't mention feeling him out," Diane cautioned with mock seriousness. "I need to stay focused on Pru."

"Is this really a good idea?" I had to ask. "Putting Pru into the hands of a total stranger . . ."

Linda frowned, considering. "He's not a gigolo, but what if he's something else shady? Like a drug dealer?"

We all sized up his lanky, easygoing posture and overall impression.

"No gold teeth, visible tattoos, or gaudy jewelry," I murmured. "No jewelry at all but a decent watch and a college ring. Definitely not pusherish."

"As if you'd know what a drug pusher looks like," Linda scorned.

Diane sighed, clearly smitten. "Georgia's right. His body language is too open to be anything but a straight-up guy."

"Oh, yeah?" Linda sized him up with a jaded eye. "Then why's he flirtin' with a bunch of women old enough to be his mother?"

"Only if you'd had him at ten," I countered. "He's at least forty."

Diane aimed a sappy stare on Cameron the Cowboy, her thoughts clearly a million miles from anything maternal. "I'd like to have him at fifty-five."

"Ohmygod," Linda said. "She's possessed." She waved her hand between Diane and the object of her fixation. "SuSu. Is that you?"

"Oh, hush up," Diane murmured absently, "and let me look."

"Yoo-hoo." Teeny snapped her fingers in front of Diane's rapt gaze. "Back to business, please."

Diane reluctantly reverted her attention to us.

"Executive decision," Teeny ruled. "The cowboy is plan B. But we can't have him take her upstairs. We've already covered that."

"The limo," I said. "We could have it waiting at the door, all packed and ready to go to the airport, with us inside. If the cowboy gets in with her, nobody will suspect anything."

The windows were tinted so dark, nobody could see in.

Teeny's blue eyes darted back and forth, unfocused, as she weighed that out. "Dr. Johnson can meet us in the limo just as easily. Once the methadone wears off, Pru will need some meds to stabilize her till she gets to rehab."

Charter jets. Black belts. Decoys. Kidnapping. A gorgeous cowboy. And a doctor who not only makes house calls, but flies cross-country with the patient?

How much more unbelievable could this get?

I had waked up in the middle of a movie. That was all there was to it.

"So, we'll all be waiting in the limo," Diane clarified.

"Jus' like a *spider*," I quoted Mammy from *Gone with the Wind*.

Linda frowned. "But when we send the cowboy after Pru, shouldn't at least one of us be there to keep watch and show him who she is? And make sure he does what he's supposed to?"

Diane had her mouth open to volunteer, but I beat her to it. "I'll keep watch. Please, y'all. Let me make up for the gigolo thing. Please, please, please."

"We're all assuming he'll do it," Teeny said.

Definitely channeling SuSu, Diane shifted like a femme fatale in her seat. "Trust me. If y'all let *me* do the asking, he'll come through."

"Should Diane tell him everything?" I questioned. "Or just ask him to get Pru to the limo?"

Diane picked up the money and folded it seductively into her slender, perfectly manicured hand. "The truth is always safest." She sucked in her tummy and smoothed the hips of her slacks. "I'm off."

"Down, girl," Linda cautioned. "Try not to look so predatory. You'll scare him off."

"Easy for you to say," Diane shot back. "You haven't been celibate for two years." She set out, her trim, middle-aged body slinking with the calculated grace of Marilyn Monroe, her eighteen-hour-encased size Cs thrust proudly forward.

We all watched with bated breath as she engaged Cameron the Cowboy in conversation.

Between the noise from the casino and the Muzak in the lounge, we could only hear the louder snatches of their conversation. After they'd talked for a few minutes, she fanned out the bills.

Teeny moaned. "So much for being delicate."

After the gigolo thing, I was in no position to throw stones.

Clearly taken aback, Cameron the Cowboy looked at the money, then at Diane, shifting his Stetson and increasing the distance between them.

Oh, no. Please don't say no. Oh please, oh please, oh please.

Falling back on her expert corporate negotiating skills, Diane backed off physically and campaigned for our cause in earnest.

Cameron bent his head to listen, his rugged face in shadow as he stared down at one extended boot. Diane finished, then wisely gave him the space to make a decision. It didn't take long. He straightened, his expression clearing, and nodded, offering his hand to seal the deal.

"Oh, thank you, thank you, thank you," Diane said as they shook.

He picked up the money and folded it three times into a tight packet, then dropped it into the deep vee of her blouse, where all well-endowed middle-aged women have a popcorn-catching bra gap.

Blushing like a missionary at an R-rated movie, Diane gave the money a pat. Then with a triumphant grin, she hooked her arm in his and all but dragged him over.

"Linda and Teeny," she said, "allow me to introduce Cameron Hodges." When Teeny's eyes widened at the use of her real name, Linda flinched. "Sorry. Cameron, this is my friend Linda and *Rose Pendergrass*." She granted me a cursory, "You've already met Georgia." Then she smiled up at the cowboy. "Cameron's here on his first visit to Las Vegas from his ranch near Austin. And he'd be delighted to help us rescue Pru."

There went those dimples again. "It's the least I could do for a lady in distress," he said with endearing humility. "Dah-anne here explained everything to me, including why y'all thought I might be a gigolo."

"And guess what?" Diane added, her hand to the hundreds. "He wouldn't take the money."

We knew. All four of us gazed at him with admiration as well as lust.

"A true gentleman," Teeny said. "We can't thank you enough for helping us. Our friend is truly in a life-or-death situation." She rose, coming only to his chest. "If you'll just excuse me for a moment, please, I'll set everything into motion." She headed for the lobby, presumably to have the manager get our stuff packed and loaded into the limo.

Poor Charles the butler. All that unpacking and ironing, just to repack us hours later.

Repacking . . . I realized he'd see my raggedy undies after all, but since we were leaving, I didn't mind so much.

I saw Mr. Phillips materialize halfway to the lobby and accompany Teeny.

Glad that things were back on track, I realized that nobody had asked Cameron to sit down. "Where are our manners?" I motioned to Teeny's vacated seat. "Please join us."

"Cain't think of anything I'd rather do." Truly the gentleman, he didn't take her chair, but drew up one from the next table and sat in the space Diane cleared between her and Linda.

The waitress returned, and Cameron insisted on picking up the tab for another round, ordering a cola for himself.

Gorgeous, courtly, sensible, chivalrous, unassuming, intelligent, and now, moderate and generous. Why wasn't this man taken?

Like a long-lost cousin, he settled in at ease and asked Linda and Diane all about themselves. But all I could think about was why nobody had snapped him up. (It never occurred to me that he might be gay.) "Are you married?" I blurted out apropos of nothing, to the horror of my more polite friends.

Cameron actually blushed. "Nope," he said. "Never had the chance. Most women aren't interested in a man who gets up at five, goes to bed at nine, works every hour of the in-between, and comes home beat."

"I was," Linda told him as Diane bit her lips to keep from volunteering. "And I still am, thirty years later. So don't give up looking."

He turned a devastatingly ingenuous, boyish glance toward the floor. "Haven't really had the time, lately." Clearly, we'd made him uncomfortable.

Why had I opened my big mouth?

Teeny provided a welcome diversion from the awkward subject by returning. "Everything's set, and the jet's being gassed up." She sat, looking more positive than I had seen her in days. "The flight plan's already filed, and Dr. Johnson's on his way. Charles is packing our stuff, and Mr. Phillips is sending it to the airport for screening, so we can take off as soon as we get there. As soon as everything's ready, he'll let us know"—she looked to me and Cameron—"and you can lead Cameron to our friend."

The waitress arrived with our drinks and set Teeny's double Black Russian in front of her. Teeny tried to hand it back. "I'm sorry, I didn't order this."

"Cameron insisted on treating us to another round," Diane gushed.

"How kind." Teeny bestowed that deceptively angelic look of hers on him. With the wisdom of our Southern heritage, she knew better than to bruise his male ego by rejecting his generosity. "Thank you ever so." She took a sip of the drink, but no more as we chatted with Cameron, who quoted Keats and turned out to have a masters in English from Yale, but had given up the academic world for the ranching he loved. Ten thousand acres of it.

When he started spouting poetry, I thought Diane was going to drool all over the table. Not that she'd have been alone.

Double woof. What a man.

I know it was wicked, but against my will, I kept picturing him in that Han So Low outfit with impressive equipment displayed through the black hole.

This had never, ever happened before. (Except that one time during the sermon when the devil flashed the image of our minister, naked and aroused, into my brain, but I had said a heartfelt prayer, so it only lasted an instant.) But this lecherous vision refused to go away. I got so embarrassed, my ears all but melted off, and I had to quit looking at him altogether. For distraction, I broke open SuSu's roll of quarters and toyed with them on the tabletop.

Twenty minutes later, Mr. Phillips came in and told us everything was ready. The limo was waiting outside the casino entrance, the doctor inside, and our luggage on its way to the plane.

That hadn't taken long! But money definitely speeds things up.

Without hesitation, we gathered our purses and stood. I scraped all but three quarters into my pocketbook, reserving those for at least one stab at the slots for SuSu.

Cameron the Cowboy unfolded to his impressive height at a more leisurely pace.

Teeny introduced him to "her security coordinator" (Mr. Phillips), and explained that the detectives would be keeping an eye on things and running interference should anything go wrong.

Diane moved in close on Cameron's other side, but he ignored her and placed his warm hand at my back to usher me toward the casino. "Nothin's gonna go wrong," he assured Teeny with absolute, calm confidence.

"What if it does?" I couldn't keep from asking.

His piercing look of conviction was even sexier than his smile. "I'll bring her to y'all, her choice. You have mah word on it."

I almost swooned.

Teeny looked hopeful, but unconvinced. "We'll be thrilled if you can just get her into the limo without attracting attention," she told him. "It's a white stretch Mercedes, and we'll be right outside the main exit. Once she's in, we'll take it from there. And the limo's yours for the rest of your visit, with my compliments."

He touched the brim of his hat. "Thank you, ma'am, but I sorta like drivin' mah Jag, if it's all the same to you."

Rich, too.

Diane looked back to him with fresh longing as Teeny herded Linda and her toward the main entrance.

Cameron's expression relaxed. "So, what's our damsel in distress wearin'?"

I stopped in my tracks, drawing a blank. Oh, Lordy. I resorted to a familiar middle-aged coping device: When you don't know the answer, answer something you *do* know and pray that what you need will come to you in the meantime. "She's tall and sort of bony, except her butt. Darkish hair with darker roots, in a ponytail high off the crown." The picture began to form. "And tight black pants." No hint of what she wore on top, just her face. "She's haggard, like a cornered animal."

Cameron the Cowboy shook his head. "Poor gal. Don't worry, I'm real good at gentlin' hurt, wild things." From anybody else, that would have sounded *too* hokey, but not from him. "It might take a while, but I'll get her to come around." He resettled his Stetson. "Keep an eye out. As soon as I get her in mah arms, start followin', but not too close."

"You're going to pick her up?"

He grinned. "Just like *An Officer and a Gentleman.* It works every time."

"And when was the last time you carried an addict out of a casino?" I couldn't resist asking.

Flirting? I was *flirting.*

There came those dimples again. "You'd be surprised."

Pru's life hung in the balance, everybody was poised to flee, and I was wasting time mooning worse than Diane. Not to mention the fact that I was happily married. I sent up a brief arrow prayer for forgiveness.

Cameron frowned as a security guard strolled past a little too slowly. He leaned in close to whisper, "Since the security guards have you marked, we probably ought to split up. I'll trail you. When you get two rows past hers, stop and signal me what seat she's in, counting from your end, then move on so security doesn't get nervous."

I couldn't lean close to whisper back; his Stetson was in the way. "But I promised to watch over things," I murmured.

He nodded. "Okay, then. Give me a few minutes, then meander back, but keep out of sight. Don't want her to spook."

He made a great show of saying good night, then wandered into the casino. I refreshed my lipstick with shaking hands before setting out in Pru's direction, suddenly conscious of how many dark blue security jackets there were among the casino's patrons.

Damn. Security was everywhere. And I could have sworn that most of them were watching me.

Cameron had been smart to keep his distance.

I got scared. My heart started bolo bouncing inside my ribs, and my mouth went dry.

Needing to make sure Cameron was still there, I pivoted—doing my best to look casual as I pretended to look for the others—and spotted him a few rows back, convincingly unaware of my attention. On his way past a cocktail waitress, he flashed her a grin.

Dazzled, she turned around and ran slap into a dollar slot, providing a minor diversion when her tray of empty glasses went tumbling.

Normally, there's nothing like a pratfall to break the tension, but I was beyond that. The stakes were too high.

I forged ahead, slowing near the back at each new row till I spotted Pru feeding the slot machine like a zombie, six seats down between two overtanned old ladies. I don't think she'd have seen me unless I shook her, but warning tingled from my extremities to my chest.

I walked two rows past as instructed, then turned in Cameron's direction and pretended to be deep in thought, counting out six on my fingers. I know I shouldn't have looked his way, but I did, and was grateful to see him nonchalantly flash the same signal for an instant. When he reached the right row, I nodded, and he turned in.

I checked my watch. One eighteen A.M. He'd said to give him a few minutes. Five should be enough.

I strolled down the row I was on, feigning great interest in the various machines, then ambled indirectly toward Pru's, wary of the security guards who circled, silent and impassive, like sharks through the crowd.

At exactly 1:23 A.M., I peeked around the corner to see Cameron playing the machine next to Pru's. As I watched, he worked her like an expert therapist. I completely forgot about circulating. At first, it was just a few remarks. Then he drew her out, got her talking. The next thing I knew, they had stopped playing and were talking in earnest, his expression one of rapt concern. Fortunately, Pru's back was to me, so I moved out for a better look.

I saw Pru's shoulders sag, her hands going to her face.

Cameron circled her shoulders and kept talking, then listening. Her head nodded.

He talked some more, taking her hand.

Her head nodded again.

He helped her to her feet, where she clung to him like a slow dancer at the prom.

Then, smooth and natural as a slow stream over polished rocks, he scooped her into his arms. Even with his height and strength, it couldn't have been easy, but he did it with no visible effort, holding her sure and steady.

She quaked with the quiet tears of an exhausted child, her face turned tight into the side of his neck as he gently swung her back and forth, one work-worn hand smoothing her hair. Then he started slowly for the other end of the row, speaking low to her all the way.

I moved gingerly after them, as instructed, careful not to get too close, till I reached the machine Pru had been playing.

Everything was under control. We were leaving. Cameron was moving slow, and I couldn't get too close.

On impulse, I took the three quarters from my pocket and slipped them in, then pulled the lever.

One odd-looking logo stopped in the window. Then two. Then three.

Then all hell broke loose. Lights flashed, bells rang, sirens went off, and the jackpot sign over the machines flashed $100,000 again and again while a canned voice boomed, "We have a winner! We have a winner!" I covered my face in horror and peeked through my fingers. People at the other seats jumped up and stared at me—some with outright hostility—and every security man within a hundred feet came running.

The overwhelming instinct to run exploded inside me, but my feet wouldn't move. Nothing would move! Seconds seemed like minutes, but I finally managed to find my voice. "Oh, shit!" It came out in slow motion.

I was supposed to keep a low profile!

Hindsight's twenty-twenty, but at that moment, all I could think of was getting away. I swear, it never occurred to me to sit tight and claim my winnings while the others went on. I was too panicked.

Hindsight being what it is, though, I can tell you, it made a hell of a diversion. Nobody was watching Cameron carry Pru to the limo.

They were too busy trying to see what happened. Or catch me.

Back at the big payoff, the noise escalated to a roar as people poured in from the rest of the casino, hopelessly clogging the aisles.

Cameras flashed, and I covered my face, half-blinded, my purse clutched to my chest like a football on a Hail Mary run.

Security guards started pushing people back and setting up bright orange cones and ropes to cordon off the area. When I saw a particularly burly guard headed for me, I finally broke out of my stupor and leapt sideways with superhuman strength, but from everywhere, hands grabbed at me to keep me from getting away.

"Let . . . *go* . . . of me, dammit!" I yelled as I tried to struggle free.

"It's okay! Don't run away! You won!"

"You're the big winner!"

The hands grasped, tugged, dragged, but I was determined to escape.

Somehow, I got to the next row (over the machines?), then dropped to a crawl and didn't come up till I came to a spot where everybody was looking toward the commotion. I stood and made for cover behind a potted palm.

There I jerked out of my navy blue blazer—not even caring that I was exposing the fat beneath the back of my bra to the world—and tried to walk as casually as I could toward the exit, hyperventilating all the way. I almost got away with it, but just as I pushed the door open and saw the limo idling only twenty feet away, I heard from behind me, "There she is! She's at the door!"

I tore outside on adrenaline overdrive.

"Let me in!" I pounded on the tinted glass in the limo's back door. "Let me—"

The door opened with force, and Cameron the Cowboy sprang forward like a jack-in-the-box, then jerked me back in and slammed the door behind us.

"Hit it!" he yelled to the driver. Immediately, our tires screeched as we pulled away in what felt like slow motion.

Meanwhile, security guards and hoards of the curious stampeded toward the exit.

Inside the limo, a good-looking older man was sitting with Pru's head in his lap (She was out cold.), but the others stared at me in confusion.

"What took you so long?" Linda asked, on top of Diane's, "What happened?"

"They're after me," I blurted out, too panicked to think or speak clearly. "I screwed everything up. We have to get out of here. Fast!" I ripped off my wig, oblivious to the matted mess underneath, and ducked below the tinted windows.

Cameron reacted with a genteel wince at the transformation.

Teeny picked up the intercom phone and said to the driver, "There's a thousand extra in it for you if you can get us to the airport without anybody catching up with us."

"Buckle up and hang on," the driver ordered over the intercom speakers as he accelerated.

Teeny reached into Diane's bodice and deftly extracted the wad of hundreds. "Sorry. You've got my driver bonus."

Diane waved off the apology. "It's yours, anyway."

The limo went into hyperdrive. (As hyper as a limo can get, which I prayed was hyper enough.)

All of us but Pru turned to see the mob pouring out of the hotel, some of them racing for their cars.

Teeny grabbed the intercom again and told the driver, "Lose 'em, and there's another five hundred in it for you."

We veered sharply onto a side street, narrowly missing a light pole.

As we careened down a series of back streets, Cameron the Cowboy took off his Stetson and ran his fingers through that thick, wavy hair, then laid the hat aside. He didn't even have hat hair. "You know, I was pure-dee bored when you ladies came into that bar, but this evenin' is turnin' out to be the most fun I've had in . . ." There went those dimples again. "Ever."

Diane slid up next to him. "How 'bout coming with us? Can I interest you in a flight to—*ow!*"

Unrepentant for pinching her, Linda chided, "I don't really think discussions of destinations would be prudent at this point, do you? We wouldn't want to get Cameron, or us, in trouble."

"Speaking of trouble," Teeny said to me. "What the heck happened back there, George?" Cameron mouthed my masculine nickname in confusion. Diane had already blown my cover by introducing us, and now Teeny was doing it again. "You didn't kill anybody, did you?"

"Worse." Totally unraveled, I burst into tears. "I hit the jackpot!"

Red Hats Fly

*E*VERY CONSCIOUS PASSENGER IN THAT LIMOUSINE SNAPPED TO IN unison with, "What?!"

We all lurched to the left as our driver navigated another turn in his evasion course to the airport.

"I hit the jackpot," I wailed, beyond caring that I was running mascara worse than Tammy Faye Baker. "Pru's slot machine . . . ," I blubbered. "I told her it was lucky, but I was just making that up." Fresh sobs assailed me, propelled by the falling-into-Tallulah-Gorge letdown from my adrenaline-crazed flight. "It wasn't even for me," I gasped out between spasms. "I swore to SuSu I'd play her quarters." Gulp. Sob. "Double-pinky promise. I had to do it."

Did I mention, I suffer from a compulsion to be justified?

The others watched, fish-faced—even the doctor.

We all listed right in another turn, then bounced out of our seats when the back tires jumped a curb.

Cameron's head contacted the roof with a daunting thud, but he barely noticed, his attention riveted on me.

"And then it did one, then two." My voice escalated. "Funny-lookin' things. Couldn't read 'em. No glasses." More sobs.

Teeny pulled a cool, damp napkin off the liter of bottled water chilling in the dwarf-height champagne bucket and handed it to me.

Instead of blotting at the wreckage on my eyes as she'd probably intended, I broke one of the most basic rules of etiquette and used the napkin for a monumental nose-blow worthy of Babar.

Diane and Teeny winced, but I didn't care.

"So two came up," Linda prompted.

"And then, the third one came up." A spastic breath. "And everything went crazy." A shuddering gulp of air. "Bells and lights and '*We have a winner*,'" I said, mimicking the basso tone of the recording. "And then everywhere, people coming and security guards. And *cones* and *ropes*. And 'Nevada gaming rules.'"

I blew again, but by then, my nose was so stopped up that it came out a truncated squeak. So I folded the napkin and dragged the unmolested side across my swollen eyes, trying to get control of myself. "Everybody in the place was after me, but all I could think about was getting away."

"How much did you win?" Diane demanded.

"*I* didn't win anything," I retorted in the round, nose-closed vowels of an FM announcer. "I told you, it was for SuSu."

Diane waved off the technicality. "How much?"

Hands over my face, I bent forward into my lap, the impact of what had happened finally coming home. "A hundred thousand dollars!" I sat up, staggered by the implication of what I'd done. "Y'all! I ran out on a hundred thousand dollars of SuSu's money!"

Cameron burst into a guffaw. "Hot damn. What a night." He reclined like a pasha. "Durndest thing I ever saw."

I peered into Linda and Diane and Teeny's stunned faces.

Teeny picked up the intercom. "Driver, pull over." She scowled. "Yes, you'll still get your bonus. Just pull over." She covered the receiver and said to me, "I can perfectly understand your reaction, sweetie. I know you were only trying to protect us all, but you didn't have to run. Pru came with us of her own accord. You are not a felon." She looked to the doctor. "Will Pru be okay if we delay leaving for a while?"

"She's stable and sedated," he said. "She'll be fine for at least another six hours."

With typical clear-headed decision, she told me, "We'll go back right now and drop you off near the casino so you can claim the money."

Relief welled inside me till the complexities of the situation sank in. If only it were that simple. I raked my fingers through my wig-matted hair. "But if I go back, won't that raise too many questions? Teeny, they knew I was staying with you. They'll find out you're not the woman who registered."

Linda's expression went grim. "Not to mention the media. If you go back and reveal your identity, it won't take the press long to figure out who the rest of us really are." Her hands framed an imaginary headline. "Atlanta housewife wins Vegas jackpot, then flees with prominent socialite-slash-tycoon masquerading as wealthy recluse."

"Big deal," Diane interrupted. "I'm sure people use assumed names all the time here. That's not news."

"Look who's the expert, all of a sudden," Linda challenged. She went back to her news story. "Also involved were an Atlanta doctor's wife, a women's wear CEO, and a Texas rancher, all of whom have declined comment."

She'd carefully left out our names this time, only to tell Cameron and the doctor we were from Atlanta. Little by little, we were blowing our cover.

True to my role as Dire Projector, I picked up the story with, "An inside source at the Parthenon Hotel and Casino states that the rancher and the women may have been involved in the abduction of an unnamed female customer.' "

"She has a point," Cameron chimed in, eliciting prim, "mind your own business" glares from me, Teeny, and Diane.

Teeny, suddenly looking haggard, rubbed her forehead. "Let me think." Scowling, she peered into the middle distance as if the solution could be found in thin air.

The intercom beeped. "Ma'am. This isn't a safe place to stop," the driver said. "Is it okay if I take you to a more secure location while you decide where you want to go?"

Teeny sighed, then straightened, her expression clearing. "Take us back to the casino, but park around the corner. We want to keep a low profile."

All I'd wanted to do my whole life was keep a low profile, but crazy stuff like this just kept happening to me. The last thing I wanted was to embarrass my best friends. "Teens, are you sure about this? I'm jinxed."

Linda exhaled sharply. "George, a person who just won a hundred thousand dollars on one pull of a slot machine cannot refer to herself as jinxed."

Cameron grinned. "More like *charmed*."

Teeny patted my arm. "One way or the other, you have to go back. No matter what happens, we're with you. And don't worry about the money. I'll make it right, regardless."

Teeny had already staked SuSu to a huge chunk of starting-over money once SuSu finally acknowledged that she wasn't getting anything from her ex. "But it's not yours to make right," I said, miserable. "It's mine."

"Oh, take off that martyr's crown," Diane scolded without rancor. "Tradition Eight."

"Tradition Eight doesn't apply," Teeny calmly asserted. "Georgia didn't blow anything. She made a generous gesture to keep a promise to one of us, and when it got out of hand, she escaped to protect us."

I thanked the good Lord again for such wonderful friends, then said a heartfelt prayer that nothing sensational or embarrassing would happen when I went back, which turned out to be one of those "be careful what you pray for" situations.

Teeny spoke into the receiver. "Please take us back to the casino, but park around the corner from the main entrance."

She hung up the intercom. "He's private security, ex-black ops, trained in high-speed evasions and antiterrorist responses. If things get hairy, just come back to the car. He'll get us to the plane."

We zoomed off, heading back by another route. Diane took advantage of the trip to hang onto Cameron, who didn't seem to mind a bit.

Cameron double-dimpled. "I cain't wait to tell the guys back home that I met five fine ladies in Vegas and had the night of my life."

At our alarmed reaction, he grinned again. "That's *all* I'll tell 'em, or anybody else, includin' the Supreme Court. A gentleman never tells."

Linda sighed. "Oh, thank you."

The doctor frowned, clearly concerned about his own involvement.

If *only* I hadn't played those quarters in that machine.

My imagination conjured a news flash: *Another hotel source stated, "I don't know why the lady in question ran when she won. Obviously she needed the money. Her granny pants were quite ragged."*

A spark of mischief brightened Diane's eye. "Exclusive," she said in an announcer's voice, as if she'd read my thoughts. "CNN has the inside scoop on Vegas escapade by eccentric Atlanta Red Hat Club. Unanswered suspicions prompt grand jury investigation. Details at eight."

"Cut it out," I grumbled. "This is not funny."

Diane grinned. "Not at the moment, but it will be."

Within minutes, we pulled up on a side street next to the casino.

I picked up the intercom. "I'll need my purse from the trunk." Driver's license, IDs, and cell phone.

"You'll need this, too," Linda said, handing me the wig and sunglasses.

I shoved them on, haphazardly tucking up the stragglers of my own hair.

"Do you want any of us to come with you?" Teeny asked.

"No!" This was my mess to straighten out.

"Okay, but call us if you need help," Teeny instructed.

I got out and retrieved my purse from the trunk.

"Good luck," the gang called from inside the tinted windows.

Cell phone on, I headed around the corner, completely unprepared for what awaited me.

Women.

Everywhere. Running for the doors. Shoving into the jammed casino.

Security men shouted, "Ladies! Please! If you don't settle down, we'll have to empty the casino!"

And two remote TV crews were setting up to film.

I froze in the middle of the sidewalk.

The stink of stale smoke assailed me when a haggard, paunchy bleached-blonde of at least seventy almost knocked me down. "Me! I'm the one! It was me!"

A fat woman in an electric wheelchair cut her off and plowed into the crowd. "It's not her! It's me!"

From inside the casino, a roar of female voices echoed the same refrain.

Word was out on the strip, and it looked like every woman who could walk, ride, or crawl was determined to claim SuSu's jackpot.

Dazed, I avoided the camera crews and headed over to the hotel entrance, which was slightly less crowded. Once inside, I worked my way through the pushing, frantic mob toward a beleaguered security man.

My situation claustrophobia kicked in, big time. Only my love for SuSu kept me going through the tangle of bodies and smells and human heat.

Halfway there, I heard a rough whisper from somewhere nearby. "Oh my God, it's her. The real one. And that hair's a wig."

How did she know? I saw my reflection in a glass case and realized my hair was on crooked. But at least I'd been recognized. A good sign.

Not!

A hand reached out, grabbed my glasses and wig in a desperate grip, and snatched them off, then disappeared.

"Hey!" Oblivious to the matted mess she'd exposed, I spun around and tried to nab the culprit, but she had melted into the throng.

This was not working out the way I'd thought it would.

Smarting, I shoved my way to the security man. "Sir! Sir!"

His face dusky with frustration, he turned to me. 'What?"

"I know you probably won't believe me, but I really was the one who ran away from the jackpot. I can show you what machine and everything."

"So can half the people in this place," he countered.

"But it really was me. And I don't want it for myself. It's for my friend. I promised her I would play the slots for her, and we were leaving, so I stuck the three quarters into the machine, and it won."

"Lady, get in line. Every woman here says she was the one." He pointed to a well-dressed brunette. "She says it's for an operation for her grandson." He pointed to the woman in the electric wheelchair. "She claims she was so excited to win that she could walk again, which made her so ecstatic, she ran just to prove to herself that she could."

I faced him squarely. "They're lying. I was the one. Look at the surveillance tapes."

The guy let out a wry bark of laughter. "Listen, lady. I've seen the tapes, and you don't look anything like her. She had straight hair, and it wasn't even the same color as yours."

"It was a wig," I protested over the clamor surrounding us. "Somebody recognized me when I came back and stole it. They took my sunglasses, too."

"Right." He shook his head, unconvinced. "I'll tell you what I told all the others: Nevada gaming regulations require winners to identify themselves. Once that woman left the casino and we lost visual contact, all we have to go on is the security tapes. I've seen them, and frankly, she was a lot heavier than you."

"Everybody knows the camera adds ten pounds!" I argued. How could I convince him? "I got away in a white limo! How many people know that?"

He wasn't impressed. "Most of them." Annoyed, he recited, "The Parthenon will make every effort to find the legitimate winner, so get in line and leave your information like all the others. Then don't call us; we'll call you."

In a flash of insight, I realized the casino was about as likely to search out the winner as it was to start handing out free chips. The machine had paid off, as it was required by regulation to do. I had left without identifying myself. My wig was gone, and somebody else was out there wearing it and claiming to be me. I didn't even look like the woman in their videotapes.

Sure, they'd go through the motions of looking for the winner. But money was money, and they had no legal obligation to find me, really.

I stood there, suddenly in a hollow, muffled void.

It was hopeless.

With no conscious decision on my part, my body started backing away.

When the crush around me thinned, I turned and headed back toward the limo.

I'd prayed that nothing drastic would happen, and I'd gotten my way. Definitely a bad-news, good-news situation.

No money, but no dire publicity, either.

At least I'd tried.

I rounded the corner in a trance of guilt and relief. The door opened, and I crawled in.

"To the airport, Jeeves." I was hoarse from shouting.

Teeny gave the word.

"Lord," Linda greeted me as we pulled away from the curb. "You're a wreck. What happened in there?"

I flopped into the seat and closed my eyes, exhausted. "Half the women in Nevada were in there claiming to be me. Somebody in the crowd recognized me and stole my glasses and my wig. It was hopeless, so I left."

A consensus of sympathy expressed itself in "Poor baby," and "At least you tried," and "I was afraid that might happen."

"The only consolation is," I said, "SuSu will never have to know what she almost had." I raised up to peer at my friends, my voice pleading and threatening at the same time. "Y'all won't tell her, will you? It would only make her feel awful."

Heads shook in confirmation. Linda zipped her lip.

I sagged back. It wasn't the first secret I'd kept from SuSu, but the weight of it already dragged me down.

I felt as if I'd barely closed my eyes when the driver announced, "We're at the airport, ma'am."

We looked out to see a guard kiosk beside the entrance to the private hangar area. The driver showed his license and signed in with the guard on duty, then the security arm lifted, and we rode past toward the hangar.

Mr. Phillips was there waiting. "Casino security tried to question us, but we got away. We'll get you through airport security as quickly as possible. I've explained to security that one of our passengers is passed out. Happens all the time, so they're set up to accommodate such situations."

The only hang-up we had was Diane, who lingered in the car saying good-bye to Cameron. Gentleman that he was, he managed to get her out without hurting her feelings, then gave me a wink and a wave. "Your secret's safe with me," he called to us, then closed the door and rode away.

Diane immediately turned and started fussing at us to hurry up. Apparently, she was channeling the *old* SuSu.

Jumpy as a cat in a foghorn factory, I followed the others through screening procedures, then boarded the plane. Only when we were airborne did I let myself go.

Teeny immediately called her people in Denver and arranged for them to take Bubba to Ashville to join his mother as soon as the doctors said Pru could see him.

"What happens now?" I asked Teeny as soon as she'd finished.

"An ambulance will be waiting for Pru and Dr. Johnson in Ashville, to take them to the recovery center. Then we'll go home."

I felt a definite anticlimax. "That's it? We just go home?"

Teeny yawned hugely, then nodded. "Yep. Until Pru's ready for family therapy. Then we all go up and act as her support network."

"Whether she wants us to or not," Diane stated, catching Teeny's yawn.

I reclined my comfortable seat and closed my eyes. "Maybe things'll go smoother from here on in."

Wishful thinking, but at least for the next hour, they did.

I went to sleep rehearsing answers to John's inevitable, "How did things go in Vegas?"

Oh, fine. I wore a wig and sunglasses while we tried to kidnap Pru, then I lusted after a literate stud of a cowboy, then I ran out on a hundred thousand dollars, got in a car chase, and was accosted when I tried to go back and claim the money. How was your weekend?

Can we say, I don't think so?

Winter

Piedmont Road, Atlanta. New Year's Day, 1967. 12:30 A.M.

I T WAS OUR FINAL NEW YEAR'S EVE OF HIGH SCHOOL, SO WE DE-
cided to ditch our dates early, throw convention to the winds,
and celebrate together in a deliciously inappropriate manner.
The heater in Linda's honkin' big black 1964 Lincoln (her mom's most
recent castoff) blasted away, fogging the windows and resurrecting the
jumble of heavy perfumes we'd slathered on five hours ago, before our
dates.

"If anything happens to this car," Linda repeated as she drove the
six of us past the Driving Club, "y'all are dead meat."

"I still can't believe we are doing this," Diane fretted.

"Me, either." Teeny sat straight and alert, her eyes bright as a bird's.
"Are you sure this is safe? Didn't somebody get knifed down there?"

She'd asked that back at my house while we were waiting for my
parents to fall asleep so we could sneak out. (Everybody else's parents
were having parties at their houses, so we'd ended up at my house by
default.)

"We'll be fine," I assured for the jillionth time. "We just need to stay
alert and keep close to each other."

"I think it's exciting." Pru rubbed a circle in the misty window and
looked at the after-midnight traffic still on the roads. (Unheard of!)
"Tyson will crepe a brick when he finds out we went by ourselves."

"I'm not so sure about this," SuSu dithered—again. "I mean, us going down there without any guys. What will people say? It could really hurt our reputations."

"Suse," I explained—again. "The six of us will be way safer than we would individually with a date. As for our reputations, Mademoiselle will be green with envy. We'll be legends."

She wasn't convinced. "Assuming we don't get killed . . . or worse."

"Silly," Pru said with her usual naïve confidence. "It's the sixties. Peaceful coexistence. People go there all the time, and nothing happens."

"At least we'll have something exciting to show for our last New Year's Eve as Mademoiselles. Beats watching some Buckhead boy get smashed, havin' to fend him off when he tries to maul you, then havin' to drive his car to get home in one piece."

Which was why we'd all cut out early on our totally predictable dates and come back to my house early from Tommy Madigan's party.

Since Brad had disappeared and taken my heart with him, I'd been at loose ends, miserable and restless. It had been my inspiration to say good-bye to 1966 in a blaze of feminist glory and sneak out to the Royal Peacock. Convincing the others had taken some heavy lobbying, but I was determined and, truth be told, they were just as curious as I was about the legendary place where nobody checked IDs.

"Watch out for the other drivers," SuSu cautioned Linda as we rolled south of Tenth Street (the hippie district). "Whoever's out this late is probably drunk. Give them plenty of room."

SuSu was so dad-gummed serious. I wished she'd cut loose occasionally.

We crossed over the Interstate Connector. "Okay," I navigated, "it's down here somewhere. Auburn Avenue. We turn left."

I heard the muted click of the power door locks as Linda made sure we were safely locked in.

Brittle with excitement and anxiety, we all searched for the street signs at the next three intersections. So far, no Auburn Avenue.

"Are you sure you know where this place is?" Linda asked, more nervous with every passing block.

"Yes. You were there when I called for directions and cover charge." Twenty dollars—awfully steep. Four nights' babysitting.

We passed another intersection. Even I was getting worried. This was not the part of town where you wanted to get lost.

"There it is!" Teeny pointed to the light ahead. "Auburn Avenue."

One left turn, and there it was, wedged into a row of brick buildings. *The* Royal Peacock.

Cars were parked everywhere.

I saw a bulky granite church farther down the way. "Ladies," I said with a welling sense of destiny, "look down there. That's Big Bethel, Dr. Martin Luther King's church. History is being made here."

Teeny laughed. "Right down the street from the Royal Peacock."

"What do you think those good Baptist ladies at Big Bethel think about that?" SuSu asked, sounding way too much like her hyperjudgmental mother.

Pru dispelled her seriousness with a chuckle and, "Honey, they're probably in there now, havin' a good time."

Red lights and white vapor appeared in the line of parked cars just ahead of us.

"Look!" Diane pointed between me and Linda. "Somebody's coming out of that parking place."

"Grab it," SuSu ordered. "At least that way, we won't be stuck in some parking lot."

"But it's parallel parking," Linda wailed.

"No sweat." I looked back and was relieved to see nobody coming behind us. "Just pull up so you're even with the driver's door of the next car. I'll talk you through it."

Five minutes later, I ended up having to get out and do it for her. Then we all piled out and hastily assembled, clutching our coats and purses and each other as we crossed the street, fused like a Roman phalanx.

Looking back, I realize why the people around us—black and white—laughed when they saw us. We were the definition of uptight.

We paid our money and moved inside, praying for a booth or table where we could all sit together. But when we opened the inner doors and stepped into the familiar haze of smoke punctuated by the smells of beer and booze and perfume and humanity, I relaxed a little. At least a fourth of the crowd was white.

I wish I could say the others relaxed, too, but I can't.

This was the era when we, as forward-thinking children of the New South, ardently supported the civil rights movement, but we superimposed our own white, middle-class mores on the black culture. And the specter of prejudice still manifested itself. We treated people of other races with respect, but wanted somebody else to be the one to break down those barriers. More than that, we still feared what we were not a part of. And we all curdled up at the sight of a mixed-race couple.

What a waste of energy.

So thanks to the cautions of our parents, the others were scared half witless to be surrounded by black people.

Except Pru. She was beaming, taking it all in, happily oblivious to the attention she'd attracted from quite a few black men. Not boys. Men.

Even I got a little nervous about that, but it wasn't her fault. She couldn't any more turn off that ingenuous sex appeal than she could pass a trig exam.

I told myself to calm down. The people who ran this place wouldn't let anything bad happen. They wanted to stay in business. Looking around, I realized the club wasn't that different from the Pink Pussycat, where my boyfriend Brad had taken me a bunch of times.

There was no music, so nobody was dancing. "I hope we're not too late for the band," I hollered above the din of conversation. "Why don't we go to the bar?" There weren't any seats there, either, but at least we could get a drink.

"Ladies and gentlemen," a voice boomed over the intercom. "The Royal Peacock is proud to welcome back Joe Pope and the Fabulous Tams for the second show."

Huge applause and cheering erupted as the band cranked up with "I've Been Hurt."

I hustled everybody to get our drinks so we could find a place to sit when the dancing got going.

It wasn't easy searching for a table in the crowded room when we were all joined at the hip, but after about fifteen minutes, Linda spotted a couple having an argument and wisely steered us over that way. Sure enough, the girl slapped her boyfriend, slid out of the large booth, then grabbed his shiny burgundy jacket by the velvet lapel and said, "Take me home!" with a snarl that brooked no disobedience.

We didn't even wait for the waitress to clear the table. We just slid in, three to a side with me and Pru on the outside, and heaved a collective sigh of relief to have found safe haven. We all ordered.

By the time our drinks came, the Tams started playing "Laugh It Off" and everybody had started to dance. Seeing the couples only made me sad. I couldn't help thinking about Brad.

Linda patted my arm. "Honey, don't think about him. The guy's a wolf. He's probably got half a dozen Gidgets out there already. Let it go."

I never was a poker face.

"Easy for you to say," I grumbled, slipping deeper into tragic mode with every sip of my screwdriver. Brad had left town a few weeks ago and nobody had heard from him since. "I tell myself a dozen times a day to let it go, but it doesn't do any good. I still miss him so much I can hardly breathe sometimes." My eyes welled with tears. "I'll be doing fine, then out of the blue, I feel like somebody slammed a baseball slap into the middle of my chest. It's physical."

"Don't cry." Teeny handed me one of the extra cocktail napkins still waiting to be cleaned up on the table. "Your mascara will run."

"It's waterproof," I whined. I'd cried so much since Brad left, I'd had to resort to that.

Pru reached across the table to pat me in consolation. "We've passed midnight," she said. "It's New Year's Day, sweetie, and you know what that means. Anything you do today, you'll do for the rest of the year. So listen to the music and eat some pretzels and have some fun. No boy's worth that kind of misery."

"Hah!" I challenged, loosened by the gin. "You wouldn't be so smug if it was Tyson who moved to California without you." Back to California. He was from there.

She sighed. "Probably not. But all we have is now. You'll find somebody else, somebody even better."

"Yeah," the others concurred.

Better than Brad? It couldn't get any better than Brad and I had been. The thought of him welled huge, overflowing my aura and beyond.

God, I missed the sex. And felt guilty, because I had justified "doing it" with him by promising myself—and God—that we were married in

His eyes, just like those romantic young couples on the soaps who said their vows in empty churches. It was that old Southern double standard, and the excuse nice girls like me had been using for generations.

Not that we Mademoiselles ever talked about our own love lives, even among ourselves. The reality of unmarried sex was far too conflicted and dangerous a topic to voice openly.

If Brad and I *didn't* get married, I would have to take responsibility for "doing it" with a man who would never be my husband. Unthinkable. But at the moment, all I could do was miss him and love him and see my life as irreparably diminished by his loss.

And cry into my screwdriver.

"Hey." A male voice invaded the booth.

We looked up to find none other than Jake Rolader, one of the semi-hoods from school, and his gang of *West Side Story* wannabes. We'd been in the same honors classes for four years, but I knew almost nothing about him beyond the fact that he and his group of friends were always tinkering over their hot rods in the school parking lot.

We Mademoiselles pruned up, especially the preppies (Teeny and Diane).

"Don't tell me y'all are here alone," he said with an insolence that put us in high dudgeon.

I adopted my Savannah great-grandmother's frosty Victorian demeanor. "And how is that any of your business, might I ask?"

He wasn't intimidated. "Nice girls like you, in a place like this? That's crazy. Askin' for it."

Our eyes and nostrils flared, our semi-feminist hackles raised.

"We are not *askin'* for anything," I bit out. "We are in a public place, mindin' our own business, and everything was just fine till you and your gang, here, came over and blocked our booth."

Clearly, he had no intention of leaving. His toadies crowded even closer, to let the waitress pass behind them.

Scanning them, Pru traded her worried expression for a grin of recognition. "Hey, Booger." She waved to the huge lug in the back, who smiled like a kid and waggled his fingers.

"Booger bought my brother's old car," Pru explained as if she'd just found a long-lost cousin. "He's a real sweet guy. Knows everything about hot rods."

Booger nodded in pride. "It's a hemi. It'll drag two hundred miles an hour, easy."

Diane and Teeny stared, clearly never having confronted anybody named Booger in their sheltered lives, much less a short-haired hot-rodder who topped six five and weighed at least 300.

"So?" Jake stood cocky, blocking our booth. "What's the story?"

"So, if you must know," SuSu took over, "we are not here alone. We are here with each other. And if we need any help, we'll call for a bouncer. As a matter of fact, I think we could use one now."

"Whoa." Jake backed off, palms raised. "We didn't come over here to start a war. We just wanted to make sure you girls were safe, that's all."

Finally. Something besides male posturing.

"Sorry." He seemed to mean it. Or else he didn't want to get kicked out. His less-than-cool gang nodded in apology, suddenly looking like the awkward, socially insecure teenagers they were.

Seeing them that way, I felt the fight go right out of me.

They were on their own looking for some slightly risky fun, just like we were.

Come to think of it, I didn't ever remember seeing them with any girls, even majorettes (the social choice of hoods). Heaven knew, the Mademoiselles never gave them a thought.

The band struck up with "What Kind of Fool," and Booger leaned in, extending a meaty hand between the two guys in front of him. "Hey, Pru. Wanta dance?"

"Sure." She popped up and took his hand.

"Pru," Linda chided. "What about Tyson?"

We weren't supposed to dance with anybody when we were steadies.

Pru looked up at the man-mountain holding her hand and laughed. "I'll just tell him to take it up with Booger." She pulled him into the crowd.

"You know, for somebody so flaky," Diane said, "that woman's got a lot of sense."

One of the boys who was actually pretty nice-looking cleared his throat, then asked Linda, "Would you like to dance?"

She took a sip of her Coke, considering, then nodded.

"Linda," Teeny gasped out. Going to the Peacock was one thing, but dancing with hoods was social suicide.

Linda's shrug said she didn't have a social life anyway, so what did it matter? We always managed to get her dates, but they only tolerated each other. She was way too grown-up for most of them.

She took the boy's arm, not his hand, and instantly, he stood a little taller as he escorted her to the dance floor.

Diane and Teeny buzzed in amazement and disapproval while SuSu scanned the room for familiar faces while she sipped her beer.

To this day, I don't see how people can drink beer. Yuk. Put it back into the horse.

"They're doing the shag," Jake said to me, trying to look cool, but showing his youth and insecurity. "How about a dance?" His pause resonated with adolescent agony. "I promise not to tell anybody."

That stung, so much that I didn't hesitate. "Tell anybody you want." Why not? Brad was gone. My life was over. "You'll have to help me brush up. I haven't done the shag in a while."

He grinned, looking almost normal.

We shagged, then went back and had a drink at the booth. Out of context the way we were, talk came easy and honest. At least, for him. I asked questions and listened. It was the first time in my life that I'd been with a boy in a social situation and not seen him as anything but another human being.

Meanwhile Pru danced with Booger, who was surprisingly light on his feet, while Linda cut a rug with whatever-his-name-was, appearing to have a great time. When the next booth came available, the remaining hoods settled in and started talking engines, betraying the fact that they were just a bunch of dorky guys who loved cars and tried to look and talk tough.

SuSu, Teeny, and Diane refused their offers to dance, which came as no surprise. Those boys didn't meet their standard for escorts. (Regardless of the rest, their pointy-toed lace-up shoes and cheap suits ruled them out.) Diane proceeded to get stiff as an ironing board on old-fashioneds, collecting the cherries to keep track. SuSu nursed a giant margarita (no salt). And Teeny sipped champagne cocktails from a flute. They rolled their eyes a lot, but when Jake sat down across from me and we started talking future plans, they actually got interested.

"So, are you planning to go to college?" I asked him.

"I haven't been busting my back making a four-oh in those honors classes for nothing."

I didn't even have a four-oh. All those years we'd been in the same classes, and I hadn't even known he was that smart. "Have you applied anywhere?"

"Yep. Annapolis."

I managed to keep my mouth from dropping open.

"My dad was killed in Korea. Medal of Honor. I've been working in my uncle's service station since I was ten, helping my mom keep a roof over our heads. But I don't plan to stay there." The boy had a fire in his belly. "I'm gonna get into the Academy. Then I'm gonna make field rank. Even if I have to go to 'Nam to do it."

I shivered at the thought. SuSu and Teeny peered at him with new respect. Diane just sat erect, staring at the middle distance and singing loudly (and off-key) with the Tams. "Be young, be foolish, and be happy . . ."

I counted four cherries beside her empty glass. I caught SuSu's eye and pointed. "I think she's had enough," I mouthed over the din.

She nodded.

Pru and Booger arrived back at the table. "Booger," she said, flushed, "could you please be a prince and get me some ice water from the bar. I'm about to melt."

He nodded. "Sure. Be right back." He disappeared into the crowd.

Pru was about to squeeze into the booth with us when somebody bumped her from behind. "Hey!"

She turned just in time to dodge a drunken black guy who had just socked his date and seemed bent on further punishment. Oblivious to the throng around him, he screamed and cursed her with rabid abandon.

The rest of us froze, panicked at the prospect of getting involved in a matter that was not only dangerous, but also on the wrong side of a racial line we'd never dreamed of crossing.

Frantic, I searched the crowd. Where was the bouncer when we needed one?

But Pru didn't bat an eyelash. She took one look at the terrified despair in the black girl's expression and the blood seeping from her lip, and pretended to stumble between the guy and his prey. "Sorry." She held up her hands to the guy. "Sorry! It's so crowded here. I'm really sorry. Somebody shoved me."

All of a sudden, she was on her own. Blacks and whites alike did the whistling toe-glance and distanced themselves from the confrontation.

The whole thing took only seconds, but we watched, horrified, as the situation played out in slow motion.

"Bitch," the drunk snarled at Pru, doing his best to get past her. Even drunk, he had no taste for taking on a white woman, and what that would mean.

Pru shot the girl a look that said, "Get out!" then grasped the guy's lapels and started smoothing his jacket and apologizing profusely, turning him away so the girl could escape.

The drunk wouldn't be deflected. He shoved Pru, hard, with a strength she was doubtless all too familiar from her daddy's binges.

She paused momentarily, the breath knocked out of her.

Where was Booger when you needed him? His back turned to us, waiting for a slot at the bar.

Jake and his friends managed to get to the drunk just as he realized his girlfriend had escaped. Pushed over the edge by pure rage and malice, the idiot tossed aside our "tough guys" without even looking at them as he whirled on Pru. "Bitch. I'll kill you for that!"

Unfazed, she shook her head. "I don't suppose there's any chance of talkin' you out of that, is there?"

Had she gone insane?

The guy let out a feral roar and charged.

Pru waited until she could see the whites of his eyes, then her muscular cheerleader's leg landed a perfectly aimed kick with lethal momentum into his groin. She hopped back, just out of range.

Eyes bugging, the drunk stopped dead in his tracks, clutched his crotch, then dropped like a fifty-foot loblolly pine, not even trying to break his fall.

A roar of laughter erupted from all around us, but we were too busy trying to get out of there to enjoy it. I grabbed Pru and beat it for the street, while SuSu shoved Diane, who insisted on collecting her cherries, after me. The others exploded out of the booth and joined the boys in fleeing for our lives. I don't even remember how we got out, just the bracing shock of cold, damp air when we left the sounds of a growing brouhaha behind us and lurched onto the sidewalk.

We ran for fifty feet, then collapsed against a brick wall, gasping for breath.

"Pru, are you crazy?" I demanded, awed and horrified in equal measure. "What were you thinking?"

She shrugged, still unruffled. "I couldn't just stand there and watch him beat that girl up, could I?"

"That's what the bouncers are for," SuSu chided.

"There weren't any bouncers," Pru defended.

"Jesus, Joseph, and Mary," Teeny panted out. "What if you'd missed?"

"Trust me, I knew what I was doing," Pru dismissed. "I never miss."

For a flake, she was the coolest cookie in combat I'd ever seen.

The boys eavesdropped in amazement.

"Crap!" Diane flapped her hand to fan her red face. "Where did you learn to do that?"

A cloud crossed Pru's ingenuous expression. "I've had plenty of practice. Daddy's drinkin' buddies get some weird ideas, sometimes." She brightened. "It always works. Most of the time, they don't even remember what hit 'em."

Booger emerged, searching for us, then headed our way. Hot on his heels, people started pouring onto the sidewalk and either heading for the hills or breaking into fights.

Jake glanced back in alarm. "We gotta get out of here, and quick. Where's your car?"

He didn't have to ask twice.

"Over there." Linda pointed back to the Lincoln, just across from the club, and the vacant space in front of it. We all made a beeline across the street.

Booger met us halfway across the pavement, loping over with surprising speed for such a big boy. "Guys," he complained to Jake. "Y'all promised you wouldn't leave again without telling me."

Can we say, oblivious?

Jake didn't even bother to try to explain what had happened. "We have to get these girls to their car. Watch our back."

Booger sobered. "You got it."

With primordial perception, I could almost smell the danger all around us.

"Keys," Jake ordered Linda. "Get your keys out."

Flustered, she groped in her purse for them. "Damn. They're in the bottom."

I heard people fighting in earnest behind us. Sharp shouts. Threats of gunplay and stabbing. The whole scenario was starting to feel like a very bad dream.

"Aha." Linda lifted the keys into the light just as the first shot went off, sounding more like somebody popping a paper bag than a gun. Not the noise we knew from TV or the movies.

"Get down!" Jake shouted.

More shots, a volley of firecrackers this time.

"Move!" Jake hustled us toward the far side of the car. To a man, those boys put themselves between us and the gunfire till we all reached cover. Lurching for safety, I banged my arm so hard against the bumper that it smarted like fire.

"Get behind the tires till it's safe to get inside," Jake warned. "The bullets can skip on the pavement and go under the cars." Clearly, he had experience in such matters.

Two more shots went off, and the side window of the car behind Linda's shattered and crazed around a ragged hole the size of your fist.

Jake saw it and bent his head. "Shit. That was a hollow point."

I came seriously close to wetting myself.

"Gimme those." He snagged the keys Linda was clutching, crept over to her passenger door and unlocked it, then slid in and started the motor, using his hand on the gas. I heard him pop the door locks open.

A siren sounded only blocks away.

Police. Thank God.

Unless they wanted to question us.

We had to get out of here. Not to mention getting away from the shooters, who were still yelling and taking occasional shots.

Jake crawled back over. "Okay. Do what I say, and everything will be okay. Y'all keep low, and get in the car. Linda, you first, but keep below the windows. There's nobody parked in front of you. I'll let you know as soon as it's safe to sit up. I'll whack the side of the car and say,

'Go.' " He sounded so calm, so organized. "As soon as you hear that, pull away at a reasonable pace and do not look back. Take the first right, then right again to Piedmont. Turn right on Piedmont, and don't stop till you're home."

"But what about y'all?" we all protested. "We can't just leave you here."

"We'll be fine," Booger said in his deep voice. "We know how to disappear." An ironic statement, considering his size.

I looked to Jake in gratitude. "I think you're gonna make a pretty good general."

"Admiral," he corrected. "Now get into that car."

Two patrol cars approached from either direction, sirens blaring. We crawled into the car, but not before Diane threw up in the gutter.

"It was the cherries," she mumbled as she crawled into the back with Teeny and Pru and closed the door behind her. Teeny started crying, and Pru comforted her, while Linda and SuSu and I lay plastered down in the front seat.

I didn't even dare pray, since this was all my fault, and we'd had no business being there in the first place.

The night exploded into red, white, and blue lights as sirens gave way to screeching tires, then shouts of "Police! Drop your weapons!"

When no more shots were fired, Jake slapped the side of the car and ordered, "Go!"

We all jumped like we'd been shot, then Linda peeked up over the dashboard and pulled slowly away, her hands shaking so hard she could barely hold onto the steering wheel. "If there's a bullet hole in this car, y'all are dead meat."

Sirens converged from everywhere. Every foot of the way, we expected to be flagged down and pulled over, but we made it back to Piedmont and looked down Auburn Avenue as we crossed it to see two men spread-eagled against the patrol cars as more units arrived.

The entire passenger compartment pulsed with adrenaline. Except Diane, who had passed out. As we left behind the scene of the crime, the rest of us burst into a din of recaps and thank Gods.

All the way north to Fourteenth, where we cut across to Northside Drive, we worried about the boys.

"I don't care what anybody says," I declared. "I'm calling Jake to-morrow to make sure they're okay."

"Mademoiselles do not call boys," SuSu reminded me. "Ever."

"Well, this one will. Those boys probably saved our lives," I drama-tized. "The least I can do is make sure they're okay."

"She's right," Teeny said. "Rules were never meant to come before humanity. I think I'll call him, too. He's a most impressive person."

As the streetlights of Fourteenth gave way to the unlit stretch of Northside Drive near the Water Works, my arm was really hurting. I held it tight, and it felt a little better. "Man. I must really have given myself a whack on that bumper. Bet I'll have some bruise."

"You don't think it's broken, do you?" SuSu asked.

I moved it, wincing. "Nah. It doesn't hurt way deep."

"Take off your coat," Pru ordered. "Let me see."

"Why don't we wait till we get home?" With three of us in the front seat, I could hardly move.

"Just humor me." When she made her mind up, there was no sense arguing.

"Well, pull over into the Howard Johnsons, then." We were coming to I-75.

Linda steered into the light of the restaurant parking lot, one of the few places besides Dobbs House that was open that late.

I shrugged my right shoulder out of my navy reefer coat and was in the process of pulling my arm free of the sleeve when the others gasped.

"What?"

I followed their horrified gazes to a slash of torn, bloody-red satin sleeve. "Well, damn. I got cut."

Pru poked her finger through two holes in the sleeve of my coat. My brand-new coat I'd just gotten off of layaway. "Honey, you didn't get cut. You got *shot!*"

"I couldn't have gotten shot. People know it when they get shot."

Pru pulled open the torn sleeve and looked at the skin beneath. "It's not deep. About four inches long. It's already closed up and stopped bleeding."

Diane reared up. "I think I'm gonna be sick again."

"For God's sakes, somebody take her to the bushes," Linda barked. "If she throws up in this car, y'all are dead meat."

"Come on, sweetie." Pru opened the door and helped her toward the hedge.

With the hubris of adolescence, I looked at the bullet holes in my sleeve and grumbled, "My brand-new coat. I was planning for that to last me all through college."

"Georgia." SuSu started to unravel. "We could have gotten killed tonight, and all you're worried about is your *coat*?"

I held my arm, starting to shake. "Forget the coat. I just want to be home in my own bed." Four of us would have to sleep in pairs on the twin mattresses, while the other two got a box spring apiece.

Pru hugged me, placing her forehead against mine. "I feel so bad. None of this would have happened if I hadn't gotten between that guy and his girlfriend."

I hugged her back. "Don't be ridiculous. Like you said, you couldn't just stand there and let him beat her up."

"Yeah," Linda chimed in. "You were braver than Mrs. Peel." Of *The Avengers* fame.

Suddenly I was so tired, I could hardly stand up. "I'm dead. Let's go."

I put my coat back on, and we all got back in and headed home. Linda parked at the top of College Circle, and we crept stealthily on foot down the sleeping street to my house.

The only time having your room in what was once the basement came in handy was when you wanted to sneak out. Or back in. My house was dark and still. We lined up against the brick foundation, lest somebody inside look out and see us, but we didn't hear a sound when SuSu raised the well-oiled transom window beside the driveway to climb in. I was helping hoist her over the sill when she started scrambling backward and fell on top of me.

"What?" I whispered, furious. She'd almost knocked the breath out of me.

My mother stuck her head out the window and looked down on the lot of us. "Why don't you girls use the door? I unlocked it."

We were doomed. That was all there was to it.

"Remember," I whispered to the others, "don't volunteer anything. And whatever you do, don't tell them where we were or what happened."

Pru hugged me. "Don't worry. It's gonna be okay."

She always believed things would work out, no matter what.

Mama would probably ground me forever and make me drop out of Mademoiselle, as it was. If she found out I'd been shot, I'd never be allowed to leave the house again.

Diane went straight to the bathroom to wash out her mouth and brush her teeth, but she still smelled like a distillery when she came back. She tried to stand straight, but wavered despite her best efforts.

At least she had the sense not to speak.

We filed into the bedroom and found Mama sitting on the box springs in her shabby quilted robe and embarrassing pink scuffies. "I won't ask you where you girls have been," she said with controlled fury. "It's obvious you've been drinking. And smoking."

"Mama, Linda didn't drink," I defended. "And she doesn't smoke."

Mama pinned me with a "splitting hairs" glare. "No. She just drives."

Uh-oh. Arguing, not a good tactic.

"I have been sitting here for two hours," Mama enunciated, "alternately wanting to take you all to the woodshed, then begging God to bring you home safe."

She pinned Linda in accusation. "Why does a sensible girl like you let Georgia talk you into these things?" Clearly, it was a rhetorical question.

"Oh, it wasn't Georgia's fault, Mrs. Peyton," Pru volunteered, earnest. "It was all my idea. I made them do it."

Bless Pru's heart. A noble gesture, but Mama wasn't buying it.

Mama ignored her. ("How can you expect anything from that poor child," Mama was always harping, "with those parents of hers?")

I cringed in embarrassment for my brave, wonderful friend.

Mama turned to Diane. "And you, young lady. You have better sense than this."

Teeny burped. (The Pabst.) Horrified at such a gaffe—never mind getting caught sneaking in at three o'clock in the morning—she colored in mortification.

Mama stood up. "There's no point trying to talk to y'all in this condition. Mr. Peyton and I will discuss this with you tomorrow." She picked up the chair from my room and set it outside my door at the base of the stairs that led to the main floor. Then she paused in the doorway. "For now, I suggest you go to bed, where you should have been all along." She left us and headed upstairs. We waited till we heard her bedroom door close on the second floor before we dared to speak in desperate whispers, wondering what would happen.

Linda cleaned my scratch (that's really all it was) with Bactine, then bandaged it neatly with gauze. By the time we finally sank into exhausted sleep, it was three-thirty.

"Pru," I whispered to her as I teetered on the edge of exhaustion. "You're my hero."

"Thanks, honey." I could hear the affirmation in her voice. "That means a lot to me."

Mama waited till we were good and gone before she marched into our room banging two huge pots together, sending us out of our skins.

We sat up, shrieking.

Mama smiled a superior smile. "Y'all kept me up all night. You didn't think I was gonna let *you* sleep now, did you?" She hit the pot another jarring whack, then marched back out and shut the door.

I hated creative parenting.

We sat there in shock, hearts racing.

Then we wordlessly flopped back to our beds.

One hour later, and every hour on the hour, Mama marched back in and raised a racket loud enough to wake the dead, which is what we were. By seven, we gave up and got up to fix breakfast.

Daddy came down and gave us a serious lecture. (I'd rather take a beating any day than have to endure one of my daddy's lectures. It was like getting chewed out by God himself. Patient. Long-suffering. Convicting.)

Then, miracle of miracles, my parents let my friends go home without telling their parents. And I wasn't even grounded.

"I hope you learned your lesson," Daddy told me.

If only he knew.

He looked at me with that God of Justice face. "I won't have you putting your mama through that again, ever. Is that clear?"

"I swear, Daddy, I won't." I meant it when I said it.

I never did tell Mama the truth. The woman would never have slept again.

Later that day, I got out the Northside student directory. Then I made my first official call to a boy and dialed up Jake Rolader to thank him for what he and his friends had done. (They'd thought it all a great adventure.)

Next, I called Pru to thank her for offering to take the blame and to tell her again how amazed I was by her courage. She laughed it off, as she did everything, but I never forgot her for it.

As for Jake and his hoods, from then on, I spoke to them in the hallways and in class.

Concerning SuSu's fears for our reputations, we discovered that it's more than fine with the In Crowd if you go to the Royal Peacock unescorted and consort with hoods, as long as those same hoods rescue you from a gun battle and you end up getting shot.

We were legends.

12

True Confessions

Atlanta. Friday, April 11, 2003.

I WAS SO EXHAUSTED WHEN WE GOT BACK TO ATLANTA THAT I didn't trust myself to drive, so I had Kal take me home. I'd pick my car up later. I rolled in just as John was getting ready to leave, in the kitchen with Katie, Matt, Al, and Ann.

"Well, that was quick." He lounged against the sink, absorbed by the Business Section in one hand and holding a mug of coffee in the other. The man hardly looked up when I dragged by. "Have a good time?" He gave me a peck when I detoured over on my way to bed.

It wasn't till I spoke that he abruptly looked up.

"I'm dead," I croaked out. "And I'm goin' to sleep all day. Please do not disturb."

He took in my faded makeup, smashed hairdo, wrinkled clothes, and deep, dark circles. (I was dehydrated from doing socially unacceptable things in the plane's little bathroom the whole way home.) "Honey! What the hell happened?"

"Tough night, that's all." I sounded like Sam Spade, I noted distantly and with satisfaction. John would never believe the truth. I didn't believe it myself.

Fluids.

John watched in shock as I took our old-fashioned glass iced-water bottle out of the refrigerator, removed the lid, and gulped down half of it straight from the lip, which only served to alarm him further.

I never drank from the bottle, ever, but Sam Spade did. And I never slept in the daytime, but I planned to that day.

"Tough night?" he repeated, skeptical. He closed into my space and took hold of my upper arms. "I'm sorry, but that ain't gonna cut it. If I rolled in from Vegas less than twenty-four hours after I'd left, looking like I'd been through the wringer, and said, 'Tough night,' you'd call your Red Hats for a sheet beatin'." He peered at me in genuine annoyance and concern. "I try not to intrude with your girl stuff, but this is ridiculous. I want to know exactly what happened, and I want to know now."

Of all times for him to turn into Macho Man.

I yawned hugely, then curled into his chest, afraid I was really, truly about to fall down. "John, honey, it was just the damned low-carb chocolate peanut butter cups. And the low-carb gummy bears. The gummy bears finished it off."

He tucked his chin in confusion. You'd think after all these years, he'd know I always got to the point eventually.

Feeling a little light-headed, I forced myself to explain. "I have no idea what's in those things, but they tore through me so bad, I spent the whole flight home in the bathroom. We are talking, explosive."

He winced.

Definitely woozy. "I've gotta lie down. Now."

I slithered down to stretch out on our hardwood kitchen floor, glad that I'd mopped it the day before. I swear, I literally could not open my eyes.

"Georgia! What is it?" John's agitation shot through the roof as he hovered over me. "Should I call nine-one-one? What? Tell me where it hurts."

He didn't even try to pick me up, which was just as well, at our age.

"Calm down, sweetie," I croaked. "I'm not having a heart attack. I'm just exhausted. And dehydrated."

"Well, tell me what to do, then," he barked.

Men always bark when they're really worried about you, so I took it for the love sign it really was. "I'm okay." I spoke slowly, partly because I was almost too tired to talk, and partly so John would get it the first time. "Give me a minute, then help me upstairs to bed, undress me, and put me in my gown"—Bigbrains require detailed instructions—"then call in sick and come to bed with me. I need you."

Bigbrains do not shift gears easily, so I didn't expect an immediate answer. He'd do the first things first, then work up to the calling in part.

Well padded though I was, the floor thing definitely wasn't working.

I waved my hand anemically and mimicked the thready plea of, "Heeeelp," our daughter Callie had used when she was four.

John braced his toes to mine. "Both hands." He had to lever me to my feet, or we'd both end up at the chiropractor's for a month. I bent my knees and took his still-strong grip in both my hands. "Okay." He drew me erect on, "Upsa-daisy."

Somehow, we made it upstairs. He undressed me with awkward briskness, as if he was in some kind of race, but despite his clumsy efforts I fell dead asleep sitting up. Four hours later when my bladder woke me, I found him curled against me, softly snoring, his hand above my head on the pillow where he'd been stroking my hair.

Stiff and an old granny, I staggered into the bathroom, relieved myself, brushed my teeth (talk about death breath!), then guzzled a quart or so of cold tap water. Worn out from those simple activities, I snuggled back in bed with my head on John's chest.

"Hey," he said when I curled against him. He stretched, glancing to the clock. "Man. It's after three." A long, satisfying yawn. "I could get used to this."

"Good. Let's." I shifted closer under his arm. "How 'bout we stay in bed for at least a week, like John and Yoko."

"Ugh." He made a Kabuki face. "Do not mention Yoko and bed in the same breath."

I felt so safe there in his arms, so much myself, quintessentially loved and protected.

Forget the female Sam Spade fantasies I'd had in Vegas.

Oh, Lord.

Vegas.

I shoved the thought into a mental closet and clung to John for dear life.

"Whoa-ho-ho," he said gently, trying to pry my face up where he could see it. "What's this?"

No way, could I keep what happened from him, even if I'd wanted to, which I didn't. So I did some quick mental editing, balancing Red Hat confidentiality against my loyalty to John, and launched into, "Pru fell off the wagon and got in some really dangerous company in Vegas. Teeny had detectives on it, but Pru was so determined to destroy herself that we all had to go after her to try to get her back into rehab."

"Whoa." John's brows slammed together. "She's in dangerous company, and y'all go traipsing out there to get her?" He snorted. "In a casino? In Vegas, where the *mob* lives?" He scowled as he assimilated the information.

"Well. I don't know about the mob or anything," I qualified, "but the detectives managed to lure Pru to the casino, away from the drug dealers, so I don't think we were in any dan—"

I felt John's body temperature rise. "Damn, Georgia, I thought you girls were just goin' out for a little harmless gamblin'." He all but squeezed the life out of me, hanging on. "What kind of an *I Love Lucy* stunt was *that*? Drug dealers . . . God knows what might have happened. Risking your lives for some hopeless addict you've only seen once in twenty years!"

We'd deal with that "hopeless addict" business later, when he'd had time to calm down.

"What else have y'all been up to that I don't know about?" he accused. "That trip to the spa in Bali . . . where were y'all, really?"

"At a spa in Bali," I fussed. Reminding myself that he had every right to be upset, I softened. "John, honey, there's no conspiracy here. Teeny's people only located Pru yesterday morning. They tried to lure her off, but she was too suspicious. We had to move—fast—or risk losing track of her forever." I kissed his chest and gave him a squeeze. "We were never within a mile of the drug dealers."

"Don't ever keep me in the dark like that again, Georgia," he said, grim, the use of my whole name warning enough. "I mean this. Put the shoe on the other foot. How would you like it if I conveniently didn't tell you I was going into a potentially dangerous situation?"

"Oh, yeah," I countered mildly. "Like that time you went to Russia right after Chernobyl. 'Don't worry, honey,'" I quoted. "'They just need technical advice. We won't get anywhere near the hot zone.'"

He'd had to wear the radiation badge for three weeks after they got back.

He paused. "Point taken."

John hated conflict between us. "We'll call it even, then," he said in truce. "From now on, though, no more significant omissions from either of us, okay?"

Rats. He would put it that way.

"Okay." Might as well bite the bullet and tell him the rest. I sat up. "There's this one other thing that happened in Vegas . . ."

He went still as stone. "What?"

I tried to distill the events into something brief and linear. (Like all scientists, John really appreciated brief and linear.) "Well, here's the thing. Pru was at the slots when we tried to talk her into coming with us, but she was like some hunted animal, and she raised such a stink, security almost gave us the bum's rush, but Teeny talked them out of it, because she had registered as some reclusive billionaire."

John's face really screwed up on that one. I probably should have left that part out.

Forestalling questions, I forged ahead. "So we regrouped and talked this adorable cowboy from Austin into carrying Pru to the limo so we could whisk her to the airport before she escaped, but just as they were leaving, I had this impulse to put SuSu's three quarters into Pru's slot machine. I'd promised SuSu I'd play some for her, you see, so I put three quarters in and pulled the lever, and it won."

It took him several seconds to catch up to that last. "You won."

"I won." I looked at him askance. "Big." He didn't get it. "Very big."

"So?"

"So, it was a disaster. I realize now how stupid I was to run, but then, all I could think of was getting to the limo so we could get away with Pru."

"You ran?" Bigbrain wheels turned behind his eyes. Abruptly, he sat up, plastering the front of his hair back with his hand. "Holy crow! *You're* her? That mystery woman?"

John levitated out of the bed to stand in at combat stance in his boxers. "It was all over the news this morning. Papers. Morning shows. They had videos, but they were pretty blurry. Didn't look like you, though."

"I was wearing sunglasses and a wig." Fortunately, he didn't question that.

He looked at me as if he'd never seen me before in his life, and I didn't like it. "That woman vaulted a slot machine from a standing start!"

This wasn't going the way I'd thought it would. I figured he'd be upset about the money, which was SuSu's, anyway. But I felt like he'd just kissed me and pulled back to find a toad. "John, don't look at me that way. You're scaring me."

Still wild-eyed, he got back into bed and leaned against the headboard, drawing me close, his heart thumping, breathing shallow. "You're that mystery woman." Staring into space, he patted my back like he was burping a baby, his bent knee waggling back and forth. "That's you in those pictures. Oh, Lord, and the tabloids. Nobody ever ran away from a hundred-thousand-dollar jackpot. This thing could get *huge*. Totally out of control." I got the toad look again. "If the tabloids find out who you are, we'll never have another moment's peace." His heartbeat sprinted, the pats on my back keeping pace.

"John, stop patting me, honey," I said, jiggly as a jackhammer operator. "You're about to poke my lungs out."

"Not good." He did, but shifted to rubbing my upper arm till the skin started to redden. "This is not good."

"I went back and tried to claim the money, but every female in Las Vegas was there doing the same thing. It was a madhouse. And somebody stole my wig and sunglasses, so I gave up and left," I explained. "It was clearly hopeless, and I didn't want to raise any questions about who we were and Teeny's not being that billionaire woman."

"And *why* did she register as this billionaire person?"

I moaned. "Lord, I don't know. It seemed like a good idea at the time."

I leaned forward, putting the pillow over my head for a muffled, "Aaargh. Why did I put that money in the machine?" I surfaced. "We could have left, and that would have been that."

"What is, is." John started rocking us in place. "We'll get through this. Just lie low. It'll all blow over."

I extracted myself from his arms and urged him toward the edge of the bed. "Pace, honey. Pace."

He did, arms akimbo, gone to whatever mental place he goes when that big brain of his is humming like a mainframe.

"The one I really feel bad for is SuSu, though," I said. "It was her money."

John returned to the mortal plane and cocked his head. "Oh, honey." He clambered back into bed to hold me, kissing the top of my head. "All you really lost was seventy-five cents. Why would you want to tell SuSu the truth, anyway? It would only make her feel terrible."

"That's what we thought, so we're not."

John lapsed into professor mode. "Good choice. When I have to make a decision like this, I project the possible outcomes and weigh the consequences for each one. Better to keep it under your hat." He hugged me tighter. "Gasp! You might have to *lie*, you little saint, you."

"Don't tease me. I feel awful enough about it already."

I settled against him, comforted by his sanity and stability after the chaos of the last twenty-four hours.

Your sins will find you out echoed from the dark recesses where I'd shoved the fine points of my conscience, prompting a worrisome thought. "What if SuSu finds out I kept it from her?"

"Let's look at this logically." John stroked my hair, gentle now. "What would you say the chances of that happening are? Ball park?"

"Very slim," I said, maybe wishful thinking. "But it's always the things you don't expect that bite you on the butt. It's the press that scares me. I swear, the *Tattler* can find anybody. As for the odds, they'll either find us, or they won't. That puts my odds at zero percent or one hundred percent. There are no fractions. That makes me nauseated."

He said the magic words every woman needs to hear when she's up to her ass in alligators: "It's gonna be okay. I promise, honey. Nobody's gonna bother you. I won't let 'em." He drew us back down and stretched out, cradling me in a protective, undemanding embrace.

"I'll tell you one thing, though," he said as we settled for another round of nap. "I will definitely be checking out the tabloids till this thing blows over."

"Just don't show them to me," I mumbled as I drifted into oblivion, consoling myself that at least Pru was safely in rehab. All we could do now was wait and pray.

For the next thirteen hours, I slept the dreamless sleep of the blessed in the warm aura of my loving husband. Then I resumed my life, reading every one of the tabloids he brought home.

13

No Bad Ink?

National Tattler *front page, Saturday, April 12, 2003 issue.*

ORTUNATELY, THE BLACK-AND-WHITE PHOTO SMEARED ACROSS the front page was blurred and unrecognizable. My mouth twisted in a grimace, my eyes looked crossed, and my hair stood on end like Carrot Top's. My own mother wouldn't know the woman above the headline.

JACKRABBIT JACKPOT WINNER FLEES $100,000 VEGAS PAYOUT

Inside, another grainy (and grossly unflattering) image ran above:

> *Reliable sources inside the Parthenon Hotel and Casino have revealed that an unknown middle-aged woman, shown here in a photo taken by vacationer Tyrone Curry, won a $100,000 progressive slot machine jackpot, only to shriek a profanity, then flee the building with casino security and onlookers in hot pursuit.*
>
> *"I don't think she was from here," said Curry. "I told her in plain English that she'd won, but she didn't get it. Must be foreign or something."*
>
> *Casino regular and witness Thelma Gribble had another theory. "She didn't even sit down. Just put the money in and pulled the lever. First pull, she hits the jackpot. The minute the lights started flashing, she froze. But when she saw security coming, she*

ran like she'd just held up a bank. Makes you wonder what she was up to."

Another witness, Mabel Oshman, stated, "I told her it was okay, that she'd won big, but when I tried to stop her, she jumped over the machines just like a jackrabbit. Never saw anything like it. Must be some kind of athlete."

Officials at the Parthenon Hotel and Casino have refused comment, but inside sources have revealed that the mystery woman may have been in the party of reclusive billionaire, Rose Pendergrass, believed to have been a hotel guest at the time.

When contacted by the Tattler, Ms. Pendergrass's representatives stated that Ms. Pendergrass has been abroad for the past two months.

Other observers have speculated that the mystery woman may have been Pendergrass, herself, which could explain her bizarre reaction.

The Tattler is offering a $10,000 reward for information confirming the identity of the Jackrabbit Jackpot Winner. For details, contact us at our Web site thevoiceoftruth.com.

Atlanta Journal-Constitution, *Sunday, April 13, 2003*
AP Las Vegas, Nevada

Numerous witnesses report that an unknown woman won a $100,000 progressive slot machine jackpot at the Parthenon Hotel and Casino here, only to evade security officials and well-meaning pursuers by escaping in a waiting white Mercedes limousine. Efforts to trace the limousine have proved unsuccessful, but the bizarre case has sparked nationwide attention and conjecture.

Initial reports that the mystery winner may have been linked to billionaire recluse Rose Pendergrass have subsequently been disproved.

Parthenon officials confirmed that a patron had won the $100,000 payout, but declined further comment.

When questioned, Nevada gaming officials said that under the circumstances, the casino's surveillance tapes would offer the winner's only hope of lodging a valid claim for the money. So far, more than 1300 women have come forward to claim the prize. Casinos *are only required to retain those tapes for seven days, so the clock is ticking as The Parthenon Casino tries to determine if any of those claims are valid.*

The story made not only the news and the tabloids, but the late-night shows. David Letterman did "Top Ten Reasons to Run Away from $100,000." (Six of them were really funny.) Leno showed the blurry photos, then said no wonder I didn't want my picture taken. Then he laid the audience in the aisles quoting from conflicting news reports, one of which said I was deaf; another, Jimmy Hoffa in drag; another, an alien; and a disturbing one that I was a transvestite, because somebody had heard me called "George" on the way to the bar.

That one was too close for comfort.

But all that went out the window when the phone rang just after supper two weeks later.

I picked up the cordless receiver, hoping it was Linda with a report from her morning appointment with the gynecologist. She'd said she'd call earlier, but hadn't answered any of her phones when I'd tried to check.

"One moment please." Wary of brain cancer, I hooked on the earpiece and plugged it into the receiver. "Hello?"

"Hey." It was Linda, and something was wrong.

Not a little wrong, but slightly breathless, tingle in your guts wrong. I could hear it, even in that single syllable.

"The good news is, I'm not pregnant," she told me, but the subtle alarm signals in her tone prompted anything but relief.

I cut to the chase. "And the bad news . . . ?"

"It's probably nothing"—please God, no. My own stomach plummeted—"But after the sonogram this morning, they did a CAT scan this afternoon and found something that needs a closer look, so they've scheduled me for a laparoscopic tomorrow morning first thing."

Bad sign. Way too instant. I did my best to conceal the fear that made me conscious of every cell in my lungs. "Tomorrow? Isn't that awfully quick?"

"Calm down. It's just professional courtesy," she said, unconvincing. "You know how doctors are. Their own wives could expire on the spot, but let another doctor's wife get so much as a splinter, and she goes to the head of the line."

"They don't do instant CAT scans and laparoscopics for splinters." I did my best to sit on Chicken Little. "What exactly are they going to be looking at?"

Her pause was two beats too long. "My right ovary."

Oh, God! Gilda Radner!

"Georgia?"

I couldn't speak.

"Oh, stop it," she scolded, sounding like herself. "I can hear you going nuts about the worst-case scenario. I almost didn't call you, 'cause I knew you'd do this. It could be a dozen things, and not all of them are dire, so cut it out."

"Sorry," I managed. "I just . . . we've all been so healthy. You hear the statistics, and you think, not one of *us*, but . . ." This wasn't coming out the way I intended at all.

"Ask me what I want you to do," Linda instructed briskly.

"What do you want me to do?"

"I want you to pick me up at six in the morning and take me to the outpatient center. Brooks offered to cancel his surgery, but I told him not to. He'd just drive my doctors nuts, so I told him I'd rather have you take me."

Doctors, plural? Another bad sign.

"I should be ready to go home by one," she went on. "Can you take me?"

In the tradition of any terrified Southern woman worth her salt, I pulled up my socks and thanked God for something constructive to do. "Honey, I'd be there with bells on even if the *National Enquirer* was waiting on your doorstep to nail me as the Jackrabbit Jackpot Woman."

She chuckled. "I think you're safe there."

Over the weekend, she and Teeny and Diane had all faxed, forwarded, and called me with gleeful updates on my notoriety, something that suddenly faded away into true perspective.

"Can I bring anything special?" I offered.

"Nope." She sounded relieved. "Just yourself." Pause. "One thing, though."

"Name it."

"Please don't tell the others. Not yet."

I surprised myself by understanding. "Whatever you want, sweetie." Why she'd chosen to trust me with this fearsome, breathless thing, I couldn't say, especially considering my big mouth and penchant for panic. But I was deeply moved that she had.

"I just . . ." Linda sighed. "I'm doing fine, really, but I'm not so sure I would be if I had to go over everything with all the others. It would make it too real, too scary. I'll call them after, once I know what's up."

I nodded, tears springing to my eyes. I couldn't cry. That was the last thing she needed. "I almost wish you were pregnant," I managed.

"Bite your tongue!" Linda softened. "You know the weird thing? I mean, truly weird?"

I knew, but let her tell me. "What?"

"I was disappointed to find out I wasn't. How crazy is that?"

"Oh, sweetie, it's not crazy at all. It's perfectly understandable."

"Not to me," she said. "A baby would have been a disaster."

"A baby is life renewed, no matter where, no matter when. It makes perfect sense for you to be glad and sad at the same time about that part of it."

"Yeah, well, we all *know* you're nuts." I could tell she felt better for telling me.

I needed to get off so I could go cry in the shower. "Pick you up at six sharp tomorrow morning."

"Bye."

Outpatient surgery recovery cubicle. Tuesday, April 29, 2003.
10:00 A.M.

The striped curtain parted, and Brooks preceded two other doctors in scrubs into the small space.

I closed my copy of *Harry Potter* and rose as Brooks introduced them quietly as Linda's surgeon and the pathologist.

My blood solidified. Pathologists never show up for good news. Pathologists never show up, period.

"She's been dozing," I managed to get out. "Would you like for me to leave?"

"'Course not." Brooks circled the bed and gave me a brief hug.

"She'd kick my can to Valdosta." His kind eyes held a worrisome, oblique cast.

Brooks leaned over to give Linda a kiss, then took her hand into his. "Hey there, peaches 'n' cream. Rise and shine."

She inhaled long and deep, then opened her eyes. At the sight of him, her features glowed. "Hey. What time is it?"

"Ten."

Her eyes closed, then fluttered back open, fixing on the other two doctors, who had the sense to sit tight till she was ready to ask the question nobody ever wants to ask. "Okay," she rasped out, still dry from the surgery. "What am I up against here?"

"Do you want it from me," Brooks asked her, "or from them?"

This wasn't happening.

Linda's grip tightened on his hand. "Them."

"There was a suspicious growth, right where the CAT scan indicated," the surgeon said, "so we removed the entire ovary and tube for biopsy. The good news is, the tumor appeared contained. And the frozen section preliminary results indicate a rare situation—not ovarian cancer, which can be far more difficult to treat, but breast cancer."

Linda's eyes went dark. "Metastatic. It's in my breast."

Translate: I'm dead.

"Not necessarily," Brooks told her.

"As I said," the surgeon went on, "this is a rare manifestation, but not unheard of."

The pathologist spoke up. "It'll be several days before we have more conclusive results, but based on the frozen section, I'm optimistic that it will confirm my original assessment."

Linda searched Brooks's face. "Optimistic?"

When he nodded, she peered at him with raw longing for what he said to be true.

Watching, I felt surreal, like I'd been dropped into a movie, and it grieved me that I'd withdrawn like that, unable to stay in the harsh reality my beloved friend was enduring.

Linda exhaled. "So, what now?"

Brooks stroked her cheek. "As soon as you feel up to it, we fly to M. D. Anderson in Houston, where they'll run a thorough battery of tests to see if this is an isolated situation or one that needs a more general approach."

"Why there?" she asked. "Why not here?"

Just what I was wondering.

"Local care is fine for most situations," he said, "but for something this out of parameter, I'd feel better taking you somewhere where they have a track record with unusual situations like this one." He smiled. "I've already spoken with the high muckety-mucks at their breast cancer department. They're eager to see you, you rare thing, you. Then they'll work out a course of treatment. Cutting edge, all the way. We're gonna lick this thing, honey."

Linda let out a harsh chuckle. "I think I'd rather be pregnant."

Brooks's smile was bittersweet. "Me, too."

She nodded to the surgeon and the pathologist. "Now that that's over, you fine gentlemen can go back to helping your other patients, with my thanks." She waved them out, then turned to us. "And y'all can lighten up. If I'm going to Houston, I'm gonna need a little more sleep."

Brooks kissed her again, lingering slightly. "I've got to check on my patients in recovery, then I'll be back."

"Take your time, honey," she said, then yawned, eyes closing. "I'm not goin' anywhere."

Only when he'd disappeared out of earshot did she reach out to me. "You know," she whispered. "It's almost better knowing than being so afraid. At least we can do something about it now.

"Poor Brooks. It's easier being me than him right now." Then she smiled with a sweet, wistful expression. "Or, y'all."

I fought to control my tears. "Yeah, well, you'd better not get within a mile of dyin', that's all I can say. 'Cause then I'd have to go and evangelize all over you, and I know that would only piss you off."

She actually laughed. "Amen to that one, sister." She settled down to a brave little smile. "Better call the troops and fill them in."

I nodded, catching some of her calm determination. "You are gonna lick this," I told her, believing it with every cosmic molecule of my soul because I had to. "And we're gonna take turns coming to Houston to help you."

"I know. Now go get yourself a Diet Coke, and don't come back till you've told the others. I'm fine by myself." She waggled that finger at me. "And tell the girls not to start sittin' shiva yet. I plan to last at least another thirty years."

I gathered my purse and headed for the parking lot, where my cell phone worked and I could cry all I wanted to when I talked to the others.

"One good thing," I heard Linda say to nobody in particular as I left. "People on chemo always lose weight."

14

Here's to Happy Endings

Swan Coach House. Tuesday, August 12, 2003. 11:20 A.M.

FOR THE FIRST TIME IN MEMORY, WE HADN'T MET AT THE SWAN Coach House for two months in a row. Instead, the second Tuesdays of June and July, we'd flown down en masse to have catered high tea (iced, of course) with Linda at the Rotary House across the street from the M. D. Anderson Cancer Center in Houston.

And in the process, we found out what hot and humid really meant. Atlanta cannot hold a candle to Houston for sheer slap-you-flat-and-run-over-the-pieces hot. From the time I got off that plane till the time I got back on it, my underwear stayed wringin' wet. If the others would have let me, I'd have gone around in one of those wet cloths knotted at the corners on my head (a red one, of course).

I mean, after visiting that place, July in Atlanta paled to bearable. Linda just joked and said she was glad she didn't have any hair, since it was so much cooler.

But we'd have gladly entered the gates of hell if that was where Linda had to go to get better. Fortunately, her stage-two breast cancer had been encapsulated, with no sign of any malignancy in her breasts or nodes, so chemo and radiation had left us all relieved and hopeful.

And it sure was good to see her walking back into the Coach House that August, where the restaurant had made a special exception for Linda and let us decorate our corner in red and purple flowers, balloons, and doo-dahs.

When Teeny escorted her inside clad in a light little embroidered knit red hat over her bald head, everybody in the restaurant, staff and patrons alike, rose with us and applauded.

We'd sworn we wouldn't cry, and we did our best, but a stray tear or two escaped.

Linda, embarrassed but clearly loving all the attention, glided through the standing ovation with a wave worthy of Queen Elizabeth II.

She sat, and the applause started to die, so she popped right back up again to solicit more applause, making the whole place laugh and putting them at their ease.

Grinning so hard my face hurt, I leaned closer. "Cute hat. Is that writing embroidered on it?"

She smiled beatifically and leaned closer so I could see. "Cancer sucks!" it said in ornate script. She patted it. "Somebody gave me a pink one at radiation therapy, but I told her I was way past pink, so I had this one made. In the interest of propriety, I got 'em to do it kinda scrolly, so you have to look close."

Perfect.

But she'd been perfect through the whole ordeal.

"And you're sure you don't want us to shave our heads by way of solidarity?" Diane asked for at least the fourth time.

"Yes, I'm sure." Linda was back in full form. "I told y'all, I want all the sympathy for myself."

SuSu adjusted her ultralight straw picture hat she had on with her slim dark purple linen shift. "So. How does it feel to be back home?"

"Wonderful," Linda said with exaggerated emphasis. "It's *so* good to be back in bed with Brooks. I cannot *tell* you."

There was a brief pause, then we all burst out laughing.

Linda went the color of her hat. "I mean . . . Oh, y'all, come on. You know I didn't . . ."

"That's okay, honey," Diane told her, dabbing tears of laughter from under her mascara. "It's been a long, dry spell, I'm sure."

Linda gave up and laughed with us. "God love the man, he won't stop actin' like a teenager. He doesn't even care that I'm bald. Or that I haven't lost one single bleedin' pound, dammit."

I shook my head. "I don't get it. How can you have three rounds of chemo and not lose weight?"

"Beats me." Linda unfolded her napkin. "It's not like I've been livin' on Häagen-Dazs, either. That chemo makes everything taste nasty. I'm off sweets altogether." She flagged Maria down as she distributed our usual summer drinks.

"Welcome back, Mrs. Murray," Maria said. "You look wonderful."

"Oh, my darling girl," Linda vamped, "you lie so well. How about a basket full of cheese straws for the table? I'm starving, and salty is all that appeals to me these days."

Maria winked. "Right away. The Coach House has been far too quiet without you and your Red Hat ladies."

Diane was eager to get to the presents. As a matter of fact, she'd been awfully chirpy in general. I made a mental note to get to the bottom of it.

"Okay." She lifted the gift wrap bag she'd brought. "Presents." Linda hadn't let us bring her any in Houston because her room was crowded enough without them.

"Joke first," I reminded them. "Whose turn is it?"

SuSu raised a red nail and covered her half-eaten cheese straw with her napkin. "That's me."

We waited for her to finish chewing.

"Okay," she started. "These two little Red Hats are riding down Peachtree, yakkin' away, and they came to a red light and just breeze right through it. So the one little Red Hat thinks, 'Ohmygod. We just ran that red light!' But she doesn't say anything to her friend, 'cause by then it was over, and they were okay.

"Well, lo and behold, miracle of miracles, they hit the next three lights on green, but when they come to the fourth, it's red, and darned if they don't run right slap through it again! Grace of God, nobody hits them, but when the little Red Hat passenger turns back to look, she sees cars screechin' and swerving every which way in their wake.

"When the poor woman turns back around, here they come to another red light, and no hint of the brakes, so she hollers, 'Red light, red light, red light!' But darned if they didn't run right through it again.

"'Louise,' she screams to her friend, 'are you trying to kill us? That's the third red light you've run!'"

"'Ohmygod,' Louise hollers back. 'You mean I'm driving?'"

SuSu waited a heartbeat, then burst into most unladylike guffaws while we gave the joke a polite, lukewarm response. "I just love that joke," she said, shaking her head.

"Now, can we do the presents?" Diane asked.

I'd swiped my gift idea from a friend of mine who's a graphic designer. It was wrapped behind me in a flat sixteen-by-twenty package.

SuSu waggled her bright red nails. "Me first!" She drew a largeish box rapped in purple foil from the floor beside her and handed it to Linda. "Welcome home."

"Y'all didn't have to do this," Linda protested without conviction as she tore into it. "On second thought, yes, you did."

Inside the box was a delicate rose-patterned teapot with a red tea cozy quilted in an intricate rose design. Beneath that lay a matching red quilted cap with a rose-blossom ruffle at the crown and woven silk ties.

"Too cute!" Completely unselfconscious, Linda whipped off her fuzzy hat to try on the quilted one. Bright eyed, she looked like a bud from an Anne Geddes portrait.

"Adorable. You look like a Mongolian princess." Diane eyed Linda in assessment. "You know what, Teens? We ought to do some attractive accessories for women taking chemo. Cute stuff, like that."

Teeny nodded to her in pride. "Go for it."

After Diane's wretched divorce, Teeny had taken advantage of her creativity and executive skills by putting her in charge of Teeny's real-women clothing line. Since then, Diane had taken the clothing industry by storm by focusing on baby boomers instead of teeny boppers. The chemo specialty items were just another of a series of practical, feminine inspirations.

No wonder Diane loved her job. She was making a difference for women like us, and doing very well in both money and acclaim.

Teeny extended a small gift bag toward Linda. "Here. It's not much, but welcome home."

Linda opened it to find a dainty little piece of framed needlepoint with rosebuds around an intricately stitched quote.

"Oh, Teens. I love it." Linda grinned. "You did it yourself, didn't you?"

Teeny preened. "For you, I figured I'd dust off my needle."

Linda turned it so we could see the message. In two lines of elegant script surrounded by rosebuds, the message said, "Whenever you're cornered, go for the nuts."

"Like Pru at the Royal Peacock when we were seniors," Diane remembered aloud.

"Damn straight," Linda said.

Diane urged her gift on Linda next. "I thought these might warm things up in bed for you and Brooks."

"Uh-oh." Linda waggled what was left of her eyebrows. "He's bad enough without encouragement."

She opened the wrapping paper and read the box. "Wild Blue Yonder?"

"I got 'em over the Internet," Diane confided. "In a plain brown wrapper."

"Oh, Lord." Linda rustled through the tissue, then let out a whoop and came up with a pair of heavy socks dangling wires. "Electric socks!" She hugged them. "I am not kiddin', I need these. They keep those doctors' offices and hospitals like meat lockers."

And cold feet were a common side effect of chemo.

Down to my gift. I handed it over.

Linda tore through the paper and sat, rapt, staring at the framed image, all the love and promise of our youth reflected in her eyes. "Oh, George, it's perfect."

I'd found a photo from the fall of '67 with all six of us posed in Pru's old Fireflight convertible, top down on a perfect football Friday. We were suntanned, gorgeous, and so full of ourselves we practically reached out of that picture and grabbed you. A graphic artist friend of mine had played with the image on the computer, stylized it, colored it, blown it up, and sealed the moment in time like some amazing semi-abstract painting.

"Georgia, this is . . ." She grinned, wordless, then murmured, "It's our youth." No sadness tainted her nostalgia.

"Show!" the others clamored.

Linda turned the image around for them to see.

SuSu stood straight up for a better look. "Ohmygod! I want one!" She flagged her napkin at it. "Seriously. I know right where to put it. In the bathroom, right over the foot of my soaker tub."

Linda shrugged toward me in question. "Ask Georgia. I'll bet that could be arranged."

"Sure." I've never been exclusive about my finds, but some people are. "If it's okay with you."

Linda peered at it again. "Absolutely fine with me."

Diane and Teeny wanted one, too, and we all decided to include Pru.

"Speaking of Pru," I asked after we ordered. "How's she doing?"

Teeny nodded. "Great. The doctors are very encouraged. And I think she's breaking some new ground."

"When are we goin' up there?" SuSu asked. " 'Cause I've been sloggin' through all that self-help stuff they told us to read, but once school starts, I won't have time to read so much as a menu if it ain't on the exam, much less 'A Merry-go-round Called Denial.' "

Ooooo. A bit hostile, there. Maybe a little too close to home.

"Dr. Chalmers thinks Pru is ready for a visit." Teeny got out her little two-year pocket planner like the ones we all lived by. "We're thinking sometime in the next few weeks. We can take the plane, so it won't be but a day. Can we coordinate?"

SuSu sniffed. "It'll have to be soon. When school starts, I'm out."

Once that was settled and our food arrived, we lapsed back into general conversation.

"So. What's up with everybody else?" Diane asked in a definite "Okay, somebody ask me about me" cue.

"Spill it," I dutifully complied. "You've been all over the place since you got here."

Diane flushed, blinking even more than her usual sensitive-eyes-with-contacts flutter. "Well, if you must know, I have a date."

Stop the presses!

"Who?" Linda asked atop Teeny's, "How'd you meet?"

"Ohmygod," SuSu said with alacrity. "Details. Leave nothing out."

"I told y'all about him," Diane said. "You remember. Clay Williams, the guy from grammar school."

With everything that had happened to Linda, it seemed like worlds ago since Diane had mentioned him.

"So?"

She was really savoring this, dragging it out, as was her due. "We've been e-mailing a lot. Then it just naturally shifted to the phone, and we both felt like we had known each other forever."

"Since sixth grade," I remembered. "I think that constitutes forever."

"All that time apart though," she said, "but we just seemed to fit. At first, I was the one who was wary. Frankly, I don't really have time for anything or anybody else in my life. But he's so sweet. And so poetic." Big blush on that one.

"Refresh me, now," SuSu told her, shifting to watchdog mode. "Let's have some stats: Divorced? Health conditions? Gainfully employed? Dentures? Children? Obnoxious pets or hobbies? Financial profile? Tattoos?"

This, from the woman who'd been widowed, then married a man who'd dumped her to marry his *other* fiancée, then came crawling back!

SuSu bristled when we glared at her. "Well, if I'd have asked that stuff, I wouldn't have ended up in the pickle I did." Never mind that we were screaming the answers at the time, but she'd ignored us. "I'm only trying to look after Diane."

Diane crossed her eyes at SuSu. "Read my lips: I am not getting married again. I just have a date. A simple date."

Famous last words. We all exchanged knowing glances.

She sighed a happy sigh. "I just want to go to the ballet. And dinner. And the movies. And maybe the symphony. He loves the symphony, too. And he even has a sailboat,"

"Kids?" I asked, doing my best to reserve judgment, which for me is never easy.

"Two daughters, grown and married," she said blithely.

Oooo, daughters with a widowed father. That would be trouble enough, but she'd discover all that later for herself.

"So," Teeny asked. "Where are y'all going for your first date?"

Diane smiled demurely. "Cancun."

SuSu's iced tea went up her nose, causing a most unladylike coughing fit.

Diane sighed as if SuSu had done it on purpose. "Oh, for heaven's sake, SuSu, it's just for the weekend, and it's separate rooms."

"Well, good for you," was all I could say, glad I wasn't out there in the modern world where a weekend in Cancun was a "simple date."

"It's about time you had some fun."

"Just be sure to let us know where you'll be and bring along your cell phone." Teeny dropped to a whisper. "And some pepper spray. Better safe than sorry."

Diane grinned. "Thank you, sweetie, but I don't think I'll be needing the pepper spray. That's not what this is about. He's a perfect gentleman."

"They all think they're gentlemen," SuSu sputtered out, "and that's always what Cancun's about." She took a sip the right way down. "But don't take my word for it. You'll have to find out for yourself."

"When is this momentous occasion?" Linda asked.

"Two weeks. He's connecting here from Birmingham, then we're flying together to the resort."

I did my version of Groucho. "Make sure your underwear matches, just in case."

"Y'all, this is me, here." Diane looked anything but smitten. "I do not do casual sex. Period."

"Period?" Teeny blinked in mock innocence. "Oh, dear. I hope you don't get your period."

God, I loved it when we were flying fast and loose that way. It was the first time the Red Hats had felt normal in months.

Diane shook her head. "If he thinks separate rooms means anything besides separate rooms, he's got another think coming." She smoothed her impeccable skirt. "I am so old-fashioned and so out of practice, so scared of *diseases*, that if he tries to French-kiss me, I'm seriously considering asking him to put a condom on his tongue."

How can you top that?

Seeing that Diane had had enough of the spotlight, I turned to SuSu for a little fishing expedition. "So, Suse, you can't study all the time. Met anybody interesting lately?"

For a fleeting fraction of a second, I saw that "secret lover" look slither back behind her eyes. "I swore off, remember? No more casual sex." She shifted in her chair, her Stay Scarlet lipstick in a sly little smile.

Must not have been anybody significant. And as I had told the others before, we couldn't expect her to quit cold turkey.

She'd tell me about it eventually. Or not.

My odds were on her telling me, but Sacred Tradition Five kept me from pestering her, even if she was breaking Sacred Tradition Seven, herself.

Then my self-righteous bubble burst when I remembered what I was keeping from her.

Humbled, I raised my water glass. "Here's to Diane, and new beginnings."

"And here's to Linda," SuSu added, "and happy endings."

"Don't say endings to a woman with cancer," Linda joked, deadpan, then dry-spit three times for luck.

Teeny, our mistress of secrets, grinned. "And here's to life's surprises. May they all be good ones."

15

Summer

Holy Spirit Presbyterian Church, Moreland, Georgia. June 20, 1968.
3:30 P.M.

*E*VER HER PUNCTUAL SELF, SUSU HAD INSISTED WE GET TO HER country grandmother's tiny little church near Newnan at least an hour before her wedding, so I'd driven her the thirty miles from College Circle. Now, thirty minutes later, I stood trying to cool my blood in front of an ancient oscillating fan in the bathroom that doubled as a bride's room.

SuSu was in the stall, trying for one last tinkle before she got dressed. I envisioned her perched in the cramped space surrounded by her veil and reams of crinolines, like some exotic human stamen to a *Tullius Grandiflora Gloriosa*. (I took four years of Latin at Northside.)

"You're getting married," I said to the door of the stall. "Shouldn't we be talking about something profound, here?" After all, it was the most momentous event of our young lives so far. "The future?" I suggested, afraid to speak what was really on my mind for fear of giving it substance. "The bomb?" *Infidelity. Divorce.* "Colonial versus Mediterranean furniture?" *Her moving away.* "The pill, or IUD?" *Trying to manage without my best friend.* "Vietnam?"

At the mention of Vietnam, a daunting thought occurred to me. "The army uses dogs. Do they ever draft vets?" Not ex-soldiers, but veterinarians, the groom's profession as of this month.

SuSu's laugh echoed off the plaster ceiling. "No. They don't draft vets; either kind. And we are not supposed to be talking about earth-shaking things. We're supposed to be trying to stay cool and get dressed."

Though both of us were used to Atlanta's heat and humidity—we'd grown up without air-conditioning—this plain little brick church had only a few trees to shade it, so the temperature was at least 90 degrees inside, despite the valiant efforts of two window units pumping away in the sanctuary. SuSu's wedding day had dawned at 88 degrees and gone up from there, so staying cool was out of the question, and we'd postponed putting on our dresses till the last possible minute.

I turned on the cold water and soaked a paper towel, wrung it till it didn't drip, then draped it above my *Cat on a Hot Tin Roof* slip. Even in the heat, I wore a gut-sucker longleg girdle from Lerner's, to make sure my turquoise, princess-line bridesmaid's dress would fit me smoothly, without lumps or "bobble" as my mother called any visible shifting of my generous curves.

In my day, those girdles were as close to birth control as well-brought-up young Southern ladies ever got. Mama knew me well enough to insist that whenever I went out, I was trussed to the teeth, which totally eliminated the possibility of impulsive nakedness.

Not that it had stopped me with Brad back in high school. But no other boy had stirred my libido in the three years since Brad had disappeared without a trace after moving to California with his parents—no clues, no note, no warning signs—leaving them and me frantic and brokenhearted. I'd remained stale and unsatisfied, still aching from my true love's loss, the mystery of his fate trailing blacker than any shadow wherever I went.

I wasn't jealous of SuSu's happiness; I was thrilled for her. But the wedding only reminded me of the love that Brad had taken with him, leaving me none to risk on anyone else.

"Guess what?" SuSu said from the stall.

"What?" I asked with forced brightness.

"I'm not wearing any underpants."

"SuSu!" That jolted me out of my pity party. I was truly shocked. SuSu had always been so straightlaced. "You can't get married without any underpants. It's not decent."

"Watch me," she said with delicious defiance. "I've got on the lace garter belt and white stockings you gave me at the lingerie shower. That's enough."

"Lord." I freshened my damp paper towel. "Why did you tell me? Now all I can think about is the fact that you don't have on any underpants."

I could hear her grin in what she said next. "You were getting way too serious. I know you, and I know what's in those sudden silences. You're probably sitting there wondering if Tom would ever cheat on me, or if we'd get divorced. Or worrying how you and I would manage without each other. I know you."

I wasn't as unselfish as she thought me, but the other things had crossed my mind. "So?" I defended. "I don't want you to get hurt."

"Trust me. It's gonna be great. And you and I will still be best friends, just like always." She paused, reading my mind more accurately this time. Her tone softened. "Your day will come, too. Then I'll be the one helping you get dressed before the ceremony. And you'll be as happy then as I am now."

I wasn't so sure. I'd been seeing John, a really sweet, boring guy who adored me, but my heart still belonged to Brad. I'd tried and tried to let him go. I'd buried him mentally, complete with shoveling the dirt into an open grave where he lay, uncovered. But he'd waked up, laughing, and jumped out, teasing me about thinking he was dead.

How could there be anybody else? I could still see Brad as clearly as the day he'd kissed me good-bye in the spring of 1967 and promised to call every week.

"All this wedding stuff has been hard for you, hasn't it?" SuSu prodded.

Was I that transparent? Guilty, I winced at myself for being such a wet blanket.

A rustle of nylon net and crinolines came from the stall. Then the rumble of the toilet-paper roll. Then a flush. Then more rustle of stiffened fabric.

She opened the stall door and came out holding up her crinolines, a vision of golden tan and artful russet curls that tumbled halfway down her back to her white strapless push-up bra. "It's dredged up that whole Brad thing, hasn't it?"

I knew her well enough to realize she wasn't going to leave me alone till I admitted it. "Some. But I'll get over it." She, alone of all the others, was safe to confide my true feelings to. Linda just told me to get past it and move on. Diane said Brad was probably surfing somewhere, not thinking of me. Teeny recommended prayer to St. Anthony, patron saint of lost things. And Pru always cited karma, saying he'd probably turn back up again when I least expected it. Only SuSu understood how fresh the loss still felt.

"But this is your day," I said brightly, "and I want you to enjoy every minute of it, because it's the beginning of your life as Mrs. Tom Harris, DVM."

"So," I diverted, "did Tom give you any hints about where y'all are going to honeymoon?"

A honeymoon—the first for our little group of Mademoiselle alumnae. I envisioned the Bahamas, or Bermuda.

"Yep," SuSu answered over a satiny rustle of white polyester and nylon tulle. "I'm pretty sure it's Gatlinburg." She wet a paper towel and dabbed at her slender neck, mottled from the heat. "Last night on the way home from the rehearsal dinner, I found a piece of paper in his car that had 'the Chalet' written on it, with the area code and phone number, so I called it this morning. It's that pretty A-frame motel up the hill above the river, on the west end of town."

Gatlinburg was fun in the winter, but a honeymoon there was pure redneck. SuSu didn't sound disappointed at all, but I sure was. Of course, Tom had to be really strapped from finishing vet school, then setting up his practice in Beaufort, SC. He wasn't being cheap. But to me, honeymoon meant the Bahamas.

Not that I would ever have one. Unless Brad came back.

SuSu looked at her veil in the mirror. "Dang. I messed up my veil. Could you fix it while I'm getting these crinolines straightened out?"

"Sure." I was glad for something to do. "Bend down," I ordered, lacking six inches on her statuesque height. "Okay. Hold it there." I checked the pins anchoring her custom-blended russet "fall" of curls, then rearranged her fine tulle veil that was securely fastened behind a pearl tiara. I couldn't help noting the flush of heat and excitement that livened SuSu's cheeks.

While her makeup seemed fine, my Silk Fashion foundation felt like it was about to melt right off my face.

We both turned to look at the dresses we had to put on. Hers hung, deflated, from a ceiling pipe in the concrete block room, while my maid of honor's dress was hooked over the side of the stall.

SuSu's aunt had made the turquoise bridesmaids' dresses from clearance drapery fabric that looked for all the world like silk shantung, even close up. The material was heavy, but at least the cut was sleeveless, with tasteful flat bows sewn over each shoulder. She'd made SuSu's gown of luminous white polyester "silk" with short, puffed sleeves, fitted bodice, and a sweetheart neckline. The embroidered bodice tapered to a deep vee below the narrow waist, with a skirt that billowed like a ball gown, just like Sleeping Beauty's.

I'd been there for the final fitting, and SuSu looked like a princess in it, only taller.

I just hoped she didn't have too many "happily ever after" illusions to go with it. Brad's disappearance had taught me that you can't take happiness for granted.

I eyed the dresses. "We've got to put them on eventually," I said. Even my dyed turquoise pumps looked too hot to be borne.

Searching for a good reason to delay dressing for a few more minutes, I remembered my maid of honor duties. (Since I'd never even been a bridesmaid, I'd had to consult my big sister and take her word for what I was supposed to do.)

I studied my oldest, bestest friend, trying to see her the way a stranger would. Already, love had erased the wary look from her past trials and disappointments. Tom's unshakable support and encouragement had given her a new confidence, and it fit her well. But I had to be sure she knew what she was doing.

Tom seemed too good to be true. And despite what she said, I had to be sure she was marrying him for the right reasons.

It struck me that in less than an hour, she'd be a married woman, and I couldn't help wondering if it would come between us. After all, our generation firmly believed that a wife's first loyalty was to her husband, not her friends.

Misting up, I laid a hand briefly to her arm as she freshened her lipstick in the wavy, dime-store mirror. "SuSu, are you sure this is what you want to do?"

"George!" She glared at my image. "Don't be ridiculous. I wouldn't be here if I wasn't sure."

I ignored her and went on. " 'Cause if you're not absolutely certain, you can postpone this. We'll take care of everything for you. Don't be afraid to speak up."

Her expression softened. "Thanks for the offer, sweetie, but I've never been so sure of anything in my life." The peace in her green eyes said it all.

"Sorry," I said. "I was just trying to be a good best friend. And maid of honor."

"You've been perfect." She pivoted to give me an air kiss and hug, careful not to disturb our teased and lacquered do's.

"I loved the lingerie shower," she told me. "I love my sexy garter belt and my satin garter." She raised the hem of her crinolines to reveal the white satin garter just below the knee—"something new" for her big day from me. "I loved the sweet stories you told and the precious toasts you made last night at my parents' restaurant."

I'd compiled all the positive stories I could remember from her complicated childhood. Telling them at the rehearsal dinner, I'd finally realized that her parents had just been doing the best they could, trying to survive.

There in the "bride's room," SuSu smiled like she hadn't since we were kids. "And I love you. But most of all, I love Tom, and I can't wait to be blissfully flea-bitten for the rest of my life, surrounded by dogs and cats and rabbits and kids. So let's get this show on the road."

I glanced at my watch and frowned. Three forty. "The others were supposed to be here at least ten minutes ago." Since there was so little room to change, Pru and Linda and Diane and Teeny were all coming dressed.

As if on cue, Miz McIntyre knocked and came in with the same motion. "Lord, SuSu where *are* those friends of yours? I swear, I don't know why you had to drag everybody all the way down here to get married. What if they got lost?" she said as she turned around and peered into the vestibule as the door closed behind her. "The church is so full nobody can breathe, and no bridesmaids."

She turned to face us, her sour expression all too familiar and her hat—a blue velvet bow with an almost invisible veil to the chin—awry.

SuSu laughed. "C'mere, Mama. Your hat's all crooked." She centered the flat bow on the crown, then rearranged the veil so its tiny matching bows near the bottom were evenly spaced below her mother's chin.

Miz McIntyre submitted with unusual docileness, but that sharp tongue of hers was still working. "Lord, SuSu! Look at you. Not even dressed. I cannot fathom why a fine man like Tom Harris would want to marry such a scatterbrain." She shot me an accusing glance. "You, too, Miss Georgia." As always, she said the nickname with aspersion, like I thought I was some kind of beauty queen. "You're the maid of honor. You're supposed to get her ready. The wedding's in twenty minutes, and she's still half-naked."

If only she knew. I had half a mind to tell her SuSu didn't have on any underpants, but the last thing SuSu needed was more trouble from her mama. "Don't worry, Miz McIntyre. We'll be ready, just like SuSu said."

She glared at me afresh. Miz McIntyre had wanted SuSu's older sister, Phoebe—now eight months pregnant and stationed with her SAC-pilot husband in Minot, North Dakota—to be matron of honor, but SuSu had insisted on me and our gang for her attendants. Phoebe had better sense than to fly or drive that far so close to her due date, but SuSu's mama remained convinced she would have come to be matron of honor, so I was on Miz McIntyre's shit list worse than usual.

Miz McIntyre glanced into the mirror, swiping a fingertip along her lower lip to stop the spread of lipstick into the tiny lines there. She was our mothers' age, but looked twice as old, gaunt and haggard even in her light-blue mother-of-the-bride suit.

At least my mama was just embarrassing in an ordinary, parental way, with goofy glasses, no sense of style, and nothing but lipstick and powder for makeup. But I loved her, and I knew she loved me, and she'd brought me up to believe I could be any damn thing I wanted. Poor Miz McIntyre didn't know how to be anything but miserable and spread it around.

But SuSu wasn't catching any misery today. "Don't worry, Mama." She caught her mama in a hug, to which Miz McIntyre responded with all the warmth of an armful of coat hangers. "Everything's going to be fine," she crooned. "Tom and I are going to get married, and my best friends are all going to be standing up with me. They'll be here in time." She released her mother, who couldn't seem to move away fast enough. SuSu regarded her with genuine sympathy. "Why don't you go help Daddy say hello to everybody and thank them for coming. The girls will be here in time. I promise."

After her mother left, I carefully washed and dried my hands, then took down SuSu's homemade wedding dress. "I don't know how you can be so calm. I'd be a wreck, even if the others were here, which they're not."

SuSu laughed. "I'm too tired to get hysterical. And too hot." She unfolded the sheet we'd brought and laid it on the floor. "Just spread the skirt out, and I'll step into it." After we got the skirt arranged, she took off her pink bedroom slippers, checked the soles of her white stockings and found them clean, then stepped across the folds of material to the middle, where she stuffed the crinolines through the waist till she could draw the bodice up into place. "Okay," she said, bracketing her waist with her hands. "Hook me."

"How come your aunt used hooks?" I asked as I focused on keeping them lined up with their proper eyes.

"She thinks zippers are too instant. Too modern. Not romantic. 'Make him work for it that first time,' she said." SuSu chuckled. "She also thinks all brides are virgins, but since she was making the dresses, I didn't want to bust her bubble. Especially since she'd tell Mama, who would probably ask the whole congregation to help pray down the Holy Ghost to convict me and Tom of our heinous sin. During the wedding."

"Tom would die." Her handsome, cultured groom would die for *sure* if he knew how much *I* knew about SuSu's calculated surrender of her virginity only months before.

I couldn't help feeling sorry for him and his family. The Harrises were just well-enough off to be embarrassed by the McIntyres' humble means and lack of social graces, but they were good people, polite enough to act as if everything were perfect.

"Your mother-in-law seems like a peach," I said as I hooked. "I'm surprised. I thought women with only sons were usually harsh on their brides, but I didn't detect a single claw."

"She's adorable." SuSu wriggled her hands through the short, puffed sleeves, then drew them to her shoulders. "She said I could be the daughter she'd always wanted."

Before I could respond to that bit of good news, the door burst open and Linda, Teeny, Diane, and Pru piled in, looking fresh in their matching turquoise dresses, their bouffant hairdos perfectly arranged and sprayed (except Pru's wild hippie mane, which we'd talked her into catching back at the nape of her neck).

"Hurry up, sugar," Linda slurred with a blast of champagne breath. "T minus three minutes and countin'."

"Dee dee *dee*, dah-dah dee dee *dee*," Diane sang in an off-key rendition of a quiz show "time's running out" theme.

They weren't staggering, but it was clear they'd been in the sauce.

"Y'all," I said in an outraged stage whisper. "I cannot believe y'all came to SuSu's wedding *high*." I almost lost count of the hooks. "Is that where you've been? Out getting' drunk somewhere? Poor Miz McIntyre's about to have a fit. Not to mention SuSu."

SuSu's good humor had faded. "Please, y'all. Just try not to trip or pass out during the ceremony," she pleaded. "Okay?"

The plastered expressions evaporated, replaced by smug grins. "Gotcha!" "Surprise." "Fooled ya."

Linda, looking like a brunette version of Teeny in her bridesmaid's dress, clapped her hands. "We just swished and spit. We're dry as Sunday, honey." Which was true back then. "Now, put some clothes on, so we can get this girl married and remedy that at the reception."

Which was at the *air-conditioned* Newnan Golf Club, thanks to the generosity of all our mothers chipping in to pay for it.

Pru handed SuSu a prism. "Here. This is for your new life. Hang it in your window. It makes rainbows." We'd had a heck of a time convincing Pru not to wear her love beads and a headband with her bridesmaid's dress. She and Tyson were really into that whole hippy thing (except for enjoying the comforts Tyson's wealthy "sold-out, perpetuating-the-war-mongers-military-industrial-complex" parents provided them).

Pru fixed SuSu with an ingenuous smile. "Whenever you get sad, just look at the rainbow and remember I love you. Peace." She made the peace sign, which I'd always, ironically, associated with Winston Churchill's vee for victory.

Diane helped me put on my dress while Linda took over with SuSu's hooks. Fortunately, SuSu's aunt didn't think zippers were too modern for bridesmaids, so I was dressed and ready in seconds, my feet imprisoned in the dyed turquoise pumps (which, they don't tell you, always shrink when they dye them).

Pru just stood by looking dreamy, which Pru did very well.

"Okay." Looking like a preteen in her pint-sized bridesmaid's dress, Teeny motioned to the door. "Linda, would you please put the trash can in front of the door?" She turned to SuSu. "Would you please close your eyes till I tell you to open them?"

A brow cocked in question, SuSu nodded and obliged.

Diane drew five candles and a lighter from a grocery bag, then handed one to each of us with an index card neatly printed with our part of the ceremony.

The wedding ritual. I'd completely forgotten.

Reading mine, I was taken back four years to that momentous day when we'd all become Mademoiselles and learned the lore, dreaming of just this moment.

Since SuSu had never been in another sorority, I found the gesture touching and appropriate.

Teeny handed out some pretty, saucered candleholders. After we'd firmly secured our tapers, she touched the lighter to the wicks. "Careful to hold them level," she whispered. "We wouldn't forgive ourselves if we got anything on the dresses, especially SuSu's."

The wax ran like water in the heat, but the saucers worked.

We circled SuSu.

"Susan Virginia McIntyre," Teeny intoned, her voice as strong as she was small. "Open your eyes and behold your sisters."

She did, and immediately, hers welled with tears.

Teeny handed her a paper towel. "This is a solemn ritual, but one of joy. Please do not ruin your makeup," she said in the same prophetic tones, which lightened things enough for SuSu to get a grip on herself.

Teeny nodded to Linda, our steadfast one.

"This day," Linda started, "you take a new name and new responsibilities as a wife, but the bond of sisterhood is not diminished." She raised her candle. "I bear the blue candle of friendship. Years may pass, distances may grow, and circumstances may change, but whenever you need friendship, we will give it. Without hesitation. Without judgment. Without thought of recompense."

When the reverent silence that followed stretched too thin, Linda nudged me. YELLOW FOLLOWS BLUE, my card said, right at the top, setting loose a sting of embarrassment. "I bear the yellow candle of truth," I, the frank one, read. "Whenever you need the truth, you may come to us, and we will give it in compassion. Without hesitation. Without judgment. Without thought of recompense."

Linda nodded to Pru, who had to turn her card right-side up. "I bear the purple candle of mercy," Pru read, an appropriate choice for her gentle spirit. "Whenever you need forgiveness, you may come to us and we will give it. Without hesitation. Without judgment. Without thought of recompense."

Diane didn't have to be prompted. Our crusader, she spoke out, clear and true. "I bear the red candle of justice. Whenever you have been wronged, you may come to us, and we will do all we can to bring justice. Without hesitation. Without judgment. Without thought of recompense."

Teeny, our well of secrets, went last. "I bear the white candle of silence," she said. "When you need to share a confidence, you may come to us, and we will keep it. Without hesitation. Without judgment, and without thought of recompense."

Teeny handed SuSu a shiny brass candlesnuffer. "As first to step beyond the days of girlhood into the solemn covenant of marriage, you are offered this solemn covenant of friendship. By extinguishing each of these candles, you accept the promises we have made, and agree to extend them to each of us in time."

With great reverence, SuSu snuffed out each candle in turn.

As the smoke increased, we shared a profound silence resonant of the change to come, not just for SuSu, but for all of us.

And then SuSu's daddy pounded on the door, causing all of us to jump. "Is everybody decent in there? 'Cause it's about time for us to have a weddin'."

"Yes, sir." Diane opened the door to find him standing in the vestibule with our bouquets in a box, while Tom's college buddies waited to file into the packed sanctuary.

Mr. McIntyre took one look at SuSu and gasped. "Dear Lord, child of mine. You look just like a queen. What a lucky boy that young man is. A lucky boy, indeed."

It was the most I'd ever heard him say in my life, and when I saw the look of love and gratitude on SuSu's face, it took all my where-withal to keep from bawling.

Her own eyes welling, Linda handed out the bouquets, then we exited the bathroom so the church lady could arrange us for the processional.

No fancy brass fanfares for SuSu. We filed in to plain old "Here Comes the Bride" on the church's Hammond. But when I saw the glow on lanky Tom Harris's face as he caught the first glimpse of his bride, everything else faded into oblivion: the heat, the humble surroundings, the uneducated accent of the minister, and most of all, the forgotten disappointments of the past.

My prayers had been answered. SuSu had finally found a love that meant no harm. And a kindly mother-in-law, to boot.

It was the best wedding ever.

16

Rehabilitation

East Winds Rehabilitation Center, near Ashville, North Carolina.
August 19, 2003. 1:00 P.M.

SINCE AUGUST NINETEENTH WAS THE ONLY DAY WE COULD ALL GO to the rehab facility before SuSu went back to school, Diane postponed her big date to Cancun till the twenty-second. Out of solidarity for Linda, we all wore our red hats when we went into the rambling stone building. We brought one for Pru, too, so she wouldn't feel left out.

The place looked like the Biltmore mansion, only on a far more human scale. When we got there, a very polite baby-girl receptionist took us to a separate room, where another young woman offered us the option of checking our bags in tasteful little lockers, or having them searched, along with our pockets. The others checked theirs, but I opted to have mine searched.

I'm cosmically attached to my purse. Every time I leave home without it, even for a little while, I end up forgetting, then having a major adrenaline spike when I think I've lost the thing. Not that there's ever more than a few hundred dollars of available credit on my two bank cards, anyway, but it would be a bitch replacing my license, photos, and the thirty or so discount cards I've accumulated.

As the pretty young security girl was searching through the haphazard contents of my bag's umpty-jillion pockets and compartments, I told her she could throw away the wadded-up fast-food receipts and gum wrappers, which she did without so much as a hint of derision.

Fortunately, she didn't notice anything odd about Teeny's flowing skirt.

Once I had my bag and she'd checked our pockets, she led us into an elegantly welcoming library where our session was scheduled.

This was the riskiest part.

Hyperconscious, I winced when Teeny's skirt rattled instead of rustled, but the security girl didn't notice, too busy explaining that Pru and the doctor would join us shortly.

I didn't breathe easy till we were alone.

Looking razor sharp in a white-knit shoulder-baring top and slim brown slacks, SuSu nervously circled the room as Linda and Diane claimed comfortable leather easy chairs. I sat at a window seat overlooking the gorgeous grounds while Teeny hovered awkwardly nearby, unable to sit for reasons that will become apparent.

SuSu scanned the orderly contents of the mahogany shelves. "Best sellers. Classics. Motivational. All that Twelve Step stuff," she enumerated. She got to the DVD collection. "Seriously great movies." She took up pacing again.

She'd been antsy as a cat on caffeine ever since we'd picked her up that morning.

I couldn't help wondering again if the whole rehab thing was a little too close for comfort. Thanks to the books about alcoholism and addiction Pru's therapist had recommended we all read, I'd learned that it wasn't my job to tell SuSu she had a drinking problem. She had to come to that realization herself.

But I sure could pray that the books and these sessions would open her eyes.

"I still can't believe y'all didn't tell me why you were going to Las Vegas," she griped, apropos of nothing, for the eighty-leventh time since we'd gotten back.

"Tradition Eight," Linda reminded her for the eighty-twelfth. "You forgave us. Remember?"

"Yes, but forgiving doesn't mean forgetting," SuSu retorted.

"Suse, would you *please* quit bitchin' about that?" Diane said without rancor. "You aced your exams, didn't you?"

Here we go again.

SuSu exhaled. "It was only twenty-four hours. I could have spared twenty-four hours. I should have been there. You might have needed legal advice."

Puh-leez.

This was where one of us was supposed to remind her that we'd had no idea how long it was going to take to rescue Pru (which I have since learned is a nasty word in rehab circles), but we were worn out playing that game.

Deliberately changing the subject, Linda perused one of the facility's bound brochures. "Good grief. Unlimited massages. Hot rock treatments. Chiropractic. Acupuncture. Waterobics. Naturopathy. Chelation. Yoga. Hypnotherapy. Personal trainers. Custom diets. This place is incredible."

Teeny nodded. "They take a holistic approach. It's why I chose them. That, and their success rate. It's double any other facility's in the world."

"That might just have something to do with the twenty-five thou a week," Diane put in, ever practical.

Teeny nodded. "This is definitely one of those situations where you get what you pay for. But the addicts also have a lot to do, themselves. It's hard work, learning a new way of life. And as soon as they're physically able, they're given jobs at the facility's farm and greenhouses just down the hill."

SuSu tapped a pointy slide on the cushy area rug. "Twenty-five thou a week, and they make you work like a field hand? I don't think so."

"Well, they're hardly pickin' cotton," Teeny said. "More like planting flowers, collecting eggs, weeding." She shifted uncomfortably, with an ominous rattle from under her skirt. "Pru wrote me that she likes working in the vegetable gardens. It's all organic. They use the crops in the kitchen. The food's wonderful."

I looked out the window to the broad sweep of rhododendron-bordered lawn that allowed a breathtaking view of the Smokies. "Do they have any job openings? I'd shovel out the stables for a chance to stay here." The place was Eden, more like a five-star spa than a hospital. "I could definitely live here."

But who would want to be cast out of a place like this? I turned back to Teeny. "How do they get people to leave?"

"By reinforcing independence as a goal from the very beginning," she explained.

SuSu shook her head. "Make me work on a farm, and I'm outta here in a New York minute."

Linda stretched out on a leather "swooning couch" like the ones in the psychiatrist cartoons. "Amen, sister. With me, it's a Jewish thing. My people don't do anything that ruins our manicures or messes up our hair, even if we don't have any hair."

"Malarkey," Diane, our gardener, said.

The door opened, and a nice-looking older man who I assumed was Dr. Chalmers ushered Pru into the room. We all sat to attention, probably as nervous as she was.

The woman who followed him was a definite improvement over the angry, emaciated, desperate Pru we'd finagled out of Las Vegas. Clean and nicely dressed in a matching set of blue knit pants and T, she'd cut and colored her hair to a much more natural style and shade, and begun to fill out in a healthy way. Her harsh life was still written on her face, but not graven nearly as deep. She even had on mascara.

But her eyes were shielded, unreadable. She frowned. "What's with the hats?"

I proffered the crushable one with the turned-up brim. "We brought one for you."

Pru balked, her expression clearly indicating that, though she might have to endure these therapy sessions with us as family whether she liked it or not, no way, was she going to wear a dumb hat.

Linda countered her resistance by whipping off her red straw panama and running her palm over the scattering of silver fuzz on her pale scalp. "They wore 'em for my sake, so I wouldn't feel self-conscious in mine."

Pru halted abruptly. "Damn, Linda. What happened?"

"Cancer," Linda said with matter-of-fact cheerfulness. "But we're not here to talk about me. We're here for you, kiddo."

Pru stood there, slightly stunned.

Nothing like throwing her off guard.

Studying Linda, Dr. Chalmers's objective façade slipped, revealing a flash of admiration and curiosity.

I rose and went to join the circle, while Teeny lagged behind by the window, standing.

"You've had your hair done," I said as I neared Pru, amazed by the effect of the loose, flattering waves that fell to her shoulders. Apparently, a makeover came with the therapy. "It's so pretty that way." I couldn't resist touching it, which made her flinch, so I backed off.

"Fabulous cut." SuSu nodded in genuine admiration of the soft, believable blond with subtle highlights. "And I love that color."

Pru's already tentative posture seemed to shrink. Apparently she wasn't ready to accept compliments.

"Why don't we all sit down and get comfortable?" Dr. Chalmers suggested.

Teeny spoke up from over by the window. "Dr. Chalmers, would you mind if I had a brief word with Pru over here before we get started? It won't take long."

He frowned, pushing his glasses up the bridge of his nose. "Well, as long as it complies with the guidelines . . ."

Which were pretty basic: no force or coercion, no shouting, no shocks or sensational unburdening, and no contraband. *Especially* no contraband.

"Of course." Teeny looked so angelic, she could have smuggled an Uzi into Congress.

Diane peered at the doctor. "You don't have a heart condition or anything, do you?"

Diverted, Dr. Chalmers tucked his chin in consternation. "No. Why?"

She smiled and patted his arm. "Just checking."

"Come on." Teeny motioned Pru closer to her. "I won't bite you."

Pru looked to the doctor, then cautiously approached. "No offense," she said to Teeny, "but I've been hugged to smithereens in this place, so if it's just the same to you, I'd—"

Teeny smiled that angelic smile. "No hugs. I promise." It wasn't until Pru came close that Teeny reached up her own skirt and ripped loose the Velcro that was holding a plastic bag of authentic-looking labeled prescription bottles slung between her legs. "Ta-daa." Teeny held the clear bag up to Pru and shook it, rattling the contents of the bottles. "We thought you might be needing these right about now."

Dr. Chalmers let out a strangled gargle as Pru shrieked "Shit!" reverting to the hunted animal she'd been in Vegas. She leapt back in horror. "Teeny! I thought y'all were here to help me!"

Uh-oh. We hadn't meant to scare her.

The doctor lunged toward Pru, but Diane and SuSu blocked his path. "Please," SuSu told him. "It's okay. I swear. Just trust us for a few minutes, and you'll see."

"Calm down, Pru, honey," Teeny soothed. "You know me well enough by now to know I'd never do anything to hurt your recovery." She drew out one of the bottles. "Here, take it. And please read the label aloud."

Neither Pru nor the doctor seemed convinced we were on the up-and-up.

"Okay." Teeny placed the "prescription" on her palm and held it where Pru could see it. "How about I hold it, and you just read the label?"

Pru shot a pleading glance to the doctor and deflected, "I don't have my glasses."

I leapt to the rescue, causing everybody to jump. "Here. Take mine." I handed her my 225s, then backed off.

Still tentative, Pru put them on.

"Please read the whole thing," Teeny instructed.

Pru bent closer. " 'Wender and Roberts Pharmacy.' " Our teenaged hangout. " 'Dr. Erasmus B. Schoen, M.D. Fifty mg' "—she said the letters instead of "milligrams"—" 'gluteus maximus removus. Take whenever ass appears on shoulders. May be repeated as often as needed.' "

It took a second to sink in, then Pru actually smiled. "Erasmus be showin'. That's *funny*."

Teeny handed her the bottle. "Open it."

Pru did, and laughed aloud. She turned to the doctor. "It's M and M's—my favorite."

"We remembered," SuSu said with a grin.

Teeny handed her another bottle.

Pru adjusted my glasses, eyebrows raised in anticipation. " 'Dr. Haywood J. Buzzoff. One hundred mg Distilled Detachment. For use with irritated asshole attacks. Works best when patient leaves the presence of said irritated asshole.'" She barked a "Ha," like a delighted child. "'Effectiveness is enhanced by calm, *I* statements. CAUTION: Shouting nullifies all benefits.'"

She grinned. "Did y'all make these up yourselves?"

"Absolutely," I told her. "Spent the whole day thinking them up and figuring out how to print the labels."

Dr. Chalmers finally eased down a bit, but remained alert.

Pru opened the bottle. "Oooh. Lemon drops. I love those, too."

Eager now, she drew another of the four remaining bottles.

"'Dr. Doan Set Yasefup. Fifty mg Extra Strength Expectation Remover. Take immediately whenever expectations about other people's behaviors crop up. Prevents resentments.'" That one just got a grin, but you can't hit a home run every time. She opened the top. "Ha. Red hots. Very appropriate."

Pru picked another. "'Dr. I. M. God.'" She let out an edgy chuckle. "I've met plenty of those M-dieties in rehab over the years, let me tell you."

A joke! She'd actually made a joke.

Pru shot Dr. Chalmers an impish smile, pulling her deep dimple. "Present company excepted."

He nodded and, much to our relief, smiled back.

Pru read on. "'One hundred mg Brainflush B (powerful mental laxative). Take as needed to banish negative projections and obsessing about other people's behavior. May be repeated up to five hundred times per day.'" Pru grinned. "I'd probably have to double the dose. But then, we all know I've got that addictive nature."

Another joke!

She looked inside. "Gummy bears!"

I raised a cautionary finger. "Low-carb gummy bears, and you gotta watch those little boogers. I ate a bunch of them on the plane back from Vegas"—I deliberately didn't mention the nine low-carb chocolate peanut butter cups that preceded them—"and within thirty minutes, it sounded like somebody was runnin' a subway through my innards. I spent the last three hours of the trip in the bathroom. Fortunately for the others, there were two bathrooms on the plane."

"Unfortunately for the others," Linda quipped, "yours wasn't sound-proofed."

Even Teeny laughed at that one.

"I'm glad I slept through it, then," Pru said.

Two and a half jokes!

She drew the next-to-last bottle, the biggest of all, with the most writing. " 'Dr. E. Gozaway.' " She frowned, trying to figure that one out.

"Egos away," Diane prompted in a stage whisper.

"Oh. I get it." Pru nodded, her face clearing. "Very clever." She shifted to her careful reading voice. " 'Two hundred mg Concentrated Crow. Specially formulated for Step Ten, but can be used as needed. May be difficult to choke down at first, but gets easier with increased use. Take with one sincere, "I was wrong" or "You may be right," though some patients have been known to choke to death on that last one.' "

Pru hooted. "Man, I cannot wait to show these to the other inmates. We need all the funny we can get." She scanned our faces. "*I* need all the funny I can get. And the candy. Sugar is my sole remaining vice. They don't even let you smoke in this place." Realizing she'd just criticized Teeny's generosity, she looked abashed and hugged the bottle. "This is too great, y'all. I don't know how to thank you. God, it feels good to laugh."

SuSu preened. "Thanks. We worked hard on it, just for you."

Dr. Chalmers nodded. "Getting folks to lighten up is one of our biggest challenges here."

Pru opened the bottle lid. "Malted milk balls. My mostest favorite of all." She took one out, paused, then put it back. "I'm gonna save these till my taste buds get straightened out."

Taste buds?

Who knew? I could only imagine what sort of havoc the drugs had wrought in her body.

"Last one." Pru took the final bottle from the bag. " 'Dr. Howe M. Portant Izzit. One hundred mg Purified Perspective. Taken at immediate onset of symptoms, prevents minor irritations from becoming emergencies.' " Pru giggled like a girl. " 'Repeat prescribing doctor's name at first sign of annoyance. May be taken as often as needed, in conjunction with Brainflush B.' "

She opened the top to find tiny peppermint drops. "Y'all are the best." Smiling, Pru closed her eyes and just stood there, head tipped back.

The silence stretched, thrumming longer and more resonant.

"So this is what it feels like to feel good," she murmured. "I'd almost forgotten."

We all misted up while she stood there savoring that small victory.

Then she took a cleansing breath and headed back to the circle. "C'mon, Teeny. I've got some work to do."

Dr. Chalmers waited until we were all seated to take his own chair. Amenities like that are so rare these days, I decided I might be able to like this guy.

Pru held up the bag of pills. "How 'bout it, doc? Can I keep 'em?"

He hesitated.

"I swear, Dr. Chalmers," Teeny reassured him, "We won't pull anything else like this. We just felt like an icebreaker would help, and this was all we could come up with."

"That was some icebreaker," he said with admiration. "Madison Avenue should be so creative." He looked at the pills, a half smile softening his professional demeanor. "Well, it's iffy, at best, on several points of appropriateness. Drugs are no joke. But as I said, getting people to lighten up is one of our main objectives. So I think we could make an exception in this case."

Sitting Indian style in a wide easy chair, Pru clutched our gift in triumph. "This is gonna rock the socks off Group Therapy."

The doctor glanced at his watch. (Don't they all?) "Well, I think we've gotten this off to a great start." He looked to Pru. "Would you like to explain your goals for this session, Pru, or would you like for me to do it?"

Her relaxed expression tightened slightly. "You."

"Pru is working through our twelve-step program for addicts. With certain minor modifications, it mirrors AA, which is also a valued part of our treatment resources." He glanced to us. "Did any of you have a chance to read any of the literature I recommended?"

Diane, still a hopeless apple-polisher, actually raised her hand. "Every word."

I nodded. "Teeny gave us all the books and pamphlets. I learned a lot."

SuSu squirmed in her seat, eyes averted. "Some."

Definitely too close to home.

"Excellent," the doctor said. "Most families don't even read the list." He settled back with his tablet in his lap, his speech calm and deliberate. "Accepting responsibility for her actions is another primary objective for Pru's successful recovery. She's spent the past seven weeks working hard on her steps. Part of that process is Step Nine."

Diane took advantage of the pause to recite, "Made direct amends to such people whenever possible, except when to do so would injure them or others." She qualified it with a quick add-on. " 'Such people' refers to 'people we had harmed,' from Step Eight."

"Thank you for clarifying that, Diane," Dr. Chalmers said gravely. "You get an A."

She blushed beet red. So much for apple-polishing.

Yep. I was beginning to like this guy.

"Pru, here's your list." He drew a sheaf of scrawled notebook paper from his clipboard and reached across to hand it to her. "Take your time. We've gone over all this. Remember, you are only responsible for your part. No expectations."

Gripping the list in one hand, she shook the bag of bottles with the other. "Definitely the time for some of those red hots."

Was she really afraid we'd reject her?

She settled back to scan the wrinkled pages covered in her large, loopy script, growing tension evident in the way she gripped the edges.

"Slow, easy breaths," Dr. Chalmers coached.

"Okay," Pru said, peering at the words she'd written. "I've got this chronological for each of you. It's everything I can remember. I know there's stuff I forgot. The booze and the drugs do that. Particularly the booze. Blackouts. You honest to God don't remember."

My heart went out to her, stalling, qualifying, summoning up the courage to admit the things she'd done.

She looked up, straight at me.

"Georgia, I'd like to start with you."

17

Changing Colors

Seaside Villas Condominiums, Panama City, Florida. Tuesday,
October 3, 1989.

*I*T WAS THE YEAR OF OUR BIG FOUR-OH. NINETEEN EIGHTY-NINE,
when I decided to dye my hair *I Love Lucy* red and get a job sell-
ing upscale houses to corporate transferees. I picked the execu-
tives up at the airport, rode them through the nicer sections of town,
fed them, showed them at least twenty good possibilities, swung back
by the Varsity, then put them on the plane to Cleveland. It did wonders
for both my bank account and my ego.

No monkey business, just a great distraction from teenagers and
the predictable routines of my marriage.

Since all five of us girls were turning forty that year, we decided to
celebrate with two weeks of sun, fun, seafood, and all the bridge
games our little brains could handle. No kids. No husbands. Just look
out, Panama City Beach, the Mademoiselles are back in town, and the
crab claws are gonna fly.

That was back in the good old days when the rates and the tourist
population plummeted at Labor Day. No half seasons. Just miles of
powder-white beaches, a three-bedroom oceanfront condo for $950 a
month (including utilities), nothing but St. Andrews State Park to the
east of us, no waiting at the restaurants, and everything on sale for half
price in the stores.

As tradition demanded, our first full day (Monday, this year) was
spent on the beach. As usual, we all got just a little too much sun, then

we went to Captain Anderson's for a little too much wine and a lot too much fabulous seafood.

So we didn't really mind it much when the next morning threatened rain. We slept late and lazed around with breakfast on the screened porch overlooking the clouds and waves from a storm out in the Gulf. I suggested we take in a matinee of *Parenthood*, *When Harry Met Sally*, or *The Adventures of Milo and Otis* after lunch, but only Linda voted with me. It was eleven before we were all dressed and reasonably presentable, and Teeny had already called her nanny twice to check on the boys.

Never mind that Bradford and Christian were safely at school and probably hadn't given her a second thought.

"Teens, darlin'," Diane said. "Those boys are big enough to play baseball. Don't you think it's time to cut that umbilical cord?"

"This is the first time I've ever left them for two weeks," Teeny protested sweetly. "I just want to make sure everything goes smoothly with the new nanny."

"New nanny?" That was news to me. "What happened to the old nanny who came last summer? I thought she was perfect." (A jewel in her midthirties who could speak three languages, cook, play soccer, and pitch like a pro.)

Teeny had the decency to squirm. "She is perfect. I just still think of her as the new nanny. I just want to make sure she doesn't have any questions."

Linda aimed a trenchant glance at Teeny. "Teens, we didn't call this a getaway for nothing. We're gonna have to work on detaching, here, babes."

SuSu yawned, scanning the local paper we'd picked up at the resident manager's office. "Great sales. Why don't we go shopping?" She waggled her perfect deep-coral nails. "We could get those guilt gifts out of the way, up front." She tapped Teeny's shoulder. "You can buy something really nice for the boys. Next time, they'll beg you to leave 'em."

Teeny was not amused. Besides our friendship, her life *was* her children. And Christ the King Catholic church and school. And the obligatory charity work expected of the wife of one of the city's leading developers. She stayed so busy looking after everybody else at home, it was probably going to take some time for her to finally let go and relax. If she still remembered how.

Linda shifted the topic to safer ground. "Shopping's good. We could have lunch at that cute little tearoom downtown." She perked up. "Oooo. That mango chicken salad. Yes."

My mouth watered at the thought of another beach favorite. "And those divine little phyllo tapioca pillows with the honey and cinnamon from the Akropol in St. Andrews. We can pick them up on the way back home."

Which was only one of many reasons (including éclairs) why I had reached my fortieth year with nothing but elastic waistbands in my wardrobe.

Diane balked. "Shouldn't we wait to go shopping till we do our colors?" she argued.

Our unofficial social director, she always brought along one or two slightly dorky activities for us to do as a group. This year, she'd rediscovered a book on choosing your colors that had swept the country more than a decade before. "I brought the book and made all the swatches. I promise, it'll be a hoot. We did it at Beanie's last month, and it was great."

"Mmmm." Linda and SuSu and I continued musing through the paper.

Diane didn't give up. "Really, we had a ball. More than twenty people came, and we all chipped in for four cosmetics artists from the salon to redo all our makeup according to our color palettes."

"I'm really looking forward to it," Teeny said with believable enthusiasm. Goodness knew, she needed help with her colors. "But if the others want to shop and do late lunch," she mediated, ever our peacemaker, "couldn't we do our colors tonight?"

The other three of us chimed in with, "Mmmmm." "Yeah." "Tonight."

Diane finally gave up. "Okay, shopping it is. But colors tonight."

I folded up the paper and faced her. "I'm not buying anything for me, anyway," I said, actually uttering those famous last words with a straight face. "Just some stuff for John and the kids."

The others exchanged significant looks that smacked entirely too much of Tradition Two (Makeover) for comfort.

From their expressions, I knew I wouldn't like the answer before I asked the question. "What?"

"I think it's time you got a new bathing suit." Linda never beat around the bush. "When the sun hits the one you had on yesterday, you can pretty much see through the fanny."

I gasped in horror. "Y'all! Why didn't you tell me?"

SuSu waved her hand. "It's not *too* bad, and nobody but us got close enough to notice. We figured we'd clue you in before you wore it again."

Mortified, I snapped, "Well, you should have told me right away."

Linda got up. "Consider yourself told. Now come on. We'll help you pick out a new one."

"As long as it looks reasonably like my old one." I might have something to learn about my colors, but I knew my swimsuits, and the only style that looked decent on me was one with a blouson top and a black, conservatively cut bottom. Attached.

Sulking, I grabbed my purse. "My ego is not up to this. I hate shopping for bathing suits."

"Necessary evil, babes," SuSu told me, snagging her bag. "Let's start up near Long Beach first. Alvins usually has a good selection."

"And Saul's past that," Linda said. "I need some more of those sandals." We all wore them, the upscale leather equivalent of flip-flops—cute and comfortable, in seven colors.

Diane picked up her sensible vinyl Liz Claiborne bag and headed for the door. "I'm just along for the ride." She always said that, but she always bought something.

As designated driver (it's a control thing, not a liquor thing. I *hate* to backtrack) I grabbed the keys to my minivan. "We can work our way to Back Beach Road, then cut over to the bridge," I navigated. "Then we can do the shops in town, have lunch, run over to Gayfer's at the mall, if we have time before the bakery closes in St. Andrews, and be home by the time the sun's over the yardarm."

Ah, for forty. Back then, we could do a day like that standing on our heads.

Teeny held the door open for us, letting a gusty land breeze funnel through the apartment. "Sounds like a plan to me."

Off we went.

When we checked out the beach shops, the others picked up a few gifts at fifty percent off, but I struck out with the suits. Didn't even find any close enough to try on. Everything was too high cut in the legs for my middle-aged Thunder Thighs. So we headed for the local department store in town.

"Definitely an improvement," I said as we walked into the attractive, upscale emporium.

SuSu made a beeline for the designer beachwear—the one display in the store without a discount sign on it. "Ohmygod! Would you look at that adorable cover-up!" She held up the intricate cutwork jacket. "Is this the cutest thing you ever saw? Oooo, and it has matching slacks. Very sexy."

Way too Miami Beach for me, but since SuSu had married Jackson, she'd developed a taste for the obviously extravagant.

"Great cut," Diane ruled, "but that teal color only really works for springs or summers, and you're a true autumn."

"Oh, poo," SuSu dismissed. "Greens are perfect for redheads. And look at the bathing suit." She held up a miniscule one-piece shaped like a deep vee, with only a few strategic bands of Lycra bridging the sides. "It's the exact cut for me."

The suit looked more like something made to fit Teeny at five feet and 90 pounds, than SuSu at five feet eleven and 130. "That thing is tiny. What size is it?"

SuSu checked the label. "An eight. Perfect."

She might be a perfect eight, but that suit sure wasn't. "Eight, my ass," I chortled. "That's probably the recommended age, not the size."

She ignored me completely. "A definite *yes*," she admired aloud.

Diane frowned. "SuSu, there's no support in the bust." Just an extra layer of tricot to *maybe* hide the nipples of SuSu's size Bs if she dared to get into the water. "You'll be able to see straight through it if it ever gets wet."

I picked up a well-known, expensive brand in my size (half price). "Look. This one's no better. It's a conspiracy," I grouched. "Just when we're all starting to sag, they come out with these ridiculous bathing suits that look like they're spray-painted onto every lump and jiggle and hair on your body, except where they mash you flat in the chest or make you look like you're smuggling prunes when you're cold. What is *with* that?"

"The idiot fashion industry," Diane said. "They go for the youngsters because they have the highest percentage of disposable income, but we're the ones who hold the purse strings for America, and we need decent, attractive, washable clothes that work with our forty-something bodies." This, from a woman who still wore gingham one-pieces with boy legs and little belts.

"Tell it, sister," Linda exhorted.

"You ought to design some," I told Diane. "You're so artistic. You'd make a million."

Diane did that "contacts" blink she did. "Oh, no. Too busy bein' a banker's wife." Her voice dropped. "Now that Harold's over a whole branch, there's all kinds of security Lee and I have to observe. No way, could I just launch out into some fashion business."

"Security?" I stopped beside her. "Like what?"

The others gathered close.

Diane shot a quick glance in either direction. "Like making sure bank robbers don't kidnap my child. Or me."

"Ohmygod," SuSu breathed out. "You mean, like they might actually take you hostage? Or Lee?"

"We don't talk about it. Nobody in the industry does, but it's a very real threat. The bank people keep it low key. They don't want to give anybody any ideas." She pulled out a boy-leg suit that had somehow survived the high-cut trend. "That's why I had Mama come up to watch after Lee instead of letting him spend the afternoons with friends while I was down here."

"It doesn't bother you, being boxed in like that, always on guard, always in danger?" Linda asked.

Diane exhaled a brief snort. "Honey, the way I look at it, Lee and I are in about as much danger of being nabbed by a bank robber as we are of having a safe fall on us." She checked the tens again. "*Two* safes. At once."

"But the security?" I said.

"All three of us pay attention to what's going on around us," she said. "That's the best protection."

Ah, for those innocent days when even she could afford to be oblivious.

Diane shrugged. "As far as the rest goes, I have very reasonable expectations for both my life and in my marriage. The three of us rock along just fine. Harold and I don't get in each other's way. I make sure Lee has plenty of fun and friends. I do the corporate wife thing. And I'm almost finished renovating the carriage house. That's rewarding enough for me."

It wouldn't be for me.

John and I were no great love match, but I had immense respect and affection for him, and he was a fabulous father for our kids. I couldn't imagine existing at tangents under the same roof, without anything in common. It sounded so empty and sad.

"Well, bummer." Linda exhaled. "Am I the only one left who's still in love with my husband?"

"Love?" SuSu qualified at the same moment I protested, "No. I love John just fine," and Diane said a flat-footed, "Yes. You are."

Linda shook her head. "You guys are gettin' depressing."

SuSu cocked her mouth in envy. "Drum up a few more like Brooks, and we'll gladly improve."

"Pah!" Linda dismissed with a grin. "None of y'all would give him a second look. He's too short. And too nice."

"I don't want to give anybody a second look," I argued, maybe with myself. "I'm perfectly happy with John."

Teeny chose that moment to arrive from the boys' department with an armful of clothes, most of them tagged at 70 percent off. A few things were from the girls', where she always found great deals for herself. Her developer husband had millions, but he kept her on a really tight financial leash.

She took one look at SuSu's extravagant selections and frowned. "There's no markdown on that rack." Thrifty as ever, she asked, "Did you check the price?"

SuSu looked at the tag and betrayed a brief flash of sticker shock. "Oh, well," she said blithely. "You get what you pay for."

Translate: *way* too much.

She pulled out her well-worn gold card. "I think Jackson wants to buy me another present."

The main advantage (the *only* advantage, as far as I was concerned) to marrying Jackson had been financial security, and SuSu had been making the most of it ever since.

"You're not gonna try it on first?" Linda asked.

SuSu shook her head. "You can't tell anything from the light in dressing rooms. I can always bring it back if it doesn't fit."

"The sign says, 'All sales final,'" Teeny pointed out.

"I'm sure that's just the clearance sale stuff." SuSu shifted the attention to me. "Come on, George. Let's find you that suit."

Subject closed. What can you do?

She did find a suit for me, though, and it was half-priced.

Six hours, one lady lunch, countless shops, a mall, five calls to the nanny, and a bakery later, we rolled back into the Seaside Villas.

After breaking out the wine, we set to work on a giant chef's salad. While Linda and Teeny chopped stuff up on the pass-through bar, SuSu set the table, and Diane and I tried to avoid bumping into each other while she boiled eggs and fried bacon, as I tried to keep up with the mess so we wouldn't have a huge cleanup afterward. (I always clean up as I go. It's so much easier in the long run.)

Diane looked at the empty counter beside the sink. "I know I got that paring knife out."

Oops. I opened the drawer and handed it to her, fresh from being washed and put away.

A few minutes later, she hunted for the potato peeler. "*This* time, I *know* I took it out."

I made a sheepish face.

She placed her fists on her hips. "Would you please quit kidnappin' my utensils," she said in a sassy, staccato rhythm, "and washin' 'em before I can even use 'em?"

The others laughed and flicked cucumber and radish peels all over me.

As soon as the salad was done, we sat under the glare of the dining room's plastic globe chandelier and enjoyed our food and wine to the sound of the surf below. Then, just when everybody was tipsy enough to need to go to bed, Diane stood up and rubbed her hands together. "Okay. Time for our colors."

A general groaning and lolling ensued, but Diane would not be put off, and we had promised.

"Everybody, wash off all your makeup," she directed. "I only brought the swatches for the ideal seasonal matches, so bring as many colors of clothes as you can find to the master bedroom. We need bad examples."

Amid much grumbling and complaining, we did as instructed, but not before Teeny stopped to call the nanny. Again.

When we arrived in the bedroom, our faces stripped, Diane had taken off the lampshades on either side of the bureau mirror and put 250-watt bulbs into the bare lamps.

"Whoa." Talk about bad lighting! "Gross," I complained as I laid my color collection onto the bed. "We all look postsurgical."

SuSu, sporting a fresh *grand vin* of Merlot, winced like a vampire in church. "Gawd. This is cruel and unusual." Without makeup, her eyes all but disappeared.

I noted in shock how many crow's feet she'd been camouflaging.

Not that I was much better. I only had a few crow's feet, but my dark circles made me look like a raccoon, and my skin was so sallow, it bordered on jaundiced.

Teeny, who didn't wear much makeup anyway, just looked a little older and wearier than usual.

Linda looked the most like herself, owing to her naturally ruddy complexion and smooth skin (the only advantage to those extra pounds).

"Here." Diane handed out stretchy headbands. "Put these on and strip down to your bras."

Goodness knows, we'd seen each other plenty in various stages of undress over the years, but the abrupt order caught me sideways. "Did y'all take off your shirts at Beanie's?"

The question conjured a hilarious mental image of supersocial, superproper Beanie perched in her elegant living room on Habersham, asking all her friends to pop their tops.

"Lord, no," Diane blustered.

SuSu laughed. "Wooo, would I love to see *that*."

"The woman who did our colors had little flesh-colored kimonos and makeup remover pads for everybody," Diane explained, ever earnest. "We changed and washed our faces in the powder room."

"And Beanie's guests actually let each other see each other with bare, bald faces?" Teeny asked, aghast.

We knew those women, and they wouldn't be caught dead in major surgery without their faces, much less in public.

"Yep. And they all looked great in the makeovers, except for the ones this one girl *way* overdid it on." Diane unbuttoned her blue oxford-cloth shirt to expose her narrow rib cage and white satin underwire bra.

"Did you get made over, too?" I asked, pulling off my white cotton shell to reveal the only nonunderwire, reasonably attractive style of beige bra I'd been able to find that offered decent support without making me feel like I was wearing a girdle on my chest.

"Yes, they did do me over," she answered, "but their products made me itch, so I washed it all off as soon as I got home."

"Did it look good?" SuSu prodded. She'd told Diane for years that she needed to snazz herself up a bit.

"Too much eye makeup," Diane knee-jerked. "I felt like a skag."

SuSu and I exchanged diabolical smiles. "I'll make you a deal," I said. "We'll do our colors if you'll let us make you over."

"No itching," SuSu hastened. "We'll use all your own stuff. But you've got to promise to go out to dinner with us in the new makeup at least once."

Diane arched an eyebrow. "You already said you'd do the colors. It's not legal to add conditions after the fact."

Linda rolled her eyes. "Spare me from lawyers' wives."

"Oh, come on. How 'bout it? Be a sport," I coaxed.

SuSu nodded. "It's for your own good, Di. Major M.O." She pointed to the mirror. "You're still wearing 'Mary Richards' eyelashes."

"You're gonna make it on your own," I serenaded.

"Y'all," Diane whined.

Linda raised a finger. "I've got an even better idea. How about, in honor of our fortieth birthdays, we make it our mission to buy at least one outfit apiece that fits our color profile and body type, even if we feel weird in it."

No guessing who that one was aimed at, but Teeny didn't seem to pick up on it. Bless her heart, Teeny's clothes and makeup were excellent quality but so drab, she all but disappeared.

"All in favor?" Linda proposed.

It was unanimous.

We'd get hold of Diane's outdated makeup yet, though.

No longer self-conscious about being in our bras, we relaxed to discover our "seasons."

"Ohmygod," SuSu said as she crawled up onto the bed with all the clothes. She pinched her sides. "Would you look at these love handles?"

"Oh, quit complainin'," I fussed, folding mine. "Yours are tiny. Mine are two inches thick."

"Ain't forty fun?" Linda unsuccessfully tried to corral a chunk of her barrel-body. "I can't even pinch mine up anymore. They've turned into a ski belt."

Slender little Teeny remained conspicuously silent, but looked on in sympathy. Meanwhile, Diane turned up the soft-rock station that was playing "We Didn't Start the Fire," by Billy Joel, then finished setting up.

SuSu jiggled her bra straps up and down to the music, bobbling her bosoms like yo-yo's. "My boobs are headin' south at an alarming rate." She watched them with a pensive frown. "Don't y'all think I should have them lifted?" she asked in all seriousness. "I mean, they're really getting bad. Look." She whipped down the straps, letting them out, and sure enough, they were getting longer and looser, but I had no desire to see for myself.

"SuSu! Put those back!" I scolded as the others shrieked and covered their eyes. "We do not need to see the ravages of time on your bust line. Our own are depressing enough."

"Amen to that," the others chorused.

SuSu recaptured her size Bs. "I definitely think I need to get a lift. And maybe just a teeny implant to fill things back out."

"Wait till you finish redecorating the house first," I deflected, hoping she'd forget it in the meantime. Not that it was any of my business, but if she started tinkering with nature at forty, she might well end up looking pulled and oddly rearranged like half the women in Highlands, NC.

"No silicone," Diane cautioned. "That stuff's dangerous." She corralled our attention back to the color setup. "All ready." She took a fortifying sip of Chablis. "Who wants to go first?"

"I will." (I always like to go first.) I plunked into the chair facing the mirror, and Teeny refilled my white Zinfandel.

"Okay," Diane ruled, "with those brown eyes and that red hair, I think you might be an autumn, but since you looked so good as a blonde all those years, I'm not sure." When she pinned back my hair and draped the autumn colors on me, only the rich dark brown, deep orange, and persimmon looked good.

"Eeyew. The off-white's awful," SuSu ruled.

"And the gold is nasty." This, from Linda.

Even Teeny winced at the olive greens.

"Definitely not an autumn." Diane flipped through the book. "But you look so good with the red hair."

Believe it or not, I'd done some modeling on the teen board eons ago and learned a lot of tricks, but none of the others had wanted to take advantage of them. "I compensated for the hair color with different makeup and clothes," I explained. "When I was blond"—from eighth grade till childbirth—"I did the same."

"What *is* your natural color?" Diane asked.

"Beats me," I confessed. "Something dark, with gray in it," I surmised.

The others started trying colors on me left and right, mostly with hoots of derision and comments like, "Bury her quick before she starts to smell!" Invariably, the colors that looked the worst came from my own wardrobe.

"That'll teach you to masquerade as an autumn," SuSu gloated.

Spring and summer were a disaster on me, except for a clear pastel pink. (My favorite color of all time.)

Diane read off the list of color rejects she'd been keeping: "Okay. No lavender, teal, olive, bluish reds, maroon, burgundy, turquoise, navy, camel, dusty pastels, tan, yellow, chartreuse, plain black, gray, or off-white."

She shook her head. "The only thing left is a winter."

"You said Mediterranean types are all winters," I protested, lifting my wineglass for a top-up. "My mama's side is straight fair-haired English stock, and my daddy's people were Welch. I can't be a winter."

"You gotta be something, sweetie." Diane draped a swatch of bright fuchsia across my chest, and there was a collective gasp behind me as the others peered at my reflection.

"Oh, my, god," SuSu said.

I looked in the mirror in amazement. My dark eyes practically jumped off my face. My sallow skin glowed like alabaster. Even my dark circles faded.

"A true winter," Diane said in reverence. She swapped the fuchsia for a clear, emerald green. Same effect.

Then she draped the fuchsia alongside the green. "Is that perfectly preppie, or what?"

The others applauded.

I'd never worn fuchsia in my life, much less at the same time as emerald green, but they looked really good together on me.

She drew out a lively red. "The scarlet works great," she demonstrated, "but not the muddy or bluish reds." Next, she switched to a length of black velvet. "You can do the black, as long as you wear it with pure white around your face." She draped a strip of white lace like a collar.

"Oooo. That's fabulous," Teeny said. "You look like a Spanish princess."

Colors, I was perfectly willing to change. The rest of my life, not.

We went through the palette, discovering that persimmon and royal blue and scarlet and deep, rich, purple all worked magic, as long as I relieved them with a little white. But that fuchsia was the one that surprised me most. "I've never even considered that color," I said, mesmerized, liking it especially with black and white.

"Okay." SuSu took hold of my upper arm and lifted me out of the chair. "Winter, she is. Now it's Linda's turn."

We had a great time with her. Linda turned out to be a winter, too, even though she had pink skin tones. She could wear plain black and look great, and she did better with a little blue in her reds. Some of my colors were terrific, and some weren't. Since her skin tones were rosier, she couldn't do the orangey shades at all, but she could tolerate some dusty pastels.

Navy blue (one of her staples) was banished, but she could wear grays with white. Clear pink looked good on her, too.

By the time we were done with her, we were all slaphappy and snockered, munching through a giant bag of Ghirardelli's Snack Mix like there was no tomorrow and getting hilarious over the slightest things. I'm telling you, a jug or two of decent wine can do wonders to soften resistance to new ideas.

In one of the lulls, I spoke as the thought hit me: "I wonder what season Pru would be?"

"Pru?" SuSu challenged. "Where in the world did *that* come from?"

"Dunno," I confessed, my lips already growing numb from the wine. "Just popped up. *Poing.*"

Diane gestured with her glass, sloshing her Chablis dangerously close to the lip. "I bet she'd be a summer."

"Who knows?" Linda sighed, then turned to SuSu. "Let's find out what SuSu is, so we can get to Teeny before I have to go to bed."

SuSu was a genuine autumn (duh!). Persimmon, rich browns, rusts, golds, livelier olives, and clearer greens looked great on her. She had to steer away from yellowy oranges and especially teals, which let out the expensive new outfit she'd bought.

It was almost midnight by the time we got to Teeny. In deference to her sensitive nature, I tried to break it to her gently as she draped her collection of drab miniprints across her chest. I heard myself slur, "Honey, I hate to tell you, but you look like the wallpaper in every one of those." It never occurred to me that she might have been compelled subconsciously to disappear in the jungle that was her marriage. "Gone. Disappeared. Pure camouflage."

So much for diplomacy.

The others pelted me with pillows and snack mix which, I was relieved to see, made Teeny laugh. As she progressed to definite color clashes, she started loosening up in earnest.

But the color of all colors for her was a clear, sunny red.

"You look better than Nancy Reagan in that color," I told her.

"I'd never have the nerve to wear it," Teeny said, clearly wishing she could.

"Sure you can. Tell you what: I'll wear fuchsia to church when we get back, if you'll wear red." Since I went to First Baptist and she went to Christ the King, we wouldn't have to worry about clashing. I stuck out my hand to shake. "Deal?"

Teeny laughed. "Oh, what the hell. Deal."

Diane got us back on track. "Teens, I really think you're a summer, but nobody's all one thing," she explained. "You've got to try everything to see what works." She brought out the "summer" swatches. "Summers are the rarest of all," she said. "Most of them are ash blondes with blue or hazel eyes, but they're not ruddy or sallow. They do better in dusty colors than clear pastels. Jade. Seafoam. Taupe. Taupe is great on summers." She draped a dusty rose across Teeny, then a soft teal. Both brought her skin to life and made her blue eyes sparkle.

We stomped and whistled, neighbors be darned.

Diane nodded. "And solid blocks of color, matching ensembles, are going to work best with your small stature, not overall prints." She held up the taupe, then paired it with soft pink. "A pink blouse or scarf with this taupe would be all the variation you need."

Teeny played with the swatches, amazed at the transformation they made. "I am going to do this," she said with tipsy deliberation. "I am going to make some clothes in these colors, matching ensembles, like you said." Teeny was an expert seamstress. She brightened. "Who knows? Maybe Reid will even notice."

It ripped me right out of the frame that she still cared what that philandering, besotted, crook of a husband thought of her. I knew the others were thinking it, too.

"Hey, wait a minute," SuSu diverted. She turned to Diane. "We haven't done you."

Diane waved her hand, yawning. "They did me at Beanie's. I'm a winter."

"Okay, then." SuSu rubbed her hands together. "Time for the makeup makeovers. Come on, Diane. You first."

It was after midnight, so serious protests erupted.

Linda giggled, "Honey, I'm so tipsy, I'd put your eye out if I got within a mile of your cornea with a liner or mascara."

I stood, then swayed. "Woooo. Bedtime for this girl."

The others started gathering their clothes and breaking up like a herd of turtles.

"Y'all, the night is young," SuSu argued. "Don't poop out on me." She brightened. "I know. We can play some bridge."

Now, I dearly love bridge. But one nice thing about being forty: I went to bed when I was ready, even if I had to pass up a bridge game to do it. "Cain't do it, sweetie," I said, dissolving into a yawn.

Diane threw in the towel, too. "Y'all can do my makeup over before dinner tomorrow night. I promise."

"Us, too." Teeny headed for the little bedroom in the middle, and Linda cleared off her spread in the master.

"You know," I said as SuSu and I carried our clothes back into our room. "It's pretty sad when you look forward more to going to bed alone than you do with your husband."

"Speak for yourself, honey." She dumped her clothes on the floor. "That's the one thing that really works with Jackson. Besides the checkbooks."

Not an image I wanted to conjure.

Yuk. I brushed my teeth twice.

And I vowed not to ask any more disturbing questions about my marriage, or anybody else's.

We had almost two more weeks left for makeovers, tanning, playing bridge, seeing movies, and shopping.

As it turned out, we did all that and more: rented jet skis, swam with the dolphins, took a sunset cruise, and parasailed (all but Linda, who didn't trust the harness).

We didn't even notice that for all of us but Linda, our fortieth year had marked a sad and silent passage from believing in true love, to accepting life without it.

We might have brightened up our wardrobes, but our secret souls were bleached of dreams, a bland and sturdy beige.

Mirror, Mirror on the Wall

East Winds Rehabilitation Center, near Ashville, North Carolina.
August 19, 2003. 1:30 P.M.

BRACING MYSELF, I LOOKED UP AT THE NINTH STEP ON THE POSTER hanging behind Pru's rehabilitation therapist. *Made direct amends to people I had harmed, except when to do so would injure them or others.*

I should have found that reassuring—it promised that Pru wasn't supposed to bring up anything that might cause harm to any of us—but I didn't. True confessions make for dangerous territory.

I could see that the others were just as edgy as I was. Especially SuSu. She popped up and started moving restlessly from point to point in the room.

"Before Pru starts with her ninth step," Dr. Chalmers said in a slow, deliberate cadence, "I'd like to give you an idea of our objectives for this session. First, I want you all to know that you're off the hook, so you can relax. When Pru raises an issue, you are not required to respond, but if you want to, feel free. Please just do it within the common rules of courtesy. Careful listening is great, but interrupting causes tension and throws things off track. For best results, it's most effective to stay focused and allow each person to finish her thought."

Linda shook her head. "Doc, we've been interrupting each other for thirty years, but for Pru's sake, we'll give it a stab."

"I appreciate that." He went on. "But please bear in mind, this process is never easy for an addict. Pru has worked hard searching her past to take responsibility for the negative things she's done. Sharing her list with you is part of getting beyond those shortcomings so she can focus on the present and work her recovery."

"Like cutting loose Marley's chains in *A Christmas Carol*," I said.

"Precisely." He granted Pru an encouraging smile.

"What about Sacred Tradition Eight?" SuSu's tone bordered on belligerent.

The psychiatrist frowned in question.

Pru recited without hesitations, "No beating ourselves or each other up when we blow it."

I was amazed she remembered.

"This has nothing to do with beating myself up," Pru explained to SuSu. "It's just the opposite. It's admitting my faults, doing my best to make up for them, and finally letting go of old sins so I can focus on the present."

Sounded good to me. "Okay. Let 'er rip."

Pru scanned the top page of her notes. "Okay. I tried to do these in order for each of you." She looked at me. "Georgia, in Home Ec, I swiped your team's milk after I spilled mine."

"Forgiven." I didn't even remember it. "No amends needed."

She shook her head. "It mattered to me, so please don't discount it that way."

Whoa! Rehab really had made a difference. Pru had never been confrontational before. At least, not when she was clean and sober.

Smarting, I said, "Sorry."

"That's okay." She smiled in irony. "I forgive you. But I know it mattered to you, whether you remember it or not. It was the only F you ever made. Ever. And I was responsible."

I'd forgotten about that. "That teacher was a total bitch about the ingredients. Wouldn't give me any more milk, and when I offered to pay for some, she gave me an F, on the spot. 'For insolence,' she said."

Funny, what you forget, till something resurrects it. I tingled with a distant twinge of the perverse pride and horror I'd felt watching that teacher mark a fat, red F in her grade book next to all the A's by my name. "I still made a B for the course." I looked to Pru. "Everybody ought to make at least one F sometime. As I said, you are fully and wholly forgiven."

Pru remained serious. "The amends I make are as much for me as for y'all. And my amends for that is, every time I buy milk, I'll remember to admit when I make a mistake instead of trying to cover it up, especially at somebody else's expense."

I should do so well. "Sounds good."

She read again. "In tenth grade, I copied your answers in the American History exam."

"I know," I said in all seriousness. "I sat catty whompus so you could see."

SuSu's mouth dropped open. "You? Miss Goody Two-shoes Honor Council member? I was terrified I'd get brought up before you."

I shrugged. "If Pru hadn't passed, they'd have held her back, and she wouldn't have been able to graduate with us." Those were the years before social promotions. Unrepentant, I looked to Pru. "So, what's the amends for that one?"

Her mouth flattened in resignation. "No cheating on my taxes. Not even a little."

The rest of us winced, conscience-stricken, except Teeny.

"Eeeyew," Diane said. "Don't you think that's a bit extreme?"

"Diane!" Teeny turned to her in genuine indignation.

"Oh, down girl," Linda said. "Everybody fudges a little."

"Not me," Teeny huffed.

Pru got back to business. "The next one's a biggie." She took a deep breath, her expression sober. "When Tyson and I hired you to work in our shop back in seventy-three, we were importing more than decorative items and teapots. We were bringing in cocaine and marijuana. Half the time, it was right in the little stockroom behind the register." Her pale blue eyes swam with shame. "I loved you, yet I exposed you to possible prosecution. You could have been arrested right along with us."

A truly daunting prospect. "I forgive you," I said without hesitation, something I might not have been able to do if I *had* been arrested.

She sighed. "I knew you would, but it sure is nice to hear."

"What I *don't* forgive you for," I said in an effort to lighten things up, "is that honkin' huge *tarantula* that crawled out of the stockroom and pinned me in the corner that time I was at the shop all by myself."

Did I mention I'm phobic about spiders? Even the teensy ones.

Diane shuddered, even more phobic than I am. "Whoa."

Linda stared at me in awe. "Why haven't I heard about this?"

"You and Brooks were in residency," Diane said.

"Oh, gosh." Pru laughed. "I'd completely forgotten about that."

"I turned around and saw that huge thing crawlin' out of the stock-room"—my fingers unconsciously mimicked the slow, creeping gait—"and vaulted right slap over the register, cash drawer be damned."

"Ha!" Diane pointed to me. "So Vegas wasn't the first time you—" Seeing the look of horror on Teeny's and Linda's and my faces, she caught herself just in time and shifted to a feeble, "jumped ten feet when you saw a spider."

Talk about close calls. She'd almost mentioned the infamous jackpot in front of SuSu. The three of us glared at her in wide-eyed rebuke.

The doctor picked up on the silent exchange but didn't pursue it. "So," he said, "what happened about the tarantula?"

I covered for my thumping adrenaline with a mommy smile. "I got the little guy from the pants shop next door to go after the hairy beast with a broom, but he got a gander at the thing and came right back out for reinforcements."

Pru laughed again. "He went hunting for something to kill it with, and ended up with half the merchant's association looking on while he dispatched it with a nine iron from the golf shop. When Tyson and I got back, they were all standing around the carcass beatin' their chests like cavemen."

Realizing he'd lost complete control of the session, Dr. Chalmers smoothed the front of his shirt and corralled us with, "Well, I'm glad that worked out. Now, if we could get back to Pru's list . . ."

"So," I asked her, "what kind of amends do I get for the tarantula?"

"Just a sincere 'I'm sorry,'" Pru said, "because it certainly wasn't anything I had any control over. But for the drugs, a vow that just for today, I will not allow my addiction to endanger the health or reputation of anyone else."

"Good one," I told her.

The next few infractions were minor ones from the era before she and Tyson were busted for wholesaling cocaine. Then she got to the one that still stuck in my craw.

Pru took a leveling breath. "After we were arrested, you tried to help me. I took the grocery money you gave me and used it for booze and drugs, instead of food for my child." She shivered.

"I knew." I had judged her for that more than anything. "So I started giving the money to your mama."

Pru's eyes widened. "I didn't know you did that."

I felt renewed gratitude that those times were so far behind us. "You weren't supposed to."

She peered at me in amazement—me, the blabbermouth of the group, who had managed to keep that secret. "How long did that go on?"

Years. "Till you moved to Oregon with Bubba without leaving a forwarding address."

I hadn't been the only one helping Mrs. Bonner. She'd hinted that the others had been, too.

Pru struggled to maintain her composure. "You knew I'd spent your money on drugs, but you're here." She looked to us. "All of you. You came to Vegas to get me, and took time to do this." Quiet tears overflowed. "Why?"

"Friendship," Linda averred.

"Grace," said Teeny.

"Personally, I've always wondered what it would be like to kidnap somebody," I quipped. "Not to mention getting to see what rehab's like from the inside without having to be the patient."

Pru wiped away her tears, shaking her head. "Trust me, this rehab is like no rehab I've ever seen, and I've seen plenty. Usually it's metal chairs, concrete block, and cracked linoleum."

SuSu got up to pace again, putting distance between herself and the process we were undergoing.

It was probably the longest she'd been without a cigarette in thirty years. Diane followed my gaze to SuSu with narrowed eyes.

Dr. Chalmers wasn't missing a trick. "Pru," he said, "would you like to continue this session as a ninth-step exercise, or shift to group discussion about the relationships represented in this room?"

Pru zeroed in on SuSu with a fatalistic, knowing smile. "Are you kiddin'? I want to get this step done and over with. Not to mention the fact that it's not exactly polite to keep draggin' these poor women up here."

She cocked her head at me. "For this amends, I need your help. What do you think would help make up for me spending the money you gave me for drugs?"

"Hmmmm." I thought hard, eyes narrowing as I eliminated the obvious as too predictable and too serious. Then it came to me. "I know! But it's a hard one."

Pru nodded. "Your word is my command."

"Okay, here goes then." I did my best to look grim. "I want you to call me every single week and talk to me about what's up in your life. The real stuff, not the fluff. And messages don't count."

Dr. Chalmers's smile widened in obvious approval.

Pru frowned. "Why that?"

"Because I don't know you anymore," I said, "but I'd like to. For old times' sake."

Pru regarded me with assessment. "So let it be written," she quoted, imitating Yul Brenner's voice from an old movie we'd watched together many times in happier days. "So let it be done."

Then she got back to business. One by one, she addressed her past sins and negotiated amends with Linda, Diane, and Teeny. Most of her transgressions we'd long since known and let go, but I realized that Pru needed to banish them from her own troubled conscience. By the time she got down to SuSu, the last, Pru had promised by way of amends to have dinner with Linda once every two weeks, to watch at least one funny movie a month with Diane, and to go with us on the next Red Hat junket Teeny planned.

Shadows had lengthened across the lawn by the time Pru turned to SuSu. "SuSu, I have only one amends to make to you, but it's the most difficult of all." She took a breath, then exhaled heavily. "Do you remember your grandmother's cameo, the one of Apollo?"

SuSu froze. She'd adored that cameo, her sole legacy from her beloved country grandmother. Some things stand for a lot, and that pin—rare, elegant, and valuable—had been SuSu's talisman against the struggles and embarrassments of her family. It had disappeared when we were on our last weekend outing as a group, when we'd dragged our husbands and babies up to Gatlinburg—just before Pru and Tyson were busted for wholesaling cocaine.

The rest of us held our breaths, praying that Pru wasn't about to say what she did.

SuSu's eyes narrowed, her forearms interlocking. "You know I remember it. It was the one truly fine thing in my life, something from my family I could be proud of."

Packing up all those years ago, SuSu had been frantic when she realized the cameo was gone. She'd called the police in tears, demanding an immediate investigation, then sent us all to retrace our steps through town, searching, while she ransacked the motel room, wailing that she never should have brought it along, but she'd been afraid to leave it unattended back in Beaufort.

Seeing her anguish when we'd finally realized it was really gone, I had vowed never to own anything that could hurt me so terribly to lose. From then on, I'd searched for her precious pin every time I saw a cameo at a jeweler's, flea market, estate sale, or antique jewelry show.

Watching SuSu there in the library with Pru, I saw that same anguish gathered like razor blades behind SuSu's expression.

Pru met SuSu's guarded stare with a mixture of shame and dignity. "Tyson stole it that last day we were all in Gatlinburg. We were tapped out from the vacation, and he needed a fix."

SuSu's face reddened with anger and disbelief. "And you just sat there and let me go crazy, knowing he had it?" The razor blades tore free, launched through the look of hate she aimed at Pru. "How could you? That's beyond cruel. Beyond sick."

"I wasn't sure till we got home, and then it was too late," Pru said, miserable. "It's no excuse. There is no excuse. The truth is, I knew he'd done it, but I didn't ask him sooner because I wouldn't have known what to do if he admitted it. I take full responsibility for that, and I ask your forgiveness. But Tyson was the father of my child, and crazy as it seems now, I loved him very much. I was terrified he might get sent to jail. I didn't know what would happen to me and Bubba if he went to jail."

"Well," SuSu lashed out, "you ended up finding out soon enough, didn't you?"

We watched in suspended animation as the fabric of their long-ago friendship shredded before our eyes, perhaps irreparably.

Pru started to shake, and Dr. Chalmers laid a steadying hand on her arm. "SuSu is entitled to her anger. Try to stay focused and detach with love."

SuSu turned on him. "Oh, can the psychobabble crap! I'm sick and tired of how everybody's suddenly had to turn themselves inside out to accommodate Pru. And now, suddenly, she's supposed to be all noble just because she's managed to stay sober for a few weeks in this glorified prison." She pointed to the Twelve Steps poster. "I thought you weren't supposed to cause harm to anybody. What about that? How did you expect I'd feel when you told me such a thing?" She marshaled the rage and disappointments that had been simmering inside her and lobbed them into, "Recovery, my ass. I hate you for this."

Pru's blue eyes welled as she reached into her pocket. "I only told you because, thanks to Teeny's help, we found it." She drew a small, flat velvet box from her pocket.

Ignoring the box, SuSu wheeled on Teeny. "You knew about this, and kept it from me?"

Pru opened the box, tears flowing down her cheeks. "You don't have to forgive me, but please take it. It meant so much to you. I want you to have it."

SuSu snatched it, her knuckles white as they closed over the long-lost treasure. "I do not forgive you."

She aimed an accusing finger at us. "And I won't forgive y'all, either, if you choose her over me."

"SuSu, nobody said anything about choosing," Teeny hastened. "We love you. You know that."

"I know you used to, till the black sheep, here, decided to come back for another shot at us. Well, you can count me out." She stomped toward the lobby. "I'm leaving." She tried to slam the door, but it was pneumatic, which just made her madder.

We sat in wide-eyed silence for several seconds before Dr. Chalmers said quietly, "People often need time to come to terms with such strong feelings." He bounced a brief look in the direction of SuSu's retreat. "Pru, what you did took great courage, and you handled things very well. You let SuSu vent her feelings without getting hooked into a confrontation. I'm really proud of you all, but I don't think it would be productive to continue under the circumstances. Let's give SuSu some time and space to sort herself out. Maybe by the next session, she'll be willing to come back and seek resolution."

The four of us exchanged skeptical glances.

We all rose, gathering our things, then hugged Pru.

"Don't worry, honey, she'll come around," Teeny assured.

"She always does," I said. "She's always popping off."

"She's right," Diane said. "This will blow over."

"What if it doesn't?" Pru asked softly.

Unthinkable.

Linda hoisted her purse straps to her shoulder. "Honey, we've survived a lost worse than this and kept on chugging. It'll all work out. It always does."

Teeny said she had a surprise for all of us as soon as Pru completed her transition back into the big, bad world (which Dr. Chalmers had told us privately should be about another seven months). But Teens refused to give us any hints about the trip beyond the fact that we'd need to pack for a month.

That helped lighten the mood considerably. Yet as we pestered her for details, I couldn't help worrying that we might have witnessed the beginning of a rift that could threaten our group as nothing else ever had.

If SuSu tried to make us take sides, we were all in deep trouble, and I wondered if the Red Hats would ever be the same.

solemn vow from Abby never to get a tattoo or become a Muslim. When Linda's hair grew back in, it was snow white and baby fine, but she hadn't lost a pound, which thrilled the doctors but royally ticked her off.

Diane went to Cancun with Clay and had a ball. (Pun intended.) We chipped in for condoms, which she accepted without comment and almost certainly didn't need. Then she came home and dived into designing a line of inexpensive, flattering, cotton clothes and accessories for cancer patients. Initial response for the niche market was phenomenal. Meanwhile, she cranked up a long-distance courtship with Clay that involved lots of late after-the-rates-drop phone calls, and fairly frequent weekend excursions into each other's turf, but no signs of further commitment. When pressed for a prognosis, Diane said, "Why mess up a good thing? Now leave me alone." So we did.

I stayed busy with church and the kids, helping Callie decorate her new apartment at school. And getting frisky with John, of course, but that doesn't bear discussing. Pru called every week, as promised, and we rediscovered each other in a comfortable, unpressured way.

SuSu pouted around after her blowup and refused to go back to rehab with us, but we just ignored her sulking and went anyway. Eventually, she slacked off, but we all knew something had to give when Pru finished her transition and came back to town. Once law school started back up, SuSu dived into her second year with such a vengeance that we scarcely heard a peep out of her except for our monthly luncheons, at which, I am proud to say, she switched from wine to iced tea, claiming it helped keep her from getting drowsy in class. Whatever the reason, I was glad to see it, but frankly, I still missed her irresponsible, promiscuous, fun-loving old self. Without her, we were all getting pretty boring, SuSu included. She got asked to interview with some really prestigious practices for her summer associate's position after the school year. She didn't even look at out-of-town firms, but had her heart set on Sutherland, Asbill, and Brennan, a top local firm.

Teeny passed the months doting on her grandchildren, quietly supervising her excellent retinue of managers and financial advisers, going to the symphony and Tech football games with a carefully vetted selection of eligible men, and taking junkets to her condo on Sanibel with anybody who wanted to go.

19

Fa La La La La,
La La La La

I LOVE WHAT SOME MIDDLE-AGED COMEDIENNE (WHOSE NAME I can't remember, of course) said about what happens to time as you age:

"When you're a little kid," she said, "there's just *now* and all those other, meaningless designations. Even 'in a minute' seems endless. A week might as well be a lifetime.

"Then you go to school, and the time between Labor Day and Christmas just crawls by, but Christmas vacation flies. Then January to June takes at least a decade, but summer vacation only seems like a few weeks.

"By the time you get to our age, though," she said with a sigh, "it's just birthday-birthday-birthday-birthday!"

All that to say, late summer and fall passed by without incident. Pru made really good progress, part of which Dr. Chalmers attributed to our healthy support (minus SuSu) and renewed relationships. We only went back twice for sessions before he told us he was hoping Pru would be ready for the halfway house in January. If everything went well there, she could be out by March, something we all anticipated and feared in equal measure.

Thanks to chemo, Linda dive-bombed through menopause without major complications (nothing like cancer to give you a sense of perspective about hot flashes and vaginal thinning). Then she finished her treatments with flying colors and rock-bottom cancer markers, but not before she took advantage of the seriousness of her illness to extract a

And the next thing you knew, Christmas and Hanukkah were upon us.

Swan Coach House. Tuesday, December 16, 2003. 11:15 A.M.
Georgia is known for its crisp, sunny winter days, but at Christmastime, I almost prefer cold, rainy ones to set off the warmth indoors and make the decorations seem at home. The Coach House was no exception. When we gathered at our corner banquette—a week later than usual so SuSu would be out for Christmas break—a cold drizzle had fogged the windows, and the smell of cranberry muffins and hot coffee permeated the air with a festive, spicy note. We all got there on time, which was a miracle, considering the fact that whenever it rains, regardless of the season, half the people in town completely forget how to drive, hopelessly snarling the roads.

Maria made us our special hot lemonade, and for once, I ordered the hot entrée du jour.

"So." Last to arrive, Linda plunked down in her tea-cozy red hat and old faithful purple sweater. "Is everybody done with their shopping?"

We'd all made a vow that we would be finished before the luncheon so we could concentrate on our families and the religious reasons for the season.

"Just a few stocking stuffers left for me." I still did them for the whole family, boyfriends and girlfriends included.

"I'm picking up Clay's overcoat on the way home, then heading for his house till New Year's," Diane told us, her dark hair tucked back onto a gorgeous red-dyed fur pillbox that set off her tailored (washable!) red suit and dark purple satin blouse.

"Ah-hah." I twiddled an imaginary mustache. "Does this mean you're 'meeting the family'?"

"It means," she said, still brooking no speculation, "that I'm going to stay at the inn, go to some parties, go dancing, eat Christmas dinner with his kids, and have some good clean fun. Period." She shifted the focus to SuSu, who had on a red wool fedora. The rest of her outfit was classic black that almost, but not quite, disguised the fact that she'd put on a few pounds. "How about your shopping?"

SuSu waved her hand in weary dismissal. "Done, such as it is."

You have to hit me in the head with a two-by-four to get my attention, but it occurred to me that she looked awfully tired. "Are you feeling okay, Suse?"

"I just need to catch up on my sleep," she deferred. "This set of exams is a bitch. But I've got good news. Sutherland, Asbill, and Brennan offered me the position for next summer." She hardly had the energy to muster up any enthusiasm.

"That's fabulous," Linda said. Seeing SuSu's lethargy, though, she faltered. "It's what you wanted, isn't it?"

"Absolutely. Like I said, I'm just bushed."

Come to think of it, she'd been awfully pensive lately. Her daughter and son-in-law had come down for Thanksgiving, but the in-laws had them for Christmas, so all of us had invited SuSu to our houses for the holiday.

"You're sure you won't come spend Christmas Eve night with us," I repeated for the third time in as many weeks. "We've got plenty of room, and Callie and Jack would love to see you."

"You're welcome at my place, too," Teeny chimed in. "The grands will all be there, so we'll have loads of fun."

SuSu shook her head, her expression distant but hardly bereft. "For the tenth time, I am looking forward to holing up in my apartment, cooking all my favorite foods, and not getting anywhere near a book for at least a week."

"Lucky you," Linda said. "I get to spend a week in my mother-in-law's two-bedroom condo in Miami, along with everything she ever owned in her life."

"Are Abby and Osama coming down?" Diane asked with a wicked smile.

"Lord, I wish they would." Linda placed her palms together in supplication. "If that doesn't finish the old battle-ax off, nothing will."

Prompted by decades of December luncheon ritual, we all dived into our waiting shopping bags and distributed the gifts we'd bought each other. We'd set a fifty-dollar maximum, but the prize—a decorated, red-foil Christmas tree hat with a Star of David on top (our addition), from Spencer's, circa 1978—went to the best gift for the least money.

The year before, SuSu had won hands down for finding a size 16 full-length mink coat for forty dollars at the estate sale of a male transvestite, whose surviving sister was a devoted PETA member. I am not makin' this up. A pair of scissors and some Super Bond 6000 (sticks anything to anything) later, SuSu presented Linda with a stunning coat at just the right length, plus a luscious muffler. Hand to God.

For this year, I'd recorded double CD's for everybody with all their favorite old songs from high school and college, duly noted in my diaries from way back when. (I like anthologies. My attention span's way too short for whole albums by anybody.)

The collections went over great, but Linda promptly knocked me out of the running. Seems she'd been taking art lessons on the sly and painted each of us a small but wonderful watercolor of our favorite flowers: bright zinnias for me, pink camellias for Teeny, delphiniums for SuSu, and salmon geraniums for Diane.

Impressed and amazed by her instant mastery of such a difficult medium, we praised her profusely.

"I had a great teacher," she deflected, basking in our praise. "I always wanted to learn watercolors, and things being the way they were, I figured there's no time like the present." She beamed. "I sent Pru a gardenia."

Diane had plundered the markets of Hong Kong on her last buying trip and brought back amazing embroidered robes for each of us in our favorite colors.

They looked so elegant, I was afraid to touch the supple fabric. "Silk?" I asked.

"Gracious, no," Diane said. "They wouldn't last past the first piece of bacon. Those babies are polyester. We're introducing them for forty-nine ninety-nine next Christmas, but y'all get them a year early."

No minks this year, but SuSu gave each of us a lifetime certificate for unlimited free domestic legal work, then wished aloud that none of us would ever need it.

Last, but not least, came Teeny. "Okay, everybody. Nothing to unwrap from me, but get out your calendars."

We dutifully obliged. Linda had already given us our new pocket-sized, twenty-eight-month calendars as she had every September since 1967, so everybody had a two-year window on the future.

"When's your spring break?" Teeny asked SuSu.

"Mid-March," SuSu answered. "I'll have to check on the dates. Why?"

Teeny scanned us. "Does anybody have anything scheduled for March?"

None of us did.

"Great. Please mark out the entire month and save it for us."

"A month?" we blurted out, almost in unison. "For what?"

Teeny's answer was far from satisfying. "A really special trip for us and Pru. Mostly for Pru."

SuSu bristled. "I can't possibly leave school for a whole month."

"Let me worry about that." Teeny remained unruffled. "I have connections. You'll get your lecture notes and handouts on line."

SuSu started to sulk, but Teeny remained calm and cheerful. "I promise, it won't set you back in your studies."

SuSu had been dead-set on keeping a four-oh average from the first day of school September before last. "Couldn't we cut it down to a week?" she grumbled.

Teeny frowned. "It's a package deal. Very exclusive. And once you find out what it's about, you'll see why."

A month, and she wasn't going to tell us where? John was *not* going to like this. Especially after our reckless rescue mission to Vegas. "Teens," I told her, "I love surprises as much as the next person, and God knows, I love the way you throw your money around on us, but John's gonna have to know where we're going. He's still smarting from Vegas." Even a man as laid-back as my absentminded professor had his limits. "He thinks you're a bad influence."

Teeny's laugh was clear and pure as birdsong. "My. I'm flattered."

"No kiddin'," Diane put in. "Four weeks is a mighty big chunk of time to be away from work."

"Or away from Brooks," Linda said. "Since I got sick, I can hardly get him to go play tennis, much less a game of golf. A month . . ."

Teeny raised her palms in surrender. "Okay. I'd planned to wait till two weeks before, but y'all have a point." She paused for dramatic effect while we awaited the big revelation. "It's a four-week plastic-surgery cruise. We'd leave on Saturday, February twenty-eighth, and come back four weeks later all healed up and looking ten years younger, with nobody the wiser."

The possibilities were boggling.

"Pru could really use some help with her looks," Teeny explained, "but I didn't want to single her out, so I thought we could do our own 'Extreme Makeover' orgy. Carte blanche, whatever you want."

"Ohmygod." The light of the universe shone from SuSu's green, near-sighted eyes. "That's the greatest idea I've ever heard of in my life. How did you find out about it?"

"It's very hush-hush," Teeny said. "Strictly word of mouth. Lots of celebrities use this ship." She reached into her purse for an understated brochure with photos of a sleek, midsized liner and roomy, elegantly appointed staterooms. "None of those Chinese-looking, assembly-line face-lifts. These doctors are masters, most of them Swiss, and the ship's a fully equipped hospital with its own medevac helicopter, in case of complications."

I grabbed the not-so-little paunch below my waistline (a trait I shared with my sisters that we'd dubbed 'the baby') and sang a chorus of "Bye, baby, bye-bye." Eyeing my sagging bust line, I mused aloud, "Do you think they could transplant some of this to my chest?"

"Absolutely," Teeny said.

We crowded over the brochure.

"They do everything," Teeny said with glee. "Lifts, lipo, peels, implants, porcelain veneers, German hormone treatments, laser eye surgery and hair removal, micro-dermabrasion, vein reductions, electrolysis, wardrobe and makeup consultation, the works."

Diane whipped out her purse mirror and scrutinized her chin, lip, and eyebrows. "No more plucking for me. I'm gonna have 'em zap every whisker from my hairline to my collarbone." She peered closer. "And micro-dermabrasion." She bared her teeth. "And bonding to close up all those nasty little gaps."

Linda patted her double chin. "After all that torture I went through just to stay alive, it'll be pretty nice to have something constructive to show for my pain. As long as my doctors okay it."

"Even if you don't want to have a procedure," Teeny told her, "they have personal trainers and physical therapists. Plus a full spa."

"Oh, I definitely want a procedure," Linda hastened. "Or two. Or five."

"You don't have to decide right away. Take your time." Teeny looked from Linda to me. "It is surgery, though."

She knew us well enough to know we'd talk it over with our husbands—not because we needed permission, but because we loved them and valued their counsel. Unless John didn't like the idea, in which case I'd probably have to overrule him.

"Brooks won't know what to do with me if I only have one chin," Linda said.

Diane chortled. "I'm not talkin' this over with anybody. Especially Clay. It's none of his business." She grinned. "I just love bein' single."

Teeny sipped her hot lemonade. "So y'all want to do it?"

We hooted our assent as SuSu crowed, "Does Miss Piggy want Kermit?"

If Teeny's gift hadn't gone galactically over the limit, we would have voted her permanent recipient of the Christmas Tree Award for that one. As it was, we gave it to Linda for our wonderful paintings, but she had to put it on over her rosebud cap, because it scratched her tender scalp.

Then she took it right off. The wearing of the tree was merely a brief, ceremonial degradation.

"So," I asked her. "What do you want for Hanukkah this year?"

"At least twenty more Hanukkahs," she said with a wistful sigh.

I raised my glass, and the others lifted theirs. "Here's to at least thirty more Hanukkahs for Linda."

"And for us all," Teeny added.

"Hear, hear."

Being together with those we loved, marking the years. It was the greatest nonspiritual gift we could ask for.

Not that I wasn't happy about the plastic surgery cruise.

I couldn't wait to tell John what I wanted done. The only question was, where to stop?

20

Spring

Fort Lauderdale, Florida. Saturday, February 28, 2004. Noon.

SUSU HAD SULKED ALL THE WAY FROM ATLANTA, BUT THE REST OF us had only acknowledged her when she was civil, so she'd eased up a bit. Still, she avoided direct conversation with Pru.

"Good grief," I said as we pulled into a long queue of limos at the far end of the pier. "Every limousine in Fort Lauderdale must be here."

Teeny nodded. "Confidentiality. Nobody wants to come in their own cars. License plates," she said in that muted tone she reserved for mentioning the unmentionable, which with Teeny was usually something minor.

Usually.

The line of stretch Mercedes, SUVs, Caddies, and Rolls Royces ended beyond all the cruise line behemoths at a sleek, white ship less than half their size. The name *Narcissus* marched across her stern in tasteful, scripted blue letters that matched the twin bands on the stacks.

Narcissus, the personification of heartless beauty from Greek mythology who fell in love with his own reflection. *Too* rich.

"Is that it?" Eyes sparkling with excitement, Pru pointed to our ship. "It's not very big."

"It only carries two hundred passengers," Teeny said, "but twice as many staff and crew."

Besides the name, the only marking on the pristine white ship was a white dove in the sky-blue band around the main stack.

Pru all but plastered her face on the glass. "Ooooo, but look at all those balconies."

"Dibs," SuSu said.

"They all have balconies," Teeny reminded us.

Pru bounced in her seat. "Cool."

It did us all good to see her so happily distracted. She'd finished her rehab with flying colors, yet there was always the specter of her addiction hovering just below the surface. But since Dr. Chalmers had cleared the cruise and let Teeny tell her, Pru had bloomed like a big, beautiful peony.

It was contagious. I hadn't felt this excited (or scared) since who knows when. I couldn't help wondering if the bubbly, slightly dangerous sensation was another of the things that age was bleeding out of us, along with our collagen, hormones, and stamina. But then, I'm always overanalyzing everything.

Chicken Little had been going nuts since I'd decided to get nipped, tucked, and sucked, but I'd countered her with a heady dose of the adolescent invulnerability we had all shared as Mademoiselles.

Nothing bad was going to happen to any of us, I told myself again. Teeny had thoroughly checked out the ship and their surgical statistics (beyond excellent). And just to be safe, she and Diane and I had prayed angels of protection and safety over the whole ship. Those doctors didn't know it, but they were getting ready to be the healing instruments of the Holy Spirit.

It was just that laser eye surgery . . .

"So," Diane asked in that way we have of picking up on each others' thoughts, "what did you end up deciding about the eye surgery?"

I curled forward. "Aaargh. I don't know."

Yaaaaa! Chicken Little did a devil-dance. *It was invented by some* Russian, *for heaven's sake! What if the equipment malfunctions? You could go blind! One tiny slip, and 'hello, triple vision.' And the correction doesn't even last! You'll just have to do it again in a few years! Why risk it?*

Linda patted my shoulder. "Chill, sweetie. If you aren't comfortable with it, forget it."

I sat back up. "Yeah, but if I *don't* have it done, I'll be the only one of us left in granny glasses."

Diane raised a finger. "Not necessarily. They won't know about my corneal implants till I see the surgeon."

"Choosing not to decide *is* a decision," Pru comforted me with one of her AA pearls of wisdom. "And that's okay, too."

Four cars ahead of us, another limo stopped beside the elegant gangway that was cloaked in dark green and white canvas so the embarking passengers were screened from the unwashed masses (or the paparazzi).

At the thought of paparazzi, I corralled my red sun hat, then groped around in my "necessary doo-dah" canvas tote for my honkin'-big Jackie O sunglasses. I was determined to keep a low profile. The Jackrabbit Jackpot winner mystery had died down at last, but it wouldn't do for some tabloid photographer to snap my photo and see a resemblance. Not that they would, of course. The casino guard had inspected me close-up without making the connection.

Linda saw me getting ready to go incognito and shook her head. "Down, girl. Somebody's liable to think you're a star or something and really start snapping away."

I hadn't thought of that.

I scanned the piers. Everybody within a city block had on a uniform and looked official. Still, though . . . "Better safe than sorry."

We were a mixed bag, indeed: Teeny was color-coordinated in dusty coral silk slacks and camp shirt. SuSu had on high-heeled slides with a white polka-dotted *Pretty Woman* halter top and brown shantung slacks. Pru was fresh-scrubbed in plain jeans and a white T that showed off her rock-hard body from months of working out in rehab. Linda was swathed in yet another of those loose, baggy dresses by that designer whose stuff all looked like floppy slipcovers to me. Diane looked professionally elegant and comfortable in a cotton cardigan jacket with matching knit pants (her own design). And last but not least, I was all about comfort in my black squishy sandals, black knit slacks, white satin camisole, and pink linen tunic.

From the back room to the boardroom, we were represented. And all of us were up for some serious improvements.

I just wondered how SuSu was going to fare with our vow not to drink on the whole trip. Teeny had insisted, for Pru's sake, and all of us but SuSu had readily agreed. SuSu had complained that she didn't see why she shouldn't be able to have a mai tai in one of the bars if Pru wasn't around, but when all of us had greeted that with prim disapproval, she'd grudgingly promised to go along with the rest of us.

And the ship was nonsmoking. Cutting out either of her remaining vices cold turkey would be a huge challenge. Doing both . . . At the worst, it could be a reality check SuSu needed. At the best, she'd manage just fine and realize she didn't need alcohol or cigarettes to have a good time.

Or, we could spend the entire trip with the whining bitch from hell.

Regardless, we'd be there for her.

We pulled closer to the gangway.

"Ohmygod." SuSu patted her chest like old Aunt Minnie with the vapors, so excited she forgot to pout. "Three more cars, and we are here. This is really happening." She grasped the elastic of her halter bra behind her neck and lifted, stretching it like a giant slingshot above her head. "Hello, pert and perky boobs. Good-bye, crow's feet. Good-bye, blotches. Good-bye, spread-ass."

At last, a glimpse of her old self.

I patted "the baby" in my lap. "Good-bye, twenty pounds." Funny. I hadn't turned a hair at the thought of liposuction—the more, the better. It was just having my vision corrected that scared me.

"Good-bye, liver spots," Teeny blurted out. Such intimacy, at such volume! We were amazed. "Good-bye, crooked bottom teeth. Good-bye, 'gone-ass.'"

"Ohmygod." SuSu's eyes widened in astonishment. "You are gettin' butt-cheeks?"

Teeny grinned. "Yes, I am. And a boob lift. And a face-lift." She hadn't said a word before this, only that she was still making up her mind.

"Yay, Teens," Diane congratulated.

"Good-bye, twenty years," Pru said. "I asked for a total body transplant, but they said I'd have to settle for the works."

Smug as a Cheshire cat, Linda thrust her jaw forward and rubbed her double chin with the side of her finger in unspoken farewell.

Pru popped that sunny little smile I remembered from our years as

Mademoiselles. She took Teeny's hand. "You've done so much already, 'thank you' is starting to lose its impact. But thank you, thank you, thank you. You do the best 'coming out' parties in the world."

"Don't thank me, sweetie," Teeny said. "Thank yourself. You wouldn't be here if you hadn't had the courage to leave Vegas behind and turn your life around."

Pru's expression showed a mixture of awe and gratitude. "I would be dead by now. I wanted to be dead."

Before things got any heavier, Diane gave Pru a good-natured poke. "Well, thank God you're not dead," she said, covering a spark of humor with a serious expression. "You just look like you are."

Teeny and Linda and Pru and I turned in horror and set upon her.

"Ow!" Diane fended off our whacks and nudges. "Well, it's the truth. Why pussyfoot around about it? The woman has a mirror." She grinned. "But ain't it great that she won't look that way when she comes back? And neither will we."

We were still laughing and trying to sort ourselves back out when the limo door opened to a dark green carpet that led up the covered gangway. Two gorgeously Nordic stewards extended their hands to assist us.

At the sight of those two hunks, SuSu let out a strangled gurgle and started plastering down her dandelion hair with her fingers.

So much for fitting in with the jet set.

But for the first time in memory, the mere presence of studly man-persons didn't set off her usual hormone grenade.

If anything, she just looked embarrassed to be seen with her hair messed up.

Watching her ignore the stewards as she got out, I wondered if maybe she was taking saltpeter.

I donned my glasses and hat, but inside the limo's tinted glass, I couldn't see well enough to find my crossword puzzle and purse, much less the three tote bags of bare necessities I was carrying. So I had to take off my sunglasses till I located my tote full of books, my other tote with all my meds and makeup and jewelry, and the third one full of my favorite postsurgical treats like peach tea and low-carb candy (I know, I know; who are we kidding?), and no-sugar-added instant hot chocolate.

Meanwhile, the others dithered up their belongings in a slow-motion frenzy worthy of a herd of octogenarians.

The stewards waited patiently and helped us out, one by one. Hat low on my forehead and sunglasses back in place, I was the last one to join the others just inside the covered gangway as we waited for the way to clear.

SuSu might not have noticed those stewards, but those short white uniforms they had on were giving me ideas. Maybe I could buy one for John. We hadn't played *Love Boat* before, but I'm a sucker for epaulets, and John's runner's legs sure would look sexy in those shorts.

Teeny nudged me. "Gracious." She shot me a knowing glance. "That's some wicked little smile, there."

Caught. I dropped my focus to the ground, smarting.

I pointed beneath our feet. "No red carpet?" I deflected.

"Oh, no," she murmured in her "unmentionable" tone. "No red anything. On the whole ship." She mouthed more than said, "Blood," then shook her head as if I'd just asked about somebody's jailbird uncle at church circle.

"What's the holdup?" SuSu asked, peering up the shaded gangway.

We heard a small dog going nuts from just inside the ship, and a guy yelling. Apparently, the man had tried to sneak his dog on the cruise, but the crew was politely having none of that. Furious, the man started cussing and insulting everybody who tried to talk to him. He sounded jacked up, like he was on something, his speech rapid and fragmented.

"He tried to smuggle his dog on the cruise," I told the others, fulfilling my role as Stater of the Obvious.

Linda bristled. "Well, he'd better smuggle it right back off. Dogs and surgery do not mix."

"Dogs and ships don't mix, period," Teeny assured her. "It has to do with international quarantines."

Lo and behold, who should come stomping over the velvet rope than the season's latest thirty-something male lead, carrying a frenzied little shih tzu in his arms.

He barreled through us, cussing a blue streak, jostling Teeny and knocking over one of my bags. "Get me a limo! Now! I need a @#%@*ing limo!"

"Ohmygosh!" Totally blowing my cool, I pointed after him. "That's . . . that guy! You know . . . the one who was in that movie last summer, the remake of that old version that I liked much better than the new one. Remember?"

Linda pointed, too. "I know. He did that sitcom a few years ago. It's him."

"Oooo, oooo!" SuSu sounded like Curly in *The Three Stooges*. "He was in *Pearl Harbor*."

"Matt Damon!" Diane guessed.

The ankle-biter dog was still going nuts, and the stewards were trying to calm the mystery movie guy, but it only made him madder. He just kept bellowing for a limo.

"No. This guy wasn't in *Pearl Harbor*." I didn't know who he was, but I knew he wasn't Matt Damon. "Matt Damon's *cute*. This is that other guy."

"Aaargh." Linda winced, trying to come up with the name that was hovering just beyond us all.

You know! The guy with close-set little eyes, and really short hair with a widow's peak, and his nostrils are kind of slashy. Frankly, I never saw what all the fuss over him was about.

And he was a lot shorter than he looked in the movies.

Meanwhile, the next limo in line pulled up and a harsh-looking, overdressed, middle-aged woman started to get out.

The maniac mystery movie guy shoved past the stewards, then hollered, "Out, bitch!" He then proceeded to jerk the woman to her feet, scaring her half to death with the rabid shih tzu, who acted like it wanted to eat her face off.

We all watched, openmouthed.

Not one to take such treatment lying down, the woman hauled off and kicked the guy in the shins with her Prada stiletto. "Who the hell are you? How dare you manhandle me that way?"

The stewards moved to defuse the situation, but the maniac movie guy appeared to have met his match.

Meanwhile, the limo driver, having heaved the woman's luggage to the concrete pier, made a beeline to the driver's door to escape. But the movie guy pointed at him and roared, "Five thousand, cash, if you'll take me to the airport."

"Ten," the woman screeched, "if you'll stay right where you are!"

"Fifteen!" The movie guy shrieked.

Wide-eyed, the driver looked to the woman for a higher bid, but she hauled off with an impressive right cross to the movie guy's jaw, prompting a fresh explosion of profanities.

Taking the highest bid, the limo driver tipped his hat to the injured celebrity. "Airport, it is." Then he ducked inside the car to avoid the fray.

The woman waggled the hand she'd used to sock the movie guy. "Shit! Now look what you made me do!" She extended it to reveal two maroon talons broken off at the quick.

We girls winced.

More profanities were exchanged, and when the guy tried to get into the limo, the woman jerked him back out with surprising strength for somebody so thin in such high heels. A shoving match followed, including a lively ping-pong of threats that asses would be sued.

Staff from the ship hurried past us and attempted to separate the two, but the dog tried to bite the woman one time too many, so she snatched it from its master by the scruff of its adorable little neck, carried it at arm's length to the edge of the pier, and dropped it into the water. (Only about four feet below the pier.) It came up swimming.

The jerk shrieked and dove in after it.

Solicitous crew members whisked the woman toward us, while other crew members helped the guy and his dog up out of the water. Dripping and furious, the guy stomped over to the limo with his dog, got inside, and slammed the door. The driver burned rubber getting out of there.

"Think he'll really give that driver fifteen thousand," I asked SuSu.

"Nah. Guys like that are the kind who'd go through a church youth group car wash, then drive off without making a donation."

Amid a murmured chorus of apologies from the staff, the woman stopped just short of us. "Well!" she huffed, straightening her clothes and hair.

Of course, I put my mouth in gear before my mind. "That man," I said to the woman, pointing after the limo. "That movie guy. Do you know his name?"

She arched a perfectly plucked auburn brow. "Mud."

Murder in her eye, she flipped open her cell phone and speed-dialed. "He picked the wrong woman to attack," she muttered as she waited for an answer. "In front of witnesses!"

She turned slightly away. "Arthur, this is Celeste. I want you to find out who just dragged me out of my limo at the *Narcissus*, and throw the book at him. Some jacked-up little Hollywood wannabe." Pause. "My usual limo service: On the Town. The guy's probably still in the car." Pause. "Of course, I want to press charges. He laid hands on me. Jerked me right out of my car and threatened me with a vicious dog."

Vicious dog? Puh-leez. From where I stood, she'd dished out a lot more than she'd taken.

"I have witnesses," Miz Gotrocks said, then thrust her phone at me. "Here. Tell Arthur who you are and what happened."

Uh-oh. And I had wanted to keep a low profile. I drew my hat lower on my forehead. "Couldn't it wait till we're on the ship? I'm feeling awfully self-conscious standing out here with all this . . ." I wanted to say "commotion," but the word went AWOL along with the stupid shih tzu guy's name.

A dozen people hung on our every word, my Red Hats among them.

"It won't take a second, darling," Miz Gotrocks insisted, waggling the phone at me, "and I'll be in your debt forever."

Oh, Lordy! I'd just wanted to know the dad-gummed guy's name, not end up in a court case!

I had a powerful urge to sprint for our staterooms, but being the good citizen that I am, I put the receiver to my ear. "Arthur?"

"Police Captain Feinburg. May I have your name, please?"

Oh, crap! Way too official. I did *not* need this, especially at that moment.

Horns started beeping. Now that the sideshow was over, people wanted to board, and we were blocking the gangway.

I prayed that Miz Gotrocks wouldn't put me on her hate list forever. "Arthur, darling," I said into the phone. "I'm afraid we'll have to talk about this later. I'm holding everyone up, here. Have your friend find me later, and we can talk."

I'd do my best to avoid her, but on a ship, the odds weren't in my favor.

I returned her phone, already backing away. "I'm so sorry for your awful experience, and I'm so glad you're all right. We'll do this later."

Miracle of miracles, she didn't raise a stink, just eyed me with shrewd assessment, as if I might be trying to put something over on her, which I wasn't. "Of course. Later."

Leaving half the staff behind to smooth her ruffled feathers, we fled to the ship.

"Who was that on the phone?" Diane asked on behalf of the others.

"Police Captain Feinburg," I rattled off. *His* name, I could remember!

Diane laughed. "What is it with you?" She shook her head. "One minute, you're just standing there like the rest of us, and the next thing we know, you're in the middle of a lawsuit, on the phone with some police captain."

Teeny's mouth flattened. "Police captains are very influential people."

"Ohmygosh." Pru's expression fell. "Teeny. Did you remember the tickets?" she asked, drawing us back to our own concerns.

"Don't worry. That's all been taken care of."

At this level of service, I guess the passengers' "people" took care of the technicalities. But I sure was glad Pru had diverted the conversation away from my propensity for disasters.

We stepped on board into a wonderland of pink. Extremely tasteful pink, balanced with the softest white trim and punctuated with pale gray, which wasn't what I'd expected.

"Your favorite color," Pru remembered.

Shades of *Color Me Beautiful*.

A flawlessly attractive older woman stepped forward (probably the human equivalent of a billboard for the company), while three tanned, buff stewards politely collected our carry-ons. "Welcome aboard, *mesdames*," the woman said with just a hint of a charming French accent. "I am Madame Reynard, director of passenger relations. We so regret the little disturbance caused by our other guest." She folded her hands over her chest like somebody posing for an icon. "Some people are quite unreasonably attached to their pets, but the regulations must be observed. Of course, we all love our little puppies and kitties. Zay simply do not belong on the ship."

She stood there smiling for an awkward beat before motioning us toward our cabins. "Your party will be staying amidships in the Neptune Suites on the starboard side of the seventh level," she said as we followed her down the hallway. "Unless you prefer otherwise, our staff will unpack your belongings."

They could unpack away. I'd bought all new underwear and nightgowns for the trip.

Madame Reynard went on. "We invite you to our midday buffet in the main dining room, or you may order from our extensive room service menu. Your nutritionists will be by this afternoon to work out your personal diet requirements. We pride ourselves on accommodating your preferences as well as your nutritional needs."

Berries. Lots and lots of fresh berries. And lobster.

"The captain's secretary will call later to arrange a private audience with your group at your earliest mutual convenience."

I wondered if anybody else had ever sprung for more people at once than Teeny.

"Due to the unique nature of our services, we dress for dinner only on the last three nights of your cruise. Otherwise, comfort is the order of the day."

She stopped to slide open a double door that pocketed silently into the wall on either side, revealing a surprisingly spacious living area with a hallway down both ends that led to the individual bedrooms and baths.

We all followed her in. Nothing in the soft-toned room stood out, but it was warm and welcoming without being fussy, thanks to an excellent watercolor collection bolted to the walls. The upholstered pieces looked comfortable and inviting in what appeared to be leather, but was probably vinyl so they could sterilize everything. Long sofas, squushy sculptured chaises bent to a natural sitting position, padded chairs, and overstuffed ottomans had been perfectly scaled to the space. The tables were made from sculpted white resin with no hard edges or glass surfaces to bump tender patients.

Madame Reynard distributed our keycards, then bowed. "If there is anything I can do to assist your stay, please do not hesitate to call me day or night. Simply dial zeh-roh." She left us to our little kingdom.

"Mesdames?" The steward rolled a cart full of our luggage to the open doorway. He knocked politely.

"Please," I said, "come in."

He stepped inside. "Do ze ladies 'ave any preferences as to state-room?"

Oooo, that was sexy, the way he rolled out "preferences" with that French accent.

"Anywhere for me," Teeny said from the galley.

"Ditto," Linda called from the balcony.

"Same," from Pru.

SuSu piped up with, "Give me an end."

"Next to the living room, left," Diane claimed. She always wanted to be near what was going on.

I couldn't resist the opportunity for a harmless flirt, a fine art in the South. I peered seductively at the steward. "Do we have any noisy neighbors?" I asked it slow and low.

The steward sent a 500-watt smile my way. A+ on the return. "But no, madame. Each of our larger suites is separated from ze others by at least three meters of service space."

"A very sensible plan." I batted my eyelashes at him, imagining John in that uniform. "Then please put my things in one of the end rooms."

He cocked his head for my name. "Madame . . . ?"

"Baker." I smiled and drawled out, "I never could stand being in the middle."

The man actually blushed.

I walked away to let him off the hook. On the balcony, I hooked Linda's arm and said, "The girl has still got it."

After all our luggage was distributed and the maids had unpacked us, we were left on our own at last.

As always, Diane acted as social director. She opened the large menu on the dining table. "Okay. Who wants to go to the buffet, and who wants to order in?"

SuSu surprised me. "Order in. I'm comfortable where I am."

She sounded almost . . . content. This was a good thing. All those attractive men around, and not a blip. Maybe she really had gotten past that frantic, fruitless quest for casual sex.

I had to ask her. "Are you takin' saltpeter?"

"George!"

The others glared at me, except Pru, who took it all in like Jane Goodall monitoring her chimps.

"It's just that you seem so oblivious to men all of a sudden."

SuSu flushed to the darker roots of her dark blond hair. "Maybe I'm just happy. True happy. Calm happy, after all this time."

Why or how, she clearly wasn't ready to share, but I couldn't remember seeing her so quietly self-assured. Quite an abrupt about-face from sulking over Pru.

"Oh, honey." I stretched out my arms, laying it on thick. "That's so great. Group hug."

All the others but Pru closed in like zombies. Pru stood by trying to decipher our private language of touch and tumble and pester and hug.

"Quit that." SuSu laughed and fussed while we descended on her. "Stop. Stop it," she protested without conviction. She'd never admit it, but it did her good to be jostled beyond her comfort zone occasionally. "I mean it. Y'aaall, quit it. Somebody order lunch!"

Knowing when enough was enough, we broke up, laughing.

SuSu snatched one of the menus. "Give me that."

Taking one for myself, I lobbed in one last shot. "When are you gonna tell us what's got you so happy all of a sudden?"

She peered through her granny glasses at the menu. "Maybe when you call *Arthur* back."

"Aaaargh." I covered my head with the menu. "Touché."

I decided to mind my own business. For the moment, anyway.

21

Renewal

The Narcissus, *Bahamas*.

AYBE IT WAS BECAUSE TEENY HAD BOOKED ALL SIX OF US, BUT IT appeared that we were first in line for everything. Room service was amazing. To die for. We were still savoring our fabulous diet-legal desserts that first afternoon when the nutritionist came, bearing a cart full of yummy food samples. While she spent hours working out our menu plans with each of us, we took turns having massages or sunning on the balcony—with a strict caution to use their custom-blended sun blocker and not overdo.

We'd get our vitamin regimens after the blood tests.

I chose a modified Atkins plan with all the lobster, crab, shrimp, steak, lamb chops, grouper, fresh mushrooms, artichokes, asparagus, fresh spinach, salad stuff, low-carb desserts, and *berries* I wanted.

Pru liked my choices, so she did the same plan. Diane opted for chicken and fish. Linda went for the clinic's custom weight-loss plan with yummy protein shakes. Teeny needed boosters to get her weight up. (World's smallest violin playing "Hearts and Flowers.") And SuSu went with their Cleansing Regimen, specially designed to help people quit smoking.

Sunday and Monday, we cruised at a leisurely pace to the company's private tropical island, a sheltered mooring whose turquoise waters, white sands, and swaying palms looked just like a travel poster. Meanwhile, a stream of attractive nurses (mostly male, and not a one of them swishy) with top-notch credentials and experience came to introduce themselves and do our pre-op testing. We played bridge and backgammon, read, and watched movies from the satellite between visits from our surgeon and all the other people who would be taking care of us.

The six of us had three nurses on each shift, just for our group. Linda's and mine looked like a Viking prince, and his name was Hans. If anything should go wrong, the ship's life-flight helicopter could get us to a top-notch Miami hospital in less than an hour.

I liked everybody we met, but especially our surgeon (of whom there were two dozen aboard). Norwegian, she was beautiful even without makeup and looked forty-something. We were all shocked when she showed us her passport, and the birth date was 1941.

"No way are you sixty-three," SuSu told her.

"Who did *you*?" Linda challenged. "That's who I want."

The doctor laughed, then opened her huge album of befores and afters she'd brought. It impressed my socks off, as did her surgical statistics for the thousands of procedures she'd done (up to date and neatly printed out by procedure for each of us). We settled on our final selections with confidence.

So, with complete confidence in the staff, we fasted after midnight on Monday, scrubbed down well with Betadine at the crack of dawn, then hugged each other good-bye as we went to the operating rooms.

The **Narcissus,** *Basa Cay.* **Tuesday, March 2, 2004.**
Pru went first, at 7:00 A.M., maybe because she was having so much done. She didn't bat an eyelash at the prospect of going through all that surgery with only her regular dose of methadone and acupuncture. Boggled the mind. And she wasn't even afraid.

I went next. It felt weird just walking with the attendant to the pre-op area which, along with the OR, was pink, too. As I lay on the table engulfed by the hollow operating room sound that roared below soft, classical music, I managed to get in one last prayer before they put the anesthetic into my IV. *God, I know this whole setup is vain, but I'm counting on You to look after me, for Your sake as much as mine. I mean, everybody knows I'm trusting You to take care of us all. So please make sure everything goes smoothly, and all the equipment works properly. Put angels to minister safety and protection over each of us while we're asleep. And please give the doctor supernatural wisdom and skill. In the name of Christ, amen.*

SuSu calls prayers like that spiritual blackmail, that God—if there was one, which she denied—wouldn't like. But the Bible says God wants to give us the desires of our hearts as long as we're in His will. So since there wasn't anything in the Good Book that said, "Thou shalt not have plastic surgery" (especially if it's free), I figured I was on pretty solid ground.

I woke up back in my stateroom to find the angel Gabriel hovering over me in a halo of afternoon sun, and the wind blowing through the cloud I was lying on. (It turned out to be a positive air-flow therapeutic mattress.)

"Hello, there," he said in a soothing tone. "Everything went well, and you did beautifully."

I didn't know Gabriel was German.

I drifted into a blessed fog, then back out again. I didn't hurt. Everybody had said it would really hurt at first, but it didn't.

The ship swayed almost imperceptibly, like a wonderful hammock.

Thirsty. I asked for some water and heard a rude, guttural "Unngghh" from somewhere close.

"Here you go." My angel placed a straw between my lips, and I greedily sucked down the cold water.

"Annnggh."

Where was that noise coming from? And why couldn't I talk?

Not that I cared . . . No wonder people got addicted to drugs.

I thought of *Oliver*: "Please, sir. I want some more," but nothing came out.

"You'll notice that you have on a pressure garment," he said. "We use these to discourage thrombosis, help the tissues reattach, and minimize swelling."

Thrombosis. Blood clots. Gotcha.

My stomach growled.

"May I bring you something to eat?" Hans the nurse asked. "Perhaps a fresh raspberry sorbet freeze?"

I nodded. "Ummm."

The next thing I knew, there was a straw in my mouth. I drew in the smooth, gloriously sweet raspberry slush.

Thank God for Splenda.

When I asked for the bedpan, Hans made me get up and go to the bathroom, and the party ended, then and there. I felt vaguely like I'd been run over by a Mercedes—several times, like that Houston orthodontist whose wife caught him with another woman.

My rearranged hips, sides, inner thighs, underarms, stomach, and belly button were all encased in a crotchless, gut-sucker body leotard that went from my wrists to my toes, as if they thought I'd fly to pieces without it.

Maybe I would.

On a scale of one to ten, I was rocking along at a six. Until I moved, then Katie bar the door.

"Der more you can walk, der better," Hans said. "Ve need to get that circulation going in der legs."

Ever dutiful, I tried to sit up.

"Dat's it. Nice and easy."

Easy? Nothing worked right, and I looked like Frankenstein meets the mummy!

Hans steadied me as I swung my legs over the side and stood in slow motion. "Take your time."

I looked at him and noticed a faint resemblance to Franz of Hans und Franz of *Saturday Night Live*, permanently branding him as Hans-und-Franz in my mind.

Despite my best efforts, I couldn't stand straighter than forty-five degrees from the waist. After Hans-und-Franz straightened my tubes, he gave me a pillow to hold against my stomach, which helped a little.

With my free hand, I clutched the IV pole for dear life. "Pain medicine?" I asked.

"Not quite yet." Which was nurse talk for at least two more hours.

Pain medication. Pru couldn't have any pain medication.

"My friend, Pru?" I asked. "The one who went first."

"Ah. She iss doing quite well. Quite well, indeed. Do you vish to go see her?"

"Tomorrow." Maybe.

I'd be lucky to make it to the bathroom today. It looked a city block away, but I made it.

Since my fanny was the only place on my torso they hadn't messed with, I sat without setting off too many pain alarms. Hans-und-Franz discreetly arranged my pink hospital gown to spare my modesty, then left me to take care of the necessaries.

Maybe I shouldn't have tried to have so much done at once.

In my condition, nothing was easy, including tearing off a length of johnny paper. A bone-deep moan escaped me when I did, summoning Hans-und-Franz in serious professional mode. "Are you all right, ma'am?"

"Fine. Fine," I lied. "I just tried to move my arm." I seriously considered drip-dry, but only for a second.

"May I assist you?" he volunteered.

"No! Thank you, no." I know it was silly, but I'd never had a male nurse before, and lipo didn't qualify as dire enough to suffer such bathroom indignities. "Just give me some time. I can do it."

"I'll be right outside." He resumed standing with his back to the open door.

Every movement set loose legions of nasty little demons.

"Serves you right," Chicken Little said. *"That's what you get for being so frivolous and risky, and not accepting yourself the way you were."*

"Oh, shut up."

Hans pivoted. "I beg your pardon?

"Nothing. I was just talking to myself."

He turned away again, his posture relaxing. "All der best people do, madam."

I laughed.

Big mistake. "Oh. Ouch. Oh. No. No laughing."

When I was finally finished and was ready to get up, I struggled to my feet, discovering a whole new set of pain neurons. "Okay. Help."

Hans took my elbow and assisted me back to bed, which was looking awfully good, even if it did make a lot of noise for a bed. I had just sat down when I heard Linda's voice coming through the monitor on Hans's belt. She was rattling on in Yiddish. I hadn't heard her say more than a sentence or two in Yiddish since her Bubbie had died when we were nineteen.

Hans carefully swung my legs onto the bed and covered me. "Madam's friend iss vaking up. If madam will pardon."

"Her name is Linda. Tell her Georgia said to feel better soon."

"I shall." He left me to sink into the wheezy mattress.

I slept most of the rest of the day, waking to hear a few faint sounds of distress from the other rooms, but nothing alarming. I woke the next morning to a statuesque black woman putting a blood-pressure cuff on my arm.

"Good mornin', missie," she said in a gentle Caribbean lilt. "My name is Shonna. I'll be your nurse today." The cuff inflated automatically, then eased. "Very good." She opened the Velcro. "One hundred over seventy-two. Light a candle to your ancestors."

I started to stretch, but immediately thought better of it. "Ow!"

"It'll be a few more days before you'll be wantin' to do that, darlin'."

"How many?" I don't know why I bothered to ask. I'd be better when I was better, and not before. "I'd like to have a date to look forward to," I justified aloud.

"Very fine idea." She stuck an electronic thermometer under my tongue. "If all goes as usual, by day four, you will feel quite human again. Sore," she qualified, "the way you would be after a strenuous workout when you haven't been to the gym for a few months."

Gym? Gym and Georgia weren't in the same dimension.

At least, until now. The physical therapy would start a week after surgery, something I wasn't looking forward to.

"Ninety-seven point seven," she read without alarm. "Do you usually run a bit low in the mornings?"

I nodded.

"Very good. Now." She put the instruments away. "Would you be wantin' to have your shower or your breakfast first?"

"Shower? I thought you couldn't get wet after surgery."

"It's not a good idea to get incisions wet, no, but we use surgical glue that seals those off very nicely. And we've found that a warm shower is quite therapeutic, both for de circulation and de morale."

I felt my hair, which was matted and bizarre. "It would feel good to wash my hair."

"Before breakfast?"

Oddly, I wasn't hungry. "Sure."

I was fine till she untied my gown, the warm shower ready and running. I looked in the long mirror on the back of the door and burst into tears. "I'm fat! Fatter than before."

Even with a girdle from head to toe, I looked like somebody had stuck a bicycle pump into my toe and added twenty pounds of pressure. My shape had lost all definition.

I did have an innie, but besides that, I looked awful.

"Ah, missie, donya cry now," she half-chuckled in sympathy. "Dat's just de swellin' from de fluids and de trauma. My word on it, darlin', you gonna come out lookin' like a bride."

The adrenaline of that wretched moment subsided, and I mopped my tears with a washcloth. "I'm gonna hold you to that. And my lady doctor."

"Trust, me, darlin', I know what I'm sayin'. I been doin' this for many years."

I stood there staring at my reflection with all my privates and incisions showing through the body girdle. "How do I get this thing off?"

Shonna laughed. "Honey, you don't. Dis de Bahamas. We do tings de easy way." She grinned and motioned me into the shower "as is." Then she got a lovely nylon scrubber and soaped up everything I couldn't reach, with just enough pressure to feel good, but not hurt.

I never would have believed it, but thirty minutes later when she was blowing dry my hair, I felt a thousand times better, even in a damp body girdle. I ate my breakfast of fresh blueberries, low-carb muffins, and broiled pork tenderloin while Shonna got Linda up. I heard the shower next door and smiled over my peach tea.

It was nine before I heard signs of life in the living room.

I was actually pretty comfortable in my bed, but when the others congregate, anytime, anywhere, I'm seized by the irresistible urge to be where they are.

John calls it herd mentality and claims men don't have it.

So I bit the bullet and put on a clean gown (one of mine), and braved the passage down the hallway, clinging to my IV pole and bent over with my girdle showing beyond my sleeves and hem. Linda's and Diane's rooms were vacant as I passed.

When I rounded the corner, I wasn't prepared for the carnage that awaited. Linda was sprawled on a chaise, her neck and head girded with a tube of the same stuff my getup was made out of. It left her face and the front of her hair corralled into an odd oval shape.

When she saw me, her eyes went wide and brimming.

I pointed to the tuft of silver hair that stuck straight up from her forehead. "You've got baby bird hair." I couldn't even see the small lipo incisions below her cheekbones and jawline.

"This brain corselet is drivin' me nuts," she said. "My ears are about to burn *up*. But the chin barely hurts." She tugged at the "brain corselet." "I've gotta get Shonna to cut holes for my ears." Unable to hide her reaction to the way I looked, she peered at me as if my head was threatening to fall off any second.

I turned to SuSu.

"Ohmygod!" Gingerly stretched out on a sofa to humor her lipo'd fanny, she stared at me in alarm, but I was staring back at her swollen face and two huge shiners with surgical markings and lines of stitches around her eyes. Not to mention the exposed stitches just inside her hair-line and down into her ears. Her thick hair was wild as an Aborigine's. Either they hadn't let her wash it, or she'd turned down the offer of a shower. She had a body girdle, but it was sleeveless. "Georgia, honey, how can you stand it?" she asked me with a wince that had to hurt.

I would have asked her the same question, but I didn't want to give her any ideas. She was enough of a whiner already.

"Actually, I feel pretty fair, considering all they did," I lied. (It's that martyr thing.) "But I don't think I'm gonna be able to stay up long." I subsided slowly into an upholstered Parsons chair.

Diane shuffled by, her lower half encased in elastic from her thigh-suck and tummy tuck, and her face swollen and distorted from the lift she'd had.

"Hey, sweetie." I air-kissed in her direction. "How's your self?"

Diane had an enormously high pain threshold. "Better than you, from the looks of it."

There was a knock at the door, which Teeny's nurse answered.

Mumble, mumble. Then, "One moment. I'll ask." The nurse came in and came over to me. "Mrs. Baker, there are flowers outside for you. Do you wish to accept them?"

"John. How sweet," I said to the others. "Please, bring them in." As she headed back to the door, I said, "Must have cost him a fortune."

Quite unlike John. He adored me, but was no romantic.

I knew something was up when the nurse opened both doors.

In came a huge exotic arrangement with enough giant tiger lilies in it to give me a headache for a week.

"Whoa." All of the others sat upright in amazement.

"What?" Linda asked. "Did you win the Kentucky Derby?"

The nurse brought over the card. "Madam."

I opened it. "Oh, for heaven's sakes."

I handed it to Teeny, who read, "So sorry to drag you into my little troubles. Feel better soon, then we'll talk. Celeste Heinz-Bitterman."

I might have known. The woman from the dogfight over the limo. She'd impressed me as the kind of person whose world ended at her skin.

Diane bristled. "Of all the nerve."

"They take up half the room," Teeny noted in dismay.

I motioned to the nurse. "Nurse, could you please have him take these away? They're lovely, but I'm allergic to lilies." I had an inspiration. "Is there a chapel onboard?"

"Yes, madam."

"Why don't we put them in there, then?"

She hesitated.

It wasn't hard to figure out why she had. "If they'll fit."

She nodded. "Perhaps with a little judicious rearranging."

The steward lugged them back out.

"Remind me not to get within a mile of the dining room," I said. "I am in no mood to talk to Celeste Heinz-Bitterman. Or *Arthur*."

With great care, I swiveled to scan the room. "Where's Teeny? And Pru?"

"Coming." Teeny's voice came down the hall. It was several minutes before she appeared, bent over a walker with wheels on the front.

"Booty call! The booty woman is here." She inched toward us. "And the bazoom babe, but you'll have to take my word for that. It hurts too much to stand up straight and show off my new boobs, but they're there. And they're even."

"I want to see," Diane prodded.

Teeny shook her head. "Not till they're well. But I promise, I'll let you see them before we dock." She took a whiff. "Whew. Something smells really cloying in here."

"That woman from the limo sent George a honkin' huge flower arrangement," SuSu told her, "tryin' to get her to testify."

"Lilies," Linda said. They all knew I was allergic.

Teeny bristled. "People have no sense of propriety anymore."

Pru's voice came from the hallway. "Ready or not, here I come. Brace yourselves." She moved easily, since she'd had little bodywork done, but her head looked twice as bad as SuSu's, not just because of the extensive work she'd had done, but mainly because of the jillion acupuncture needles sticking out of her head and neck.

"I know," she said through the mask that was her face. "I look like Pinhead in *Hellraiser* after a barroom brawl."

SuSu laughed. "Ow, ow, ow," she said between spates.

I was happy to see them communicating. If Pru was going to be one of us again, we had to treat her like one of us, not some wounded victim you had to handle with kid gloves.

"You are gruesome. No two ways about it," I said evenly. "But ain't we all? I decided I was 'Frankenstein Meets the Mummy.'"

Linda motioned to her brain corselet. "Yeah, well, what's this, then?"

"Big bird," Diane and Teeny said in unison, then laughed, which sent them both into a wave of complaints.

"The damnedest thing is," Pru said, "the acupuncture works. I am not kiddin' y'all. I've been really comfortable."

"Well, send the guy to me," I said.

"Ditto," from SuSu. "God, I need a cigarette," she whined. "And a *drink!*"

We all froze. Except Pru.

"You don't need a drink, honey," she said in a flat-footed, practical tone. "Or a cigarette. You just *want* one. Big difference."

Uh-oh.

SuSu bristled.

"It's okay," Pru went on. "I want one, too. The difference is, I know that all it takes is just that *one* to screw up my life. And another thing I know is, wanting something isn't the worst thing that can happen." She said it with such poise and calm.

SuSu's defenses went up, her tone harsh. "Will it ever go away?" she asked. "The wanting?"

"God, I hope so." A smile escaped Pru, which made her moan in discomfort.

The pain bug must have gotten loose just then, because we all shifted positions and made it a whine-in.

Stooped, I started the long shuffle toward my room. "I gotta lie back down. Teens, my darling, it seemed like a good idea at the time."

She did her best to smile, but it came out as a semiwince. "Talk to me in three weeks. I think you'll be very happy."

"Are we gonna show each other the final results?" Pru asked.

SuSu waggled her hand. "I want to see the lipo and the boob jobs."

"Of course, I'm only a chin," Linda qualified, "but I've got to admit, I really would like to see the final results."

"What?" I couldn't believe it. Linda, of all people. She was even more modest than I was. "Just to satisfy your curiosity, y'all want me and Diane and Teeny to get nekkid?" I left out SuSu, because she'd long since lost her inhibitions about her body.

Linda spread her hands in a soothing gesture. "That's an awful blunt way to put it."

"Yeah, well, nekkid's nekkid," I said. (That's Southern for naked and up to no good.)

SuSu snorted. "Big deal. We used to take group showers getting ready for our dates at Pru's."

"Yeah, but we were all seventeen. And we were all nekkid," I said. "I'm sorry, but I don't feel comfortable baring all while Pru and Linda sit by with their clothes on."

Pru perked up. "Then we'll all get nekkid, like we did back then. That's simple enough, isn't it?"

I wasn't too keen on that, either. "What? Just strip off in our rooms and come out like nudists or something?"

Clearly, that didn't go down with Linda or Diane, either.

Pru lifted her chin. "It could be my initiation into the Red Hats."

"Honey, we had that when we gave you the hat," Linda said.

"I know," Teeny piped up. "We'll order some great room service, then lock the suite and play Strip Bridge."

That made us all laugh, then go all ouchy.

SuSu jumped in and lobbied hard for that option, chiding us for how inhibited we'd all gotten. Eventually, she won me over.

"Oh, what the hell. Why not? It's hardly prurient," I admitted. We were just curious, not perverted.

"But I don't know how to play bridge," Pru confessed.

"Now that you're a Red Hat, you need to know how to play bridge," Teeny said. "We've got three and a half weeks. We can teach you."

"All in favor of Strip Bridge and a floor show?" SuSu said. "Raise your hands."

Everybody but Linda and Diane voted yes.

"Hah," SuSu said through her mask of a face. "You're outvoted. Strip Bridge, it is."

"When?" Diane asked.

"Last day at sea?" Linda suggested, putting it off as long as possible.

We all scanned each other, finding no objection.

"Last day, it is," Teeny ruled. "We can stock up on food and start about four."

"Y'all are seriously crazy," I had to say.

Pru laughed. "Ow. That's what I've always loved best about y'all. That, and your good hearts."

Diane went over in slow motion and hugged her, careful not to disturb her needles. "Ditto, sweetie. Welcome back."

"Strip Bridge it is," SuSu exulted.

Maybe we really were crazy.

Oh, Lordy. That meant I'd have to work really hard to get in shape, darn it.

22

Turning Points

The **Narcissus, Bahamas. March 2004.**

SHONNA KNEW WHAT SHE WAS TALKING ABOUT. FOUR DAYS AFTER our surgeries, we were all starting to believe that life as we knew it was possible. And the swelling had gone down a lot, especially when they took us off IVs. Day by day after that, we felt and looked significantly better.

The longer SuSu went without a drink or a cigarette, the crankier she got (usually aimed at Pru). Pru managed to stay detached, as she called it. Still, I knew SuSu, and there was trouble brewing. She'd gotten it into her head, consciously or not, that Pru's presence in our midst somehow took away from hers, but all we could do was try to show her otherwise and wait for her to come around.

Thank goodness there was plenty to keep us distracted. The next two and a half weeks rolled by in one long, dreamlike succession of body rubs, pampering at the spa, fabulous diet food that didn't leave us feeling a bit deprived, physical therapy, teeth brightening, dental work for Teeny and Pru, micro-dermabrasion for everybody but Teeny, and electrolysis. The electrolysis hurt like bees, but it was worth it not to have to pluck anymore.

All that pampering was punctuated by a steady succession of expensive gifts from Miz Gotrocks, who at least shifted from flowers to things we could eat, including Beluga caviar, which SuSu loves, but I think is the grossest food known to man. Not just raw fish eggs—

yuk—but *black* ones. I tried, but I could not get them down, even with tons of crumbled hard-boiled egg on a superthin cracker. I wasn't impressed with the truffles, either. I mean, what's all the brouhaha about something that basically tastes like dirt? Nice, loamy dirt, but dirt nonetheless.

We tried sending the stuff back with polite thanks, but that only made her more determined, so we started giving away what we didn't want to the nurses, who were most appreciative. I imagine the whole thing was highly entertaining "below stairs."

At one point, I seriously considered meeting with Miz Gotrocks and signing a simple statement as to what we'd seen, just to get rid of her. But Teeny called her lawyers for advice, and they strongly recommended we not sign anything till they'd reviewed the situation and vetted any documents.

I just wanted to be left alone to heal and enjoy my cruise, and I told the woman so, but she was obviously unaccustomed to taking no for an answer. And she must have been seriously rich and powerful, because I got little help from the staff, beyond updates on when the coast was clear. So I focused on getting myself into shape for the big unveiling and stayed away from the dining room.

How surreal was that? Me acting like Greta Garbo, when there were probably at least two dozen celebrities aboard.

Not that I suffered any hardships. I discovered that working out isn't so bad when you have a personal trainer and friends to keep you company. And that I love sugar rubs, and paraffin dips for my hands and feet, and having an expert give me a fabulously believable and flattering hair color, to name a few. Forget those cheesy makeover shows with the horsetail highlights. I'm talking been-for-my-daily-walk-down-a-Vermont-country-road subtle. I also discovered that dieting is no problem when people bring you wonderful, healthy things to eat six times a day. Sunning was strictly prohibited, but we could get a spray-on tan when we were further along.

The best thing I discovered was that SuSu, though cranky, seemed to be managing without her cigarettes and her booze. She spent a lot of time in the ship's Internet center, getting her lecture notes from her infamous Mattress Man study partner, then curling up on a chaise to study. As her swelling went down, I watched the cumulative rest and relaxation begin to wash some of the harshness from her, but I still sensed that something more than going cold turkey was troubling her.

And then there was her one-sided feud with Pru. SuSu refused to rotate into our bridge games when Pru was getting lessons from Teeny. We didn't buy into her "beg me" game, which only made her madder.

As for Pru, once she got the bridge basics down, she did surprisingly well.

We played a lot of bridge. And backgammon. They were just the sort of compulsive, inconsequential activities that kept our minds off all the trials and temptations waiting for us back in the real world. Like Miz Gotrocks and *Arthur*.

But now that we were more than two weeks in, everybody was restless. It was a perfect night, a warm breeze blowing in from the balcony.

SuSu paced the living room. "Y'all, I've gotta get out of this suite, or I'm gonna go crazy."

Linda trumped my ace. "Go, sweetie. Nobody's stopping you."

The way my cards had been going lately, I'd be buck naked on our last night before anybody else had their socks off.

SuSu circled the table, forearms interlocked. "I don't want to go by myself."

Pru put down the magazine she was reading. "Wanta go to the gym? We can work out. Or swim." She glanced at her watch. "It's almost nine." Too late for her AA meeting.

SuSu looked daggers at her. "No. I'm sick of the gym. And that pool's practically a hot tub. You can't swim decent laps."

We all knew it was SuSu's cravings talking. Nothing would suit her.

Pru had told me AAs called it "jonesing." She said it felt like you had ants in your blood, and you couldn't sit still or think straight when it happened.

SuSu went out onto the balcony, but came right back and flopped down into a chaise. "Ow." (We were better, but flopping down on the lipo was not a good idea.)

Diane didn't even look up from her cards. "There's tons of stuff to do on the boat. Dancing. Bingo."

Pru narrowed her eyes. "I know what you need. A little time on a slot machine."

My insides tingled with dread at the mere mention of the word.

"The casino." SuSu liked the idea so well she forgot to be rude to Pru. "Yeah."

Linda and I exchanged worried glances.

All else aside, I questioned the advisability of setting loose two seriously addictive personalities in a casino.

Teeny laid down her cards. "You know, that sounds like a great idea. I think I'll go, too. What kind of limit do you think we should set?"

Leave it to her to come up with a diplomatic way to draw some boundaries.

"Tell you what," she said. "How about I stake us to a hundred bucks apiece? If we win, we keep on playing. If we run out of money, we quit. Last one playing gets the grand prize."

"What's the prize?" I asked.

"Mmmmm. How about a weave?" Her blond brows rose in expectation. "Does that work for y'all?"

Diane got up. "Honey, it works for me. Just let me get some makeup on."

Linda pulled off her chin strap. "Ditto. I need to do something with this hair."

Which left me. "Y'all go ahead. I don't want to run into Miz Gotrocks." Not to mention the fact that I'd probably throw up if I even saw a slot machine. Heaven knew what guilt would do to me at the sight of SuSu playing one.

"Come on," SuSu urged me. "You need to get out of here, too. We'll keep a lookout for Miz Gotrocks."

"She'd probably be just as happy to get hold of one of you," I pointed out. "You were there when the shih tzu hit the fan, too. Next thing you know, you could be talking to *Arthur*."

SuSu took hold of my arm. "Don't be such a stick-in-the-mud. Come with us."

Teeny gently laid her hand on SuSu's. "If she wants to stay, let her stay."

SuSu narrowed her eyes at me. "Do you really want to stay here, or are you bein' Baptist?"

"Trust me," I said, "I have no objection to gambling, as long as the money's truly disposable."

"I'll say she doesn't," Linda chortled out, only to receive a sharp nudge from Diane.

I glared at her.

SuSu heaved an exasperated sigh. "Okay then. Be that way."

They scattered to get ready. When all of them but Pru reassembled—definitely the better for a little makeup—SuSu hollered back down the far hall. "C'mon, Pru. You're the cow's tail."

I still found it ironic that SuSu had come full circle from the compulsively prompt teenager she had once been, to the pathologically late adult, then back to "we're waiting."

"I'm coming," Pru answered. "I've got more mess to cover up than y'all."

"I can't talk you into going with us?" SuSu prodded me.

"Thanks, but I could use a little alone time," I lied. Well, half-lied.

"Did y'all hear that?" she said. "She's sick of our faces."

"That is not what I said."

Pru arrived, already looking ten times better than she had when we boarded, even this soon after the surgeries.

Impulse and conscience are a dangerous combination. As the others were about to leave, I raised a finger. "SuSu, wait. I have something for you." I got my purse and came back with five twenties. "Here." I extended the money to SuSu. "Play this, too. My gift." I looked to the floor. "You didn't get to go to Vegas with us, and since I didn't bring home any winnings, I want you to have it."

Her face scrunched in confusion as she stared at the bills. "That doesn't make sense. You didn't win in Vegas, so you're giving me money?"

Diane and Linda exchanged "uh-oh" looks.

Rats! I should never have opened my mouth. "That's not exactly what I said . . ."

"That's very generous of you, George." Teeny, eyes wide, plucked the money out of my hand and folded it into onto SuSu's. "Be gracious, SuSu. Say thank you, and let's go win something."

SuSu shrugged. "Okay. Thanks." She aimed a sunset-flame fingernail at me. "But if I win anything with this," she told me, "we're splitting it."

I started to protest, but Linda and Diane hustled them on their way.

Once the suite was empty, I realized just how much I really had wanted some alone time. I soaked in the silence, something I cherished in my time at home. I sat out on the balcony, watching the water and the moonlight and missing John for the first time.

It felt good to miss him. It would feel even better to curl up against him in bed when I got back and feel the comforting bulk of his warmth around me.

Sitting there in the gentle sea breeze, I caught up on my prayers. I had gotten out of my routines since we'd left, so I had some catching up to do. It calmed me immensely.

Then I went inside and called John, feeling guilty about the extravagance, but hungry for the sound of his voice.

"H'lo."

"Hey," I said. "Miss me? 'Cause I sure miss you."

I could hear his grin. "Who is this?"

It was a very old joke between us. "Your wife."

He chuckled. "Honey, I'm rattlin' around this place without you like a bunch of BBs in a sardine can. And horny as hell."

I chuckled, stabbed by a frisson of desire. "Me, too. But save that Han So Low costume for when I get back."

"Damn straight."

"Oh, I hope so." We talked about the kids, and his work, and what was going on during our cruise. Then my conscience caught up with me about the ship-to-shore rates, and I wrapped it up. "Call me, if you want to. Anytime. I miss talking to you."

He yawned. "I didn't want to intrude on your girl thing."

"Intrude, intrude. Girl thing for twenty-four-seven in close quarters could use some interruptions."

I heard him shift in the bed. "Are y'all getting on each others' nerves?"

"Nothing like that. We have lots of activities we can go to alone. I just miss you."

"I miss you, too."

"Call me."

"Will do." I knew he meant it at the time, but doubted he would remember. John really was an absentminded professor. We hung up, and I felt better just for having heard his voice and knowing he *was* rattling around without me.

I went to bed with a good book and fell asleep after only three pages. The next thing I knew, SuSu was straddled over me, and I smelled folding money.

"Wake up, Sleeping Beauty. We won, honey, and we won big."

I was still in a fugue state. "Ow. You're squushing my lipo. Get off!"

She flounced off and settled on the bed beside me, fanning a seriously large wad of bills. "I lost all the money Teens gave us on the progressive slots, so I started into yours, and I was almost out of that, too, when I put in three quarters and *won*!" She giggled like a kid, nuzzling the bills.

I grasped her hand holding the bills and thrust it to focus length. (I still hadn't made up my mind about the laser eye surgery.) "What are those? Ones?"

"No, honey. They are *hundreds!* C-notes. Three hundred and fifty of those babies."

I sat, stunned, trying to clear the fog out of my brain and let it sink in.

She riffled the stack in front of my nose. "Now that, my deario, is what I call perfume." Another infectious burble of laughter. "Seventeen thousand five hundred dollars each."

"No, it's yours. All of it. I meant that." It wasn't anywhere near a hundred thousand, but it sure went a long way toward making me feel better.

Surely, the Good Lord hadn't done this just to ease my guilty conscience. After all, my poker-playing, smoking, drinking country Baptist granny had been adamant that gambling was the devil's domain. Still, there was something so cosmically balanced about the way this had worked out that I recognized a familiar divine pattern.

"No way," SuSu brushed off. "We're fifty-fifty on this."

I grasped her shoulders. "Suse, honey, I have a confession to make. On my way out of the casino in Vegas, I put your quarters in a slot and pulled it. One play. And it won, big time." I couldn't bring myself to say the amount, which was probably wise. "But we were trying to get Pru out, so I ran away from the jackpot."

I probably shouldn't have used the word jackpot, but I seriously doubted her study schedule left time for tabloids.

"I've felt so guilty about it since then, I could hardly breathe. So trust me, I want you to have this money. Every penny."

"So that was what you've been keeping from me. I knew it was something." She hugged me. "Oh, sweetie. You could have told me. I understand completely. I mean, it's not like I had the money, and you took it. Neither one of us really had it, so there's nothing actually lost."

Please, Lord, don't let her ask how much. She might never recover.

Blessedly, she didn't. "I still want you to have half of this," she said. "If you won't take it for yourself, take it for John's sake."

I leveled her with a look that meant business. "The money is yours. It's the only way I can sleep at night. Take it. *Please.*"

SuSu ruffled the bills back and forth against her palm. "The others told me you'd do this." A light went on inside her head. "They knew, didn't they?"

"Not Pru. She had problems enough without knowing about that."

Predictably, SuSu shifted the subject away from Pru. "Consider the whole thing forgotten."

I decided to take her statement at face value and move on, which sent my inner martyr into paroxysms. "Thanks. That means a lot to me." *No! We're not through being guilty!*

I ignored the strident inner voice and let go of that burden, feeling it lift with the gentle tug of a helium balloon. "So. Now that I've made my confession, how about you? Something's going on, and I'm not talking about Pru."

SuSu fixed her gaze on the coverlet, her features in sharp profile. "My life's just so complicated right now." A softness permeated her tone. "There are so many wonderful, truly wonderful things happening. Y'all. This makeover." She lifted the fan of bills. "This money. School . . . And other things." Then the glow faded. "But there's all this anger I can't shake, like with Pru. I don't know why I can't get past what she did, but I can't. And there are other things, really scary ones." She turned her eyes toward the water. "Terrifying, actually."

My insides contorted. "Oh, God. Please don't tell me you have AIDS or something horrible like that."

Even in the darkness, her exasperation was apparent. "Of course, I don't have AIDS. Give me some credit. I told you, I've sworn off casual sex."

"Sorry." Me and my big mouth. I'd probably destroyed any chance of her confiding what was really bothering her now. She'd come in so happy and full of life, and look what a wet blanket I'd been. "Please, just promise me you'll come to me if you need help."

She sighed. "Some things I have to work out for myself."

Suddenly she seemed small and lonely. Then she pulled herself up, literally and figuratively. "It's late, and I'm way past ready for bed."

Desperate to restore her good humor, I reached for the money. "Before you get out of here so I can go back to sleep"—I waggled my eyebrows—"can I play with your money?"

She laughed, showering me with bills. "Honey, you can *sleep* with my money." She yawned. "See you in the morning. Try not to have *too* much fun with it."

I brushed a stack across my chin. "Bite your tongue." As she headed into the hall, I called after her. "Tomorrow morning, though, it all goes back to you."

"We shall see, my dear," she said. "We shall see."

I stared into the empty doorway for long seconds after she was gone, wondering if her craving for alcohol was what frightened her so.

She would tell us eventually—she always did—and I could wait till she was ready. Thirty-plus years of friendship had taught us all to appreciate the cycles of distance to closeness at work in every relationship.

I took a long whiff of the money, then stacked it neatly on my bedside table, then went back to sleep and dreamed of making love to John.

The next morning, SuSu was still sleeping at eleven, while the rest of us were up and had our red hats on, ready to go on a hydrofoil excursion to a nearby island for some shopping and terra firma.

"The tour's leaving in an hour," Teeny said. "SuSu's probably dead after all the excitement last night. Why don't we just let her sleep?"

"Lawd, no." Linda raised a staying hand. "She's been grumpy enough, as it is. She'd flip if we all went off and left her without even asking."

"Wups." Pru searched her straw bag. "Forgot my camera." She headed back to her room.

I followed down the same hallway toward SuSu's room. "I'll ask SuSu what she wants to do."

I passed Pru's room and listened in at SuSu's door at the end of the hall. No signs of life. I tapped, calling softly. "Suse?"

I heard an indistinguishable mumble from inside. "SuSu," I called louder, opening the door just as Pru emerged from her room. What I saw inside SuSu's room stopped me dead in my tracks. "SuSu! Oh, honey."

One look at my face, and she let out a feral cry, trying to hide the minibottle of booze she'd just drained, and using her knee to sweep aside the other half-dozen empties on the bed.

Etched into my brain, the seedy, desperate tableau was straight out of *Days of Wine and Roses*. SuSu's hair was ruined, anguish distorted her tear-swollen features, shame darkened her green eyes, and mascara blackened her lower lids.

In one of those terrible turning points in life, I saw the extent of her self-loathing and dependence on booze. I almost threw up.

"Don't look at me!" she cried, turning away.

Pru rushed over. "What's wrong?" she asked with subdued urgency. Before I could stop her, she moved past me for a look.

Oh, Lord. The last thing Pru needed was to see this!

But she surprised me. Taking it all in, she turned back to holler down the hallway toward the others, "Y'all go on to breakfast if you want to. We'll be there in a few minutes." Then she urged me inside and closed the door behind us.

"SuSu," I moaned out, my mouth in gear before my mind, as usual. "What have you done?" My heart broke to see the shame on her face. Even though she'd been angry with Pru, I knew she'd meant it when she promised not to drink.

I turned to Pru. "If this is hard for you, I can take care of her."

"I can handle this," Pru said with quiet compassion. "Been there, done that." She focused on me. "I just hope you understand that she didn't do this to me, or to y'all. She did it to herself, and it's easy to see she's completely miserable about the whole thing."

Paralyzed with recrimination, SuSu watched Pru collect the bottles and lay them on the dresser.

Pru acted as if nothing had happened, speaking casually to SuSu. "We came back to see if you wanted to go with the rest of us on the hydrofoil to Nassau for shopping." She smiled that sunny Gidget smile of hers. "Spend some of those winnings."

SuSu peered at her as if she were speaking Russian.

Unruffled, Pru coaxed her to sit at the dressing table. "How about it? We can help you get dressed." She picked up SuSu's brush and started working gently through the tangles.

Agonized, SuSu spun around and caught Pru's wrist. "You're not mad?"

Pru met her anguish with assurance. "No."

Fresh tears welled in SuSu's eyes. "Why aren't you mad? I drank."

"Because I know how it feels to be where you are right now, which is worse than anything anybody else can do to you. Why would I want to cause you any more pain than I already have? You're my friend, even though I haven't been a very good one for the past few decades."

That was *it*? Something as dreadfully momentous as this, and Pru just blows it off? I felt like Alice at the Mad Hatter's.

Then I saw the truth dawn in SuSu's eyes, huge and terrible. Shame and denial did a tug of war in her expression as the raw reality finally pushed its way into the glaring light of what we'd seen. She gripped the edge of the dressing table for dear life.

Pru looked to me. "Georgia's not mad, either. Are you?"

When she put it like that, I realized I wasn't. I felt only an aching sadness for SuSu. "No. I'm not mad."

SuSu crumbled, sobbing. "Ohmygod, ohmygod, ohmygod. It owns me. I *am* an alcoholic."

I burst into tears, too, and knelt beside her, gripping her hand. My heart broke for her, but I didn't know what to say. I'd prayed so hard for this to happen, but never thought past it. SuSu was my best friend, but I realized, despite the overwhelming emotion of the moment, that Pru was the one she needed just then.

Pru put her arms around SuSu and soothed, "Oh, honey, just let it out. I'm so proud of you for facing that at last. Doesn't it feel better to finally stop running away from the truth? That's the first step to getting your life back—yourself back."

SuSu clung to her and sobbed out all the pain and fear until she was spent, exhausted and hollow from grieving the truth. "Why are you being so nice to me?" she asked Pru in a leaden tone. "I've been so nasty to you."

"You had damn good reason to be angry." Pru calmly picked up the brush and started working gingerly to salvage her hairdo. "Let's get you ready. The shopping tour leaves in forty-five minutes, so we need to hustle."

"God, no," SuSu moaned out. "I don't want to go anywhere. I just want to get under the covers and never come out."

"Ah, sweetie. That won't help anything. Trust me; I know." Pru smoothed back the hair from her forehead. "Do you really want to be alone right now? It's your choice, but I wish you'd come with us. It'll be a healthy distraction, and we need you. You know how much we missed Georgia last night at the casino. It won't seem right without you."

I nodded. "Please. For us."

SuSu closed her eyes, deflated. "Whatever."

"Good decision," Pru said. "As for the others, we can keep this between us, if you want to."

"Mum's the word," I added. SuSu would tell them when she was ready.

"Thanks." SuSu nodded in weary gratitude. "I don't think I could face them if they knew." That settled, she registered her reflection in the mirror and winced at the wreckage her crying jag had caused. "Ohmygod. I look like Quasimodo."

Pru laughed. "We'll get you fixed up. And your red hat will draw attention away from the puffiness."

"Absolutely." I brought over some makeup remover with a warm washcloth, then started in gingerly on SuSu's face. "Tell Pru what you want to wear, so she can get it out for you."

"The . . . black linen capris and the white Marilyn Monroe top."

She sat quiet while we got her cleaned up, then made up. After she'd dressed, she stopped abruptly and asked Pru, "Will you take me to one of those meetings you go to?"

They had AA meetings onboard every night at eight. "Going to see the friends of Bill W," Pru called it.

"Sure," Pru said brightly. "But first, let's go shopping."

As my granny used to say, "The Lord can use even our sins to work His greater good," and this was just one of those cases.

The others noted SuSu's tear-swollen face, but the big news was the way she gravitated to Pru all day. One by one, Linda and Teeny and Diane pulled me aside and asked what had happened. I gave them our stock "I'm-not-talking" answer—"I really couldn't say"—even though I was dying to tell them about SuSu's breakthrough.

On the hydroplane trip over to Nassau, the sea air revived us all, and the day went really well. By lunchtime at the Atlantis, SuSu emerged as her old self, and all of us settled into a comfortable camaraderie.

For the rest of the cruise, Pru and SuSu were inseparable. They walked the decks and worked out and sat out on the balcony for hours "talking program." And every night at eight, they went to see Bill W. With every meeting, I watched SuSu grow a little bit stronger and saner.

Now, *that's* what I call a makeover.

23

"Don't Let Them Out!"

**The Narcissus, *en route to Fort Lauderdale. Friday, March 26, 2004.*
4:00 P.M.**

-DAY. WE'D TONED AND HEALED AND MOISTURIZED AND buffed and exfoliated and depilatoried. Then, as the crowning touch, we'd had the full treatment at the salon, including spray-on tans. (Quite convincing and flattering. This was something I could learn to love.)

FYI: I had finally decided to have my vision corrected. What a great thing. And Linda's corneal implants were working wonderfully. She almost didn't look like herself without her habitual "contacts blink."

For the last two weeks, we'd all dressed in baggy, comfortable clothes that didn't bind, but also concealed the cumulative results of all those workouts. And tonight, we'd play Strip Bridge and unveil the results of the cruise.

Part of me was proud and eager to show off my new shape, but the rest of me was properly horrified at the idea of exposing all my many remaining faults and foibles. The only thing that kept me determined to do it was the fact that I'd broken out of my inhibitions with John, and that had been a smashing success. Maybe it was time to *get over* my locker-room physical self-consciousness.

Gussied to the max and dressed in as many layers of clothing as the heat would allow, I joined the others in the living room for the fateful game.

"Lord, Georgia," Linda said as the others pointed to my feet and laughed.

"I told you'd she'd have on socks," Diane crowed. "Pay up."

Linda dug out our standard bet, a dime. "Who brings *socks* to the Caribbean? I ask you."

I just sat back and enjoyed myself. They might get me nekkid, but it was gonna take some doing.

Diane and Teeny were almost as bundled up as I was, including several necklaces and their red hats, shower caps, and two visors.

I'd thought of hats but hadn't wanted to mess up my hair. I kicked myself, though, for not thinking of the necklaces. I started back toward my room for my cross, pearls, and gold chain.

"Oh, no," SuSu intervened, self-appointed sergeant at arms. "No going back to your room. Once you're here, you're here for the duration."

"Oh, yeah? Says who?"

"The *rules*," SuSu gloated out.

"And whose rules would those be?" I asked.

"*The* rules. So sit those no-longer-boxy hips down and make yourself comfortable."

Teeny had done herself proud ordering the buffet. We had sparkling cider and all our favorites, including a devastating array of pastries.

"Ooooo. Éclairs. And that apricot flan looks like to die for." (I ended up falling off the wagon and eating two-thirds of it.)

The sun was low, so Diane walked over to the drapes and started to pull them shut.

"Ah-ah-ah." SuSu waggled her index finger. "Are we women or are we wimps? Don't tell me you plan to hide these glorious bodies we just got through working so hard to get?"

"Glorious bodies?" Diane scanned the room. "Better check that eye job they did on you."

"We *are* glorious," SuSu insisted. "Women in our primes. Flaunt it, baby."

Linda started loading rare roast beef and shrimp on her plate. "Just 'cause you'd run nekkid down Main Street if the dogcatcher asked you," she said evenly, "doesn't mean the rest of us would. It's this concept called modesty, honey. I'm sure you've heard of it."

"Baloney." SuSu was positively manic. "That's just another word for shame. And the only reason we're ashamed is because of all that Madison Avenue garbage that says you're supposed to look like those women in the magazines with wretched hair and anorexic bodies. We're not talking about public indecency here."

"No," Linda said. "It's *private* indecency, but that was the group conscience, so here I am."

"It's only indecent in private if you're ashamed," SuSu argued.

I sure was glad SuSu was going into a line of work where she'd be paid for such nonsense. "I swear, I didn't see a soapbox when we came in." I looked under the table. "Did somebody let Oprah in here?"

I got a reasonably decent laugh in response.

Then Teeny surprised us all with, "I'm with SuSu. Leave 'em open."

"Teeny!" Linda straightened.

Teeny smiled. "She's right. We definitely need to loosen up about ourselves. And as for modesty, what do you think are the odds of some freighter or fishing boat being out there carrying some guy who just happens to have binoculars trained on this ship, and not just on this ship, but trained on our stateroom balcony, out of all the balconies on this ship, so he can see a small and very erratic—because we are on the ocean—glimpse of whatever isn't hidden by the table or these upholstered Parsons chairs? And all that happens exactly when we've lost enough to be nekkid in the first place?"

Teeny hadn't said that many words at once in ten years.

She was right, of course. But as Southern ladies, we'd been trained from our cribs to believe that we must conduct ourselves at all times as if somebody is always watching.

Your character is what you do when no one's looking.

Diane tucked her chin. "Tell you what: How about we just draw the sheers till it gets dark, then we can decide. That'll let in the breeze and the light, but keep our privacy."

"Fine with me." Teeny poured herself a flute of icy sparkling apple juice. "But if there are no boats out there when it gets dark, promise me y'all will at least consider leaving them open."

"Teeny, what has come over you?" I asked. "Strip Bridge. Open drapes. What next? A nudist retreat?"

Beyond unthinkable.

Teeny laughed. "I don't know. I just finally got tired of being so dad-gummed proper. One night I went to bed proper as a pin, and the next morning, I woke up . . . unpredictable." She shrugged, deadpan. "Maybe it's something in that new arthritis drug I'm taking. It happened about then."

"Remind me to get the name of that from you," Linda said. "I'll warn Brooks not to give it to his patients."

Pru walked in, and all of us stopped in our tracks. She'd fluffed the soft blond cut they'd given her and put on just enough makeup to bring out her blue eyes and long lashes.

Thanks to micro-dermabrasion and the porcelain crowns she'd gotten (plus months without cigarettes), her skin glowed and her teeth shone white and straight. And though they'd tightened her skin considerably, she still had her dimple.

SuSu spoke for all of us. "Pru, you're gorgeous. Truly. Seeing it all put together, I'm speechless."

Pru grinned, then gave Teeny a hug. "I can't really believe it, either. After I got the makeup on, I just sat there and stared."

We all exchanged hugs and compliments, then dove into the buffet.

I have to admit it, our gatherings were different without wine or booze. It wasn't worse, just different, but over the course of the month, we'd adjusted. Still, I had a wistful thought that a little wine would go a long way with Teeny and Linda and Diane and me when it came to playing Strip Bridge. Then I kicked myself for such a disloyal idea.

Half of us were still eating when SuSu took it upon herself to move things along. "Finish up, ladies, and let's get this show on the road." She picked up my plate to whisk it away, but I grabbed it back. "I am not finished."

"Well, hurry up. I want to be done by eight."

"What's the big deal about eight?" Then I remembered: The meetings started at eight. But how long could it take us to finish stripping? The way we'd set up the scoring, two people lost on every hand. I doubted it would take us even an hour to get down to the buff. "Chill. We've got plenty of time." I wanted at least one more piece of that low-carb flan.

Linda stood. "I want some more of everything."

"Linda," SuSu scolded. She placed her fists to her hips. "Y'all, it's already five. We've been eatin' for an hour. Enough is enough. Let the games begin."

"I want some more, too," Pru said, getting up. Clearly enjoying the chance to assert herself, she leaned in close as she passed SuSu on the way back to the buffet. "You're not the boss of me," she said, resurrected from our schoolyard days.

The rest of us applauded, opera-style: one hand slightly raised and immobile, while the fingers of the other patted politely in the palm.

SuSu laughed. "Make some people gorgeous, and they go all uppity on you."

The others started cutting up, but I just sat back and enjoyed it. It occurred to me that these four weeks had been Teeny's superdeluxe equivalent of boot camp: shared ordeals in close quarters. A guaranteed formula for bonding.

It had worked. Pru was no longer an outsider and an observer. She held her place among us now with dignity.

Amazing, what you can accomplish in four short weeks. With umpty-jillion dollars, U.S.

After we'd eaten, the game started in earnest.

"Low scores on every hand have to take something off," Teeny rattled off. "Partners rotate every hand. We do play one-bids. No Coke hands." (Throwing in a hand if one player has no face cards.) "We don't pass the deal on a passout, and anybody who reneges has to go to the buff, immediately." (A lot of card jargon, for you nonbridge players, but it all means something in bridge. Except going to the buff. That just means getting nekkid, like it sounds.)

Teeny gently shook a bowl above eye level. "Here're your tallies." One by one, we drew. It's not the easiest thing to rotate six people, but she had figured it out, so we swapped seats a lot to make the pairings.

By the time we were all down to our underwear, it was getting dark outside. Personally, I was okay with that. We'd run around in front of each other in our underwear on vacations forever.

The only hang-up was SuSu. "Oh, for cryin' in a bucket, woman," she said when I took off my second pair of sweats to reveal my underpants. "Tell me you are gonna go home and *burn* those granny pants. You do not need them anymore."

Rather than get defensive, I just smiled. "You're not the boss of me."

Cards were put down for more opera-style applause.

"One word," she said. "Thong."

"Honey, if you want to wear a string up your fanny and call it un- derwear, that's your business. I just don't want to hear about it." Made me uncomfortable just to think about it. I had long since reached the point where less was worse when it came to underwear. Even with my new shape.

Next, one by one, bras were lost.

Linda lost hers first. She had on a substantial t-strap that hooked in the front. When she unhooked the front, I thought of that scene in *A New Leaf* where a predatory middle-aged widow unhooks the top of her two-piece bathing suit in Walter Matthau's face. "Don't let them out!" he screams, heading for the hills.

When a chuckle escaped me, Linda covered herself with her cards. "Please tell me you did not laugh at me."

The others jumped on it. "Yeah, what's so funny?"

They couldn't just let it pass. Noooo. "Really, I just thought of some- thing else, something from a movie," I explained. "It's no big deal." But laughter gathered in my chest and welled dangerously close to the surface. It was like that episode of *The Mary Tyler Moore Show* when she got the hysterical giggles at the funeral of Chuckles the Clown.

SuSu decided to rib me about it. "Oh, really? Linda bared her chest, and you snicker? I think some amends are in order here." She was en- joying this way too much.

I turned to Linda. "I swear. I wasn't laughing at you." Oh, good grief. "The whole situation just made me think about this funny scene in *A New Leaf* where this widow takes off her top . . ."

The others seemed to be enjoying putting me on the spot.

"Okay, sorry. I deeply and humbly apologize for snickering. By way of restitution, you all have my permission to snicker at me at will."

"I'll forgive you," Linda said. "If you'll take your bra off right now."

Opera applause.

I raised my palms in resignation. "Okay. Okay."

I took down the straps, then reached around back and unhooked the clasp. When it let go, I flunked the bra test. It didn't fall off. Even with my boob lift, there was still enough sag to hold the front of my bra band in place. I looked down, sanguine. "Guess I should have gotten me a little filler, too."

Linda's mouth folded inward and her nostrils elongated as she fought the laughter rising in her.

"See there." I waggled my finger at her. "Just like Chuckles the Clown."

She let it rip, and so did I. It was contagious, all that pent-up nervous energy.

Between spasms, I told them about the scene with Walter Matthau, which didn't go over a fraction as funny as the movie.

Then Diane had to take off her bra, unhooking it and baring her chest with the deliberate grace of the ballet dancer she'd once been. She cloaked herself in dignity, without comment, so we didn't harass her.

Pru lost hers next. She surprised us by being shy, but I guess it was a question of context. Our Red Hat sensibilities were a million miles from the things she'd done to support her drug habit, but she was with us now, so she reacted accordingly. She responded with blushes when we complimented the smooth new skin on her chest and shoulders from her peel.

Next, Teeny lost hers—a size B+ she'd brought to fit her new chest. "It's about time!" She proudly displayed her firm, pert new bustline. "I couldn't wait to show these puppies off."

"Wow. Great job," I admired.

"They look so natural," SuSu marveled.

Linda and Diane pointed to each other and said in unison, "Don't they look natural?" the standard funeral home comment when viewing the body.

That funnied them the most.

Linda peered at Teeny's masterpieces. "Do they feel weird?"

Teeny looked down at them as if she were assessing a new belt or necklace. "Not weird. Just a little different. At first, I was conscious of the extra weight. And they're definitely firmer than the real ones, which was one reason I had them done."

No-longer-shy Di narrowed her eyes. "Would it be too weird if I asked to see what they feel like?" She looked up, earnest. "Nothing spooky. Just a poke."

Teeny laughed. "Poke away."

Diane reached out and gingerly did just that. "Wow. You're right. Definitely firmer, but not fakey feeling."

Curiosity overcame my deeply rooted inhibitions. "May I?"

"Honey," Teeny said, "y'all can all check them out if you want to. But after this, that privilege is reserved for Mr. Right, should he come along. So poke now or forever hold your peace."

I don't know what I was expecting, but they were quite natural in a nubile way.

SuSu passed up the opportunity, cupping her own enhanced bustline, which was still encased in her sexy red lace bra. (Wouldn't you know, the exhibitionist lost last?) "I know what they feel like."

Pru waved off her turn with another blush.

"Okay." Teeny faced SuSu. "Last but not least. Off."

SuSu feigned protest. "I thought we were playing Strip Bridge."

"We are, but when we get down to the last person, it's a waste of time waiting for her to lose."

"Oh, yeah?" SuSu said, her tone light. "Who says?"

"The rules," I was delighted to say.

"Whose rules?" she parried.

"*The* rules."

We both laughed.

Her smile went wide and smug. "Okay. Prepare yourselves for perfection." She unhooked her bra and whipped it off. "Ta-daaa!"

A sixteen-year-old would be jealous.

"Wow," I said, "I can hardly even see the scars."

She nodded. "I've been using their custom scar treatment."

You know, nekkid's not nekkid when you're just admiring the handiwork.

We were still the same people, even without our clothes. And it's amazing how quickly our initial awkwardness had evaporated once we focused on our surgeries instead of our exposed imperfections.

But there was still the matter of our underpants. (I never heard anybody in my region and generation call them "panties.") Losing those was going to be another animal entirely. I hadn't run around barebottomed since I was two.

I found myself wishing I'd never agreed to this hairbrained scheme.

"Okay," SuSu said. "Who's partnered for the next hand?"

We got back to the game, watching the play but deliberately not looking at each other.

Fate had it in for Linda. She lost her underpants first, again.

Thank God the table wasn't glass. Its opaque surface made the final round a lot easier than I'd feared. One by one, we got down to our newly altered birthday suits and assessed the results of the last month with a purely objective eye.

When Diane lost, she stood up and we admired her slimmer hips and narrower waist and firm bustline. SuSu's tightened fanny looked great. But it was when I got up that everybody went nuts.

They rose and circled me to admire the doctor's handiwork.

"Ohmygod." SuSu grasped my forearm and scanned my newly svelte body. "You lost the baby!"

I looked down, quite pleased with myself. "Yep."

"And those hips," Diane admired. "Smooth as they can be."

Linda pointed. "And look at that innie! How buff is that?"

"She did a great job on that," I conceded. "It was the hernia repair behind it, though, that hurt the worst of everything."

"Oh . . . my . . . gosh." Teeny stood there, arms akimbo. "Cher, eat your heart out. I can see daylight between those thighs."

I smoothed a palm across my upper leg. "They sucked the outsides, too."

"And look at those ribs," Pru said. "Not a love handle in sight."

Teeny opened the coat closet where she'd stashed our red hats. "Okay," she said as she handed them to their owners. "Hats on, everybody. I've got a proposition for you. And a present." While we donned our hats, SuSu helped her distribute six shoe boxes labeled with our names on Post-its. "I brought these along as farewell gifts. The sizes are right; I just hope they fit."

I opened my box to find a wild pair of pumps with red heels and toes connected by purple sides, as good-looking as a pair of purple and red pumps could possibly be. And they looked comfortable: stable, one-and-a-half inch heels, cushioned soles, moderately pointed toes. In the box with them, Teeny had added a pair of sassy red-jeweled sunglasses encrusted with brilliant crystals.

I checked the size in the shoe. "Eight and a half, wide. Just my size." I put them on with delight, then stood and added the glasses.

Everybody else modeled theirs. If we weren't a sight!

"This is too priceless for words," Linda said.

"That's what I wanted to talk to y'all about," Teeny said. "You saw that movie *Calendar Girls*."

"Loved it," we all concurred.

"Well, I brought a digital camera with a tripod, and a docking station that puts out prints to do our group portrait. And I was just wondering if y'all had the guts to do one in what we have on now?"

"Ha!" Pru said.

"Love it." This from SuSu.

But Linda and Diane and I launched into immediate protests.

Teeny raised her palms to calm us. "Nobody else ever has to see them. We can burn the chip after we make the prints, as far as I care." She smiled. "I'm not trying to force anything onto anybody. I'm just asking you to consider doing something that I guarantee will make you laugh every time you look at it for the rest of your life."

She had a point there. "If it were that simple, I wouldn't hesitate," I told her. "It's just that things have a way of getting out. How could we be sure nobody but us would ever see them? And I mean, no husbands, no boyfriends, no children, nobody. Ever."

"We could do a triple-pinky oath and spit," SuSu said, deadpan.

Pru lifted her index finger. "We could each leave a sealed envelope telling where the picture was, to be opened by the Red Hats upon our death, and the rest of us would make a solemn ritual of burning the picture."

Now, that made me laugh.

Diane swatted my arm. "This is not funny."

"Yes it is," I said. "If the survivors have to be naked at the disposal of the photo. Ancient naked old ladies gathered around the sacred flame are pretty funny, in my book."

"You always were too weird for panty hose." Diane sniffed.

Linda frowned, considering. "I would do it," she said, "but only if y'all would let me show it to Abby. Just once. I mean, the payback potential there would be glorious."

SuSu and I laughed, but Diane remained unconvinced.

That was enough to win my vote. "I'd do it, too," I said. "And I'd let you show it to Abby. Serves that child right, all she's put you through."

Teeny turned to Diane, the last holdout. "I don't want to coerce anybody. We all do it, or we don't do it. Just think about it for a minute. Years from now, is this something you'll look back on and wish you had done? Or wish you hadn't?"

Diane's nostrils flared. "Well, hell. Why not? I still think you're all insane. But I also know that I'm way too inhibited, so let's do it." She waved her hand, "But get on with it. I want to put my clothes back on."

Teeny put SuSu and Diane and me standing behind three ottomans where the others sat, then positioned the camera on the tripod for a delayed shot. On her way back to her seat, she ran by the drapes and jerked them open, giving us the balcony as a backdrop. While Diane complained, Teeny made it to her seat just in time to say "cheese" when the flash went off.

Destiny being what it was, that was the exact moment when the cabin doors opened wide, and who should barge right in but Miz Gotrocks, depositions in one hand and a magnum of champagne in the other, trailed by a properly horrified woman who appeared to be her personal assistant.

Standing there in nothing but high heels, jeweled sunglasses, and our red hats, we shrieked and scrambled for anything we could find to cover up. I grabbed a sofa cushion and hid behind it.

Miz Gotrocks didn't even seem to notice. She put the champagne on the table, right in front of Pru, then closed in on me. Everybody else scrambled for their clothes. Pru, bless her heart, got the doors closed first, then covered herself.

"Oh, darling," Miz Gotrocks said to me, "I know it's inexcusable to invite myself in this way, but I just had to talk to you about this little statement before we docked, and you, you naughty girl, you, have been avoiding me, haven't you?"

I have rarely been speechless in my life, but I was then, overwhelmed by the soulless, selfish audacity of the woman.

Her expression congealed. "He hasn't paid you off, has he? Because if he has, I'll double the offer, and let you use one of our guest condos in New York whenever you'd like. We cannot let a hoodlum like that Hollywood trash go around roughing up defenseless women like me, can we?"

I finally found my tongue. "Are . . . you . . . crazy? That door was locked! How did you get in here?"

She waved her hand. "Darling, money fixes everything. Now, all I need is for you and your friends to sign these little sworn statements. It's simply a brief and straightforward account of what happened. Just asking you to do your civic duty. Of course, you'll be generously compensated for your inconvenience. My assistant will witness and notarize them, and we'll be out of your hair. You can go right back to your little . . ."

She finally registered the others. ". . . party."

Teeny strode forward, her robe wrapped around her. "How dare you? This is outrageous!" I'd never seen her so angry. "Get out of here, now! Now!" She picked up the phone. "Operator, this is the Neptune Suite. Someone has broken into our rooms and refuses to leave. Please send security at once!"

"Now, now," Miz Gotrocks said, monumentally unimpressed. "We wouldn't want to get ugly about this, would we?" She sneered at our bizarre outfits (or lack of them). "Nobody likes a lot of ugly publicity. I mean, I'm as liberal as they come. I have tons of lesbian friends, but not all of them have come out. If this should get into the press . . ."

She actually had the nerve to reach for the camera, but SuSu snatched it up, tripod and all, and growled out, "If you're trying to add felony larceny to criminal trespass, I'd think again." She started shooting pictures of Miz Gotrocks and her assistant for the record, but I was too offended to move.

I thought I was going to have an aneurysm. "You poisonous bitch!" I told the woman. "We are Red Hats. We are *not* lesbians. We were just showing off our surgeries."

"For the camera?" She smiled a snakey smile and proffered the statement. "Whatever you say."

Just then, a spotlight flashed into our cabin, and we looked out to see the lights of a fishing boat approach.

"Judas, Jonah, and Jezebel!" Diane roared. "Somebody pull the drapes!"

Linda dived for them and got them shut in record time, but dropped her cushion in the process.

At the distraction, Pru disappeared into the bedroom, then came back with a cotton thermal blanket. She snagged SuSu, who handed the camera to Linda for safekeeping, and they put their heads together. Plans were afoot. I backed away from Miz Gotrocks, who rose and followed, yammering away about why I should sign the statement. She kept right on yammering till SuSu and Pru caught her in the blanket, wrapped it around her (ignoring her shrieks), and hustled her out the door.

The four of us managed to get the door closed and keep it that way, despite her quick escape from the blanket and insistent efforts to get back in.

"I'm only going to come back in," the witch of the world called through the less-than-sturdy doors. "Believe me, you'd rather handle this the easy way. I can subpoena you, you know." More banging.

Teeny handed me my robe, and I gratefully covered up, then sank back against the door, purple pumps braced to keep it from sliding.

Miz Gotrocks's terrified assistant held up her hands like a bank robbery hostage. "Please don't hurt me." She lowered her voice. "I think she's horrible, too. I hate her, but the pay's so good . . . I'm so sorry she interrupted your . . ." Her eyes widened even further at the gaffe. "Let me go, and I swear, I'll never get within a mile of you again, even if it costs me my job."

"Oh, please." SuSu jerked on her sweatpants then, in a move worthy of *Fear and Loathing in Las Vegas*, slipped her feet back into the purple and red pumps.

By that point, we were all decently covered, albeit underwearless.

We heard a shift in the disturbance outside the doors. Men's voices. Irate Miz Gotrocks. More men's voices.

"Thank God," Teeny said, tightening her robe around her. "Security." Irate Miz Gotrocks got fainter.

Teeny picked up the phone. "Security, please." She waited. The hallway outside fell silent. "Yes. This is the Neptune Suite. Has the intruder been removed?" She made a wry face. "Very good. How long will it be before we have new coding for our locks?" Frown. "I'm afraid that's unacceptable. The intruder was very persistent." Her features relaxed. "Make that two, and you have a deal." Pause. "Fine. Please have them knock, to let us know they're there. And it's perfectly fine for them to sit." She exhaled heavily. "Are we still in international waters? I see. Please have the captain call me immediately. I'd like to speak to him before I contact my attorneys." She hung up.

Dressed and minus her hat and sunglasses, SuSu confronted the hapless assistant. "I'm going to list just a few of the laws you and your boss broke tonight." She sat, and we watched as she wrote out law after law, down to the numbers and decimals. "If we're in international waters, this could go even worse for her," she bluffed. "As an officer of the court, I strongly recommend that your employer seeks legal counsel before she tries to get within a city block of any of us." She paused, then wrote at the bottom. "Sometimes money doesn't fix everything." She handed over the list. "As her agent, you are just as guilty as she is. Trust me, it will be to both your advantages for her to back off and leave us alone."

There was a knock on the door. Pru opened them a narrow slit, then pulled them wide to reveal two security guards. They touched the brims of their hats. "Not to worry, madam," one said in a German accent. "There shall be no further trouble."

SuSu escorted the grateful assistant into the hallway. "This woman was one of the intruders. Please get her personal information before you let her go back to her employer. And see that we get the information immediately, please."

She closed the doors, and we were finally alone.

With a honkin' huge magnum of champagne.

Teeny and Diane and Linda and I all noticed it at once, and looked in horror to Pru and SuSu.

Pru took the bull by the horns. "SuSu, you want that champagne?"

SuSu smiled. "Heck, yeah, I want that champagne. But I don't need it. How 'bout you?"

"Ditto."

We all went boneless with relief.

"What do you think we should do with it?" Pru asked.

"How about sending it to the captain," SuSu suggested, "with our compliments and a big, fat lawsuit?"

"Whoa." Teeny stood with her arms akimbo, her voice a tight whisper. "We are not suing anybody. I just wanted to put the fear of God into these crazypeople." (In the South, crazypeople is one word.)

Pru and SuSu grinned at Teeny. "Gotcha," SuSu said.

"Y'all," Teeny chided without conviction. "Do not tease me. I have been seriously traumatized."

Diane cocked an eyebrow. "Could we hear that speech again, the one about the odds against anybody seeing us through the window?"

Linda strolled over, eating a piece of apricot flan with her bare hands. (It had been a trying night.) "Was all that stuff you told her assistant true?" she asked SuSu.

"The U.S. laws were accurate, but I might have stretched a bit with the assault and blackmail statutes. And I won't be an officer of the court till I graduate next year. As for the international stuff, that was smoke screen. We haven't done maritime law yet."

Diane went for a slice of flan, herself. "I am never gettin' nekkid again in front of anybody. Ever."

"Not even Clay?"

"Not even my gynecologist."

SuSu was reaching for the phone when it rang. "Hello?" Pause. "Oh, hi."

"The captain?" Teeny mouthed.

SuSu shook her head. She extended the receiver to me. "It's John." When she saw my face fall, she hastened to add, "Ship to shore. No emergency."

Thank goodness.

Or not. What was I going to tell him? "Hello?"

"Hey, honey. Sorry to bother y'all. I tried to make it till tomorrow, but I had to hear your voice. I've decided you must never die. I don't like the world without you in it."

It was as close to poetry as the man was capable of.

Everything else that had happened melted away. I loved him so much in that moment, I felt like my lungs were going to walk out and head for Atlanta. "I miss you, too. So much. So much." Why couldn't I come up with something better than that to say? I was an English major.

"So, what have you girls been up to on your last night? Nothing too wild, I hope."

I glanced at the others, poised. No way, was I ever going to tell him the truth about tonight. If I did, he'd never let me play with the Red Hats again. Plus, being a man, he'd make it into something kinky that it wasn't. "Oh, just depends on what you call wild. We played some bridge."

The girls covered their mouths and crossed their eyes.

"Teeny gave us some red and purple heels and red rhinestone sunglasses as lovely parting gifts." They rolled around in exaggerated mime. "Oh, and guess what? SuSu won thirty-five thousand dollars at the slots in the casinos. Not tonight. A couple of weeks ago."

"I swear, woman, you have a direct channel to heaven. That makes up for a lot, doesn't it?"

"Absolutely." I had to get off, or I couldn't answer for what I might blurt out. "Honey, thanks so much for calling. You are the sweetest thing that ever drew breath."

He paused. "Are you okay?"

Of all times for him to pick up on the subtleties. "I'm just homesick for you and our house and our bed. A month is way too long to be away."

"Well, you'll be happy to know that I called a maid service, and the house is all clean. They even changed the bed. And they didn't break a thing." For a Bigbrain, such domestic initiative constituted a Red Sea miracle.

"That is so wonderful. Now we can just hole up and enjoy each other."

Then he said something he demonstrated regularly but didn't say often. "I love you," he said. "I loved you the way you were before you left."

"Well, honey, you're gonna really love me now. Except when the Visa bills come in. I'm gonna need some new clothes."

I could hear his dear, quiet smile. "Why don't you hit SuSu up for a loan?"

"Nut. I love you. Bye."

I was past ready to be home.

The captain arrived five minutes later, looking harried and concerned. Teeny gave it to him with a velvet glove, then sent him on his way with the champagne. Exhausted, we packed, then went to bed.

The next morning, there was no sign of Miz Gotrocks, thanks be to God.

But we were still ambushed.

When we cleared customs and headed for our limo, who should be waiting outside for us but the jerk with the shih tzu and a cart full of roses, clearly with earning our good will in mind. He called us by name and pushed the cart toward us. We took one look at him, died laughing, and kept on walking. All but Pru. She ran over to snag the card he was proffering, then she kissed him, long and hard. He stood there like a scarecrow, in shock, and staggered when she laughed and let him go. Then she caught back up with us, giggling like she'd just pulled some innocuous sorority stunt. "I've done a lot of things in my life, but I never kissed a movie star, jerk or otherwise. Couldn't pass that up."

Encouraged, the jerk pushed the cart full of roses after us. "Just a few minutes, ladies! I brought you these flowers! And I'd love to take you out for lunch before you go back to Atlanta."

He did his best to cut off the limo with the cart, but it was too unwieldy.

Meanwhile, a man who looked vaguely familiar got out of a limo with an armful of delphiniums (SuSu's favorite) and headed straight across the parking lot toward SuSu.

"Ohmygod," she said, her expression one of alarm. "What's *he* doing here?"

Then I realized who he was. "The Mattress Man!" SuSu's study partner, the one she was always complaining about. "What, has he got a crush on you or something?"

"The man's the most irritating human being in the world!" she fumed. "He's an idiot, with no sense of propriety."

We'd certainly attracted our share of those lately. Behind us, the jerk movie star was doing his best to bribe Linda and Diane to lie for him.

As the Mattress Man approached, SuSu waved the rest of us toward the limousine. "I'll take care of this. Y'all go on. I'll catch up with you at the airport."

For obvious reasons, we hesitated.

"Please!" she pleaded. "I'll be fine. Just go. Damn, this is embarrassin'."

He was getting closer.

Diane frowned. "At least let one of us go with you, for security."

"No!" SuSu thrust both palms forward. "No. I can handle this myself. I'm begging you, just go."

Eyes on her, we reluctantly headed back to our limo, trailed by the movie star, who hadn't stopped for breath in at least five minutes, and his cart of roses.

SuSu stomped up to the Mattress Man, bloody murder in her face, snatched the flowers he proffered, then started flailing away on his head with them and fussing him out to beat the band. But she didn't look afraid, so I relaxed.

Undaunted, the Mattress Man laughed and did his best to fend off the blows as she whipped him back to his waiting limo and got in. He followed, and his driver closed the door behind them. Just as the limo pulled away, the Mattress Man rolled down the window and heaved the denuded stalks out the window.

"What was *that?*" Linda huffed.

"Come on." I urged them toward our car. "Let's get to the airport so she can tell us."

As we piled in, the movie star sped up in our wake, talking even faster and louder. When he tried to push the cart off the curb, it turned sideways, spilling water and flowers everywhere.

We took advantage of the diversion to escape.

Diane turned around and looked out the back window. "All those roses." She shook her head. "What a waste." She pointed. "Oh, look. He's giving them away now. That's good." Her thrifty Presbyterian soul could relax.

Linda bristled. "He knew who we were. I thought that ship was sooooo confidential."

Teeny arched an eyebrow. "So did I."

"Man," Linda groused. "It galls the schmoo out of me how much any Tom, Dick, or Harry can find out about you these days."

"Don't worry, sweetie," Teeny consoled. "My lawyers will make this go away."

"And how much will that cost you?" I grumped. "It isn't fair. We did nothing wrong, and you end up having to clean up this mess to the tune of goodness-knows-what."

She patted my arm. "My lawyers are on retainer. It won't cost me a penny extra."

Pru pointed skyward. "Oh, I forgot." She took the card out of her pocket. "I got his card."

Finally! The jerk's name.

We huddled over it.

Roy Finklestein?

"Have you ever heard of Roy Finklestein?" Linda asked.

None of us had.

"Maybe that's his real name," Teeny offered.

"More likely," Linda said, "it's his agent or one of his underlings."

"That guy?" I frowned. "You think he's big enough to have underlings?" I shook my head.

"Regardless," Teeny said, "He's the lawyers' problem now, not ours."

Why couldn't things just be simple?

At least we looked good, I consoled myself. Damned good.

As for the Mattress Man incident, SuSu was waiting for us at the gate, alone.

"SuSu! Thank goodness!"

We descended on her, full of questions.

"What was your study partner doing down here? And with flowers? I thought you couldn't stand him."

She arched a perfect eyebrow. "Like I said, the man's an idiot. I told him to get lost, and he did."

I repeated the same question I'd asked back at the pier. "Has he got a crush on you, or something?"

She sat down and opened a copy of *Elle*. "Something."

We all waited for the rest, but she seemed intent on the magazine.

"That's it?" I prodded. "This is us, honey. We want details."

SuSu didn't look up. "Sorry. He embarrassed me. I sent him packing. End of story. Tradition Five." (Mind your own business.)

The melody to "Breaking up Is Hard to Do" erupted in my brain, but the words were, *Backing off is hard to do-oo.*

The rest of us exchanged looks that ranged from consternation to annoyance to acceptance.

I hate when people throw up boundaries and get all firm about them. After all the excitement of our trip and the debarkation, there we were in a bubble of anticlimax.

"Okay, then," Pru said in her new capacity as SuSu's mentor. "There's an ice cream stand back there. Who wants to top off our trip with a final blast of carbs?"

Linda raised a finger. "Count me in."

Diane shot SuSu one last glance, then joined them.

Teeny looked to me. "Coming?"

"Might as well, as they say in Buford." I took SuSu's arm. "Come on. You started this trip poutin'. I'll be darned if you're gonna end it this way. Let's all get high on sugar."

SuSu rose. "Now *there's* a proposition."

We took our gorgeous selves to the ice cream shop and did the place proud, which is what Red Hats are supposed to do.

24

Red Hats Rule

Swan Coach House. Tuesday, April 13, 2004. 11:15 A.M.

JOHN SAYS IT'S MY SMILE THAT TURNS HEADS SINCE I GOT BACK, how happy I am. But he always has been oblivious to the bald realities of life. Plain and simple, the bod makes a difference. Saleswomen were more deferential, and my new clothes fit and looked more like the women in the magazines.

Well, maybe I was smiling more, more confident. That doesn't hurt. But it sure was fun getting a little attention after all these years. Even the valets at the Coach House stood back and took notice when I drove up.

The studly young blond sized me up with genuine "man eyes." "Lookin' mighty fine today, Miz Baker," he purred out. "Mighty fine indeed." He opened my door with a flourish.

I stepped out into the dappled shade under the huge, tasseled oaks to the sight and scent of massed azaleas, Japanese magnolia blossoms, and bulbs galore.

Every year, I marveled afresh at how gorgeous the season is in Atlanta. If you could only breathe.

Oh, gosh. I hadn't snorted my spray that filled up all the parking spaces in my nose so the pollen couldn't attach and drive me crazy. I pulled the little pump dealie out of my purse and was about to use it when I sensed the valets still looking at me. I turned, and sure enough, they waved.

Histamine be damned. I was too sassy to do such nerdy things in public anymore. I strode into the restaurant and sashayed all the way down to a stall in the bathroom to take care of my sinuses. Then I sashayed back up to find Pru waiting at our corner banquette.

People noticed as I crossed the dining room. Heads turned. Assessing looks peeked above hands that sheltered speculative whispers. I couldn't wait till they saw the others. Not that the differences were glaring. We all just looked like improved versions of ourselves.

Pru and I had talked on the phone a lot, so I knew she was doing great. But seeing her again for the first time after our cruise, I was struck anew at the transformation, inside and out. She looked so happy in her stylish purple pantsuit and red picture hat with violets at the crown. And she had on the purple and red shoes Teeny had given us. (Mine were at home. I only wear heels when I have to.)

"Hey, there, gorgeous." I hugged as close as our hats allowed. "How's Bubba doing?"

"Believe it or not, he loves that job Teeny got him with the recording studio downtown. He started day before yesterday, and it seems the boy is a whiz with all those amps and things. He's happy as a clam."

"How about Pru?"

She popped that dimple. "Pru is . . . Pru again. Thanks to y'all, and a lot of hard work. And a program that works."

"Is it hard all the time?" I couldn't imagine. I couldn't even stay off *carbs*.

"Terrible. Wonderful. Hard, hard, hard," she said evenly. "But just for today, it's good. Very good. And it helps that SuSu and I can support each other."

Linda arrived with Diane.

Heads turned for them, too. Diane's toned-up shape looked even better in her own designs. Linda, still just glad to be alive, kept her chin slightly elevated, the only indication of her pride in her shapely new neck and resurrected cheekbones. She'd lost twenty pounds, but thanks to her slimmer face, it looked like twice that.

"Hey." We all air-kissed and hugged.

Odd, how the passage of only two weeks had triggered just a whiff of awkwardness between us. After four weeks in such close quarters on the cruise, we'd pretty much kept to ourselves the past sixteen days. But I wasn't worried. By the end of lunch, we'd have things back in balance.

"So," I said to Linda. "How are Abby and Osama?"

She snorted in a most unladylike fashion. "They're talking about getting married."

Uh-oh. "Specifically, or generally?"

"Specifically, as it happens." Predictably, Linda was less than thrilled, to put it mildly, but what can you do? The "kids" were almost thirty.

"Have they said what kind of service they want?"

Linda's bosom swelled even further. "Rastafarian."

We all exchanged pregnant glances. "So," Pru ventured, "what kind of service is that?"

"Sarongs, I would imagine," Linda said in a long-suffering tone she was perfectly entitled to. "Lots of large, matted hair. As for the ceremony itself, there will probably be assorted farm animals sacrificed to idols, and plenty of communal pot-smoking and heavy metal music."

"Probably won't be having the reception at the Standard Club, then, huh?"

Linda shook her head in full martyr mode.

Pru laughed. "Linda. Are you serious, or are you just making up all that idol stuff?"

That succeeded in getting a smile out of her. "Busted. But they really do want a Rastafarian service. With a rabbi, too, of all things." She shook her head again. "How schizophrenic is that?"

"I'd say it just about fits the situation," I said.

Diane gave Linda a shoulder hug. "Oh, sweetie. At least she hasn't rejected the faith of your fathers completely."

"Oy." Linda rolled her eyes. "Crush glass, then jump over the broom . . . ? Oy, oy, oy."

I tried not to laugh, really I did.

Fortunately, SuSu strode in looking like one of those luminous space-beings from *Cocoon,* her hair drawn back into a classic chignon at the nape.

"Ohmygosh," Diane said as she approached. "Can you believe how fabulous she looks? She's radiant."

She'd practically dropped off the world after we got back, which was understandable considering the makeup work she had to do in addition to her regular assignments. I'd forced myself not to obsess about her progress with AA in the past two weeks, but it was clear to see she'd done well.

Pru spoke what the rest of us were thinking. "Getting sober and facing down your demons can do that for a girl."

I glanced at her with a smile of pride. "We know. You showed us."

A dozen feet behind SuSu, I caught a glimpse of Teeny coming in through the gathering crowd in the lobby and felt that reassuring sense of completion I always got when we were all together.

"Hey, Suse," I greeted her as the others made nice. Something was definitely up.

Diane eyed her shrewdly. "You look mighty happy."

She flounced into her seat. (Safe to do now that six weeks had passed since having her fanny sucked.) "I am." She grinned. "I made a perfect score on two major tests. And I'm getting excited about being a summer associate at Sutherland, Asbill, and Brennan."

"Couldn't get on with Injuries R Us, huh?" I joked.

"SuSu, that's great," Pru said. "I never made a perfect score on anything. What an accomplishment!"

Especially considering the difficult changes she'd made. Not to mention missing three weeks of classes.

"Was it awful," I asked her, "trying to get caught up when you got back to school?"

SuSu exhaled with satisfaction. "I have quite literally lived with my study group since the day I got home."

I deliberately didn't ask about having to study with the Mattress Man. She'd bring that up if she wanted to. But obviously, his presence hadn't hurt her work. It must have been awkward, especially since studying requires you to focus deeply. Still, I couldn't help envying the linear concentration of SuSu's life. Working with a tight-knit group to achieve a lofty goal. Blazing trails at our age.

Teeny bustled over to the table and sat, pretty radiant, herself. "Y'all are not gonna believe what happened last Saturday night."

"What?" Diane dutifully asked.

"I went to this charity gala, and there was a party afterward with a bunch of the entertainers, and I met Paul McCartney and Michael

Collins and Cyndi Lauper and Billy Joel and a bunch of other people, but you want to know the one I liked best of all?" She forged ahead. "Elton John. I was sitting in a quiet corner with an empty chair, and he came over and struck up a conversation, and when he found out I practically lived across the street from where he had those penthouses, he just jumped right in, and by the end of the evening, we were like old friends. And I am here to tell you, that little man can still sing the ceiling off." She took a sip of iced water. "Not that the others were any slouches. They were great. It was really a fun evening."

Another soliloquy! The woman was getting downright talkative in her old age. Give the girl some boobs, and you can't shut 'er up.

"I don't remember hearing about anything like that," Diane said.

"Sorry." Teeny daintily spread her napkin. "I forgot to mention, it wasn't here. It was in New York."

"You little jet-setter, you," SuSu kidded.

Maria arrived with warm bread and took our drink orders. You've gotta love somebody who asks you what you want every month for years as if she really believes you might order something besides your usual.

I ordered unsweet iced tea with no lemon, then turned to Diane. "So. How are things with you?"

"Busy, busy, busy. We got the cancer-patient products fabricated and started production in record time. Had to be divine intervention. The advance orders are phenomenal, particularly from hospital gift shops, but we project that direct orders from the Web site will be our hottest market."

No mention of Clay?

Linda asked the question for me. "What does Clay think about your working such long hours?"

Diane brushed it off. "He pounds his chest like Willie B"—Zoo Atlanta's late, lamented silverback gorilla—"but I just ignore it. The old adage is true: The less available you are, the more men want you."

"Don't you miss him?" Pru asked.

Diane considered. "Yes, I do, in the moments when I've had the time to notice I'm alone. Yes, I miss him very much, then." She picked up a mini muffin. "But most of the time, I have a ball tearin' it up at work, come home late, nuke a nice frozen dinner and have a glass of wine, then curl up with my cat and a good book and fall asleep. Unless it's Wednesday; then I watch *West Wing.*"

"Not very exciting," Teeny commiserated. "I've been telling you, you work too hard."

"Need I remind you, boss," Diane said evenly, "I just took a month off."

"Well, maybe you need to take another one. With a man."

Diane reared back. "Can y'all believe this? Our little Miss Mass-Every-Morning, advising me to go off with a man who's not my husband. For the second time."

"I said it before. I'm just suggesting y'all might benefit from getting away together for a while, that's all," Teeny clarified. "Anything else is between you and God. And Clay, of course," she qualified with an impish grin.

"Tsk, tsk, tsk. Do I hear qualitative morals?" I pruned up like the church lady. "Teens, that was worthy of a Unitarian."

"Thenk yew." Teeny said, dodging the barb entirely.

"I really like your Twelve Sacred Traditions," Pru interjected. "Especially the religious and political part, the way you respect each other's beliefs even when you disagree with them. It's the same way in my twelve-step program."

"Our Twelve Sacred Traditions are yours now, too," SuSu reminded her.

Pru smiled. "I know. I just wanted to say that."

Like a lot of things Pru popped up with, it had seemed like a non sequitur. But I recognized that she'd steered us away from potential conflict by gently and obliquely reminding us of our own rules.

"So. Who has the joke?" Linda asked.

We looked around. Nobody's light went on.

"Don't tell me nobody had the joke. Who did it last?"

We pointed to Teeny.

That meant Diane was supposed to be next.

"Oh, crud," Diane said. "I totally forgot."

"Have your secretary put it in your tickler file," Linda suggested.

Which reminded me. "We need to add Pru to the rotation," I said.

"Listen, y'all," Pru said, "I cannot tell a joke right to save my life."

SuSu briskly patted her shoulder. "Good. Teeny can't, either. She'll be delighted to have some company."

"Does this mean we don't get a joke?" Teeny asked, disappointed.

Maria arrived with our drinks and more muffins.

"We must have our joke," Linda whined.

"You need a joke?" Maria asked us. It was the first time she'd ever intruded into our personal conversation, but it was welcome.

"Absolutely," I said. The others nodded.

"Okay. I give you a joke," she said in her soft Hispanic accent. Coffeepot poised, she leaned in to be heard.

"Just before mating season, Pedro the pig farmer's prize boar gets loose and, *bam!* gets hit by a truck, so Pedro has a big feast for all the village with the meat. Then the next morning, he must take his fifteen lady pigs to Farmer Manuel's boar to be mated."

We hung on her every word.

"When he comes back that night to pick them up, he asks Farmer Manuel how he will know if they have mated successfully. Manuel tells him that if the pigs are grazing, they are pregnant. Since pigs do not graze, this is an easy way to tell. The next morning, Farmer Pedro gets up, and the pigs are not grazing, so he takes them back for another day.

"The next morning, none of the pigs are grazing, so he loads them back up and returns them to the boar for another day.

"Still no grazing. Back they go.

"The morning after that, Pedro is afraid to look, so he asks his wife, 'Maria, are the pigs grazing?'

"She shakes her head. 'No, I am sad to say. They are not grazing.'

" 'Well then,' Pedro asks, 'what *are* they doing?'

"His wife looks out the window. 'They are all in the truck, and one of them is honking the horn.' "

She beamed at us, waiting for the light to go on.

There was a pulse of silence, then delighted laughter.

Maria grinned.

"Maria, that was wonderful." Teeny pulled off her pert little straw pillbox with the turned-up brim. "Here." She handed it to Maria. "I make you an honorary Red Hat."

Maria bobbed a happy bow, but didn't attempt to put the hat on over the thick ponytail at the nape of her neck. "I am truly honored to have such a gift from my gracious ladies." She headed back for the kitchen. "Your meals will be right out."

"So." Pru turned to Linda, shifting gears abruptly. "When's Abby's wedding?"

"They're talking about August," Linda said. "Outside. I ask you, who gets married in August, anyway, much less outside? You bake your brains out."

"What happened to 'glad to be alive'?" I chided.

"Oh, can it," Linda retorted. "Think of your Callie as the bride, then tell me, 'glad to be alive.'"

Pru cocked her head. "I love weddings. They're so romantic. People have such hopes. Hope is a good thing." She looked to Linda. "Are they happy together?"

Linda's silver brows lifted. "Yes," she admitted. "But he's a pot-head."

"So is Bubba," Pru said without offense. "I can't do anything about that, but you can't love people in pieces. So I accept him as he is. No expectations."

"Well, whatever kind of calico wedding it turns out to be," Linda said briskly, "I'm expecting all of you to be there for moral support, August or not."

"Wouldn't miss it for the world," Diane said.

We all assured Linda we would be there for her. We always are.

SuSu scanned the five of us, something clearly on her mind. "Y'all, I'd like to ask you a favor. I've been working like a field hand for the past two years, March excepted. After exams at the end of this month, I want to kick back and have some fun—sober fun. So I'd like to throw a Red Hat bash to celebrate. Here, upstairs, the Monday after exams. That's May third. Do you think y'all could come?"

Her first stab at a dry party? I'd come in just my red hat, purple-and-red shoes, and sunglasses if it would guarantee a success, which I absolutely, positively knew it would not, so John—and the party—were safe.

"Come in your best Red Hat duds," she instructed. "I really want y'all to meet my study group and friends from school. We can show those nerdy twenty-somethings how to have a good time without anesthesia. We'll have music and dancing."

Conspicuous omission of reference to the Mattress Man.

Maybe when I saw him in person, I could figure out what the heck was going on.

Linda laughed. "Sweetie, we were sold when you said you wanted us to come to a party."

SuSu relaxed. "I won't have time to do invitations, but I'll call and let you know the particulars."

"Works for me." Wups. John. "I hope this includes dates?"

"Oh, definitely. I want everybody to have somebody to dance with."

"Good." Linda lifted her single chin toward Diane. "We can all meet Clay."

Diane nodded.

SuSu looked to Teeny and Pru. "That means you two, too. I don't care if it's the mailman, just bring somebody to dance with."

The gauntlet had been thrown.

Teeny nodded to Pru. "We can do this. Call me."

We settled back and ate our lunches, weaving a more intricate pattern of friendship enriched by the once-missing thread that was back in our design.

Until Phoebe Abercrombie waltzed over and stopped Linda in midanecdote. "Y'all, I apologize for intrudin' this way, but I could not eat another bite until I asked you one question. Where have you been, and what have you done? We are talkin' de Soto's dream here. Fountain of youth." She scanned our group with envy. "Don't be selfish, *please.* Tell."

We looked to each other askance, lips literally curled inward.

Teeny, of course, smoothed things over. "Fresh carrot juice," she whispered in deadly earnest.

Phoebe frowned. "Carrot juice?"

Teeny nodded. "Fresh. At least a quart a day." She leaned in closer. "Plus saline high colonics once a month. Those are very important." We were all trying desperately to keep a straight face. "And the Carrot

Juice Workout, of course. But the fresh carrot juice and the high colonics really put it over the top. I tell you, it does miracles. Totally rejuvenates the skin and melts cellulite deposits. We're the proof."

Phoebe grasped her hand. "Thank you so much, darling. I swear, I won't tell a soul." She laid her finger to her lips, then hurried back to her table, where she immediately huddled with three of her closest friends from the Opera Guild.

Diane nudged Teeny with a broad, flat smile. "You are so bad."

Teeny laughed. "Oh, it won't hurt 'em."

Two weeks later, women all over Buckhead were looking decidedly orange, the enema business was booming, health food stores couldn't keep fresh carrot juice on the shelves, and every gym in town offered the Carrot Juice Workout.

Sometimes it's fun just to be alive.

25

"I Hope You Dance . . ."

Swan Coach House, upstairs sun porch. Monday, May 3, 2004. 8:00 P.M.

JOHN AND I CROWDED INTO THE TINY ELEVATOR. "I CANNOT BElieve she sprang for valet parking," I said, adjusting my red rhinestone tiara.

"It's her money," John said in that live-and-let-live way he had.

I grasped his lapels and gave him a good wiggle where it counted. "Now remember, you promised to be charming, which we all know you can be. And you promised not to go off with the men and forget I'm there."

He wiggled back, smiling on me with a half-lidded blend of lust and affection. "This, from Miss Sputnik, who's always off in orbit somewhere as soon as we get to a party?"

"Guilty as charged," I said as the little elevator wheezed to a stop at the second floor. "But not tonight. Tonight, I won't run off and leave you. I want a good, old-fashioned date." The doors opened. "Can we do that?"

He shot me a sexy look, then swept me into his arms and danced me right out of the elevator and into an attractive, tall, stocky man.

Oh, Lord. The Mattress Man. But then, he would be there. He was SuSu's study partner.

"Sorry." John kept his arm behind me, but moved alongside me to speak to the man. "I was just dancing my bride to the party."

"I'm all for dancin' our brides." The guy stuck out his hand. "You must be John and Georgia."

He and John shook. "We met," I said, bristling. "Sort of."

John was oblivious. "And you're . . ."

The Mattress Man colored. "Oh, gosh, I'm sorry I didn't introduce myself. I'm a little nervous, meetin' SuSu's friends and all. I'm Stan McCann."

"The Mattress Man," I bit out. "From those annoying commercials on the TV at night."

John's eyes widened at my complete lapse of social graces. "You look much thinner in person," he offered in an awkward effort to smooth things over.

But Stan McCann didn't turn a hair. "It's the ukulele," he said, deadpan. "And the baby bonnet." He shook his head. "Adds forty pounds."

I sputtered a laugh. In spite of myself, I couldn't help liking somebody so unpretentious.

The way SuSu had described him that first year, I'd expected him to be chomping on a fat, half-smoked cigar, but he was really charming.

"She told me you were the prettiest one," he complimented with just the right mix of flattery and decorum. "You're a lucky man, John."

I sensed John's territorial hackles rise and was delighted. "Thanks, Stan," he said, aloof. "I know it."

Stan motioned across the landing. "SuSu's on the sun porch with the bar and the finger foods. She put me here to send everybody out there till the ballroom's ready."

Ballroom? I'd hardly call it a ballroom. The largest of the private rooms had a dance floor, true, but even it was a pretty intimate space.

"Thanks, Stan." John steered me toward the glassed-in balcony. "C'mon, honey. Let's go meet some of those legal eaglets SuSu's been telling us about."

We stepped down onto the slightly sloping floor of what had once been outdoors. The balcony remained, but it had long since been glassed in.

At the far corner by a formidable collection of nonalcoholic beverages, SuSu was talking to three young couples I assumed were the infamous legal eaglets. She had on an amazing purple sequined halter top that made the most of the new puppies and her peel, with a long bell of red satin skirt. Her hair was caught up at the crown and decorated with a charming explosion of red feathers and sparkles. She looked even more radiant than four weeks ago.

I was pretty sure why. She must have aced her exams.

"Wow." John looked down the left side of the room at an impressive array of fresh fruits and chocolate fondue, lovely crudités with dips, mushrooms stuffed with sausage, and fried crab claws with cocktail sauce. "She's going first-class all the way on this one."

SuSu glanced over and spotted us. "Georgia! John!" She turned to the younger set. "Please excuse me. I'll be right back with some people you're going to enjoy." Then she rushed to us. "I got it! Number one in my class!"

She didn't mention her other achievement—almost two months sober—but she didn't need to. We could all tell from her clear-eyed glow.

She wriggled between us and hooked our arms. "C'mon. I want you to meet some of my study group. Craig's incredible with researching case law." She led us to the thin, callow young man who looked decidedly subterranean. "Georgia and John Baker, allow me to present Craig Maier and his date, Megan." Another child of the night, with a lank, butcher-job haircut and no makeup. They both had on baggy clothes and looked like they needed transfusions. "Megan and Craig, these are two of my very best friends."

"SuSu's told me so much about you, Craig," I said as I shook his hand, which felt like it was made out of damp sponge rubber. I managed not to cringe.

John was charming to Megan. "Are you in school?" he asked her.

She nodded. "Tech. Postdoctorate."

That waif could not possibly be postdoctoral. She'd have had to graduate when she was twelve.

John brightened. "I teach at Tech."

"I know. I've read several of your papers on string theory."

"Really?" He straightened, smoothing his hand down his tie, a strong subliminal indicator of the direction his brain was taking. "What's your field?"

Behind those raggedy bangs, Megan actually batted her almost-invisible eyelashes at him. "I'm doing postdoctoral research with fractals."

John's smile widened. "Fractals. Fascinating stuff. Tell me what you're doing."

Megan looked up at him with patent lust as she started rattling off random theory jargon, one of the love languages of the Bigbrain physics tribe. Whether her lust was intellectual or otherwise, it was my turn to get territorial.

Two years ago, I wouldn't even have noticed. Now that I was hopelessly besotted with the man, I cared very much.

"Oh, look, John. There's Brooks and Linda." Hooking his arm, I beamed at Megan. "Please excuse us for a moment." Or forever. "We need to speak to our friends."

"We'll talk later," John called back as I steered him across the room.

SuSu, who had been enjoying the whole thing, waggled her fingers good-bye.

I hugged Brooks warmly when we reached them. "Hey, honey. How are things in the OR?"

"Bloody mahvelous," he quipped in response, as he had for the past thirty years.

Meanwhile, John hugged Linda, as he always did when we met. That, I did not mind one whit.

Brooks turned to John, his arm around my shoulders. "You'd better hang onto this girl. Since she got back from that cruise, she's man-bait."

"I know." John drew me close, anything but threatened.

I felt feisty and jealous and more than a little turned on.

"Hey," I said to Linda. "You look mahvelous."

Linda bobbed a tiny curtsy. "So do you. Very slinky." She inclined her head toward Craig and Megan. "What was that all about?"

"Oh. Megan. Just another in a long line of baby Bigbrains on the make. She was after his *mind*. I just wasn't in the mood for it tonight."

John moved around behind me and circled my arms, his chin perched just behind my tiara. "Yes, she was after my mind," John teased, enjoying my jealousy. "And more."

I swatted at him. "Cut that out."

He laughed like a boy and swung me into a Fred Astaire and Ginger Rogers whirl the likes of which we hadn't done in years. I thanked the good Lord I had on heels with slippery enough soles to make the moves with him.

Polite applause broke out from the legal eaglets and their dates.

Megan took a swat at Craig. "How come you never do anything like that with me?" she complained.

John and I laughed and came to rest back beside Brooks and Linda.

Linda let out a satisfied sigh. "Y'all are so disgusting. Keep it up."

"Oh, yeah? How about us?" Brooks stepped back, erect with arms poised, humming the opening notes of a tango. (They'd been taking lessons.) Linda stepped into a slow, seductive rendition that made all of us who were watching forget that they were two round little gray-haired people.

We heard applause from the doorway, and looked over to see Pru walk in with a tall, apologetic-looking man I didn't recognize.

SuSu hurried over and greeted them, then introduced the guy as Doyle Travers. He had kind, tired eyes, but seemed awkward and out of his element.

"Doyle and I met through a mutual friend," Pru explained. "He's the best dancer I know, so I asked him to come with me tonight." She fixed a reassuring look of pride on him, and he stood a little straighter. Pru looked comfortable but attractive in a deep purple pantsuit with a red camisole.

Then Doyle saw the food, and I knew where he was headed. "Can I get you a plate?" he asked Pru.

"You go ahead. I'll be right here."

There was something in the air. I couldn't put my finger on it, but I sensed a tidal shift in our cosmos, which made no sense, because we were all firmly anchored in our lives.

Who wasn't there?

Teeny. Clay and Diane.

Oooo. Maybe that was it. Maybe Diane and Clay had reached an understanding.

Speak of the devil, Diane walked in looking smashing in royal purple leather jeans and boots, a fringed satin western shirt with a modestly plunging neckline, and topping it off, a perfectly scaled red cowboy hat with feathers and rhinestones around the crown.

We all went over to greet her, anxious to meet the elusive Clay.

When it became obvious she was alone, Linda peered out into the landing. "Where's Clay?"

Diane smiled, a touch of wistfulness in the resolution she showed. "North Carolina would be my guess."

I had a bad feeling about this. "He couldn't come?"

"He wasn't invited."

The men had sense enough to drift away and leave the Red Hats to deal with such touchy woman stuff.

"Okay," SuSu said. "Enough with the one-word answers. What's going on here?"

"Well, I decided to take Teeny's advice and go away with Clay for a while. And guess what? He proposed."

"That's good," Pru said. "Isn't it?"

"Not if he wants me to commute to North Carolina every weekend. And holiday. And give him unlimited access to all my assets, with no prenuptial." Her features hardened with disappointment. "And especially not when I checked up on his financial status and found out he was in debt up to his eyeballs. The house, the cars, his businesses, the condo in the mountains. All of it was hocked to the hilt. No wonder his kids were so friendly. They were hoping I would bail him out."

"Sonofabitch," SuSu said. "A gold digger."

"Oh, Diane." I hugged her, but she was too embarrassed to hug me back.

"Do we need to get a gun?" Pru asked. " 'Cause I know where we can get one that's untraceable, cheap."

"Pru!" Diane exhaled in exasperation.

Pru shot a finger-gun at her with a grin. "Gotcha."

"Oh, sweetie," Linda said. "So you're here all by yourself?"

Diane perked right up. "Nope. I've got a date, but he had a meeting out of town, so he had to meet me here." She went sly on us. "You know him."

I tried to think of somebody we knew who traveled in his work that Diane might invite, but came up dry. "Okay, we give. Who is it?"

"You'll see." Diane hardly looked brokenhearted. She left us and went over to greet John and Brooks, who introduced her to Doyle.

The caterer came in and snagged SuSu, leading her away toward the room with the dance floor. When they opened the door across the landing, we heard the sounds of a band setting up.

Linda tucked her semisingle chin. "Live music?"

"Sounds like it." I poked my head out onto the landing, but the ballroom door had closed. "Band must have been late. Guess that's the hang-up."

It was already almost 8:30.

"Any ideas about Diane's date?" Pru asked.

"Not a clue," Linda said. "If I'd have had anybody in mind, I would have fixed her up with them."

"Somebody we know," Pru mused.

I raised a finger. "Come to think of it, where's *SuSu's* date?"

"Good question."

SuSu reappeared, only to be accosted by the Red Hats.

"Where's your date?" I asked her.

SuSu walked over to the window overlooking the parking area and peered into the darkness. "In due time." She shooed us over toward her study group, who had congregated at the far end of the buffet and didn't appear to be having a very good time. "Now would y'all please mingle? I asked you all here so you could meet each other. I'm telling you, these are very wonderful people. Please go and charm them."

"Oh, all right." We'd just have to wait till the mystery dates arrived to find out what was up.

We were mingling away when I saw Diane look over toward the doorway and light up like a Christmas tree.

In unison, the five of us followed her line of vision to a tall, gorgeous hunk of cowboy.

"Cameron!"

Cameron and John, in the same room? I almost passed out from an orgasm, on the spot.

Stetson in hand, Cameron ambled over to Diane and met the men, then turned and came alone to Pru. "Do you remember me?"

Impulsive as the teenager she had once been, Pru jumped on him like a monkey, wrapping her legs around his waist and clapping him on the back. "Do I? Man, you saved my life!" She pointed to him, announcing to the room, "This man saved my life. Perfect stranger, he talked me into leaving Vegas when I was hell-bent on destruction."

Doyle tipped his Coke in Cameron's direction. "Mighty nice of you."

Cameron just stood there, smiling graciously as if he didn't have a grateful addict wrapped around his waist.

Diane came over and tapped Pru on the shoulder. "That's my date, sweetie. You think you could let go of that leg lock so we can say hello?"

Pru flushed the color of her hat. She ejected backward, almost flattening Linda in the process.

"Easy, tiger." Cameron caught her arm in time to prevent a tumble.

Watching him turn to Diane, I could almost see the hormones pulsing between them, even stronger than they had in Vegas.

Gazing up at him, she murmured, "Cameron's takin' me back to the ranch for a couple of weeks."

Good for her. That was some tidal change.

SuSu acted more nervous by the minute. "I wonder where Teeny is." She looked at her watch. "She's never this late." She turned to me, apropos of nothing, and said, "I asked my kids and their significant others, but they had other things to do."

Kids. One night, to help celebrate their mother's accomplishments, and they couldn't be bothered. I made a mental note to do some godmotherly phone scolding.

I heard a car pull in and looked outside to see a limo. "Here's somebody." Either Teens or SuSu's date.

"Georgia, come here, please." John summoned my attention away from the window. "I want you to meet Andrew. He got four book awards his first year."

"Just a second, honey." I looked back to see I'd missed the passengers' getting out.

Rats.

I crossed to meet the boy who had won one more book award than even SuSu (a serious coup in Law School). John was really in his element. These were very brilliant kids.

I wondered if any of them had even heard of the Shag or the Stroll. Well, once the band finally cranked up, they'd learn tonight.

"Hey, everybody," Teeny's voice came from the landing. She

stepped into the doorway, a vision in purple bangles, boas, and beads, with a jewel-encrusted red toque that practically flamed around her face. She drew a plump little man forward. "Elton, say hello to my friends."

Elton John rushed across the room, clasping our hands in effusive recognition. "Oh, and you must be George and John." He beamed. "Love the sound of that." With a contagious cackle, he moved on. "And you must be Pru."

I went over to Teeny. "Teeny," I whispered, "you know this man is gay, right?"

"Of course." She gave me a nudge. "I only want to dance with him, honey."

"Just checking."

"Georgia, I never was *that* naïve."

Pretty soon, Elton had us all in stitches.

"See? Isn't he great?" Teeny asked. "The sweetest, most fun man."

Only SuSu didn't get in the swing of things. She started to pace.

"What's the matter?" Linda asked her. "Can we help?"

She shot a pregnant glance at Linda. "We're just missing one couple, then we can get started."

I heard the elevator bell chime downstairs.

"Maybe that's them."

The bell dinged on our floor, and the room poised at the sound of the doors opening, then footsteps.

In walked our collective goddaughter, Abby, with a tall brown man as elegant as a Byzantine icon, in a dashiki and baggy pants, his intricate body art peeking out of the neckline and the sleeves.

Linda pasted a frozen smile on her face.

Osama came over and bowed to Brooks, then her, with what appeared to be genuine deference.

Abby wasn't so reserved. She hugged her mother, then flew to all of us distributing more hugs.

When Osama came to meet me, I looked into his eyes and saw intelligence and compassion. Maybe Abby wasn't doomed, after all. "What happened to your dreadlocks?" I asked him.

He glanced with love toward Abby. "Life is a journey. When a man becomes a man, he is willing to put away certain unnecessary things to bring happiness to those he loves. I did not need the dreadlocks anymore."

You wanted them, but you didn't need them.

"Finally," SuSu announced. "We're all here, including the band, so if y'all could all move into the ballroom, I have a very special surprise for all of you."

I clung to John's arm. "If this one is anything like Elton John, hold me up. I am serious. I'm not sure I can handle it."

My John closed his hand around mine. "Gotcha covered, honey."

We walked into the ballroom to find a fairyland of tables decorated in purple and red with tiny, bright lights, centered around a canopy draped with scads of tulle and flowers in the same color scheme. SuSu's parents were beaming in front of the canopy, decked out to beat the band alongside her grown children, with pride and happiness alight on all their faces.

I couldn't remember seeing the McIntyres so happy. Or so stylish. SuSu mounted the two stairs to the canopy and stood there, alone and radiant. "Beloved friends," she said in a clear voice that carried all the way to the back of the room. "I have asked you all here to celebrate a very special event." She extended her hand to the audience, where Stan McCann, the Mattress Man, rose and came forward to take it.

SuSu gazed at him with open adoration. "I want you all to meet the man I'm going to marry." They shared an impish smile. "Tonight. With all the people we love and care about as witnesses."

Their study group burst into applause and "I told you so's," but we Red Hats take longer to digest such revelations. We sat there, stunned.

SuSu looked to us. "Now, if all the Red Hats will please join me in the other room for a few minutes, the band will entertain the rest of y'all with some kick-ass Beach Music, so y'all cut a rug, and we'll be right back." Stan kissed her hand and let her go.

We followed, not knowing what to expect. She opened the door to the long private dining room lit only by two pillar candles on the table, motioned us in ahead of her, then joined us, closing out the rest of the party. There on the tablecloth, neatly laid out beside the glowing pillars, lay a butane match, a dull brass candle snuffer, and five colored tapers, each candle with an aged index card written in slightly faded ink.

The cards from our sisterhood ritual at her first wedding!

My knees went weak, tears springing to my eyes, my hand over my mouth.

All four of the others were crying, too.

We sounded like a funeral instead of a wedding, and SuSu didn't help by saying softly, "I saved everything from the first time." Silent tears were running down her cheeks, too, and she helped herself from a box of Kleenex and passed them down.

She cleared her throat, taking hold of herself, and said in a stronger voice, "This time is so special, y'all. So right. He drove me crazy, at first. He really did. But then, he wormed his way into my heart by being just plain wonderful. I wanted to tell y'all, but I was terrified I'd blow it, that he'd find out about my past and run screaming into the night. I was so afraid, I broke it off myself, right before the cruise. But when we got back, there he was, determined not to let me go. He proposed to me and said he never wanted me to leave him again. We could still have our own lives, but just with each other." She laughed, wiping tears. "He said that even though I looked like a spring chicken, we weren't, and he wants to make the most of every day God gives us."

God! She said God, respectfully!

"I knew then, I had to tell him. I couldn't lie anymore. He deserves the truth. It was the first time I prayed in a long time, but I asked God to give me strength to tell Stan everything, and He did."

She prayed! She actually prayed!

"What did he do when you told him?" Linda dutifully prompted.

"He laughed and hugged me and said he was so relieved. He thought I was going to banish him to the outer darkness because he was so uncouth. Then he said it didn't matter what had gone on before, he just thanked God I was exactly the way I am now, and he loved every part of me."

"Oh, that's so romantic," Diane wept out.

"He's a big softie," SuSu said through her own tears. "So I told him it was mutual, and I even loved his sweet, snuggly stomach and all his redneck family and his corny jokes and his loud laugh."

I laid my hand over my swelling heart, ecstatic. She'd found true love at last, both spiritual and human.

She searched our faces. "We would have told you about the wedding, really, but all this only happened when I got back. And we had exams, so we decided to keep it small and surprise everybody."

SuSu's green eyes pleaded with us. "I want your blessings. May I have them?"

Fresh waves of tears all but drowned out our assent.

Every hand was shaking as each of us picked up her candle and stood ready, getting a grip on ourselves so we could read the words we'd said almost a quarter of a century ago, when all of us still believed in everything.

We circled SuSu, who closed her eyes.

Teeny cleared her throat and straightened. "Susan Virginia McIntyre Harris Cates," she said, her voice strong. "Open your eyes and behold your sisters."

Teeny turned to Linda, who lit her candle and held the card up to its light. "This day, you take a new name and new responsibilities as a wife," Linda, her life now fragile, read. "But the bond of sisterhood is not diminished." She raised her candle. "I bear the blue candle of friendship. Years may pass, distances may grow, and circumstances may change, but whenever you need friendship, we will give it. Without hesitation. Without judgment. Without thought of recompense."

YELLOW FOLLOWS BLUE, my card said across the top, but this time I didn't miss my cue. I swallowed, hard, to ease the lump in my throat. "I bear the yellow candle of truth," I, the frank one, read. "Whenever you need the truth, you may come to us, and we will give it in compassion. Without hesitation. Without judgment. Without thought of recompense."

Pru lit her candle next. "I bear the purple candle of mercy," she, the prodigal, read. "Whenever you need forgiveness, you may come to us and we will give it. Without hesitation. Without judgment. Without thought of recompense."

Diane, still a crusader, spoke out clear and true through trembling lips. "I bear the red candle of justice. Whenever you have been wronged, you may come to us, and we will do all we can to bring justice. Without hesitation. Without judgment. Without thought of recompense."

Teeny, still our well of secrets, brought the ritual full-circle. "I bear the white candle of silence," she said. "When you need to share a confidence, you may come to us, and we will keep it. Without hesitation. Without judgment, and without thought of recompense." She paused briefly, then added a crisp, "Including telling us you're getting married."

We all chuckled, breaking the tension.

Teeny handed SuSu the no-longer shiny brass candle-snuffer. Off the cuff, she adapted the closing portion to perfection. "As you make this most recent step beyond the days of solitude into the solemn covenant of marriage, you are offered this solemn covenant of friendship. By extinguishing each of these candles, you accept the promises we have made, and agree to extend them to each of us in turn."

With great reverence, SuSu snuffed out each candle.

We all shared a group hug-in, laugh-in, cry-in.

Then we did as good a patch job on our makeup as we could manage, and walked back, high and proud.

When Stan saw us escorting his bride back to the canopy, he started leaking tears worthy of the big baby he portrayed in his commercials, the softie, which all of us thought was adorable.

SuSu squeezed his hand, hard, when she joined him in front of the robed minister. (Not a judge!)

The minister stepped forward and opened his well-worn Order of Service. "Dearly beloved, we are gathered in the sight of God and before this company to join this man and this woman in the bonds of Holy matrimony . . ."

I hugged John to my side and gave heartfelt thanks for new beginnings. For so many blessings, my mind could barely contain them.

And with a kiss, SuSu became SuSu Virginia McIntyre Harris Cates McCann. She promptly started introducing Stan as her third and final husband.

After the ceremony, I cornered her. "You said you prayed. And you had a minister do the service. Is this significant?"

She nodded with a joy I hadn't recognized until that moment. "Well, I finally realized I was being pretty silly. Like the mole tellin' the moon it didn't exist. I was just mad. I learned so much more than torts from Stan. He's a man of simple, boundless faith. I learned about self-respect and real love and what really matters from him. He adored me just like I was, made me believe I was worthy of love and happiness."

She closed her eyes briefly, like a weary pilgrim who has finally found her way home. "He didn't tell me that was how God loved me. He showed me."

What do you say to something so profound?

I wanted to laugh and cry and shout and kiss Stan McCann the Mattress Man on the lips, but I didn't do any of those things.

As the band cranked up, I told SuSu, "Mazel tov!" and sent her back to her husband. Then I grabbed the love of my life, and I danced.

Haywood's Favorite Low-Carb Recipe

I know, this is a novel, not a cookbook. But due to popular demand, I'm including one of my favorite recipes—Dark Chicken Salad with Wonderful Low-Carb Blender Mayo. Hope you like it as much as I do, even if I do say so myself.

Dark Chicken Salad

A make-ahead dish. Serves four for luncheon.

Though no self-respecting Southern lady of my generation would dream of putting dark meat into her chicken salad, I rebelled and made up this yeast-free, low-carb recipe that's all dark meat, and even the staunchest Junior Leaguers love it. The steps are simple, but just require a little advance notice. May be doubled, but increase the simmer time on the chicken.

2 cans Sweet Sue Chicken stock or 2 cups homemade stock
6–8 chicken thighs or 12–15 drumsticks
1–2 lb. roasted pecan pieces
fresh ground pepper
salt
dash of fresh lime juice
Wonderful Low-Carb Blender Mayo (see recipe)

AT LEAST ONE DAY BEFORE:

Place chicken in pot with stock to cover. Bring to boil, then reduce heat immediately and cover. Simmer until tender (30 mins. to 1 hour). Cool, covered, then refrigerate in the stock for 4 hours to one day. (This is the secret to moist salad that needs less mayo.)

NEXT DAY:

1. Preheat oven to 350 degrees and roast pecan pieces, thinly scattered in flat pan, for 15 to 20 minutes or until they lose their raw taste. Keep an eye on them so they don't overbrown and turn bitter. Cool.

2. Take the chicken out of the stock, then remove skin, bones, and icky stuff. Coarsely chop the meat and place in a generous-sized bowl.

3. Add pecans, coarse pepper, salt, dash of lime juice, and low-carb mayo to taste.

PRESENTATION:

1. Mound on a bed of romaine or Buttercrunch lettuce and garnish with lots of fresh berries, or sliced tomatoes, avocado slices, and cucumber sticks. OR

2. Roll in lettuce leaves and serve as finger food, whole or sliced into rounds. A thin, narrow strip of cucumber peel makes a nice tie to secure the roll. OR

3. Spread onto low-carb whole-wheat (no yeast) flour tortilla and either top with another tortilla and slice into wedges, or roll like a burrito and slice on the diagonal, garnished with fruit or low-carb crudités. OR

4. If you're not counting carbs, spread generously onto mayo-coated Pepperidge Farm white bread. Yum. (Men especially like it this way.)

Wonderful Low-Carb Blender Mayo

Makes 2–3 cups (yeast-free). Keeps several weeks in refrigerator.
2 pasteurized uncooked eggs (Check with your grocer to get these.)
⅓–½ teaspoon salt (I use ½.)

¾ teaspoons dry mustard
dash of sweet paprika
2–4 Sweet'N Low packets or Splenda packets to taste
(I use 4 Sweet'N Lows.)
2 cups cold-pressed saffron or clear sesame or almond oil
(Almond is the best, but pricey.)
3 tablespoons fresh or Nellie & Joe's Lime juice (no substitutes)

PREPARATION:

1. Place eggs, salt, spices, and artificial sweetener in blender. Process at high speed for 30 seconds. (The friction sort of "cooks" the eggs.)
2. With blender running, gradually add ¼ cup of the oil.
3. Blender still running, add lime juice and blend till creamy.
4. Gradually drizzle in the rest of the oil, so the mixture doesn't "break" (separate).
5. Spoon into extra-clean jar or container. The more sterile the container, the longer the mayo will keep.